Malediction

Sparkling Books

British Library Cataloguing in Publication Data. A catalogue record for this book is available from the British Library.

Cover image © Ryan Burke

2.0

BIC code: FH

ISBN: 978-1-907230-41-7

Printed in the United Kingdom by Short Run Press

For more information visit *www.sparklingbooks.com*

PRAISE FOR SALLY SPEDDING

"Malediction is a horrifying parable of poisoned faith. No one does the darker side of noir like Sally Spedding"

Andrew Taylor, *winner of the Crime Writers' Association diamond dagger*

"Her writing is so distinctly unique it will truly chill you to the bone."

Sally Meseg for *Dreamcatcher*

"Sally Spedding is a font of creepy stories, the kind of tales which wheedle their way back into your mind, hours maybe days and weeks later..."

Western Mail

"Spedding knows that before delivering the set-pieces it's essential to carefully build suspense through both unsettling incident and sense of locale – at both, she's unquestionably got what it takes."

Barry Forshaw, *Crime Time*

"Sally Spedding... has been credited with being a latter day Du Maurier..."

Crime Squad

"Sally Spedding is the mistress of her craft."

Welsh Books Council

SALLY SPEDDING was born in Wales and studied sculpture at Manchester and at St. Martin's, London. Having won an international short story competition, she began writing seriously and her work has won many awards including the H.E. Bates Short Story Prize and the Anne Tibble Award for Poetry. She is the author of six acclaimed crime mystery novels and a short story collection. Other short stories have regularly appeared in the Crime Writers Association anthologies. She is a full member of the CWA and Literature Wales for services to literature in Wales, and adjudicates national writing competitions. She finds both Wales and France complex and fascinating countries – full of unfinished business – and has a bolt-hole in the Pyrenees where most of her writing and dreaming is done.

www.sallyspedding.com

ALSO BY SALLY SPEDDING

To Clare and Basil from Lansac. With Love.

MALEDICTION

List of Characters

Colette Bataille	- mother of Bertrand *aka* Sister Barbara.
Bertrand Bataille	- her son, *aka* Le Bébé.
Nelly Augot	- her new-found friend *aka* Yveline.
Guy Baralet	- Director of Medex. Colette's boss.
Lise Baralet	- his wife. A florist.
Robert Vidal	- Father Jean-Baptiste of La Sainte Vierge in Lanvière-sur-Meuse. Colette's lover.
Francke Duvivier	- Father André of Ste Trinité in Les Pradels, Provence. *aka* Thibaut/Kommandant/Haupsturmführer.
Michel Plagnol	- Father Jérôme of Notre-Dame-de-la-Consolation in Drancy, Paris. *aka* The Pigface.
Éric Cacheux	- Father Christophe de la Bonté of St. Honoré in the Corbières.
Dominique Mathieu	- Father Xavier-Marie of La Motte Mauron in Perros Guirec.
Christian Désespoir	- Abbot of Legrange Vivray, founder of Les Pauvres Soeurs de la Souffrance.
René Martin	- Deacon of Les Bourreux.
Raôul Boura	- Bishop of Kervecamp.
Henri Pereire	- Bishop of Beauregard.
Philippe Toussirot	- Dominican Bishop of Ramonville.
Georges Déchaux	- General with NATO peace-keeping forces *aka* Hauptsturmbannführer for the ACJ.
Nina Zeresche	- police switchboard trainee.

Antoinette Ruffiac	-	*aka* Claude Lefêbvre. Receptionist at St. Anne's hostel/Déchaux's chauffeur in Paris.
Christine Souchier	-	*aka* Romy Kirchner/ 'ma souris rouge.'
Giselle Subradière	-	*aka* Simone Haubrey/Patrice Sassoule.
Marie-Claude Huron	-	temp at Medex (where Colette worked) *aka* Julie Borel.
Sister Agnès	-	recruiting nun for Les Pauvres Soeurs.
Sister Marie-Ange	-	Sister Superior.
Sister Cecilia	-	the Inquisitor *aka* 'the Percheron.'
Sister Rose	-	cleaner.
Yves Jalibert	-	ACJ co-ordinator in Paris.
Marcel Jalibert	-	his son.
Mordecai Fraenkel	-	hotelier at the King David Hotel near the Loire.
Pauline Fraenkel	-	his wife.
Leila Fraenkel	-	their daughter. An artist.
Michèle Bauer-Lutyens	-	receptionist at the King David Hotel.

INTROIT

Wednesday August 20ᵗʰ 1997

The wine had gathered in unexpected places, but most, from Raymond Tessier's mouth, coursed down his cheek, into the clavicle and out again. A blood river, dulling on the sheet below.

"Lie still, damn you." The younger, dark-haired man pressed down on the other priest's wrists for his own lips to slide south to the left nipple. Warmer than the rest of that pale flesh, but not enough to alter their bristling as each aureole hardened under his licking tongue.

"Anges de Dieu," Tessier sighed. The rapist who would destroy a man's ambition. His reason to go on living.

"Leave them out of it," snorted the other, now busy draining his victim's navel. Hardly a round goblet which wanteth not liquor, more a ferment of secrets and lies, fucking up his promised release from this Boot Camp near Béziers. Then to the business that pushed itself hard against his chin.

Poor Tessier wanted comfort. Any comfort, but that teasing mouth stayed wilfully closed. No more wine, and definitely nothing else worth drinking. He had the power. As always. The other man's foreskin hung like an old Tricolore as he breathed along the purple vein raised in desire. Saw the scrotum bald and red against those sunless thighs, then tightened the cord around them until the man's screams filled his cell.

Afterwards, as he ran from the scene, the killer checked his watch. Raymond Tessier had taken precisely two minutes, thirty-five seconds to die.

Now you shall not offer to the Lord anything with its testes bruised or crushed or torn or cut. Exactly. Thank you, Leviticus, though the best is yet to come.

And the next time these gifts will be perfect.

I

Colette Bataille could hear the kids down below in the Rue St. Léger on their way to the new roller-skating rink. Snatches of taunts and chants were scarred by the run of blades on tarmac and the sudden staccato jumps on and off the kerb. "Hades must be like this," she muttered, reviving her lips with a new lipstick, and enlarging both eyes with a soft crayon. Eyes that in two hours' time she'd use to search her lover's face for any trace of his old longing. Father Jean-Baptiste – Robert Vidal – priest and assistant choirmaster of the Église de la Sainte Vierge at Lanvière, who'd been put away for three weeks at the Villerscourt Boot Camp for reasons never fully explained.

There'd been whispers, of course – the most consistent being that his driving ambition with his young church choir here in Lanvière, had spilled over into obsession. That he'd worked them too hard, too long and issued threats to those who'd been absent. But who had dared betray him?

Lips had stayed sealed.

She rinsed her hands then checked her watch before peering round her son Bertrand's bedroom door, as though this would somehow return him to his refuge. She then left the apartment. Twenty steps of black marble down into the catacomb of post-war design, before the sudden slab of sunlight. She squinted up to her windows – saw the red pelagoniums drifted against the down pipe, and her neighbour Dolina Levy's withered eyes unmoving. Colette waved, too briefly she knew. But not briefly enough. No time to listen, yet again, to tales of her life in Cracow; of her husband and sister taken at gun-point and her flight into the Vosges disguised as a Red Cross nurse. She was late.

"Another sheep for Le Pape?" growled the old woman.

"Safety in numbers." Colette's voice was thin and unconvincing. Besides, the Peugeot was boiling and she needed to find its key.

"No safety for us. Never was."

"I'm sorry. Everyone is."

"Not everyone, and you'd better believe it. Just listen to them out there. And they're still children."

"It's shocking, I know."

The widow craned over her tiny balcony. Two fur slippers poked through the railings next to her cat, 'Mitzvah', corpse-like in the sun.

"Got to go, really." Colette stored the bags in the boot. His and hers and a decent picnic, then covered them over with Bertrand's old baby blanket. "Look, I'll call in when I'm back. That's a promise." She waved again, but her neighbour's face stayed grimly fearful in her mirror as she turned out into the square.

***

Her radio, always tuned to France Musique, was offering a preview of a newly-commissioned work for the Feast of Saint Bartholemew. Atonal chords over a pulsing drum filled her small space. Hardly saintly for the tanner, or the poor Huguenots, she thought on the roundabout for the The Forêt de Dieulet, but then she wasn't feeling particularly saintly either.

Ten past nine. He'd taught her that. Always to keep a note of the time. Whatever. Wherever. She smiled. Three weeks had been a long time without him, and she'd allowed work to take up her evenings, staying late at the office, staring at his church through its blinds imagining him without her. So there was no guilt when she'd asked her boss for two days off to attend the Pope's Mass at Longchamp – he'd even said the break would do her good.

Now the sun was high enough over the trees to heat her face, and she saw skin forty-four years old. Not tanned exactly, but the way Robert had always liked it. And a curve of hair, gold as the corn of Limousin, he'd once said, newly shaped for the occasion.

Her heel touched the floor. There was no other traffic, for this was a weekend route to the deer parks and the walks near Nazairolles. She thought of the modest hotel in Paris she'd booked. Just for the two of them, and her hands trembled as the road ahead melted into the haze between trees where a horse and rider cantered along the dark edge of pines.

She saw the sign for Pouilly, their agreed rendezvous, and suddenly she slowed down. Something was wrong. Two men when there should have been one, black against black like crows, and Robert's hand raised as though she was a taxi. Feeling cheated, Colette found a lay-by and swung round to meet them head on.

The Dominicans were running.

"No questions, please." Robert held the door for his companion and the chassis dropped as the big man plunged on to the seat next to her. She smelt the institution on them. Incense, cabbage, and something else. "Just go." Her lover slammed his rear door behind him and clicked his seat belt. "I'll explain when we're out of here."

"Thanks." She said drily taking first left and in the stifling silence joined the road to Reims.

"Turn that crap off."

And she obeyed.

"By the way, Thibaut," his tone changed. "This is Colette. And Colette, this is Thibaut." Robert's teeth were shining, but she knew he'd lied, and the

2

breathless tension trapped them like wasps in a glass of warm beer.

After ten minutes he cleared his throat and Colette glanced in her mirror to see eyes on fire with a torch for the world, but not for her. Oh no, nothing for her. To him she was invisible, while the other passenger's sideways stare never moved.

"So, you're a priest as well?" Her small flattery broke the deadlock.

"I've tried, God knows."

"Such modesty." Vidal smiled. "The hillbillies of Les Pradels are lucky to have sucked from your soul for so long."

"What's left of it."

"Well now, that came from the heart."

Their collusion excluded her. She tried to gauge how close they'd grown at the Villerscourt Boot Camp and crashed the gears pulling up at lights, attracting the wrong sort of attention. Robert by now was lying flat on the rear seat, almost face down.

"In six kilometres there's a sign on the right. Frites, junk-shit, etcetera. Turn in there," he ordered, his voice muffled.

"Why are you hiding like this?" she challenged.

"I said no questions. Just keep going."

Through Nazairolles, the last village before the autoroute and still the two men hid below the windows. Vidal's breath heavy in his throat. A cyclist drew up alongside. Some boy racer, glancing in, his buttocks perched neatly on the saddle. Colette thought of her own son, Bertrand, inseparable from his wheels, and she surged ahead to lose the rider out beyond the straggle of new houses to the lines of poplars and the brow of a hill. Suddenly Robert reared up. His breath in her hair.

"Here it is."

On to rubble and dust. No shade except under the caravan awning. Beaten up, derelict, its stained Miko sign askew and shutters half open to darkness. Colette parked under a dead hawthorn littered with used toilet paper and attendant flies.

"Got my things?" Robert was already by the boot. His body language nervous and impatient.

She opened the boot, peeled back Bertrand's blanket and their hands met. Just a touch, a brief promise until she looked up and gave a little cry. Her other passenger was also waiting, and for the first time she saw him close-up in gruesome technicolour. His left cheek pitted like a sponge and eyes sunk so deep they reflected no light.

He laughed at her fear, ducked his bulk behind the Peugeot then lifted his *soutane* over his head. Her lover the same, but he caught her staring and pierced her with a smile she couldn't return. "Good enough for His Holiness now? What do you think?" Robert asked, his denims tight round his thighs, arms brown below the sleeves from work in the Villerscourt gardens. She wanted him for herself. To lead him to the field at the back and feel him inside her, like old times. But now it would never be even a memory.

"It's a Youth Festival for God's sake, man. Slick your hair back a bit," Thibaut growled, then the priest whose real name meant 'of the fish pond,' slunk off to squat behind the caravan. Robert Vidal glanced up, saw that same cyclist pass by in a rush of sound. Then he turned to face her.

"You're lovelier than ever, I have to say, Madame Bataille." His hands around each of her arms.

"Robert, don't."

But he pulled her to him, his body lean and firm against hers, so the new mobile in his pocket dug into her hip.

"What's that for?" she asked, searching his face.

"So none of us gets lost."

"You've never bothered before."

"Paris is a big place, remember?"

She looked again at his olive skin, his melting eyes, and something about the day's strange encounter told her this might be the last time they'd ever be so close.

"Just five minutes, Robert. Your friend can wait," she murmured, finding his mouth, but the priest eased away studying with unnerving detachment her oval face and its interrupted lips. He touched her chin then tweaked its errant hook of hair that caught the sun. He'd been looking for a flaw, a way out of his predicament. And this would do.

***

"Best be off," he said as the older man appeared, zipping up his boots. "Done your bit for nature and for God, I see." Robert pulled his own shirt from his armpits. Suddenly Duvivier stopped. Fixed him with the same cold disdain he'd shown at the graves in Carpentras. Whitebait eyes. Dead already.

In that moment, Colette knew the score. This creature was obviously in charge. *Le chef de parti.* And theirs was no pilgrimage but a sick charade, to what end she wasn't yet sure.

"It'll take three hours with the traffic," she said, arranging her skirt and setting her sunglasses in place.

Better to think of Bertrand. Something at least redeeming. I wonder if I'll spot him in all those crowds. Maybe he'll pretend not to know me...

The ex-student had saved up all his dole money since April for this, his first trip away since a final-year visit to the Futuroscope. Now it was Longchamp for World Peace Day and the Pope's Mass, just a day before, and two weeks from his twenty-fourth birthday.

He'd put his precious bike on the train at Vouziers and when she'd asked where he'd be staying, he'd been more than evasive. That he'd find somewhere cheap nearby. But as a loving mother, Colette had needed to know. She'd begged him not to take his chance on the streets, prey to all the weirdos and perverts hanging around. But that had just made him surly and silent, and he'd left her without saying goodbye. That was the worst. That's what was nagging at her. And all she'd managed to say at the time was, had he remembered his cycle lock?

Oh, douce Marie, what have I done?

This time, Robert sat in front next to her, his long legs stretched into the darkness under the dashboard.

"I'm a proud son of Provence." The other suddenly spoke. "Fishing family. We go back to the 17th century in Cavalaire. First place God made."

Fishers of men, thought Colette, repulsed already by his small filleting hands glazed with sweat.

"See, I have the Fisherman's ring too, the same as His Holiness." He wiggled a prawn-like finger in the air. "And three parishes at the last count. Ste Trinité in Les Pradels for the past twenty-two years."

In fact he looked as if he'd been buried for twenty-two years.

"Forget Thibaut. Real name's Duvivier," he said. "Francke Duvivier. Within the church, I'm Father André. Can't bear to deceive a lady, as God's my witness." He let a thin smile pucker his face and Robert turned round concerned he was giving too much away. "Don't worry, my friend. I knew from the moment we saw her, she'd be our comrade in arms."

Colette stared.

He's mad. Comrade in arms? What the Hell's going on?

Robert shrugged helplessness then fiddled with the glove box and found a melted jelly sweet. Kept it between his teeth.

"Arms against evil, wouldn't you say, sire? The blight of the world?" Duvivier chuckled as Colette drove like an automaton, bewildered and frightened in turn. "Which is precisely why we're going to listen first hand to our dear Papa. Spiritual refurbishment and all that. And thank you Madame for making it possible." A thick hand fell on her shoulder. The touch of a man who had never known a woman.

***

"How long were you at Villerscourt?" Colette asked suddenly, having stared at Duvivier in the mirror.

"My, we are curious. Shall I tell her?" The other man finally looked at Vidal who reluctantly nodded. "Well, if you must know, from the Saint of repentant sinners to the Poor Clare."

"Week before me." Robert's eyes were on the road behind. The sweet had slipped involuntarily down his throat.

"It was long enough."

"What were you in for?" she dared.

"No problem."

The Aisne and the Ardennes Canal lay below darkened by coal barges from Charleville Méziers. The bridge rumbled hollow under the car like the cobbles down to Tartarus, and for a moment, she thought of Dolina Levy.

"I let someone have it, that's all."

"Who?"

"One of my flock, I'm ashamed to say." The sun scoured his cheek. "He was getting too personal. Some of them forget who I am, you know."

"Surely not?"

"At least the charming Bishop of Beauregard backed me up. He's not without sin either, mind." He smiled. "Partial to small boys I do believe."

"That's worse than anything you've done, surely?" said Colette.

"Ah, but he's part of the hierarchy. There's the rub."

"I think that's enough." Robert checked his watch then caught her eye. "Did you bring any lunch?" he asked.

"I did."

But not for the thug, thank you very much.

"We'll stop at the next Services. They'll do."

Colette bit her lip to restrain herself. This showing off was pathetic.

"Now my friend here," Duvivier repositioned himself in the corner to continue his account, "had to make ten confessions altogether. Three in one morning, on our Founder's day, as I recall. That was fun, wasn't it, Father Jean-Baptiste?"

"I was on my belly. Prostatis come morte."

"More than a few liked that, you old tease."

"Less of the old, Kommandant, if you don't mind."

Colette blinked.

Kommandant? Am I hearing things?

She glanced from one to the other while slowing down at the *Péage* entrance. Having snatched at the ticket, she stuffed it down her camisole. "What's the point of those places if you come out worse than before?"

"Good question, Madame."

"Raymond Tessier was pushing it. Every bloody day." Robert's tone had grown peevish. "And I was supposed to take his prick whenever he felt like it,

6

or else."

"Ah, Tessier."

"Still, I got my revenge."

Colette shivered, drawing up her window despite the heat. The suspicions she'd had about Robert since before Villerscourt were growing like black tumours inside her soul.

"I made him squeeze himself to death. Poor little capon," Vidal lied fluently.

"And you know what they say about self-abuse. Thomas Aquinas declared it a greater sin than harlotry." Duvivier grinned, and she was relieved to see Services – petrol and toilets. She drove towards the pumps where a dark-haired boy, in a baseball cap and a nose too big for his face, was ready and waiting for her windscreen. "No thanks. It's fine." She told him, but he'd already dipped his rubber phalange in the bucket to lose the flies.

"You heard the lady," Duvivier snarled as petrol gurgled into the tank. "You a Yid by any chance?" The boy stared. "Pity you missed the last truck, then."

Colette's stomach tightened to a knot. She looked into the car from one to the other. Proof if she needed it was being served up on the Devil's plate.

"That's disgusting." She replaced the hose and ran after the lad who'd disappeared into the shop. She found him near the scarves and model cars, his lip trembling. "Look, I'm really sorry. That man's nothing to do with me."

"It's OK. I get quite a bit of that round here."

"You shouldn't have to put up with it. Not these days." She picked up a bag of Haribo gums, Bertrand's favourites, paid up and passed them to the boy.

"Thanks." He grinned.

"No eating on the job, Louis. Hand them over," shouted the woman at the till.

"Excuse me, we were just having a conversation," Colette retorted.

"I pay him, not you, Madame. Now, boy, get back to work."

With a heavy heart, Colette followed him into the sun. Saw the two men darkened behind glass. Their world, not hers. Then suddenly and unexpectedly Robert smiled as though he actually still loved her, and for a moment, torn by distrust and longing, she turned away.

II

Duvivier hogged the baguette that was big enough for three. Shreds of cheese lodged in the corners of his mouth and when he drank, they fell into the Stella Artois.

"Lord above," he muttered between mouthfuls. "It's twelve o'clock."

Colette edged away and pulled out her rosary beads. Blood red like garnets, they'd once belonged to her grandmother and had moved between her old fingers for seventy years. Now they winked in the picnicking sun, promising the comfort of the Angelus.

"Hail Mary full of Grace, blessed is the fruit of Thy womb, Jesus..." she whispered, trying to ignore the Latin duet issuing from the men of God, while wasps circled the litter bin.

"Got any more drink?" Vidal stood up full height, his lips shining. His shadow cutting her in two as she obliged. She watched the water sluice down his throat as Duvivier laughed to himself.

"What's up?" asked Robert.

"Shoot it and you die."

"What the fuck do you mean?"

"Shoot the dog and man's demon soul within shall live. Shoot the shadow and it dies." He cracked his fingers like gunfire making Colette start. She tried to focus on saving leftovers for later, if there was going to be one. A triangle of pizza denuded of olives, and two plum tomatoes hot in her hands.

"I can't go on much more with all this," she announced, getting up, her suit skirt furred by grass cuttings. "Count me out of whatever it is." The silence that followed seemed to choke any response there might be. A spray of yellowed leaves drifted from above and settled in her hair. Duvivier tore one into pieces.

"Your boy at Longchamp, then?"

Colette looked at Robert who gave nothing away.

"How did you know I had a child?"

"My dear Madame Bataille, I can tell immediately if a woman has enriched the population. She possesses a certain *je ne sais quoi* which I've always found most alluring."

Vidal forced him against the table and felt in his own pocket. He was armed and ready. Colette turned pale. "I think Herr Kommandant we need to consider territory. Now mine is off limits for your amusement."

"My dear friend," the older man tried to wriggle out from underneath him. "I was about to say that my own mother was the most beautiful creature

8

before having me, and even more so after." His voice broke off. Vidal took his throat and felt the carotid pumping between his hands. How easy it would be to finish him off in that quiet place with the screen of empty lorries that littered the kerb. His mouth pressed against Duvivier's ear.

"Show some respect for Madame Bataille here, or I'll tell the others that the only thing your cock's ever known is your own dirty little hands."

In turmoil, Colette ran to her car.

Who are these others? What's going on? She could make a dash for it – the exit was only a few metres away. But suddenly the sun cut out. Vidal had imprisoned her against him, his fingers hard into her skin.

"He's a nothing," he said. "And I'm not going to apologise for him."

"So why are you even seeing him? I don't understand." Her voice rose in fear. "We were supposed to be having a weekend together."

"Father André and myself have things to do. Things which are necessary for our souls."

"How can he have one? Or is he Faustus by any chance?"

"Colette!" hissed Vidal. "Ssshh… "

"Did I hear my alter ego being taken in vain?" Duvivier was behind them, pulling at the door handle. He kicked the sill when it didn't open.

"Hey! D'you mind?" she shouted. "That's my car!"

"Indeed, Madame, and as you'll discover on your terrestrial journey, such material baggage soon becomes burdensome. Now if you'll excuse me, I'd prefer to sit down."

She again obeyed with more self-loathing than even Bertrand would surely have felt. Her rigorous, upright son in an unfair world, still desperately searching for something to believe in. "Who are these so-called others, then?" she asked as nonchalantly as she could, joining the motorway. Robert coughed and pressed his face closer to the window.

"My, we are curious today." Duvivier, three years her senior, smiled irregular yellow teeth as he succumbed. "If you must know, we shall be joining Messieurs Cacheux, Plagnol and Mathieu for the festivities. Quite the Holy Trinity don't you agree, Robert?"

But Vidal was watching the farms and bare curved fields slip by. The hay, cut earlier than the previous year, slumbered in monolithic bales, each with its own stark shadow.

The stupid cunt can't stop talking. He'll live to regret it. Now she knows all our secular names. Hélas!

"Are they from the Church as well?" she persevered.

"Indeed they are. And the quintet of Dominus Cani will howl above the mob. Won't we, Robert? Go on, tell her."

9

"Yes, we'll sing. I suppose."

"Remembering of course that he who sings prays twice. And who are we to disagree with the great Augustine?"

She looked across to see Vidal's frown had deepened, but once Duvivier had started the first bars of *"Fleurissez, fleurs du Rosaire,"* he joined in, adding a slow pulsing harmony which filled the small car, but left his face unaltered.

III

The Café d'Auteuil in the heart of the 16th was full. Students mainly, still on vacation and mostly foreign. Duvivier's damaged, putty face had hardened. His movements more precise and deliberate, and Colette suddenly felt an infinite pity for the poor, helpless creatures from the sea who'd come under his knife. Robert's thighs touched hers.

He sat closer to her than Duvivier, so close like old times, but now was different. Once she would have said she'd always be there for him even if he didn't always want her. But she couldn't. Not now. She'd decided. Never mind that without him her life would be as bleak as ever, after caring for an invalid husband who'd only wanted to die, and watching her son demoralised without work. Robert Vidal had been the one illumination, the one candle lit by her spirit for her spirit. But her prayers that his hatred and bigotry might dissolve; that his time at Villerscourt would show him a man of God is a man of love, had gone unanswered.

She blushed and used the napkin to hide her face as he stirred his espresso with his crucifix and sucked its conjoined legs dry till the platinum sang on his tongue. The *garçon*, a Filipino, flicked him the kind of smile he was used to and Colette saw it, so he straightened instead with his full tray to watch the growing crowd surge past the tables towards the Allée de Longchamp.

Duvivier returned from the toilet and sat down. His scarred cheek bright as a birth mark dividing his face in two.

"I know why you're staring at me," he snapped at the boy.

"What d'you mean, sir?"

"Not *sir*. Father. I'd have thought you had enough to do without being discourteous."

"I don't understand."

"Of course, how could you? Probably grew inside a pea pod. See my face?"

"It looks OK."

"The colour of a rose, wouldn't you say? Does that mean anything to you?" By now the nearby tables were heaped with rubbish and the owner stood in the doorway, hands on hips.

"No, sir, Father," as a pile of sugar sachets fell to the ground.

"St. Rose of Lima, you yellow worm. 1586 -1617. Your patron saint. Not that you deserve one, least of all someone who blistered her skin with pepper and hardened her hands with lime."

"Excuse me." The boy backed away, spilling yet more things as he went.

"Bit unfair, that." Vidal, all too aware of Colette's eyes, studied instead the sunlight trapped in his cup.

11

"So are most things, I regret to say." Duvivier shielded himself with the menu. "I'd say eleven rodent ulcers was unfair, too; wouldn't you? A gift from my gorgeous but genetically chaotic maman."

Suddenly Colette leapt up, tilting the table. Duvivier's lager toppled into his lap giving him a huge incontinence-like stain.

"Bertrand!"

She edged through the mêlée and out on to the thoroughfare to where a tall slightly-stooped figure loped ahead, a rucksack skewed over a shoulder, from which dangled a tin mug and old cutlery. She reached him, then tapped his back. She noticed headphones – his own little world, even here. Typical of the boy. But there was a suntan where her Bertrand was white, and her heart stopped.

"Ja, mevrouw?" He turned. Wrong eyes. Wrong everything.

"Oh? I'm so sorry."

The young Dutchman was soon one of many on the Avenue Mancy, then lost altogether, leaving Colette staring after him with feelings of emptiness then alarm.

***

"You owe me one." Duvivier muttered when she got back.

"I know he's not here."

"Who?"

"My son."

"My dear Madame Bataille, take it on my authority, there'll be at least a million coming to listen tomorrow, God bless them. Just have faith."

Vidal laughed sourly and tipped back in his chair. "But he is one in a million to you, *hein*?"

She didn't reply, instead kept her eyes on the tide of humanity passing by.

"Tell you what." Duvivier stood up and straightened his crucifix. Crumbs still lay in his lap, stuck to the dampness. "Give me a brief description. Thumbnail type of thing. You never know."

But I do, you bastard. I do.

Then Colette thought hard for a moment. Any eyes were better than none. But not theirs. She shook her head. "No thanks."

Robert looked round, surprised.

"Well don't forget, there's always the eye of the Almighty to call upon. Remember *Machtgeful*." Duvivier turned his back so the favourite word was lost amongst other tongues. Her lover followed him like his shadow.

"Bloody cheek." Colette's voice faded, wedged in by Austrians to the left and Britons to the right, grappling with the menu.

"We've got stuff to do." Vidal whispered as he passed her. "Sorry."

"No you're not."

His glance was of sly disdain as Duvivier pulled his sleeve. "See you back here at 16.00 hours." His watch to his ear, checking as always it wouldn't let him down. That its metronome was in tune with his heart, the only constant. They left her alone with the detritus, discarded like herself. *Persona non grata,* but seething nevertheless.

Damn.

Colette stuck out her chin then foraged for a cigarette.

"Have you a light, please?" She turned to the English couple who'd just fathomed the mysteries of a *croque-monsieur*. The man liked her instantly, she could tell. The woman did not. He worked his Sealink lighter, apologising until it delivered.

"Thanks." She funnelled the smoke upwards. She could easily be taken for a native Parisian with the beige linen suit and her well-cared for heels. Always the give-away.

"Left on yer own, then?" He tried and she was grateful.

"My boy's here somewhere. He came up for the Mass tomorrow." Her English was good. With Medex it had to be.

"Same as us, isn't it, Pet?" His hair lay grizzled above his ears, and both faces bore the legacy of a fortnight in the sun. "We've just turned up on the off-chance. The last camp site was shite so we thought, nothing to lose. Not that I'm much of a believer. More the wife..."

She in turn squinted into her compact mirror, clicked it shut as though to end things, but the man was obviously enjoying his new company.

"Well I hope you find him in all this lot. We're going to see if we can get a room in Neuilly somewhere."

Colette smiled at his pronunciation. "La Défense might be better."

"Ta, thanks. We're Bartley by the way." He reached over to shake her hand. A working hand, unlike Robert's.

"I'm Bataille. Quite similar."

"Mansfield we're from. Near Nottingham. Ever heard of Robin Hood by any chance?"

"I learnt that legend in school. Where I come from, we have many."

"Oh?"

"The most famous one's about dogs." She drew hard on her cigarette and let the smoke bypass his eager face. "I believe it's mediaeval."

"We've got a dog. A Sealydale. Jimmy."

"No. Not that sort at all." Colette managed a smile, and stubbed out her dimp more decisively than anything else she'd done so far.

"Go on, then."

"Demons force men's souls to enter the bodies of dogs – the great white dogs of the mountains..."

"Blimey."

"They say that if you shoot at the dog and hit him, the soul will be delivered, but if the arrow or whatever falls on the shadow, the soul will immediately die."

Silence as the tourists' mouths hung open.

"Wait a mo," the man said suddenly quick to change the subject, turned to his wife. "We've an Abel label we can give her, haven't we, Pet?" he asked, but she wasn't going to open her bag again, so he pressed out a used napkin and wrote on it, making holes with his Biro.

"I really don't think that's necessary," frowned The Pet. "We don't know who she is. Besides, I didn't like that story at all."

"Oh come on, it were harmless enough. Look, I'm just doing my little bit to help Europe open up. Remember our car sticker? All those stars?"

"Merci." Colette slipped the napkin into her pocket.

All those stars...

"If ever you're in Angleterre..." the Midlander began.

"I will, thank you."

He looked back at her. His European trophy, bright in the sun.

"Might see you around tomorrow," he said.

"I do hope you find a bed."

Soon they were no more than echoes while the same Filipino stood attentive at new, ungrateful shoulders.

***

16.03

Colette got her bearings. Rue des Sables, south west, blinded by the sun as Carmelites, straight from the Martyr's Field at Picpus, Sisters of Mercy, the Order of the Poor Clares, women who'd given up on the world kicked up the leaves, letting the light kiss their cheeks as they walked.

No men, no Bertrand, but still something made her follow the last cohort of some twenty young women swathed in coarse, loose robes. She listened for any discernible dialect but there were too few words, and those that reached her were of a holy nature, in Latin. Other travellers stared as the procession of grey, black and white flowed by.

She felt magnetised, somehow connected to their purpose. She'd recently started taking the Eucharist again for the first time since Bertrand's birth, to lend more mystery, something more other-worldly to her existence. But there was no need for the Confessional – she'd been martyr enough what with her late husband whom she'd nursed for three years, and the shame of Bertrand entering the world without a father. Too much pain, too many burdens – until Robert Vidal had arrived. The man with the eyes of fire.

***

Like vast colanders, the foliage above spotted sunlight on to the heads of the Pauvres Soeurs des Souffrances. Just as in the Forêt de Woëvres in 1980, where her parents, Marguerite and Noah Rigaud had attached themselves to a new umbilical – the rubber variety – brought from his tidy garage on the birthday of The Blessed Virgin Mary, with bells from everywhere pealing the celebration...

Dust reached her eyes as though conspiring to keep her and her son apart. Her pavement shoes felt suddenly hard and inhospitable, so she removed them and drew closer, close enough to recognise "Tantum ergo Sacramentum," choir and solo parts to de Chambéry's limpid tune. The priest had always chosen Haydn, with his older boys taking the alto, but no matter, she joined in, her voice rising with theirs past the *Lac pour le Patinage* and campers settling down for the night. No longer anxious for her son or the fact she was alone. Forgetting her lover's manipulation and neglect, she touched the nun in front and gave her name.

IV

Vidal led the Provençal down the Avenue de Madrid away from the Bois de Boulogne, but Duvivier, ever the strategist, caught up, his breath rasping from his lungs.

"You come second. Always. Semper. Remember that, my friend." He pushed a finger into Vidal's coccyx until he was allowed to draw alongside.

"It's not a problem for me."

"I disagree."

They fell silent, in step broken just once by Vidal stopping to buy *Le Figaro*. He rolled it up to beat a fly away from his head as they followed signs for the cemetery. "That queer Tessier," Duvivier began, out of the blue. "Are you sure there's no family to cause trouble?"

"All in the Afterlife, I'm pleased to report."

"We don't want complications. Not now."

"Look, they'd have found the cord round his balls. Felo de se."

"A kick would have done the trick."

"Oh, really? How would you have liked his fist up your arse every night? Besides, he was unreliable. A dismantler."

Of my dreams, my ambition...

"What d'you mean?"

"Nothing."

"Our new boy Matthieu had better be able to hold a camera."

"He will."

The cemetery seemed to heap up on itself below the hazy Paris skyline. Its population of granite and marble rendered to earth colours over the centuries. A huge wing here, a Bible there, red iron oxide like blood, leaking and staining. Instinctively, Vidal crossed himself as Duvivier's half-formed eyes scoured the site.

***

17.03

For some reason the Lanvière priest thought of Colette and her light, thinning hair. How hard she'd tried with her appearance. How all in vain.

"Where are the cunts?" Duvivier forged ahead, his rolling gait at odds with the stifling rigidity of the place. In the distance, a couple with fresh flowers hunted for a grave and an old woman in black bent low, replenishing water.

"Heil!" came from behind a row of family tombs. Duvivier spun round.

"Cacheux! Good, where's the other one?"

"We're joined at the hip, Herr Kommandant." A long hand from an immaculate linen cuff sought his, but Duvivier was nervous. Some obvious aftershave Vidal couldn't quite place. Then Plagnol the Pigface appeared, unhealthily pink against a black polo neck and dark jeans. His eyes already dangerous.

Both produced posies of freesias. Éric Cacheux's deliberately the bigger of the two, and Vidal pretended to draw in their scent.

"Plastic, I see," he said. "How generous."

"They'll do." Duvivier came between, and with appropriate solemnity for the benefit of a wheelchair and carer passing by, the tributes were laid on a slab whose letters had long disappeared.

"We're seeing our new *copain* at 17.45 by the south gate. Any news or problems so far?" Duvivier stopped and Vidal offered him a Camel from the pack then lit up himself, pleased the others had noticed.

"Our *Bébé* was too fucking loud. We had to sort him out." Plagnol said matter-of-factly.

"What d'you mean?" Vidal frowned.

"Like I said."

"Please explain." Duvivier exhaled, then a cough underpinned by phlegm.

"We gave him a shot of something. Nothing traceable."

"*You* did, not me." Cacheux picked out one of the flowers and slotted it into his button hole.

"Does it matter for God's sake? Fact is, he'll have a quiet night. Got too many meddlers hanging around there for my liking."

"And Jews."

"It's Drancy. So what's new?"

The quartet clustered inside a marble portico with its six drawers, still empty and the name Famille El Fazoukt in gold leaf. "Noirs got rich." Duvivier sneered, then spat on his finger, drawing it across the name. "Look here, I know what I'm talking about." He repeated his little defamation on the tomb and watched it dry. "Nothing hasty in our *Bébé's* nursery now. We need patience."

"Easy for you to say that." Plagnol's fleshy mouth down-turned to a sulk. "The noisy brat hasn't let up since he got there."

"Just do as you're told." Duvivier stared at another name from the past. "Because I have another little anxiety."

"What's that, then?" Cacheux anxious to capitalise; to elicit a confidence, but the Provençal ignored him.

"This Mathieu could prove tricky. Not had the same vetting. No time. So he mustn't know too much. Only what I allow. Is that clear?" He dropped his cigarette on the gravel and buried it with the toe of his boot.

"Is he one of us? A Dominican?" Vidal asked.

"Look at his first name. His dear mother insisted on it. Dominique. Can't get much better than that, bless her."

"Trial period?" Cacheux's eyes on the beautiful man from Lanvière.

"Not possible. But my friend the Bishop of Kervecamp recommended him most highly."

"What for?" Plagnol's wispy eyebrows almost disappeared under his hairline.

"Domus, my new charity. Homeless stuff. Very à-propos, don't you think?"

Vidal stared at the man who could spin lies more easily than Satan himself. Who could cast his devious net far wider than any other man of the sea. "But let's not forget, at the end of the day, the poor fucker's looking for love. His words not mine on his letter of application to join us. So let's be nice to him. And another thing..."

"What?"

"His was the first reply we got."

"We?"

"I mean, I." Duvivier said quickly.

"Well, he's come to the right place." Vidal tossed his Camel butt over a cherub's head as they followed the overgrown walkway to the far end. "Just watch him, in case. By the way, how long do we keep our *Bébé*?"

"Like I said. Long as it takes." Duvivier slid him a teasing glance.

"Nobody asks if I mind playing nanny." Plagnol bleated. "We've not all struck lucky getting a vast bloody presbytery like you."

"It befits my station." The Provençal snarled again. "And my years of service. Besides, Les Pradels is too far away for our purpose."

"You get extra pay, don't you?" Cacheux flicked invisible flecks off his sleeve as Vidal held Plagnol back.

"Remember," he said, "if anything happens to the *Bébé*, I'll be taking it very personally. Got it?"

"He gave us no choice. It's all up to maman now."

Vidal coloured, his fists tightening to flint. "Leave her out of this."

"Can't have fanny and freedom, now be fair." Plagnol's teeth showed like tiny pearls. Vidal had the urge to stuff them down his throat.

"Boys, boys." Duvivier parked his bulk in front of them. "Let's not spoil it, eh?" He produced a comb clotted with grease. Ran it once through his hair. "Re our questions for the show tomorrow. Are we prepared?" Three heads nodded, but Vidal was deep in thought. "Your parishioners, bless them, your Bishops, Deacons, sub-Deacons, curse them, will all be watching. So we make ourselves obvious." He hawked phlegm back down his throat. "Just remember, our piety and concern are our alibis. Seeing will truly be believing. Right, we have two minutes."

And as the sun moved behind the Eiffel tower silhouetting its skyward journey, the small company finished their rehearsal and went to introduce themselves to the new recruit from Perros-Guirec.

V

Colette's beige suit was no longer smart. Its jacket flopped open and the skirt clung to her thighs as she walked, stretching and bagging with every step. The nun whom she'd tried to distract, merely continued singing, not from perversity but a fervour that seemed to grip them all.

"Please slow down." Colette called out, for her feet were now grey around the edges and dirt-speckled above.

The woman – or girl, she couldn't quite tell – who strode alongside, had eyes only for the way ahead, to the space reserved for the Pauvres Soeurs des Souffrances marked by a flag. 'Bienvenue, Toutes les Femmes Sans Espoir.' In bold red letters altering on the breeze.

So, someone at least cares in this city. God has obviously touched their hearts...

"I'm Colette. Colette Bataille," she repeated.

The nun turned with a pitying look on her face. A face of the purest and, if it were possible, the most translucent ivory. Her eyes without eyelashes, lined by pale blood, could have come from the brush of Van der Weyden.

"Here, use this." She pulled a cotton square from her pocket. In the corner, an 'A' was embroidered above the letters PSS.

"Thank you." Colette wiped her forehead, then between her breasts. "Is that for Anne by any chance?"

"No. Agnès. Sister Agnès. Look, we're nearly there."

The singing had resumed, more subdued and hesitant as the leaders crossed the flattened grass towards the site of the vigil.

"Caniculares Dies." The young woman smiled to herself. "Except that according to tradition, they were over by the 11th. This is most unusual, don't you think?"

"What is?"

"The heat of course. It can turn the brain."

"I'm sure." Colette was glad of the turf between her toes like a long cold towel.

"Maybe that's part of the problem."

"Problem?"

"Not now. I must go."

But Colette held her arm. "Agnès, something's very wrong here. I know it."

"How come? Five hundred thousand for the Youth Camp and over a million for the vigil. The Holy Father couldn't have wished for more."

"But it's my son, Bertrand. He's supposed to be here!"

"He will be."

"What do you do with feelings like this? I'm not mad, am I?"

Agnès paused, her eyes on the woman old enough to be her mother.

"Ascribe them to the forces of darkness. Today and tomorrow we have light." She pressed her hand in Colette's, then removed it.

"Can I be at the vigil with you, Agnès? It is important."

"Look, I shouldn't even be talking to you now. We must keep our own counsel in public, or suffer seven days alone."

"Seven?"

"More if I'm not careful." She looked to see if any of her Order had noticed so far, but to them, the shoeless woman from Lanvière was just another lost soul caught up in the expectation of miracles.

"So you call it suffering to be alone?"

"One is never truly alone of course," Agnès turned to her, "but to be without the little reassurances, the smiles of life, is surely to be in Hell."

"I spend most of my time there, then." Colette managed a grin.

"You see," the nun's eyes suddenly became intense, "we are as veins and arteries. By us and through us, from one to the next, is the precious Faith carried."

Suddenly a tannoy announcement amongst the trees sent the bird population heavenward from chestnuts and oaks overloaded by stale summer and brown in the dying sun. Soon the preparations for the Mass would be ready with the elevated dais and the requisites for it centred for all to see.

"My prayers to you and Bertrand." Agnès whispered, before flying over the grass to rejoin her group. "I'll see you again, I know."

"Me too." Colette stared after her, then realised her watch showed 17.50.

***

"Colette, this is Father Jérôme and Father Christophe de la Bonté. Two more loyal followers of our Holy Father." Vidal was forced to shout her name with theirs as the hordes who'd gathered by the Eiffel tower were now invading the park from the west. Against his better judgement, the Kommandant had decided after all it was best to be transparent. Besides, he'd argued, the men of God had nothing to hide.

She looked the priests up and down, unable to respond, for the fat one was focussed on her breasts, while his companion's gaze rested solely on Robert. "And finally, Father Xavier-Marie."

A young man with sun-bleached brown hair stepped forward, doing his best to smile. "Hi."

He was the same height as Bertrand and almost the same colouring, but tension made him awkward and hesitant. As a mother, she could tell.

Traffic stalled in the street, embalmed by fumes as motorbikes brazenly snaked their way through. Vidal stared after each one, remembering his own

Deauville bike on the open road – its surge of freedom between his thighs, the wind in his throat.

The lights changed and the five picked their way across.

Colette was hot and dishevelled, her make-up awry and her hair continually pulled from her head by a mocking breeze, but Mathieu was alongside and it would have been rude to ignore him. "Where are you from?" she asked, and his eyes rested on hers without a trace of guile.

"Brittany. Perros Guirec."

She was about to say her parents had once been there on a honeymoon visit, but Duvivier got in first. "We have a Celt among us, you see, Madame." He barked, once more in the lead. He could equally have said Pagan or Peasant, such was his tone. "And I'm afraid they can be tricky."

"St. Jean de Motte Mauron's my main base," the Breton added, ignoring him.

"I think they have the stapes from his ear." Cacheux kept checking his suit, aware of his turn-ups rucking on his shoes. "Or whatever."

The newcomer watched in obvious disgust, clearly feeling no desire to correct him. The fact it was the Saint's left thumbnail now seemed irrelevant.

***

The Bar Auréole was full at the front, but Duvivier had made prior arrangements. At the far end, in poor light between the *Toilettes* and a pair of fruit machines, stood two tables pulled together, with *Réservé* scrawled on one of their beer mats.

"Well done, sire." Plagnol straight away settled his plumpness on the bistro chair to study his new purchases. Two cassette tapes – Fuch's *Die Freiheit* and Karl Lorenz's *Das Bleiweiss*. White wolves, black skies with wreaths of yellow stars. Both new releases on the Gammadion label.

"Ladies first if you don't mind." Duvivier hauled him up by the shoulder, and Colette, shocked by the sudden violence, subsided on to his warm seat. She would watch and remember these things, for this was just the beginning, the unfolding, and she the silent witness until her time.

After the *pastis*, the company relaxed, leaning in on one another, wedging Mathieu tight, elbows and smoke mingling. Anonymous boys on the town. Recklessness in the talk, the laughter, and Colette heard every word.

"Any sign of Bertrand, then?" Robert shouted suddenly from the other table, causing her eyes to dart to the door past the silhouetted army that clustered round the till. Guilty she'd forgotten him.

"No, but it's OK."

"Is Bertrand your husband?" Mathieu, solicitously out of place.

"No. Her big boy." Plagnol laughed, fattening his formless cheeks and

showing the baby teeth again, studded behind his lips.

"How did *you* know I have a son?"

"Just chatting." Robert smiled then tilted his glass for the ice cube to meet his lips. "Gossip isn't only the prerogative of women, you know."

Colette felt her anger rising. Her neck reddening. "It's *my* business. Do you mind?"

"Like the lady says." Duvivier passed her the menu. "Her business."

VI

The Hôtel Marionnette in the Rue Goncourt, that Colette had booked for herself and Robert, was also full. Its lobby a landscape of rucksacks and rolled up mats, while the one leatherette bench was covered in dismembered newspapers. Not what she'd imagined at all.

The receptionist, a flustered woman of Colette's age whose label read Laetitia Lacroix, checked passports and dispensed keys. Everyone sported either crucifixes or bleeding hearts or both, and although dress was distinctly summer casual, there was nevertheless an underlying solemnity.

Before Colette could step in, she was giving Duvivier his room number. "Twenty-five for Father André. To include Father Jean-Baptiste, Father Jérôme, Father Christophe de la Bonté and Father Xavier-Marie. Is that right?" As her pen ticked off their names.

"Perfect."

But to Colette, excluded, the list read more like some grotesque Indulgence.

"Excuse me," she began.

"One moment." Madame Lacroix instead peered over her glasses at the young Breton. "You were a last-minute booking, yes?"

"Correct." Duvivier spoke for him, his hand eager for the key. "Two double beds and a single. En suite bathroom and w.c."

She glanced again at Colette close to his elbow. "Five men together in one room isn't our usual practice I must admit, but Hélas, we are in special times." She handed Duvivier the key, but Colette snatched it in mid-air.

"This was *my* booking," she said. "I'm Madame Bataille from Lanvière-sur--Meuse. I wanted one double room, one double bed." The fob, like an orb, was heavy and empowering in her hand.

"I *don't* think so." Robert took it from her, avoiding her eyes. "On this unique occasion, Madame, we've too much praying to do and need the space."

Cacheux looked at him, smiling his own secrets.

"Indeed." Duvivier concurred as Plagnol spluttered on his cigarette.

The embarrassed receptionist was now trying to compensate. "I'm sorry, Madame Bataille, it appears your request was amended by the gentleman here."

"Gentleman?" Colette glared at Vidal, but he turned away.

"We do have a small room near the linen store," the woman said. "Number 38. All we have left."

Colette went up to her lover. Saw his face, blank like an unworked canvas, bleached of love. She hardened her lips and pressed the room key into his hand.

"You can stuff it!"

"You could reconsider..." said Duvivier, the biggest coward of them all. But, as Vidal moved away to pick up his bag, Colette took a deep breath.

"They're all priests. God's servants," she shouted at the receptionist, "but I tell you they are wolves in lambs' clothing. Don't be fooled. They're dangerous."

***

Colette met the evening crowds, her high heels skewering as Death, the dancing partner, let her reel and spin between the faithful on the road to Hell. Nothing followed, except Vidal's eyes, while Duvivier hid his rage behind a hard, still mask. He knew where she'd be alright, like some stupid bitch on heat – out in the woods, looking for her son.

VII

The Longchamp Vigil had begun, and Pope John Paul faced the multitude of sunburnt faces turned towards him, drinking in his piety, his humanity. Amongst this crowd five men stood together in their black *soutanes*. Anonymous, keeping themselves to themselves, making the right gestures and responses yet all the while thinking of how easily their bishops and colleagues had been fooled. How easy it is to keep the dark heart hidden.

"On the eve of August the 22nd, we cannot forget the sad massacre of St. Bartholomew's Day, an event of very obscure causes in the political and religious history of France. Christians did things which the gospel condemns..." The weary Pontiff continued, occasionally wiping his forehead. His colourless gaze fixed over his flock that reached into the dusky distance. "Belonging to different religious traditions must not constitute today a source of opposition and tension..."

"Tell that to those killed in Souhane!" someone yelled, before a soft, lowing boo wafted upwards.

"Laudate Dominum!" Plagnol shouted, crossing himself.

"Bravo!" Cacheux stretched to clap over his head and all but one of the group positioned within range of the TV1 cameras, applauded in turn. Then Robert Vidal kissed his crucifix, fixing his fervent eyes on the nearest camera lens until it swung away. The Holy Father's words washed over him like the stream that had shaped his grandparents' garden at *Les Cailles* near the Vosges, for as long as he could remember. But each time his gaze fell on the little group of Dominicans, the signal for visible action came in the form of a whistle from between his teeth.

"We pray for the lost sheep of our parishes!" roared Duvivier on cue. "That their souls shall never be sullied by hatred."

"I, too, am here to remember!" Cacheux's voice a clear treble above the mêlée.

"And me!"

Those closest in the crowd touched them, especially Vidal, as if somehow in that moment he'd become holy. The true *alter Christus*. Only Mathieu remained silent and Duvivier drew him to one side, his thumb embedded in his wrist.

"This is your fucking alibi too, remember?"

Mathieu stared in disbelief.

"Alibi?"

"Correct. You must let your parishioners see your fervour," he hissed.

"Why? I don't understand. They already know I'm a diligent priest. Even the Bishop."

"My friend, you may have scant regard for your own mortality, but certainly we need ours." Again the camera was on them. "Say something, damn you!"

The young man faltered. His cheeks ashen.

"Deo Gratias," he intoned three times, as Duvivier cut off his blood supply. He tried to break free but the fisherman whose arms had once harboured half the Corniche des Maures, held him fast.

The Pope raised his hands, and silence descended over the thousands of the young, bereft of dreams, whose heads bent low as Mathieu trembled amongst his fellows. The Pater Noster took an eternity and its amen, like a gathering wave, rose and fell, scattering its syllables into the Paris night, and when all the candles had blurred into life around the dais, the Te Deum began.

***

From her hiding place behind a souvenir kiosk, Colette saw the five priests make their exit, still mouthing the sacred words and Duvivier keeping his fist in Mathieu's back. When they reached the privacy of the first open space, still unaware she was following, the Provençal spat in his ear.

"You are either with us or..."

"Or?" Plagnol interrupted, and soon regretted it.

"Or the door to Hell will open."

Mathieu crossed himself non-stop at high speed, his confession incoherent.

"I only wanted love," he said. "That's why I replied to your notice in the first place."

"Love, my arse." Vidal crushed leaves between his fingers and watched them fall. "Whatever we have told our Bishops and parishioners, we are here this weekend to prepare for a major offensive in thirty-six days' time. You're on board now, and you stay on board."

"You're also duplicitous." Duvivier kept his weight on Mathieu's foot. "And what act of contrition do we advise for such as this?"

"A crucifixion?" Cacheux smiled.

"We can go one better. Something much more original, though it's only recently been done..." He looked at Vidal.

"What's that, then?"

"A little testicular tomfoolery."

Plagnol roared with delight as the chant from the crowd reached its climax drawing Colette back into its midst to look for Bertrand among its prayers.

"*You're* the liars." Mathieu suddenly pulled away, dried spit sealing the corners of his mouth. "I met that Simone Haubrey in good faith. One lonely heart to another... or so I thought. It's you who've deceived me."

Cacheux tittered. Duvivier's knuckles now like white silk. Vidal felt tension snake up his body. "Are we not all lonely hearts?" he said. "But at least we beat as one."

Duvivier gave him a withering look.

"We've got a runt from the Breton backwoods with too much to say for himself."

"Shall we put him with our *Bébé*?" Cacheux was on a roll. "Then they can keep each other company." Duvivier's fist sprang to his chin. Bone on bone, and a chilling hurt to silence.

"What *Bébé*?" Fear quickened Mathieu's tongue.

For the first time Duvivier looked unsettled.

"Do we trust him?"

"Got to, now."

The Provençal glared at Cacheux who was still doubled up in pain.

"The secretary's son." Was no more than a scornful whisper, yet it bought Vidal a flush of guilt. "We're keeping an eye on him, that's all." he said.

You evil dogs.

"Why? What's he done?" Mathieu persisted.

"Alles, *mein Freund*."

Mathieu gulped, but a student selling bagels bumped him with his tray.

"Where is he, then?"

"No more questions, eh?" Duvivier was close. "*I do the talking.*"

They looked one to the other, except Cacheux who was dealing with a spot of blood on his chest.

"You are now one of the chosen few, Father Xavier-Marie, replacing somewhat urgently an old queen with a small talent in photography."

Mathieu thought hard and quickly. Not of the captive son, but of testicles. His own. "I do take a mean shot," he said. "Specially urban stuff, you know, streets, buildings. Compositions with people."

"Perfect." Duvivier allowed a weak smile. "God is with us. I can tell." He pressed his mouth into Mathieu's ear and spelt out in detail the group's two forthcoming missions while Plagnol held him, the stink of fermented beer on his breath. Afterwards, the young Breton crumpled between them until Duvivier hauled him upright.

"But any more trouble my friend, and you'll be dipping in your shroud pocket to pay the ferryman."

Still safe. Still alive.

No-one around as Colette and the crowds dispersed, grey upon grey, and the lights of the city came on to match the stars.

VIII

Colette hadn't eaten since midday, and her energy had all but gone. What remained was a numbing anxiety beginning to blur her judgement. Every young man, even every tall girl with short hair, was a possibility as she peered into the tents and makeshift shelters springing up under the trees. Shadows and solid mass as one, she a mere pawn in the tricks of the summer night. Was her breath drawing on her son's air? Was her path his path?

Suddenly a firework spun into the sky scarring the moon's vacuous face with an arc of fire. Then a siren, underpinning all her terrors and the remnants of faraway lives searching for a bed in that foreign place. She cupped her hands around her mouth and called his name.

"Bertrand!" rose with the city birds into the darkness and died as yet another rocket angling north, ejaculated sparks at her feet.

People had mysteriously vanished. The comfort of closeness taken away, and all her losses seemed to multiply, echoing in that wide oasis. Not since she'd lain in the Hôpital de la Charité in Metz with her fatherless child had she felt so alone. As it was September 6th, she'd named him from the Napoleonic list. Some respectability, some recognition at least. But at visiting times she'd covered her face and blocked up her ears pretending to be a corpse, while sounds of joy and pride had swilled around conspiring in her anguish.

And now again, that same hollowness, except that her child had grown to be an adult in the world, but not of the world. She knew something was amiss.

Robert and Duvivier's promises to look for him were no more than the slender breeze and Dominique Mathieu, poor blind innocent, had flung himself into their arms.

"Madame?"

Colette turned. Garlic breath and cigarettes. She recognised the voice before his shape.

"Come, dinner is waiting." Duvivier found her wrist. "Don't make things difficult, I beg you."

She recoiled away from him.

"Besides, as I'm sure you can appreciate, we all need an apology."

"I'm not interested. I'm looking for Bertrand."

"I thought you might be." His grip tightened. Iron on bird bone, her blood cut off.

In the distance, traffic on the Avenue de la Grande Armée hurtled towards the night life on the Champs-Elysées leaving her stranded with the man in black. Rigor mortis already in her throat, revulsion in her eyes as he brought her hand up to feel his cheek whose surface bubbled underneath her fingers. Her scream was silent.

"Now you have felt the worst, you can have your reward." He kept her fingers locked in his, down over the taut barrel-chest, the waist thickened on good living, to below...

Colette was powerless. This was a monster whose flaccid lump she had to harden between their closeness. He jerked in a sudden spasm, silencing her scream with his mouth – his gasps into her lungs, filling her with stench.

"That's better. Now we go," he whispered as he rearranged his *soutane*, and something else, harder still bored into her side. "Any games and you get this..." The 9 millimetre gun touched her ribs. "The filth will think you're just some tart who got too clever."

She saw his profile half a step ahead. The man her lover had chosen over her kept his gaze erect, his flattened nose and Neanderthal jaw caught by the street lamps at the end of the Allée Cavalière. Their sickly orange haze like the afterglow of war was too public, and in his split-second hesitation, she ducked and headed back towards the darkness. Her shoes like stilts took her into the trees whose trunks on the southern side formed a sheltering screen. A shot sang in pursuit and dulled into wood. Then another, spraying earth and leaves into her hair.

She stopped to listen. Just her breath and endless cars. Nothing else, she was sure, as the priest of three parishes in Les Pradels, worked his way through the traffic back to the hotel. He cursed as he went. The tart was like an unlucky card and he'd blown it yet again. Questions would be asked. From above.

Oh Merde.

IX

"Stupid bitch." Duvivier overloaded his breaded sole with pepper so it looked diseased on his plate. "We can't afford any loose cannons. Not now. She knows us and can recognise us."

But you gave her the names, you abruti. Remember?

Robert pushed his lettuce to one side and took a long draught of Vittel.

"Look, she's more bothered about her kid than anything," he said quietly.

"Quite." Cacheux played with his lemon. Dandled it on the end of his tongue, hoping Vidal would notice.

The five sat in the middle of the Hôtel Marionnette's busy dining room. The pink tablecloth already stained, draped their legs in stiff folds. Two bottles of house red and a carafe of water stood already depleted and Cacheux clicked for more, but Vidal wasn't going to weaken. He wanted a clear head for the next stage. The planning. "We'll have to take that chance," he said.

"You wait. When she gets back to Lanvière and finds her precious bastard's missing..." Plagnol smirked.

"*If* she gets back," Vidal said, busily extracting meat from his teeth. "Leave her to me."

Mathieu stared from one to the other, glad of the red wine warming his throat.

Both Plagnol and Cacheux tried not to look impressed, instead pulled at their steak tartares as if they were carrion. Five priests of the Church, with good appetites and new cash in their pockets. The manager smiled his hospitality, but wondered where the woman in the beige suit had gone. Laetitia Lacroix wasn't one for fairy tales. He brought over another red and watched as the fat one sampled half a glass, rolling it around in his mouth.

"You had a little problem earlier, I believe, Father. Is one of your party missing?"

"Just some streetwalker." Duvivier lit up and kept the smoke till the last moment. "Very persistent, and also quite mad."

"Sounded like it from what I heard." But the manager seemed unconvinced.

"Even called herself Magdalene, would you believe?" Plagnol smiled a string of tarnished pearls. "Pity about the sell-by date."

"Well, you'd know all about wallowing places for fat pigs," Vidal murmured into his glass.

"The Magdalene was the first to witness the risen Christ, remember." Mathieu aligned his knife and fork in a prayerful position, not fully aware of the rising tension around him. "And she's still the biggest mystery of all the synoptic gospels, so we shouldn't take her name in vain."

Cacheux groaned embarrassment under his breath.

"D'you think she might even have been married to Him?" The manager hovered, ignoring the sudden silence. It wasn't every day he had five priests to himself. In fact, he doubted if there were as many in the whole of the 16ième, but when he saw Duvivier's expression change like a thunder cloud over the sun, he collected up their remains and placed a circle of chocolates in the middle of the table. "Still, plenty of takers tonight, no doubt." He brushed the Provençal's ash into his own hand.

"No, this woman was different," said Vidal suddenly, and Mathieu realised she was still important to him.

"You could say that."

"I was her Confessor," Duvivier boasted, whereupon Vidal promptly kicked him under the table. "She liked to talk, you see."

"Oh?"

"Got a kid to support, rent keeps going up, so I just helped her out..." Duvivier's voice tailed away.

"A true Christian, then." The manager returned with the coffee and the bill upside down on a saucer. "But it's never enough is it? Types like that want more and more. A lot of that round here, I'm afraid. Specially Turks." He set down the tray at Duvivier's elbow, but the coffee was ignored. "We've got an eighty-year-old bitch from Bulgaria who hangs round the kitchen – not just for scraps, either."

"Will the Devil's dry old Gateway be open tonight, I wonder?" Plagnol retched laughter without his napkin.

"She's late. Probably found somewhere else." The manager moved away as if to hide his embarrassment.

"Well let's hope His Holiness soon addresses the burden of the dispossessed and the feeble-minded. Long overdue." Duvivier helped himself to the new wine.

"We'll drink to that." Five glasses chimed together as one, while *le patron* busied himself at the bar. And then with Mathieu enlivened by the additive in his drink, the conversation turned to more pressing matters. To the third of October. The second day of Rosh Hashanah.

X

By ten o'clock, with the bell of nearby St. Martin pealing dolefully into the night, Colette, with a mother's instinct, knew something was terribly wrong. She knew that her son hadn't shared the air she now drew into her lungs. That his feet hadn't walked the routes through these trees or his grey replica eyes yet seen The Holy Father offer prayers for the Youth of the world. Prayers he needed more than anyone.

She stood for a moment, locked into the stillness, racked by indecision. She had to seek help, but from whom? To search, but which way? No longer the meticulous office organiser, the one senior secretary on whom Guy Baralet at Medex depended, she was now a stranger, three hundred kilometres away from home and splashing water from a small fountain on to her face and finally Duvivier's filth. The napkin with the Nottingham address dissolved as quickly as the man who'd written on it, leaving glutinous shreds stuck to her fingers and nothing else to wipe on.

She remembered her box of rainbow tissues still in the car, but worse, Bertrand's baby blanket smelling the same as all those years ago. Instead she took out her beads and prayed from the rosary to that other mother who'd watched her own son's shared blood run from his body.

"Vierge Marie, mère de douleurs
Rendez la vie aux pauvres pécheurs.
Pleurons sur l'agonie de notre doux Sauveur,
Et gravons sa douleur
En notre âme attendrie..."

"Come." A gentle voice interrupted. It was Agnès, her cowl drawn up over her head. Her fudge-brown eyes cast quickly over Colette's damp clothes. "We're staying not far from here. I've been looking out for you."

Colette gratefully took her hand, while the other let her shoulder bag trawl through the leaves, barefoot once more.

"Is there any news of your son?"

"You must think I'm crazy, just because I haven't caught a glimpse."

"A mother's love is never madness."

Colette smiled a little. At least she'd not said "Have faith" like the disgusting Duvivier.

"Do you know where he might be spending the night?"

"He just said he was going to find somewhere near. And cheap."

"Has he got camping things?"

"No. Just a few bits." Colette thought of that young Dutchman with his house on his back. But then Bertrand was everything and everyone.

33

"There is a place. Near the Porte d'Auteuil," Agnès volunteered, then seemed to regret it. "Strictly Catholic, of course. Only for those who regularly take Communion." She looked at Colette who remained unperturbed. "Besides, one of our girls said it was now quite full. I think you'd be wasting your time."

But Colette's candle flame of hope was refusing to die.

"That's no problem. Thank you. I'll try there."

"It's quite a way."

"I like walking."

"I'll accompany you, then."

"You can't, surely. You once said if you were seen... Anyhow, you've probably got lots to do."

"Prayers can wait." Agnès crossed herself then locked her arm in Colette's before striding towards the Hippodrome as the moon swathed by clouds suddenly hung free high above the trees.

***

The St. Anne's Hostel marked the corner of a former six-storey apartment block, and its occupants, preferring the great outdoors, took up most of the pavement. They spilled out from the hallway, smoking and wisecracking in languages Colette couldn't decipher, but nevertheless they moved aside politely as the two women approached.

She thought she recognised the same backpacker, but was wrong. The universal traveller duplicated a hundred times on that Paris street, was blond and tall with a serious intent about the eyes.

"I'm looking for a boy called Bertrand," she addressed a group perched on the steps. "Bertrand Bataille from Lanvière, near Metz. He's nearly twenty-four. He has a red bicycle."

They conferred, briefly amused by the word 'bicycle', and also by Agnès who'd pulled a tiny notepad and pen from her pocket.

"Sorry. Best to ask inside. People are coming and going all the time round here," a bronzed Belgian boy volunteered.

Colette and the nun stepped over their belongings, up into the foyer, where a crucifixion hung twisting desultorily from the ceiling. A pay phone and a notice board of taxi phone numbers and local Church services took up one wall; while opposite, behind a sheet of perforated glass marked ACCUEIL, a young woman with dark bobbed hair chatted confidently into the telephone receiver tucked under her cheek. A flicker of recognition for the nun before she gestured to them both to wait while her saga continued.

"Excuse me..." Colette's mouth touched the glass in front of her. "This is urgent."

The Sister of the Pauvres Soeurs meanwhile stood acknowledging the stares of those nearby with a benign smile, as if feeling the spark of kinship that stirred her memory.

"I too was young, aeons ago," she said suddenly.

"You still are." Colette kept her eyes on the receptionist, as she tapped out her impatience.

"Just like a butterfly..." Agnès continued. "One minute this, the next, something else."

"Bertrand's just the opposite." His mother turned away from the irritating employee. "Always so... how shall I say, so safe, so dependable. He'd do anything I wanted."

"Anything?" Agnès looked surprised, causing Colette to reflect for a moment on a recent – and in her eyes – not an unreasonable request. "Really? Do tell me."

"About a month ago I gave him the key to a friend of mine's house to take a look round. Silly really." Colette paused. "But I was sure this friend was up to something, you know, racist, neo-Nazi business. There's been a lot of it recently in Lanvière."

"Oh goodness." The nun looked genuinely concerned. "This is something we could pray about tomorrow perhaps."

Her empathy made Colette continue.

"You see, I try to be a good neighbour to an old Jewish lady on the next floor. She'd had phone calls, poison pen letters, you name it. Bertrand treats her like his own *mamie*, of course, and we both get so upset by all this abuse, but as I work full time, this search was too difficult for me to undertake. Besides, I might have been recognised by someone in the street."

"And he not?"

"No. He wore his stepfather's old coat and a black *képi*. And I did pay him."

"Oh?"

"He's unemployed, you see; so he was glad of it. Meant he could afford to come here, which was very important to him..." Her voice tailed away.

"So what did he find?" Agnès picked a speck out of her eye with her handkerchief corner.

"Nothing. He just laughed and said it had been money for old rope."

Agnès smiled.

"It seems to me you're both very caring people, and that's rare. You are blessed indeed Colette, to have such a son. But where he might be now, well, I don't want to upset you, but maybe he had some private reason to be here. Perhaps to meet a friend."

"He hasn't got any," Colette blurted out, tears suddenly stinging her eyes.

"That's the trouble."

"Are you quite sure?"

This unwelcome doubt suddenly brought all the props of his life into clear and awful focus. His mug with its neat monogram BMB, his coat hangers arranged in size and colour. Clothes from long to short, and not forgetting the pyjamas panda...

"No way. He always told me everything. That was his security. He was an open book."

"I see."

By now, the telephonist had finished and looked up. Colette pushed her face through the gap in the glass designed for parcels.

"Has a Bertrand Bataille from Lanvière-sur-Meuse booked in for tonight?"

The young woman swivelled round to her PC and scrolled the screen backwards and forwards without apparent success. "No-one of that name here I'm afraid. We have a Bartley and a Baxter from England. The closest I can find..."

"Are you sure nobody's just turned up on spec, last-minute, sharing, etcetera?" Colette demanded, resentful of the Britons' good fortune.

"We do have fire regulations, Madame, and now we're full." The young woman's hand finally left the keyboard and all its possibilities as her phone rang again.

"Thank you for trying, Antoinette. We do appreciate it." The nun said unexpectedly.

"That's OK."

Antoinette?

Colette swung round. "You know her, then?"

"Of course not." The nun quickly steered her away towards the entrance and took her hand.

"I could swear her label said Claude Lefêbvre."

"Do not swear at all, Colette, either by Heaven – since that is God's throne – or by earth, since that is the city of the great King. Do not swear by your own head either, since you cannot turn a single hair white or black."

Colette glanced up at her change of tone, but there was no time to react as they were out on the street waiting for the lights to change. The nun still in command, stepping up the pace until they reached the island.

"Oh, by the way," said Agnès, as if anxious to change the subject. "A thought. Did anyone else know of your son's plans?"

Colette stared hard. What made her ask that? Why could that be significant? And then like the creeping dawn clears away the night, she realised that both Vidal and Duvivier knew, probably the others as well, and that for her, the nightmare was only just beginning.

"Don't give up, now." Agnès led her away past more squatters and into the park. "Tomorrow will bring your reward, you'll see. God will answer you." But Colette felt despair leach into her heart, a bleak pervasive melancholy that tainted everything around her. The laughter of other youngsters roaming the streets and boulevards for a bed. Even the appetising smells from the bars and restaurants they passed, had failed to touch her hunger.

"Come back with me." Agnès plucked a leaf from her shoulder. "We've just taken in two homeless girls, but there's still some spare space. Nothing luxurious you understand, just basic..."

"That's very kind, but I must get back."

"Where?"

"The Hôtel Marionnette."

"What on earth for?" The other's eyes widened. "Is it *you* who's come with a friend by any chance?"

"Good Heavens, no." Was too quick, too nervous and the nun wasn't fooled.

"Well, it seems to me like the last thing you really want to do."

"True. You must be a mind-reader," Colette smiled. "But I've too many worries to be on my own tonight." She wanted to confide in her about Duvivier and the trap Vidal and Mathieu had already entered, but a day can only bear so much dislocation. She reached for the nun's hand again and they walked north away from her car, the lonely hotel bed and the winking arteries into the city, back to the solace of trees.

XI

"It's too easy to say the *youpins* are scum. Scum isn't that clever." Plagnol took his shoes off and spread out his fat toes inside his socks.

"Exactement." Duvivier was investigating his ears with the end of a ballpoint's cap, before studying the brown wax he'd pulled out and nibbling it. "Look at that coin of theirs, the ten agorot. If that's not the big give-away, then I'm a bloody Kohen Gadol." He chortled. "And given this Zionist ambition, the social emancipation of the Jew is the emancipation of society from Judaism. I quote from the Red Giant himself."

"What pray is the difference between a Zionist and a Jew?" Cacheux had just resewn a button on his cuff and was biting the thread.

"Our friend Thiriart dismisses that distinction as a subtlety for intellectuals only." Duvivier looked round the room. "So there we can leave it."

"They're all maggoty fruit suckled by the tree of lies. Trouble is, the tree's never bare, the crop perennially abundant, and on the Jewish question, left or right, up or down makes no bloody difference." The Pigface snorted unaware of the slight.

"They eat their greens, that's why. Spinach shit." Cacheux grimaced, having severed the cotton. Vidal looked up from reading a well-thumbed pamphlet of Dégrelle's Rexist speeches which he always kept close like a second skin.

"What's more interesting is this," he said quietly. "When our friend Léon here wrote his open letter to His newly-appointed Holiness not to give credence to the 'myth' of Auschwitz, can anyone remember the reply?" Silence followed, thickened by five breaths. "Then I rest my case."

***

Room 25 – which apart from a dressing table – was filled by three low beds. It was also airless and smelt vaguely of drains. The carpet near the door was worn to the underlay and a plumbing symphony stopped and started from the en suite. Duvivier had installed two bottles of Burgundy and deliberately taken Cacheux's bed, knowing it would cause offence. The priest from the Corbières watched as first his right boot then his left dirtied the cover.

The others in a subtle hierarchy, shared the two remaining beds, with Mathieu placed at The Pigface's feet.

"All I know is they never fast for long enough, that's the problem. Still, I have news." Duvivier shifted his bulk so his lumpen head was propped against the wall. "But first can I reassure everyone this room is clean."

"Clean?" Cacheux's plucked eyebrows arched in disbelief.

"No bugs, you ponce." Vidal laughed, seeing Duvivier's eyes hard as gun barrels. "Anyhow, just to be safe, I checked as well."

"Good dog." Plagnol smirked as Duvivier opened his yellow snakeskin filofax.

"We have the second day of Tishrei in mind. Fun and games for all."

Mathieu looked from one to the other, his ears the first to betray his nervousness, burned crimson. "That's the second day of the Jewish New Year, isn't it?" he volunteered.

"My God, a theologian in our midst," Vidal purred.

"Indeed. Joy and Judgement joined at the hip. Who will live, and who will die." Duvivier's laughter wasn't catching and Mathieu lowered his head. The last of his wine a mere stain in the glass as the Provençal gargled phlegm in his throat and swallowed it. Then he perused the plan. "Right, Code names first. I'm Melon. Vidal is our Water Rat, Cacheux our Wine Merchant and Plagnol our Driving Instructor." Duvivier focussed on him. "Never, ever use a white car. Get rid."

The man nodded but Vidal knew it meant nothing; that The Pigface would always please himself until it was too late. "So who's left?"

All eyes on Mathieu, his knees drawn together, his large hands locking and unlocking in a mime of nerves.

"Our Camera Man. Fill him up." Duvivier passed the bottle over. "When wine goes in, the secret comes out, *n'est-ce-pas*? And what's yours, my friend? What are you hiding from us?"

The Breton whose only crime had been the public admission of loneliness, emptied his glass in one gulp, feeling his own Judas lodge in his soul.

My Lord and St. Thérèse forgive me.

"I loathe all Jews," he began, "they're the black worms of our planet..."

In the deadening silence he saw his mother's eyes widen in horror. Angélique Mathieu, the woman he'd adored, who'd given him his precious name and whose own rosary was lodged in his pocket. "I see them as a plague on all our earthly lives."

Far below, a siren impeded by the crowds, wailed through the streets, but Vidal fixed on the man who'd just spoken. Every muscle tremor, every drop of his eyelashes. The assistant choirmaster from Lanvière needed no persuading.

Mensonge...

"He's lying," he said. "Lose him before it's too late."

"I disagree." Cacheux straightened his cuffs. "Our new friend's quite delightful."

But before Vidal could respond, Duvivier had leant forward and nodded to Plagnol. "Fill him up again. I'm fascinated."

The young Breton drank again and wiped his mouth with his hand.

"I have never knowingly lied in my life." He crossed himself inaccurately and Vidal sneered derision. Undeterred, Mathieu went on. "The Black Death will come again. I have seen it in dreams..." His glass was refilled a third and fourth time, from the last bottle, to loosen his brain and his tongue still further, to bring to life things that the less naïve would have drowned at birth. "I also think," he slurred, "the whole notion of roasting a sheep's head, as opposed to the rest of it, is just to promote the illusion that they are superior. That *they* are the head of things.... and the rest of us are aresholes..."

Plagnol clapped, his pink face glazed with sweat.

"Better and better." Duvivier leant over and dragged his holdall up on to his knees. "And for your peace of mind, Father Xavier-Marie, I can assure you that what you've just said so succinctly is now on record." The rewind on his recorder made the voice lighter, more frantic, a *zizanie* of evil, and Mathieu leapt to his feet, tried to run. But a wink from Duvivier sent Vidal and Plagnol to work.

They threw him on the bed, pinned him down.

"You're one of us, now. The Armée Contre Juifs. Never *ever* forget," the Kommandant's finger scythed a line round his own throat, "or it will be *Nacht und Nebel* for you as well."

Mathieu burbled a whole chaplet from the rosary until the black blood from his nose, filled his mouth.

"Fetch him something!" Duvivier snapped and Cacheux who'd escaped to the bathroom to wash his cuffs, threw over a towel.

"Now then. Jobs for the boys." Duvivier nudged the pages of his filofax with his small thumb, till he found what he wanted. "Pont de L'Alma. Bridge of the soul. How apt," he smiled. "Except our punters won't have one between them. It's to be a luncheon, you understand. One o'clock..." He paused to let corridor footsteps pass by. "A celebration of the sea, no less. Fins and scales only, naturellement. Eight hundred francs per head."

Plagnol whistled, but Mathieu despite his pain, tried to concentrate on every syllable as Duvivier continued. "My contact, Jalibert, tells me the boat is cleaned out at six every morning. Fresh linen first – God what a waste – then comestibles for refrigeration. The only personnel on board is the night watchman Hermans, who leaves at seven."

"Any dogs?" Vidal asked, tossing the bloodied towel back to Cacheux who let it drop.

"I like dogs." Plagnol made a playful barking sound, thinking more of bitches weighted by rows of soft pink teats...

"Only us. Get it? And no to your question. The security beam comes round every thirty seconds. Remember all external doors are alarmed."

"Who exactly are the floaters?" Cacheux had repositioned himself on the bed and was running his thumb and forefinger up and down each trouser crease.

"Mostly in furnishings, textiles. Top brass. What Vidal senior aspired to be, if my memory serves me." He glanced at Robert and saw his expression harden. "But these are the upper, upper echelons." His finger under his nose. "Sheep's heads as you so rightly say, Father Xavier-Marie. Thirty-eight of them."

"Baaaa."

"Orthodox, Religious or Secular?"

"Immaterial. They're all greedy." The Drancy man clamped the wine bottle to his mouth but Duvivier snatched it away.

"You have thirty-six days to dry out, Monsieur. I'm only sorry I can't lay on a wilderness for you."

Plagnol let his fat, moist tongue rest a moment between his teeth, not quite bold enough to go all the way, while Vidal eased his leather jacket over his shoulders and went to the window. "This Jalibert, can we trust him?"

"I take that as an affront, Father."

"How many others know our plan? I mean, why don't we just give France Musique the full works and let them slot it between Fauré and Brahms?"

"Requiems." Mathieu murmured to himself.

"Exactly." Plagnol roared then belched. Vidal's boot got his shin.

"Fat *crétin*."

"Mes enfants, attendez..." Duvivier pulled out a pristine sheet of professional indents and margins. Their mission's title in bold at the top. "Now you were all, except our Breton friend here, sent one of these on June 22nd. Your very own personal invitations."

"Who typed it up for you?" Vidal asked as Duvivier pinned it proudly to his chest. "Is it still on file somewhere?"

The blemished half of the Provençal's face coloured in the silence seasoned by the smell of men. Mathieu grabbed Vidal's leg as he lunged at Duvivier's bed.

"Leave it," he whispered.

"More to the point, who is Kommandant here?" Duvivier snarled. "Who is it will give us glory, not just here on earth, but in the hereafter?" The orator was back once more in his Church of Ste Trinité, letting his words touch the vaulted sky and its ancient, faded stars.

"Count me out till I know who else knows." Vidal held on.

"Well, if we must split hairs, let's talk about your tart. Your Magdalena..."

Cacheux and Plagnol edged away to free the area for a fight. Mathieu held his breath, but Vidal stood motionless, except for his jaw pulsing below each ear.

"Say that again," he said as the siren outside returned

"D'you want an overview or details?" Duvivier smirked. "Like I touched her cunt out there tonight and she brought me off?"

Vidal landed on target while the others huddled by the door, listening to the corridor as new blood speckled the wall. Afterwards, the music lover from Lanvière crossed himself and rinsed his hands. Then, with Mathieu in tow, left the Kommandant to finish his confession.

XII

Outside, neon and sodium mingled against the night sky. The stark uncompromising moon had chilled the air and people camping along the Cavalière des Bouleaux were anticipating an early frost, with extra hats and blankets. Around the tents, cooking smells dispersed in the aura of music and laughter, excluding the two priests who strode without purpose nearby.

Dominique Mathieu loped alongside Robert Vidal, his hands slotted into his jeans, most of his thoughts too rapid to muster. "St. Thérèse is praying for us," he said finally.

"Stuff it."

But Mathieu clung like an eager puppy to its master.

"She knew not all priests were good holy men."

"Well that's alright then."

"And that her vocation in life was to pray for them."

"She was fourteen with a moustache. Look chum, haven't you got anything more intellectually rigorous to say?"

"I adore her. She's my life."

If she'll still have me.

Vidal stopped. Overhead lights slung between the trees honed his nose, sharp as a file. Both hands heavy on the other man's shoulders like a gymnast poised to spring on to his leather horse.

"To me, the Carmelite Reform is irrelevant and unfocussed. Our dear late sister should have done her worldly homework, then she'd have known it's the Cabbalists, running amok on our planet, that are the primary cancers. Lymphatic stuff. Subtle destruction. I agree with Barshakov. They divided two great Aryan peoples: Russians and Germans. The War was their idea."

"But the Protocols of Zion was a complete fabrication, everybody knows that. The Czarist police made it up and look who got hold of it. My God. The power of the word..."

"And the Word was made God." Vidal smiled to himself as Mathieu's true feelings deserted him. But Thérèse's radiant eyes stayed constant.

"Still, a Sainthood's not bad." He kicked a pile of leaves into a sudden spray.

"They got a quickie through to shut the women up." Vidal chuckled without mirth. "So don't be hoodwinked."

"That's just how you see *me*, isn't it? Naïve and gullible?"

"Is it important what I think?"

"Of course."

"I still say you're a dissembler. Duvivier's the simpleton."

Mathieu tried to break the awkward silence that followed. To keep things light with the man he couldn't fathom. A man with the Devil singing in his heart. "Anyhow, Thérèse will be made a Doctor of the Church next month," he said, grinning.

"Marvellous."

"You wait. There'll be a woman Pontiff one day. Ask old Balasuriya." Mathieu pulled down a branch and let it sigh back into place, bringing down a veil of beech leaves. Then he stopped. "There's no escape, is there?"

"No."

"What'll he do to you now?"

"Who?"

"Duvivier."

"Oh, it won't be the first time. At Villerscourt he tried..."

"Villerscourt? That place?"

"Three weeks hard labour my friend. But he was there first. Put one of his flock in an oxygen mask, so the story goes..."

Mathieu gasped, fear tingeing the blood in his veins.

"My God, he really is irredeemable."

Beads of traffic threaded along the Allée de la Reine Marguerite, and although a clear run lay ahead, both men slowed as if their respective thoughts had fused into a single yoke across their shoulders. Mathieu needed to know what had taken his elegant companion to that final outpost of disgrace, and asked as delicately as he could.

"I loved a woman. Once," Vidal said simply.

"The one at the hotel? Colette?"

The newcomer had remembered, and Vidal felt a fleeting shame.

"That's it."

"Funny thing. She reminds me so much of my mother. The way she speaks, the way she dresses even. You couldn't have been more cruel." He was all too aware of the other man's eyes. Burgundy still on his breath.

"Cruel to be kind, *mon ami*. I've got to keep her away for the time being."

"But she brought you here, the poor woman."

"Another of Duvivier's teases. She can know a little, but then he decides it's too much. That makes her an enemy. That's his addiction."

"I can't see someone like her being anybody's enemy." Mathieu could barely say the word.

"She's in the same boat as you, but at least I'm giving her the chance to swim."

"What about me, then?"

A shrug.

"I can't say."

Mathieu stared up into the leafless sky, pierced by faraway headlights. A plane winked its way north to de Gaulle as an empty fear gripped his insides. God was out there somewhere, waiting for his prayer, so he touched his Jesus and mouthed Colette's name.

"At the Marionnette, if I'd known about her son, I'd have told her."

"You'd have been a stiff in ten seconds."

Mathieu fell silent, then when he'd recovered, tried a different tack.

"What's he like?"

"OK. I suppose. Trouble was though, she kept trying to push him on to me. Said he needed a role model, a father figure. For God's sake..." Vidal swept a hand through his hair. "She wanted him in the choir. That was her thing. Every Saturday she'd send him over to me with a begging letter."

"A maman's love, no less."

"I told her she was more like a Jewish mother. She didn't like that at all. Just kept saying it would do him good, build up his confidence. But that's something he was never short of. Cocky little shit if you must know. He could never leave it alone."

"What exactly?" Mathieu startled by the change in tone.

"The fact we were seeing each other. He used to hang around the flat, always bloody there like mould on a cheese – once when we thought he was out, he was hiding. Actually caught us at it..."

"Oh, Lord."

"Can't prove it, but I think he let old Toussirot know."

"The Bishop of Ramonville?"

"Correct. And the rest is history, including Villerscourt."

Spasms of shouting from one of the encampments ended the brief silence.

"He must be about my age."

"Near enough but old enough to know better." Vidal's face had changed. He'd said too much already and Mathieu knew it.

"Something's wrong, isn't it?"

Robert Vidal spun round, and lengthening his stride soon reached the bridle path back to the Avenue Goncourt. Then once on firmer ground, began to run.

Mathieu willed the angels to lift his own reluctant legs. He ignored the welcoming litter of camp lights, instead kept his sights on the shape in front and his ears tuned to the shift of leaves. They were suddenly past the pavilion, the hubbub of the Porte Dauphine and down into the slime and wetness of another season. Both men close, leaping like hurdlers over the beggars and drunks ranged along the wall.

Mathieu reached out, got a grip of Vidal's jacket and kept it. The other trod air for a few strides then slumped to a standstill as two shirt-sleeved gendarmes strutted from the Metro end. One was swearing into his receiver. Four eyes fixed on Mathieu who immediately let go.

"Problem?" The taller officer asked, while the other flicked in the aerial.

"Lover's tiff, is it? Or do we check for héro...?"

"I can explain." Mathieu went for his crucifix again, but Vidal took his hand and fondled it until the police drew back, smiling.

"I see we have some liberal Catholics here, Micha. Well try to keep that little pleasure to yourselves, guys. We've got half of bloody Europe out there to deal with."

The men from the north and the east watched as those other shadows like daggers, ever lengthening, followed them along the tunnel until they were just another part of the lurking night.

"Fascist pricks." Vidal squinted at his watch and readjusted his jacket. "Did you know at least twenty percent of them are in the FN?"

"My father's an ex-flic. Do you mind?" To Mathieu it seemed as good a time as any to say this, but nothing prepared him for the look on Vidal's face. "You can trust me," the Breton said sweetly, his heart pumping overtime.

"I bloody hope so."

Duvivier's not done his homework again, obviously. Merde.

"I meant it."

"Words, words..."

Still that madness. To Mathieu it was frightening and he was quite alone, like he'd been so many times before in the worst of weather on the N12 caught in a crossfire of Atlantic and Channel storms. Was Vidal armed? He wondered. He wasn't sure.

He made a move and Vidal came up behind. Closer than he'd planned and close enough for the running breath to catch his neck.

"Wait."

Mathieu obeyed. For his life. Saw his mother's eyes close as soon his would be closed. A one-second prayer...

"Amen."

Vidal closed his arms around him, neither in love nor desire, but to save something of his soul. "I've got something to tell you. Very, very private. Understand?"

Mathieu stared.

"They've taken Bertrand," he said it as if the very name felt a burden in his mouth, "to The Pigface's flat in Drancy."

XIII

The temporary night quarters for the Pauvres Soeurs des Souffrances were spacious but dark, lit not warmed by small flame-shaped bulbs at each room corner. Light enough for bodily functions, sombre enough for prayer, and on her oblong of tatted rag, Colette prayed with all her heart.

The midnight Benediction had just ended and traffic tearing past in the Boulevard de Neuilly drowned her murmurs. She was asking too much, but He had to know she was bereft, and needing a sign, any sign, that Bertrand was alright. After twice through the rosary and a minute of intense supplication, her propped-up crucifix suddenly fell to the floor.

"I'll get it," a young girl's voice, followed by a perfume half-recognised. She set it straight and crossed herself. "There. Jesus says thank you. I'm Nelly, by the way. Nelly Augot."

Colette saw a stocky girl in tee shirt and jeans, thick black hair and spectacle frames to match. "Your perfume," she said. "I'm trying to remember..."

"Doesn't matter." A plump, warm hand touched hers. "It's only Dune. I never feel dressed without it."

"I'm just the same." But it was as though she was referring to a stranger.

"My mama's favourite is Je Reviens."

"That's nice."

It's mine as well, isn't it?

Nelly knelt alongside and squeezed her eyes shut, like a child at bedtime.

"Did Agnès bring you here?"

"Yes, she's been really kind..."

"I hadn't eaten for nearly a week when she found me."

"Goodness. But – what about your mama?"

Nelly pulled a face. "I can't go back there. It's not a home any more."

Colette sat back on her heels, trying to recall her own apartment, but all she could see was Dolina Levy's old frightened face.

"Mine's not much better."

"Where's that, then?"

She had to think for a moment.

"Near Stenay. On the Meuse."

"Got a job?"

"Probably not any more."

Nelly stared, as if surprised by her apparent lack of regret.

"I did English at the Sorbonne. Been hoping to get translation work. Anything really."

"And...?"

"Bloody nothing. Whoops! That's got to be three Hail Marys." But behind the smile lay a familiar bleakness, the same Colette had seen in Bertrand and the other jobless young on the streets of Lanvière.

"It's harder for you than it ever was for us."

"But my mate Chloë's even worse off. Least I didn't get pregnant."

"Is she here as well?"

"Yes. Somewhere, poor cow. I've sort of been trying to find her, but I'm not that bothered. Honestly."

"Why's that?"

"She's too needy. Know the type I mean? And I can't cope with that. Least not at the moment."

"And the baby?"

"Good Lord, no." Nelly whispered close up. "She got rid of it."

Colette frowned, trying to imagine ending a life when she'd tried so hard to nurture one.

"I'm sorry."

"Now she just wants to get out. Don't we all?" Nelly quipped, pulling at bits on her rug. "Says she's going to hang around in Évry. That her baby's still there even if it was flushed down the toilet."

Nelly suddenly stopped because someone else was in the room, gliding towards them. Colette instinctively stood up as the tall, slender figure in white with a vermilion heart appliquéd to her chest came closer. She gave a tiny, powerful smile until Nelly too got to her feet.

"Sister Marie-Ange, Sister Superior." Her hand cool and smooth from little more than page-turning went from one to the other. "Welcome both of you to our brief abode, although I have of course already met Mademoiselle Augot."

Her ethereal beauty mesmerised Colette. It was as though Heaven itself had brushed her skin with milk and honey. Her eyes of no one colour were set baldly between their lids like those of the Silver Bream. "I trust you've been given some refreshment and that Sister Agnès has shown you your night spaces."

"Indeed, thank you." But it was someone else with a lisp and one foot shorter than the other, who'd performed that task and been too anxious to get away. "Excuse me asking," Colette then ventured, "but is there any sort of bathroom round here?"

Nelly snickered then did her best to disguise it. But the nun paused for a terrible tense second.

"That will be dealt with I can assure you, Madame Bataille. We do in the meantime have contingency plans. Naturally, once the Holy Father has completed his programme tomorrow, we shall be returning to Libourne and a semblance of normality."

Libourne?

Colette wondered what these contingency plans were, until memories of vineyards where the Dordogne and the Garonne meet at the Bec d'Ambes came flooding back.

The summer before her Bac, she and some school friends studying François Mauriac had camped in the very pine woods that had so imprisoned poor Thérèse Desqueyroux. A place of black, pillared trees and the Atlantic wind roaring its exclusion through the days and nights.

"It will then take the rest of the week to resume our routine, but I'm sure the good Lord will forgive us." The Sister Superior turned to the bespectacled ex-student of English. "And what are your plans, young woman?" Are you reconsidering your decision, or are the Pauvres Soeurs merely a convenient rock in the midst of your particular torrent?"

Nelly glanced at Colette, pushed her glasses further up her nose and cleared her throat. "Your analogy of a river, Sister Superior, is excellent, and I admit to being a worthless piece of flotsam adrift in our state of advanced capitalism, but if we're talking about brides of Christ, then I'd rather be a demoiselle d'honneur." Her gappy smile failed to disarm, and Colette looked on, embarrassed.

"Allow me to clarify one small point, Mademoiselle Augot. We are not simply a contemplative Order. Our prayers are in equal measure to our good works..." She paused. "Or you for one wouldn't be here."

"Nor me." Colette was trying to surmise what colour Marie-Ange's hair might be under her veil.

"Precisely. And like yourselves, there are many others who have benefited from our charity. In fact, all over France."

"D'you mean they come to you?" Colette asked.

"Yes, but we also reach out to them."

Colette and Nelly exchanged glances.

"We set up our 'Bienvenue' Centres wherever the young of our country are congregated. Be it a religious festival, folk festival, it makes no difference."

"Good Heavens." Colette tried to grasp the logistics of such an enterprise.

"But I would emphasise our requirements are not for the faint-hearted." The senior nun pulled out a fob watch from a side pocket and rewound it. "I'll speak with you again in the morning after matins. In the meantime, let us hope the Lord's sleep will clear your heads."

Her audience of two stared after her and stayed silent long after the doors had closed.

"Can you imagine some low-life rasta seeking this lot out?" Nelly looked bemused.

"It's possible."

"Well, on second thoughts, I'd rather be faint-hearted. How about you?"

"I can't be. I'm supposed to be looking for someone."

"Oh? Who's that then?"

"My son. Bertrand. A student."

The girl patted her arm encouragingly.

"Well don't worry. When we're out of here, I'll help you."

Colette saw the halo of window light around her unruly hair. The brightness enlarging, fixing her in its power and instead of saying the Mater Christi, or other soulful pleadings, the secretary from Lanvière simply closed her eyes.

"It's very sweet of you, Nelly, but I really don't think you can."

XIV

Breakfast was a cold brioche and a thin conserve of doubtful origins, while coffee, too long on the simmer switch, came out like black tar. The impermanence of paper plates and cups, with their attendant flimsy stirrers would soon, in the Refuge des Pauvres Soeurs at Libourne, be pine and sycamore; heavy apostle spoons and napkin rings engraved with each member's name.

Colette ate slowly, trying to get her bearings, aware of everyone's stares, and isolated by the absence of those who'd earlier made her acquaintance. The sole diner in a worldly suit, she sat near the self-service trestle where she could ignore the curious and watch instead the three helpers, set apart from the rest in vivid red, whose identical features looked pale and swollen like dough. Triplets, she guessed, performing their tasks slowly yet with the thoroughness of the blind. She'd wondered why they'd been taken in, if they had parents, but when she'd tried conversing with the girls, someone behind her whispered a warning.

Colette scoured the queue for either Nelly or Agnès, as gradually her table filled up with more strangers. Their robes billowed out behind as they sat down bringing with them a faint smell of urine.

After scrutinising her, they set to, guzzling from their trays as though that would be their lot for the day. Grace had been a brief mumbled affair by a novice to a half-empty room, as sunlight bored through the window on to her already etiolated face and the pile of suitcases behind her.

Colette still felt light-headed, for her early morning conversation with Sister Marie-Ange had been little more than a one-sided confession. Maybe she'd said too much, maybe not enough. Whatever, an eddy of efficient succour had caught her, and somewhere, far away on the bank and fading in the heat, someone familiar had been waving.

"I'm sorry," she said to the novice next to her as her stirrer flipped into new territory. "This is all new to me."

"Me, too. I've only been here twelve hours and that's twelve hours too many."

"You didn't have to stay."

"Oh, didn't I? " She showed Colette the inside of her elbow where the basilic vein was raised more purple than blue, making her neighbour wince. And one look at her rice paper cheeks, old before their time, and the tense pucker round her mouth made Colette edge further along the bench.

"You're not coming *here* are you?" her neighbour asked.

"Oh, yes." Colette used her napkin to wipe her knife, then as it was more usefully thick than the last one, hid it for later, in case it was bedpans again that night. "So you see, I've got nothing to lose."

Her pale companion stared then shook her head.

"What's your name?" Colette deflected.

"Chloë. Sister Marthe now, so they tell me."

"I've heard about you," Colette spoke softly, aware that other ears were close by.

"Oh, yeah?"

Colette wanted to ask about her baby but judging by her pallor it was best to leave it. Instead she rejoined the coffee queue.

Suddenly the room fell silent. Outside the window the drone of incoming traffic was interrupted by the sudden, violent thud of a blackbird hitting the glass. Colette saw it fall to the ground in a sorry, dead heap.

Another little gasp rose up as the Sister Superior with Agnès close behind came through the door. All activity ceased, and the meagre cutlery laid down with a sense of occasion.

"We shall muster at nine-thirty with those newest to the Pauvres Soeurs bringing up the rear when we leave for the Mass," said the Sister Superior.

Colette thought Chloë looked about to faint.

"No personal effects, no pens or paper either as we are recording the whole celebration for everyone's later use. Besides, you will need both hands free for prayer."

Agnès nodded agreement and Colette tried in vain to catch her eye, but the signal came for eating to resume and the two Sisters moved away to a far table. Of Nelly, still no sign.

Doubly disappointed, Colette held out her beaker and stared at the identical threesome more closely. Each had the same fringe below the same red veil, but their eyes, the weirdest of all, were like little beads fixed on to puckered skin. Even when Colette passed her hand in front of them and tried to ask their names again, it was as though the dead stared back.

"They're glass," a voice whispered. "Born blind with just holes for eyes."

Colette spun round spilling her drink down her skirt. Nelly was helping herself to a butter pat. "But they're such poor girls, and they look so unhappy," she said.

"Wouldn't *you* be, stuck here with this lot?"

Colette ignored the coffee stains that had spread to form a leopardskin pattern. Instead, she pointed to Chloë. "And have you seen her? The poor girl looks really ill."

"She's had it." Nelly still in her street clothes, found an end space and moved along, but Colette stayed standing.

"I could try and help. Someone's got to."

"I don't think so, somehow. Her mind – I mean she wasn't all there after you know what..."

"Well I suppose at least she'll get looked after here. Better than sleeping rough anyhow."

"I suppose," Nelly said wrily.

But the chance for further contact had gone as Agnès was marshalling everyone before her, including the triplets who'd finally left their post.

"May I see you for a moment, over there?" The Sister Superior was silently upon them with a frown spoiling her forehead. Colette's coffee jumped in her throat.

"Fine. No problem." Nelly misjudged the gaze and got up.

"I mean Madame Bataille."

The student subsided to watch her confidante led away to a side door marked S. S.

***

"We have five minutes. Our Lord cannot spare more." Sister Marie-Ange used her desk as an island, around which she appeared to float in perpetual motion. A bare prop for her performance, with no blotter or pens to detract from its deliberately sparse symbolism. "It is now time to ask." She smiled, locking her hands together in anticipation. "Do you wish to become one of us?"

For a moment, Colette's heart seemed to stop. So this is how it had been for Chloë. Poor sad Chloë, and yet...

"I've certainly given the idea a lot of thought." Was truthful but desperately procrastinating.

"One can consider things for the rest of one's life, Madame Bataille. The pit of uncertainty is like the pit of Hell." She pulled out her rosary beads, mother of pearl, the colour of tears, and began to recite of charity towards one's fellow being in a manner that became almost singing. And when she'd finished, stroked Colette's hair. "Just think, with us you will find here a true and deeply satisfying happiness. A refuge from the troublesome world, and I know this is what has sorely vexed you for so long. That you, who have a kind spirit, have suffered more than most."

Had Agnès been talking, or had she herself unwittingly added to the Sister Superior's armoury? Colette's heart again uneven, and sweat bubbled hot on her forehead.

"I'm not sure..."

"We are here to grant you peace. The closest you will ever come to that of eternal rest, with benediction for your body and salvation for your soul." Her voice possessed such sweet monotony that Colette grew dizzy in the searing shaft of sunlight. She gripped the desk as the words washed round her like a silent, numbing sea.

Suddenly, as if from nowhere, a sheet of cream vellum appeared with the letters P S S in gold, across the top. The Sister Superior's very own pen was in her hand. Her fingers closing over it. "Anywhere will do for your signature. And I know St. Barbara is already beginning to welcome you as her namesake."

A tiny bell tinkled from somewhere on her body and the door opened. Not Agnès, but that lame nun again who limped over and, after the signing, helped drag the new recruit to a small adjoining annexe that doubled as a stock room. There the Sisters of Charity left her and locked the door.

XV

Eight stops under the Seine to the north east where the nondescript suburb of Drancy lies excluded from roads curving to the warm south. Its name obscure on any map, makes a small mean sound in the mouth. Its railway to the Vistula, however, has been a generous source of trade in human cargo and now entwines with the new TGV route from Lille. Goods of a different kind move in perpetual motion while the rising and landing planes of Charles de Gaulle scrape the skies above.

Plagnol's territory.

The two priests sat motionless throughout save for the widening irises of each eye as stations loomed out of the blackness then vanished.

"Next stop," was the only thing Vidal said, though it wasn't for want of thinking. The address and key, for emergencies only, lay in his wallet together with new phone cards and an assortment of foreign coins. In his inside pocket, a coil of fuse wire and a spring, used already at Villerscourt to pay his final call on Tessier. Also a Browning semi-automatic he'd bought last year.

He watched Mathieu study the map above the carriage window – a country mouse fathoming the city's hidden arcana – and felt a small satisfaction that in this situation he, Robert Vidal, would have the upper hand. The Breton had visited the metropolis just once before, with his mother, to the Mass for Toussaint during his last year at the Seminary. The whole experience had proved so crushing, so burdensome to his spirit, that the closeness of his mother had seemed then the only escape.

DRANCY. Works in progress, widening the platform. The drilling made a fog of dust, lit up by arc lights. Vidal slotted both their tickets into the exit gate and led the way up the steps past two *beurs* squatting close together in badly stained Arab dress.

"A few francs, sir?" one of them asked in bad French.

Mathieu paused, searching his pocket.

"Leave them," snapped Vidal.

"I can't."

The taller man pulled him away.

"Noir shit. I'm trying not to breathe."

Mathieu still managed to throw down his coins, and the beggar yelped as they hit him.

"Sorry, mate."

"Allah will save you, sir," said his companion.

"He's done alright for you, I see." Vidal sneered, bounding out into the forecourt where a solitary taxi waited with its four doors wide open and sounds of Roch Voisine drifting into the night. Mathieu looked back to check they weren't being followed. Saw Vidal's profile cut-glass hard, giving nothing away. "We'll walk."

Mathieu sensed this man, who liked to disappoint, needed time to think. He therefore bided his time, keeping up a determined camaraderie as they turned into the Avenue Gambetta. Like everything else, Vidal knew the address off by heart.

"It's just past the Renault place. 15a, le Passage..." His voice different, quieter. He was obviously troubled and slowing down. "Look, this wasn't my doing, understand?"

"You could have stopped them."

"As The Holy Mother's my witness, I knew nothing. It was all stitched up with Duvivier while he was holidaying at Villerscourt the week before me. They're real bloody fools. Whatever the stupid kid's done, this isn't the answer."

Vidal's face tightened to a splinter under the street light. A dog barked from somewhere as the traitor double checked his watch.

Mathieu wondered where the Jewish deportees' collection point and the memorial were. Where the blind terror of the tunnellers, shot like rats, and those fresh from the Vél d'Hiver round ups, had coalesced into a quiet futility.

And where, God, were you? Surely an answer after half a century isn't too much to ask?

Then he recalled his own shameful words from the Hôtel Marionnette's bedroom and looked up to the stars as though they were the Almighty's eyes winking admonishment.

That's all very well but at least now I'm trying to help, to make amends...

But in reality, there was nothing to choose between him and the accomplice next to him, dressed for the night in black leather. He crossed himself repeatedly, then quickened.

"Not so fast, pal." The assistant choirmaster caught up and kept his hand on his shoulder as they reached the Renault showroom taking up a large corner plot, topped by limp flags. Sleek new cars like glossy aubergines reposed on a thick-pile carpet in the showroom. The luxury end of the market at odds with its grim surroundings, and where Plagnol had not long ago indulged himself by buying his white Laguna outright with cash.

Beyond, an apartment block of ochre concrete reached above the street lamps, its balconies inlaid, plain and body length. Ready and waiting, Mathieu thought, like the Étagères de la Nuit with their morbid array of skulls, in St. Paul de Léon.

Suddenly a starling shot out from the entrance, beating its wings in terror.

He jumped, for a moment clutching Vidal's arm.

"Nice place." Vidal disengaged himself while Mathieu hung back, taking in the dirt, the neglect on what was a typical example of post-war urban architecture. It had a secret and forbidding air. Even the list of occupants individually encased behind plexiglass were almost bleached out, and Vidal's finger trailed from top to bottom without much fervour.

"Where's Plagnol's name?" Mathieu asked.

"Idiot. It's Lautin. Charles Lautin. Very clever, I must say." Then Vidal stopped, took a step back. "I can't."

"What d'you mean, can't? We've got to see if Bertrand's alright."

Vidal scanned the building and shivered. It was as silent as a house of the Dead, and for the first time, he looked Mathieu squarely in the eye.

"Come on. Let's get back."

"No. I'm going in."

Vidal restrained him and Mathieu felt his panic as if it was his own. He took the advantage and pressed the buzzer faintly marked C. L. No sound, nothing, and no intercom either. *Merde.*

"You're on your own."

"I'm not, damn you."

"What are you saying, then?"

"Haven't you heard of God?" And as though fortified, Mathieu pressed another with *SUZELLE Mme,* in pale italics.

Vidal struck him across the mouth. Warm blood cradled his tongue so that when the elderly occupant of flat 7 called from above, he was unable to reply.

"Who's there?" she cried. "I'll call the police."

"That's what we want," Mathieu managed to burble.

"Shut up you!" Vidal hit him again. "It's er... just a little disagreement Madame. Sorry to disturb you..."

"There's someone in 15 who could be dying!" the Breton yelled, free for a split second. "It's urgent!"

"You imbecile." Vidal had him by the hair and crushed him against the wall with a silent strength. "We came, we cannot see because there is after all, nothing to see, and we leave because I do not wish to be maggot fodder just yet. OK?"

Suddenly the sound of keys and a cobwebbed light over the door giving them no quarter.

"Don't move." Vidal, the music-lover tried an embrace, but Mathieu was ready, pushing the old woman to one side and taking the stairs behind her three at a time. "Come back you bloody fool!" boomed up the stairwell behind him, as on the fourth floor he found 15a on a scruffy red door, and heard a low moaning in the brief stillness before Vidal reached him. Mathieu's fists pummelled the wood. He shrieked to Bertrand that his maman and Jesus still loved him and not to lose his faith, before Vidal felled him against the banisters.

A door opposite opened briefly then closed and Madame Suzelle's screams diminished as she too found sanctuary.

Vidal's watch was fast and in frustration he slapped Mathieu some more before wiping away the worst of the mess. He pressed his ear tight to the paintwork. *Le Bébé* was calling for his mother, calling and choking, and a trickle of something invaded the landing, reaching his boot. His own lips moved on a whisper, not a prayer, then he dragged Mathieu down past the bedridden and the drunks, down towards the sound of the one o'clock bell from Notre-Dame-de-la-Consolation. Plagnol's Gothic church darkly spearing the sky.

Just as they rounded the corner for the station, a white saloon surged down the Rue Gambetta. Vidal saw two silhouettes as familiar as himself and quickly pulled Mathieu into a doorway so he could stare at the disappearing lights of the Laguna. The give-away car, carrying The Kommandant and The Pigface towards their prey.

XVI

"You awake?"

Colette felt the touch of a hand on her elbow. One touch too many, and she pressed it tight against her body.

"It's me. Nelly. I've been hunting everywhere for you. Some idiot must have forgotten to lock the door, thank God." The girl eased Colette's arm round to see exactly the same marks as Chloë's. Then she studied her face and gasped. "What in Hell's name have they done to you?" Her lovely eyelashes had gone, and it was obvious the pretty pink varnish had been hurriedly scraped from her nails.

The latest recruit opened her eyes to see a stranger with thick glasses and a conspicuous gap between two front teeth.

"Who are you?" she asked with a glazed expression.

"Come on," Nelly whispered, "let's get you out of here."

"I can't... I need rest."

"It'll be *in aeternum* at this rate." She tried to raise her, to properly open her eyes, but Colette slumped to one side, like a rag doll.

"Oh Christ!" Nelly kept a check on the door. She'd managed to prise the small window apart and pull the shutters behind her, but soon someone was bound to notice even though most of the Order had gone over to the Mass.

"I want to stay. Can't you see? The world is too evil for me. I want to forget everything. Everything."

Nelly panicked. She could see neither bag nor belongings. The woman had been stripped to a cotton shift with that same bloody red heart on the chest.

"They've nicked all your gear, hoping you weren't going to wake up till Bordeaux... What have they done that for?"

"I don't care any more. I don't care..."

"Well, somebody's got to. They're leaving at five. Then, where will you be?"

"I'm alright. Just leave me alone."

"What about your son?"

"Who?"

"Oh God..."

Nelly was under the camp bed, her arms like a swimmer, searching for anything they might have overlooked. But the floor was bare save for a few feathers.

She crawled out and knelt next to the woman twice her age. A mother she'd have far preferred, otherwise what else was she doing here putting herself on the line?

59

"Chloë was Number 43," she said. "You're 44 and I overheard yesterday they need forty-five."

"Forty-five? What? Apples on a tree? Dairy cows?" Colette's lips moved on the possibilities.

"Yeah, or else no money to keep going. Finito."

Colette turned towards her. Her eyes half hooded, still bloodshot.

"I don't understand..."

"Yesterday, after Nones, Sister Superior was whispering to Sister Agnès. I was pretending to do up my laces. She said the Abbot de Lagrange Vivray would keep his fist tight unless the Soeurs recruit that magic number by All Souls. So you see, that makes us very special. They won't want to lose you and they need one more. Me. But I'm not that desperate. Ever seen those huge cockerels bursting out of their crates in the Rue des Rosiers? That's what it'd be like for me. Look, I confess, I just used this lot to get a meal and a bed. I can't live without the sky..."

She crooked her arms under Colette's shoulder and began to pull, when all at once something passed by the window, breaking the filament of light.

"That was her. Quick!"

"Please, just let me be..."

"Can't you see they came here to trawl for poor needy bastards like us." She tore a corner off the Pater Noster sheet. "Here's my mama's address and phone number. Hide it." As the key rasped in the lock, and the door handle lowered in slow motion, Sister Marie-Ange swept into the room, but Nelly charged past her. Out into the other less dangerous world.

***

And Nelly got her sky but took no pleasure in it. She should have stayed, put up a fight to get Colette out, but, she thought, staring at the ground between her knees, maybe God had his reasons.

She sat hunched on a bench near the Porte d'Auteuil, tense and frightened despite all her bravado at the Résidence. She'd been grateful at first, like anybody would after a week of slumming it, with a tumble drier for a stomach. But she'd been more clever than Colette, dodging round the nutters, keeping one step ahead, even sleeping propped up with a giant hairpin at the ready. She also hadn't signed anything.

But why was Colette so important to them? Why had she been sedated so quickly in a separate room, and all her things taken? And what about the son she'd mentioned? It just didn't make sense.

Nelly looked up at two swallows curving and teasing above her head, so obscenely at liberty it was unbearable. They flew off, arching noisily on neurotic little wings towards the river.

Two things she now had to do. The first was to get enough money together to rescue Colette, and the second, find a bed. The only reason she'd tagged on to the nuns in the first place was to get away from her mother's sordid existence and living on her terms fifteen floors up. But the night was only hours away, and she was exhausted.

Nelly found a phone, dialled the Numéro Vert – Student Helpline – and lied she was still in her second year. After an agonising wait she was finally told the Catholic St. Anne's hostel had one bed left. A cancellation five minutes ago, and lucky she'd phoned. Forty francs a night with a communal bathroom and prayers compulsory.

Thank you God and merciful Jesus.

Next, thirdly and importantly, she must find herself a crucifix.

XVII

Mathieu and Vidal reached the Hôtel Marionnette at 01.45 hours. The night receptionist gave the two men a cursory glance then returned to his *Tiercé* list for St. Cloud the next day.

The place was hushed as though all the faithful had retired for contemplation and, by the time they reached the third floor, the already stagnant air had noticeably thickened.

Vidal had checked the parking round the back. No Laguna, so there was time to slide into bed and feign sleep, but as they approached Room 25, a line of brightness edged the bottom of the door. Like some feral night creature, Vidal stood with his dark head cocked, picking up every small sound.

"Cards," he whispered. "And Cacheux's losing."

As expected, the priest from the Languedoc showed no interest in their return, instead he glowered at what he'd dealt himself. Suddenly his mobile burped inside his pocket. He pressed descramble, his sloe eye on his room mates, watching their every move.

"Father Christophe de la Bonté's playing with himself again, I see," Vidal sneered, but Cacheux ignored him as he concentrated.

"Got the artichokes in? Yes sir," he said. "Two tons. One minute thirty-seven seconds exactly. No. Not had a chance... Be unloading immediately. Right on, sir..." Then smugly back to the Solitaire while Mathieu watered his face and Vidal, having unzipped his fly, peeled off his jeans.

"What's all that crap, eh?" he asked. "Bloody artichokes now, are we?"

"You should have been here."

Vidal folded his socks into his boots, a habit from Seminary days, and patted the Browning in his nightshirt pocket. The queer was stealing his thunder.

Not good.

Then he checked Mathieu was out of earshot. "Where are the others?"

"You're mad."

"I said where?"

Cacheux cringed over his game.

"Went out for a drink, that's all."

"Liar." Vidal's fingers tightened on the nape of his neck, like he was a dog who'd just fouled the floor.

"Ask them."

"I'm asking you." His nine millimetre on the man's atlas bone, cold and hard.

"Pont Neuf. For a quick drop, if you must know."

God have mercy… So that's why the Laguna had been in Drancy.

Vidal let go as Mathieu veered towards his bed, his head swathed in the stale, bloodied towel. Never in the confessional had he been privy to such a terrible secret. He got into bed fully dressed. Even the rosary he'd overworked all the way back couldn't ease his torment. In his mind's eye he saw Colette, then his own mother and rolled back and fore, covering his face with his hands. At one point, on the brink of sleep, he called out to St. Thérèse to help him.

"Fat chance." Cacheux toyed with the card pack, stacking it then letting the cards slide into a path of graceful submission. "Anyhow, what's up with him?" He tried to soften Vidal up. After all, this was a bedroom and they were almost on their own.

"Too many Schnapps."

"My, my. Boys' night out, eh?"

Vidal was still close, so he could also see out of the window. He elbowed a clear patch through the condensation. All quiet in the Rue Goncourt, or so it seemed – shop lights still on with offices above on timers, casting in intermittent darkness the kerb crawlers, the odd lost tourist, and winos using the pavement as their dance floor. *Thou God seest us...* he mused, then snatched his breath. A white car he recognised was creeping round to the parking.

"Into bed," he ordered Cacheux. "Not a sound. Move."

The forty-year-old priest hung up his jacket and dropped his trousers over the chair back, hurriedly checking the creases.

"Leave them."

Then Vidal slunk behind the door, his gun ready.

Voices he recognised. A shared bonhomie that suddenly sickened him as Plagnol's underwater laugh swelled to fill the hotel. "A good night's work, *ja?*"

"Ausgezeichnet."

They were dishevelled. Duvivier's duffel coat damp and stained on the arms, his neck as red as Plagnol's. He turned his best side to the priest from Lanvière, avoiding his eyes.

"No choice, my friend. His tongue was longer than the Loire. We'd have had it if he and his *liebe Mütter* had met up again."

Vidal put his lips to the pulpy ear, to black wax and the smell of a grave.

"It's a pity your memory has let you down Father André," he hissed. "Someone's taking the piss. *I'm* Number 2, not that pervert."

Suddenly cold hands closed round his throat for blood and river water to rain down his neck. Plagnol was enjoying himself but not smiling while Duvivier helped himself to the gun. "We still have a small problem, my friend.

You see, our *Bébé* couldn't stop talking, even at the end. He swore that just before we arrived, someone, maybe two people had come to jump him. Naturally, we wonder who they might have been. And then to cap it all, he hoped Jesus and his own maman would still love him. I ask you..."

"He was entitled to something, poor bastard." Vidal murmured. "Big mistake. As long as I don't live to regret it."

"If she hadn't run off it might have been different, and now Monsieur le *curé*, we have other things to attend to which are far more important." Duvivier nodded to The Pigface to let go. "We must finalise plans for October 3rd. Order new phones and equipment etcetera. We won't need any 'pianists' after all. Sorry about that, Number 4." He looked over to where Cacheux was simply a lump in the bedding. "I know how much you were looking forward to twiddling with your own transmitter, but the good Lord has put better technology at our disposal. And finally," he pushed Vidal against the wall and placed his parchment lips on his cheek, "most urgent of all, we hunt the tart."

Vidal stared, his thoughts in delirium. "You can't."

"Insubordination. Tut, tut. Such a disagreeable trait, don't you think, Father Jérôme?"

The Parisian from Drancy chuckled as he pulled back the covers to see if Mathieu and Cacheux were really asleep. "Absolutely."

"However, our friend here knows the score..." The Provençal's voice rose to its full preaching height. "Any more of that and we'll have mother and son meeting up at last. As fish food. And bon appétit to that." The words were intoned like his grim Sunday bell in Les Pradels, and Mathieu who'd woken on their return then tried to sustain the rhythm of sleep, heard every word as invisible tears burned his blindness.

XVIII

The cream and green Vacances Mémorables coach left the Résidence over an hour late and the driver, a mannish woman in her early forties, wearing a black open-necked shirt, wove in and out of departing traffic on the capital's outer Périphérique, to gain any small advantage.

With a clearer run after the Porte d'Orléans, she touched 100 kms an hour and her steady speed lulled the party of Pauvres Soeurs into a sleepy trance. No radio or video, instead it was interminable rewinds of the Holy Father's message that invaded their sleepy minds while silent prayers and other more personal convocations lay on their lips.

Colette opened her eyes. Warm next to the window in the westerly sun, she saw a huge silver sculpture, brazen white in parts, then the low buildings of a flying club and posters peeled by the long summer diminishing into countryside. Trees and more trees, cattle grazing uphill. Suddenly a hand she didn't recognise on hers and a voice whispering urgently in the silence.

"It's me, Chloë. I kept trying to find you, but you weren't at the Mass..."

"Oh?"

"So they've got you too now. Join the club." Resignation and resentment in equal measure, but her fellow passenger hardly noticed.

"This is just the beginning for me..."

"What do you mean?"

"My new journey..." Colette's veiled head rested against the view. Bone directly on glass, as all her cushioning hair had gone.

Her hair... The colour of Limousin corn, he'd said...

But it didn't matter, like all the rest of her worldly goods as the wheels droned south through fields flattened by the sky, stained by an early sunset.

"I'm thirty-nine kilometres from my dead baby," Chloë announced. "Thirty-nine and a half... forty..." She'd worked it all out and her frail hand tapped on her knee, keeping tracks.

"I had one once," Colette said dreamily, seeing a gypsy with a papoose strapped to her back, picking weeds by the roadside. Then Chloë nudged her.

"They're coming."

Suddenly a commotion rose from the far end. The aisle was blocked by both senior nuns making their way towards the back of the bus. A stack of bedpans rattled underneath as Sister Agnès advanced with a trolleyful of brown paper picnic parcels. The driver took no notice. After eighteen months with the PSS, she was used to all their idiosyncrasies.

"You're looking much better today, Sister Barbara." The tall, young woman stooped over Colette. "But it's time for your multivitamins again." Four capsules were shaken from a little box and handed over.

"She doesn't need anything. She's fine." Chloë kept eye contact, and her hand on Colette's.

"I think I ought to be the judge of that. Are you ready, Sister Barbara?"

Colette opened her mouth to take the offering, uneasy about her new name. *Wasn't Barbara shut up in a tower somewhere? Oh God, why can't I remember...?*

"Good. Well done."

But when her back was turned, Chloë made her stick out her tongue and removed all the pink fragments. "Vitamins, my foot." She stuffed them in the ashtray, then craned forwards, worried she'd missed some kilometres as signs for Fontainebleau and its châteaux came and went. "Can't you see they're trying to bloody kill us?"

The Sister Superior who followed the trolley suddenly rang her bell causing the driver to turn and look in her mirror. She then switched off the tape.

"We now have Grace." She folded her hands but kept her eyes on each picnic package as it was seized. "Benedicite, benedic, Domine, nos et haec tua dona..."

A piece of yesterday's baguette, a tomato, and portion of chicory heart. The Pauvres Soeurs, including the triplets, tore off the wrappings and crammed their cheeks full.

"Since when have we become swine at the trough?" glowered the Sister Superior. "You and you," she pointed to the main culprits, Sisters Ursula and Margaret, who blushed red and began choking, "will say three Aves, and Sister Cecilia will hear your confession when we arrive." She then put her mouth near their ears and hissed. "We can't afford to put our débutantes off. Do you understand?"

"See, they're worse than the bloody Gestapo." Chloë left her snack untouched. "And this stuff's got God knows what in it." She took Colette's bread and sniffed it. "Told you so. Look, from now on, you and me are going to move Heaven and earth to get out of this..."

"This is a relative Heaven to me already." Colette murmured. "Why should I want to leave?"

"That's such crap! See those poor fuckers?" Chloë pointed to the front of the coach, to where triplets Stéphanie, Victorine and Adèle, still in red, sat squashed together on one seat. "That's how we'll end up, I'm bloody telling you..."

Colette recalled their simple faces, their eyes of the blind before birth. What she'd been once and could be again. But other things were slowly imposing themselves like a mosaic reconstructed, bit by bit. A man's body brushed with dark hairs, the weight of him warm and firm seemed to press on her in that very space. His scent from somewhere, and then another, different, softer, *Bébé Bise* talc. White, with a pink top and a matching nappy-wearing rabbit on the side.

That was it.

Unforgettable. And the child himself had been so sanguine, so easy... Her *"petit bâtard"* whose face she could no longer find.

"You OK?"

"I don't know."

Evening shadows fingered the land as the coach headed into the dying sun, and Madame Falco who'd pulled her visor down, shouted she needed the *toilettes*. The Sisters Marie-Ange and Agnès stood up. "As you know," said the older nun, "when we stop, it's for our driver only. You're all to stay on board and the usual arrangements will apply."

"It's disgusting." Chloë's voice too loud. "Worse than the cattle trucks!"

"Hush."

"They were sent from near here, you know. Beaune la Rolande."

"And Pithiviers." Colette stared out looking for evidence of those hateful railway lines amongst the flat, shaved land. "We're no different."

Once signs for Blois and its châteaux had come and gone, the driver turned into the Aire de Mauvoy. She leapt from the cab, stretched her arms then jogged towards the shop. Forty pairs of eyes followed her every move, every smallest show of freedom, and of course, she exaggerated for their benefit, Chloë could tell.

"Bitch."

Immediately the Sister Superior sprung to her feet and like a wraith, flew up the aisle.

"The Devil has lodged in your soul, Sister Marthe. I knew that from the moment we took you in."

"Let me go, then."

A wary silence descended as all heads turned.

"Alas, that is a luxury we cannot grant you. You will serve your penance at Libourne and make good the evil that is now your incubus."

"You're murderers!"

"And what are you, pray? See everyone, how our Sister here is digging worse than her own grave. She would be wise to consider her fate, and the soul of the child she murdered."

Chloë tried to wriggle free but the woman with the advantage of height, held her down as Sister Agnès shot Natolyn deep into her arm. Colette was helpless, but something made her gasp. She recognised the phial and its lettering. Natolyn was the latest product from Medex. For sleep and truth. The most effective yet developed and also if misused, the most deadly.

This doesn't make sense... no sense at all... what's going on?

Chloë's head slumped into the gangway. Colette tried to shake her, anything to rouse her but she looked like death and Colette called out in fright.

"You'll be next if you keep that up." Sister Agnès was giving out bedpans to the few with their hands up. No longer the kindly soul Colette had met in the Paris park, but someone with duties to perform and a régime to sustain. Her face seemed to belong to someone else, her mouth just tight skin showing her age.

"You're a heretic of the lowest order," she spat as Colette cowered against the window. "The things you've told us, upon Our Lady's Heart, you will live to regret. Our partners in Christ – our brothers, the priesthood – have been defamed and defiled by your treacherous words, and by implication, the whole of our mother Church. We will remove the honour of St. Barbara's name unless you recant."

Colette screamed but nothing would clear her head.

Recant what? For the love of God, what have I done?

"We know that Father André is one of the most dedicated of priests in the south and that Father Jean-Baptiste of Ste Trinité has raised the stature of his church through his great love of music. How dare you!" Her breath strong enough to move the sunset from the sky, fan flames of terror into the safety of the coach. There was no escaping the witches' fire. No escape.

Colette felt for the comfort of her string of garnets, her grandmother's precious gift, but realised with growing horror, the rosary had gone.

XIX

Vidal's watch was still showing fast. He slipped it off his wrist and flung it into the metal bin. The noise made Duvivier rear up; go for his gun under the bolster.

"Holy Jesus!"

"That's trash. I need new."

"OK, so we're shopping today."

"Good." Vidal was first into the bathroom to shave and shower, then first to dress. It was important, and more so without his timekeeper. Duvivier eased his white legs from the warmth of his bed and Vidal saw calves flabby off the bone and toenails edged in dirt.

"By eleven-thirty you'll all be fixed up. Professionally." Duvivier gargled Aqua Vit and dribbled it back into the glass while the other rolled up his robes carefully. There'd be no time to iron anything back in Lanvière, what with Vespers at six and his chief choir master Moussac griping as usual.

He stored his razor inside his spare socks and zipped up his bag with the noisy finality of someone who must stay on top. To make sure the Provençal had too much to do to go hunting for Colette. He'd failed once. He wasn't going to fail again.

The others stirred. Mathieu looked dazed and rubbed his eyes open while Plagnol strolled naked across to the en suite. Vidal stared in disgust. He'd always been partial to blancmange, even as a kid, but no longer. The man was an aberration. Pappy breasts and a groin-overhang lined by red sweat.

"You've a Jew's prick," he observed. "How come?"

"He asks how it comes. I'll show you." Plagnol started to work it but Duvivier pushed him through the door.

"What advantage then hath the Jew?" he said. "Or what profit is there of circumcision? Much every way; chiefly because that unto them were committed the oracles of God. So, my man," he sneered, "consider yourself in exalted company. Now cover it up."

"What a pity," Cacheux smirked. "I was just beginning to enjoy myself."

"You filthy little runt." Vidal raised his shoulders and clenched his fists like the boxer he'd once been at school.

"Hush please." Duvivier opened his Breviary, its pages ochre against the tabletop. "We have more pressing matters. First an Indulgence to the Lord then breakfast. After that, you'll go to the Entrepôt Tronchet warehouse with my list. They're expecting you at ten. By the way, my good friends, feedback suggests that yesterday at the Mass was an unmitigated success. No doubt you'll find your flocks increased upon your return. That'll keep the shekels rolling in."

Plagnol emerged from the en suite accompanied by the toilet flush, his hair wet, smooth as a mole. He struggled into a pair of dingy underpants while Mathieu chose to dress under cover as Duvivier continued. "Even though we'll be scrambling and descrambling with new codes, we continue with our Trucker-speak on our phones. Understood? These numbers are the only ones we use, so log them into your brains. This way the G.I.C. won't be able to touch us. Hincel are market leaders, so we'll have the best."

To Plagnol first, he passed a sheet of lavatory paper bearing five lines of personal digits. The Pigface was too slow in memorising them so Vidal relieved him of it, scowling. "It should have come to me first."

"Who says?"

"I'm second in command. Correct?" He searched Duvivier's face for agreement, but the brief generosity had expired.

"That is no more than an abstract notion. Like the argument of Seraphim versus Cherubim. I will use whoever I choose, sire. Now," he turned to Mathieu, "I've ordered a 125 mm zoom. Pocket size. I want trial shots by the 30th and the real thing by the birth of the Blessed Virgin. Understood?"

The Breton nodded his unruly head and fixed his flies with shaking fingers. "You fill me with such confidence," Duvivier sneered. "And you," his pock-eyes fell on Plagnol, "will sort that fucking white car. No sale, no trade in, just dump it. It's not your woman for God's sake though you act like it is. Plenty of possibilities between here and Drancy I'd have thought."

Mathieu shivered at that name as his comb made an uneven parting on his head.

"We'll be hiring on the day."

Cacheux, who'd been cleaning his shoes with the sanitary towel provided in the bathroom, looked up. "In whose name?"

"Never you mind." Duvivier's finger pressed the prayer book pages open and closed his eyes. "Oh God and gentle Jesus, we kneel in your presence and pray to you with all our souls to engrave in our hearts the feeling of hope and charity."

Then, with the Pater over and the timetable of the skills and fitness programme in place, together with weapons allocation, the occupants of Room 25 made their way down to the dining room.

Vidal rehearsed his questions, including the identity of Duvivier's typist – enough to last the half hour and delay the chase for Colette. But the southerner's appetite didn't extend to answers, just ham, the hard-boiled eggs and a noxious bowl of prunes.

He was on his own, as he always would be. The Breton, no longer biddable, just stared from one to the other, while Duvivier having pinched his biceps told him that by the Feast of St. Jérôme he wanted to feel iron instead of muscle under his skin, and hear an engine instead of a heart. "We're the new Jagdverbande, remember. The hunting élite." He ejected a black prune stone in the youngest priest's direction.

And Vidal thought of pigs with wings.

XX

Saturday August 23rd

It was 09.15 by the Breton's watch and still no mention of Colette. He'd tried phoning her flat. No reply, but something told him her line was tapped. Probably by the exchange in Lanvière, or the Caserne de Latour Maubourg's octopus had spread its tentacles east.

By the time the small party had gathered outside the hotel, Vidal knew from every syllable that had issued from Duvivier's mouth, that the Kommandant did indeed have other things on his mind, and his distracted handshake on the corner of the Rue Goncourt and the Boulevard Ara seemed to bear this out.

"Gare de l'Est at noon," he said. "We'll debrief during lunch before our various departures. On this occasion, the flesh has parity with the soul. Amen." Duvivier's hat cast the top half of his face in shadow so Vidal couldn't read his eyes. "If by chance I'm detained, be so good as to wait." With that he slipped his case under his arm and set off in the direction of the Pont d'Iena and the Eiffel Tower.

Vidal was tempted to follow, to find out what the southern snake was up to, but the warehouse was twelve stops away in the 20ième, and trains were likely to be busy.

"Forty-one minutes." He conferred with Cacheux. "And when we get there, I'm the front man, OK?"

"Oh yes?" Plagnol's face alive with anger, but after Cacheux whispered a sweet something, he backed off.

Mathieu slouched along, making no attempt to dodge the happy and confident tourists who strode through him as though he was invisible. Sometimes he lurched between the other two collaborators who let him rebound one to the other like a pinball. Gone the clinging novice, now a man dizzy with guilt.

"Sort him out!" Vidal snapped, keeping his distance in front. Something in the air refuelled him, reminded him of Eberswïhr at the end of summer 1982. The day his father got his 'licenciement' from his employers Goldman and Berger after almost forty years of impeccable timekeeping and maintaining the looms to perfection. The same late sunlight on the wax tablecloth and the big man-tears shining the backs of his hands.

Sepp Goldman, whom the young seminarian had met only once, had ended his dismissal with a helpful quote from the Torah. "Return you backsliding children and I will heal your backsliding..."

The Jew from Lübeck had dished out the final insult. After that, father and son both joined the Croix de Feu, agitating in secret and daubing their croix gammées on the 'Jews' Tower' apartment block.

Vidal began to jog, to fill his diving lungs and flex his legs moving at last towards his mission with a clear conscience. Like Christ on the waters of Galilee, the tide of Paris life seemed to recede before him. At last, justice for the Gentile underclass. The Aryan indigene. After all, hadn't S.S. Sturmbannführer Sommer torched a few Paris synagogues in his time with plastic bombs, and his own late *copain* Pol Marnon fire bombed the 'Jewish Barracks' at Sachsenhausen? Not to mention the youthful Pope's employment at I. G. Farben?

He'd not felt so uplifted since leaving Dégrelle's funeral three years before. His hero, who'd likened the Waffen-SS to a holy order of young apostles, carried by a faith nothing could check, had spoken to him from the grave and now it was his turn. He was one of the chosen race, the Kingdom of priests.

The vision of his choir too, fuelled his spirits to new heights – never mind he had The Pigface, the queen and the misfit in the Cause, the Armée Contre Juifs was now his second Saviour, and the memory of Sepp Goldman's heartless smile spurred him on.

XXI

Duvivier was sweating with nervous anticipation after only ten minutes yet, when he stopped to cross the Avenue Gustav Eiffel, he introduced a tie to his neck. He then rolled his duffel coat and hat tight under his arm and straightened his cuffs, flattered by the girl who stood close enough alongside for him to feel her body through his clothes.

"Hi." She groped for his hand. "You busy?"

Another Magdalene, a ten-a-penny whore, when his mother and all the other women he'd admired had been regally tall, this one was too small and her cheap perfume overdone.

"I am."

"Well, I can wait. I like you."

Never in his whole life had anyone ever said that to him. Neither the girls who used to hang around until dawn for the fishing boat *Delphine* to come in, only to take his brother Hubert away to bedrooms he'd never know. Nor even his mother, Madeleine Irma Büber.

Two earnest blue eyes bore the hair-line edges of contact lenses, her lips full and red lay half open ready to mouth his reply.

"And what do they call you?" he asked.

"Yveline. And I'm not what you think."

"Where you from?" Not that he was interested, but questions had over the years become a habit.

"Montrouge. Off the Rue de Bagneux."

"Ah. You must know the Maison des Tisserands, then?" If she was lying, this would do it. He'd once stayed in the pension next door while visiting his grandfather, old Jean Büber, just before he died.

"They're the best craftsmen in all the world," she said with authority.

"That is truly amazing, Mademoiselle, considering they'd all departed this life by 1875. It's now a Museum. Ten francs a go."

"Oh." The girl blushed.

"So what's all this about? Who set you up?" His grip tightened and her rodent cry gave him a frisson of excitement.

"No-one. I just thought..."

"You're coming with me, Mademoiselle." He glanced right then left before stepping off the kerb, and then with the Champs de Mars under his feet, he began to march and holler the Marseilleise. They made an odd pair, but in the aftermath of the Mass, there was enough camouflage with other couples still mooching about the tourist attractions.

Suddenly his smell became a problem as Jacques Ange-Gabriel's entrance to the École Militaire loomed up in front. It suffused her, choked her. Garlic and neglect.

"Let me go!" She struggled, disadvantaged from the start, trailing him up the steps.

"I have certain business matters here, and while I attend to them you're to remain in the vestibule under observation. Understood?"

She fell silent, using that interlude of collusion to study and remember as much as she could. The maps of sweat under each armpit. That damaged face he could never quite keep hidden, and the hat she knew he never usually wore. Things had gone wrong but her wits hadn't yet deserted her.

"Look, I could be your daughter, your mistress even."

Her naïvety was repellent and, as his nail found her elbow vein, she paled in pain.

"You imposed yourself, remember?"

He nodded to a guard who'd just redirected a family of Germans outside. "Bloody cheek, eh? Think they can come crawling all over our country as though nothing happened. Schmutzigen Krauten." He grinned then pointed to the girl. "By the way, see this one doesn't move from here." His voice echoed like the rough unpredictable sea in that formal place, assembly line of the brave.

He left his companion on one of the replica Louis XV chairs and leant over into Visitor Reception where his pass was scrutinised, and the indigo thumbprint checked. Within the minute, Duvivier was through the vast double doors and heading with his noticeable sailor's gait towards the Instruction Centre. His steps following those of the great Bonaparte with, as far as he was concerned, the same purpose.

Ten o'clock, and with Vidal and the others safely out of the way at the warehouse collecting his gear, he allowed himself a smile as a subaltern in Swiss uniform gave him further directions to office Number 53 belonging to the formidable général Georges Déchaux.

***

After thirty metres of corridor lined with prints of the Prussian War, another young officer again checked his papers and kept them.

The man's wart was the first thing Duvivier noticed. Bigger than last time and more brown – like his hands – contrasting with the rest of his skin that resembled the lightest Carrara marble. The old friends' handclasp was warm and prolonged with Déchaux's thumb impressing three times for the Father, Son and Holy Ghost. Just like old times. He could even have shared Duvivier's genes, with the same stockiness and pugnacious profile, however, the chief difference was his baldness waxed by the sun to resemble an artificial fruit. He poured his friend a coffee from the fluted Sèvres service on his desk, then helped himself.

"So, Number 5 is now one of us?" he asked, nimbly lifting a sugar cube from the bowl using pewter tongs. "I confess, Father, I've never replied to a Lonely Heart in my life." The cube plopped discreetly into his cup. "But then we live in desperate times." He took another. "Our friend was very smitten by Giselle Subradière, obviously."

"Obviously."

The priest too long constrained by the twin reins of the Humanae Vitae and the Pastores Dabo Vobis, felt old jealousies return.

"Giselle, or should I say, Simone – and Patrice, let's not forget – is a girl of many parts. Doing well." Déchaux filled his mouth with coffee, and let it ease down his throat. "Lucky for us her catch was a fervent Dominican. I want dogs, not bitches in the front line. They have other attributes."

"He knows the score." Duvivier set his hat and duffel coat aside, deciding to say nothing about Cacheux's proclivities. "But we do have another little problem."

"Oh? You mean Papa is an ex-flic?"

Duvivier stalled, discomfited.

Merde.

"I didn't know that."

"It's not your place to know everything, *mon ami*. But let me put your mind at rest. Jean-Girard Mathieu is a Front National Founder member. In the good old days I recall, he used to nuzzle next to our friends Remer and Dégrelle very nicely. In fact," he leant forwards as though they were in a public place and might be overheard, "he took his lovely wife on holiday several times to the Costa del Soldaten. Left her on the beach so he and Léon could chinwag over the sangria." He sat back smiling only with his mouth. "Now he's running some workshop or other for *chômeurs* in Orléans. Noble stuff. Clean as a whistle, but he may be very useful. If his kid starts squealing, he'll just be pissing in the wind. So what's this problem of yours then?"

Duvivier tried to keep it light, but the man's dead-flesh face was fixed.

"*Le Bébé's* dear maman. There were too many halfwits hanging about at Longchamp for me to keep hold of her. She could identify us all. Holy Jesus knows I did my best..."

Anger, black and visible moved under the ice. The général wasn't convinced.

"How long has she been missing?" He refilled both coffee cups, deliberately slopping Duvivier's as he passed it over.

"Twelve hours."

The Hauptsturmbannführer studied his Kommandant. Thick set, peasant stock whose only refinement came from the German side and six years in the hortus conclusis of a Roman seminary. A layer which like the false pelt on a motherless dog would never grow, rather it could be all too easily dislodged. Nurture again defeated by nature, and the reason he wouldn't know just yet why the Bataille boy was being detained. Duvivier was too free with his mouth, and that could make Vidal take matters into his own hands, driving maman into further dangerous waters.

Déchaux licked his lips.

"I heard she gave you two a lift to the Bois de Boulogne. How come you agreed to that?"

This unexpected question made Duvivier's eyes disappear altogether.

How the fuck do you know? Did you bug the bloody car or what?

He desperately tried to adopt a man-to-man banter to pre-empt any retribution from the one whose whole body language spelt out dismay.

"I suppose she was good-looking – for a tart anyhow." He saw Déchaux pick up a pen. "It was sunny, you know the sort of thing, summer sap rising... I am not as some would suppose, a cold fish. I do have red blood in my veins, whatever any Papal magisterium might try to deny."

Déchaux rolled his pen between his fingers. He normally enjoyed farce, but this was stretching things. Perilously.

"Celibacy was your choice, Father André."

"At least I don't violate my own kind. Not like Tessier," the priest added, still on the defensive. But the military man from Reims had all the while sketched a *croix gammée* on to his pad and was now intensifying it with short incisive marks. His safety valve, and equally importantly, his emblem of luck.

"He's immaterial. But Number 2 should have put a stop to things instead of letting her see you... Risky, very risky..." He stared at the man who'd scored highly on detail in the Rorschach test, but had often missed the broader picture. His recruit, who'd smashed headstones at Carpentras so thoroughly, wasn't one for implications.

"My apologies, mon Général." Duvivier knew how to play it. He'd had enough dealings with him to know when to bow out.

"She must be found." Déchaux picked up his second phone and dialled Internal Operations; an eyebrow raised to the sweating priest as he was connected. He covered the mouthpiece. "But keep our *Bébé* content until then, OK? We don't want complications."

Duvivier felt blood surge to his head and turned the offending side of his face away as the général impatiently tapped his pen.

"Description?"

"Mid, late forties. Beige suit. Blondish. Good legs." *Leading to a nice little cunt...*

"Full name?"

"Colette Marine Bataille. Madame."

"Where's her car?"

But Duvivier felt the man knew everything. This was just a cover, a formality, and it was insulting.

"Still at Neuilly for all I know."

"We'll trash it." Déchaux covered the mouthpiece and Duvivier noticed the tanned hand at odds with his face, the squared-off nails. Luxury and efficiency. Chicken and egg. "That was the first thing you should have dealt with."

"Again my apologies."

"Address?"

"Apartments Cornay. Six or eight, not sure. Rue St. Léger. Lanvière-sur-Meuse. Block of flats. The général clicked down a list on his pc and smiled.

"Got it." He barked into the phone. The widow was now a nuisance, whose number was coming up. "Two guards, two shifts. Penis heads, bikers. Line and Ferey will do. They have keys." Déchaux scratched above his ear. "By the way, don't forget the old Jew in Flat 3. Get the Apparats to deal with that too." He put the phone down and faced the priest. "Is there anything else I need to know? Any other little private follies that might affect our operations?"

For a split second the Provençal looked stricken.

What did he mean? What else did he know?

Was August 20th 1967 of any significance? The night his brother Hubert slithered off the *Delphine's* deck into the dark hiding sea? Slippery with fish juice, the deck slats no longer wood but silver moonstone where he'd fallen... blood spots erased with his foot then a prayer to the sky for his mother's heart, that he, Francke the ugly one, would take his brother's place in her warm bed.

Duvivier searched Déchaux's face for clues but the man, whose Waffen SS father had witnessed the capitulation of the German army in 1945, hadn't scaled the peacetime heights through stupidity; and for a moment the other felt rudderless and unnerved. Nourished on reactions and give-aways, his every move had always been designed to elicit nothing less, so now in this arid climate, his gratitude had turned to fear.

"I asked if there was anything else?"

Duvivier took his hat and coat in both hands as if gripping a lifebelt.

"No, but..."

"Secrets are the aphrodisiacs of power, and in this venture, my friend, we have none. We are all equal."

Duvivier tried to clear his throat.

"Some *poule* tried to pick me up near the Eiffel. Called herself Yveline, little liar. There was something about her not quite right. More a bloody schoolgirl if you ask me, but I had the feeling she was after something..."

"Where's she now?"

"In the entrance. I told the guard to keep her there."

Déchaux swivelled in his chair to face a small monitor at the end of his desk.

"Let's take a look, shall we?"

Duvivier came round and saw that same orderliness unusual in men of a physical nature. The screen showed a suited man at Visitor Reception, the guard dusting his boots. Nothing more. The girl had gone.

Salope.

"Oh dear, Francke," Déchaux tutted. "What did you tell this one?"

"Nothing, for God's sake. Just that I had some business here."

Déchaux saw the other's mouth shrink to a grim line.

"Look here, none of my business, Father, but..." he redialled Internal with his pen, while his free thumb caressed his wart, "a small step into the world of women during your formative years wouldn't have come amiss. As for this – my how shall I call it, addendum to my nose – has never been a problem. Some, especially the young, actually like a challenge. Almost like having two cocks."

Duvivier coloured and fingered the crucifix in his pocket. His prayer a miscarriage of memory.

This man's wart is nothing to my burden.

"Romy, kindly see if there's a young female hanging about. Denims, blue contacts, cropped hair..."

"Thanks." Duvivier picked up his hat and his case.

Romy? Another of his women?

"A bird in the hand may yet take us to the biggy in the bush. Ah, by the way, Melon, how did you find my typing?" He offered Duvivier a Panatella, but the door was more inviting.

"Excellent, Georges. You're quite the Renaissance man."

"Number 2 rehearses in water next week, yes?" Déchaux lit the end and inhaled.

"Correct."

"Four sessions with our diving chaps should brush him up nicely. No need to go to Quelern. We can do it all here. He's cleared with Toussirot by the way. Senile old fart. Although to be fair, he has of late been exceedingly useful."

"Putting him away for fucking was a good idea." Duvivier observed

Déchaux's alarmingly white face in front of him. The man whose chief possession – knowledge – was more tangible and powerful than any faith.

"I agree. But at least it gave us a chance to put our *Bébé* to bed for a while. Has Number 2 any problem with this? Do say."

"No more than usual."

"Keep him sweet, Father. We don't want him shitting in the nest."

Someone else is doing that. Duvivier nodded.

"He's the best we've got. Can't have him getting sentimental. Do you think I'd have recruited him with these encumbrances if he'd not been worth it?" He held the coffee pot upside down for the last of the black liquid to escape the spout.

Duvivier watched the drips hypnotised.

Stigmata, all over again. Hélas.

"What happens if we find her?"

"Not if, when."

"Alright, then. When?"

Déchaux looked up, his lips stained like some character from the Commedia dell'arte. "They can play happy families, of course." He smiled. "Somewhere in the Elusion pedion, no doubt." He smacked down his cup.

Duvivier knew there was something else, but his discomfiture had returned with a vengeance, so no more questions.

"By the way, we've got the Xantia for Number 3. Red. See he uses it. Now listen." Déchaux's tone barely a whisper. "I'll be in Szrebreniza on September 30th. New thing. Just come up. NATO needs me and that's all I can say. Memorise my code." He repeated six numbers until the priest got it right, stood up and gripped Duvivier's shoulder. "To La Patrie."

"La Patrie."

Once outside, the Provençal checked for any sign of the girl, extracted his beads and with a heavy heart added his new secret to the other Sorrowful Mysteries of the rosary, while indoors in Room 53, the général took a helpful call from Libourne.

XXII

By 9 p.m., the gunmetal clouds had rolled in from the Atlantic and entirely conquered the sky. One month before the vendage, and already the heavy vines along the Dordogne could only nod in the gathering wind, their greenness sombre in the ominous dark. From the distant Church of St. Fiacre came the tolling not just of the hour but continuously to save the harvest from the storm, and this Colette heard in her mirrorless cell as she wiped the long sleep from her face.

Meanwhile in the room adjoining the Chapel, Sister Rose busied herself with making it up for its next purpose. "Something's upset the Almighty," she said, setting out four chairs, three to go behind a trestle table, and the last on a lower level in front. "There'll be trouble, you'll see."

She spread out a white table cloth, making sure its red heart border hung as prettily as though for a party.

Though God knows I've done plenty of those in my time, what the two now at rest and the triplets...

Her rough hands kept smoothing the top, echoing her contentment. Peace at last with her secrets all shared, her burdens lifted.

Sister Rose smiled at her handiwork, then from a Champion supermarket bag pulled out her silver polish and a cloth. The silver things were in a box under the window, and the best bit was seeing the little treasures rub up a treat for the glory of God. By now she knew the arrangement inside out, although not what it was all for, just as much of life at this Refuge in the Rue de l'Abbaye lay beyond her understanding.

Bedpans one day, or setting out like this on another and although some tasks were more pleasant than others, she nevertheless began each with a prayer of thanks for being spared any further vicissitudes of life with a drunken husband who'd damaged his triplet daughters for soiling. Now they too had sanctuary, and for that she was grateful, even if she'd had to lie and say they'd been born blind.

Two candlesticks, thirty-three centimetres apart, one inkwell together with pens arranged to form a cross, and finally a small salver of sand. The little woman stepped back and bowed before scuttling out in time for Vespers.

The open half of the window played host to the night wind's rising moan until Sister Cecilia swept into the room to pull the black curtains across, whereupon they swelled up like vast malignant sails. Best to have some air on these occasions, she thought, teasing the wicks into life with a taper.

She then crossed herself and sat down on the right hand chair, as was the custom for the Confessor. It was also her duty to be first *in situ* with her special little book opened ready with a feather marker. Her bulbous eyes stayed constant on the door as it jarred like a death rattle in its frame. She'd heard enough of those during the past year to last a lifetime, lost souls cast out without even the comfort of the Prayer for the Dead.

"De profundis clamavi ad te..." she began it to herself in readiness as suddenly the door opened against the draught and slammed like a thunder clap.

The Sister Superior, Sister Agnès and Colette processed towards the table. Colette kept her head bowed, her hands in prayer, the way her parents with the help of a ruler had shown before her Confirmation. And now in this room, this place of women, she would not disappoint them.

She knew from her dream that her very life lay in the balance.

Thunder and bells echoed simultaneously outside as the two Sisters joined the oldest of the Pauvres Soeurs and the most experienced of her calling. Sister Cecilia. A woman whose face so closely resembled a draught horse, that in her home village in the Mayenne, she'd been known as 'The Percheron.'

There was no invitation for Colette to sit. The chair was simply a ruse, nevertheless she clung to it as the three began the Credo. Then Sister Cecilia was ready, her pen poised above the Book of Sin...

"Sister, do you know why you are here?"

"I do not."

"Then," she made a show of conferring, "it is our duty as Pauvres Soeurs des Souffrances who are joined with our Holy Lord and His Holy Mother for all eternity, to read out your wrongdoing."

"Wrongdoing?"

"We in our Christian wisdom call your allegations Heresy, Sister Barbara. What have you to say?"

Colette trembled. Then a pause to save herself.

"You are mistaken as God's my witness..."

Her interrogators exchanged glances of derision.

"Come come." The Sister Superior leant forwards, her fingers forming a pious arch, her intimacy unnerving. "You had enough to say for yourself when last we spoke. It's all down in here." She waved the book aloft as new thunder drowned her last words and the curtains tore at their moorings.

"You've got the wrong person. I don't understand..."

"But I think you do."

"Consider your soul if nothing else." Sister Agnès added. Her total detachment making her an eerie stranger.

"We heard you again during sleep and your accusations remain constant."

"Exactly." The Confessor licked her finger and turned down another page as the candle flames wavered and suddenly died. "Now you will not interrupt until I have reached the end. Then you may explain your evil storytelling." She stood up, balancing the evidence on her open palm.

"You have known carnal lust with a man appointed by God and the Holy Father in Rome to lead the sick and depraved towards a purer life. You have allowed yourself to be aroused by his tongue and his hands and your body to be a receptacle for his seed. Not only this, but in your out-pouring of lies you accuse Father Jean-Baptiste of the Église de la Sainte Vierge, Father André of Sainte Trinité and other Godly representatives of planning murder and mayhem. What is your response?"

The Percheron put down her book and waited, not once deflected by the turbulence in the Heavens nor the lightening that startled the room. The nuns looked at one another, then Agnès got up and heaved the window shut as another deafening strike shook the Refuge.

"God is disturbed" she said. "And rightly so." She crossed herself, then whispered to Sister Cecilia. "He sees His Kingdom rent by spells and devilry, and you, Sister are a poor hapless creature caught up in the plans of Satan."

"With respect, I don't agree she is a poor hapless creature." The Sister Superior's cheeks were tinged with a vicious blush. "We have before us a knowing and insidious mind. I could tell the moment we met. And of course, this is not her first sin..."

"What is the other, pray?" Agnès asked.

"She gave birth to a child out of wedlock. A son."

"Well, that puts me in good company, then." Colette retorted.

"Excuse me?"

"The Virgin was no different."

Six eyes focussed on her in disbelief, and Sister Agnès tried to leave her seat, but was restrained. There was more conferring while the bells of St. Fiacre overruled the din from the skies with their own agitation.

Colette swayed to the recurring vision of wide water and fields of reeds stretching back to pasture. That same young man with her colouring and her eyes, still brandishing his arms as if each wave would be his last.

"With this viewpoint, Sister, by equating your shame with such imaginings, you have placed yourself amongst the lowest orders of human life and we have no Absolution for such defilement." Sister Cecilia's voice grew louder. "You are a contagion and therefore, we must think how best to contain you."

The pen shrieked on each downward stroke, and the Confessor could barely record quickly enough, the anger in her heart.

"You are equating your son with Christ, is that it?" asked Sister Agnès in an even more alien tone that Colette could only stare at the transformation. She gripped the chair so hard that its wood and her bones felt as one; her mouth disabled, until those two words "Your son" had finally registered. She, Colette Bataille wasn't mad after all, despite everything, and now his face grew clear. The boy on the banks of the Meuse was her own flesh and blood. Her Bertrand.

She took a deep breath, steeled herself inwardly, giving nothing away, but then set her hands for prayer, openly begging for the mercy of the Lord to descend. The Sister Superior – Marie-Ange – sniggered contemptuously, then whispered to Sister Cecilia, who put down her pen.

"But we digress," she said. "I agree. Sister Agnès, it is tempting to dwell upon this other matter, but I wish to return our heretic to my first question." She left her seat and came to stand at Colette's shoulder. Again a whiff of urine, and this time, cabbage.

Thibaut – Duvivier, Father André of Sainte Trinité and all the other deceptions of his sordid little life, his sperm on her hand, his loathing in her mouth...

"You *must* listen to me," said Colette. "They are Jew haters. To them, the chosen people are the ones chosen to die. And these priests will do whatever it takes to succeed."

The Percheron heaved her towards the door as the clamour outside reached its climax and all the lights went out. Total darkness as they skirted the chapel where Vespers was just ending. The merging of echoes as the other two behind harshly chanted the Confiteor as though it were a plea for damnation.

Colette tried to keep Bertrand's image alive in her mind – the only brightness – as they followed wet stone stairs down to the Cave under the Refectory, and pushed the apostate in.

XXIII

Cacheux emerged from the Public Urinal fretting about the lack of soap. Vidal could tell from his forehead's red, plucked skin that he'd had another go at his eyebrows specially for the journey home. They looked more like two sticks of charcoal strangely detached from his face... The priest from Lanvière laughed out loud.

"What's the joke, eh?" Cacheux felt a deep blush spread up from his neck.

"Everything." Vidal secured his Monoprix bags between his knees, keeping a lookout for Duvivier. "The fact we're stuck here, for God's sake."

Still in anonymous casuals among the steady flow of late holidaymakers and students looking for a couple of cut-price days in the smoke, his new timepiece with all its intricacies on view showed twelve eighteen. Also diving depths, speeds of currents – micro technology heavier on his wrist than his last watch, but luminously purposeful.

He watched the day's brightness desiccate the figures outside on the Concourse into Giacometti-like thins as they neared the station. His eye on them all not just to pick out the fisherman but also the woman he'd lost, and in the purity of that light, that spectral whiteness of her absence, his outlawed soul drifted black as a mote towards Hell.

"Did you get everything you need?" Duvivier came from nowhere.

Vidal could tell he'd made time for a couple of cognacs at their expense but didn't push it. He was on his way back, to where she'd come from, her place in the Rue St. Léger. Empty rooms and cut flowers browning on the sill, the doormat with a green *Bienvenue* woven into it. His hunger wasn't important.

"See you after our scholar Jérôme's day, then." Duvivier strolled over to where Mathieu was checking his luggage. The Breton's mother had insisted on collecting him, but he, Vidal had done the decent thing advising against it, and now the novice was trying to lose him, he could tell. Itching for his other life, the sails in the sunset and a baptism in the morning. Some other woman's child, he thought.

This is not a suitable world for the very young.

He saw him head towards the Metro for Montparnasse, and then Duvivier as an afterthought, detain him with both hands, covering all eventualities. Covering himself. But it was a minute too long, and Mathieu pushed him away.

Hélas! That one will never learn...

In thirty six minutes the Frankfurt train would be in. Time enough to see Plagnol stocking up with panini and salami, and watching the way the girl in the deli reached over, her breasts white as eggs in the V of her overall.

Duvivier had told him to take one of his mother's small rooms in the Avenue St. Quentin for the duration, and to make the trip back to Drancy in the Laguna his last. So he was compensating, Vidal could tell.

The 12.14 for Zurich pulled out with a sigh and disappeared into the haze as Duvivier came over, his mouth open at the ready.

"That Breton's *fou*, and Plagnol's a *pétain*."

"Not my problem." Vidal gathered up his things.

"He won't be paid unless he takes the Xantia."

"His problem."

"Before you go, tell him."

Vidal stared in surprise.

For the first time the fucker was asking for help.

"No man can serve two masters, Father. He despises me even more than you."

"Thank you for that little snippet, my friend." As Duvivier turned towards The Pigface, he caught a glimpse of his own cheek in the photo-booth glass, let his fingers roam like ramblers over some familiar landscape.

I look like a citron. Worse, Esrog. Thank God this doesn't represent my heart...

"It's getting worse, don't you know?"

"All flesh is corrupt." Vidal smiled, slicking back his hair. "Why should we be exempt?"

He saw Cacheux take Plagnol's hand before leaving. Another disobedience that Duvivier missed as he stared around like a lost traveller. There were still too many unanswered questions, such as: where had he been while they were at the warehouse? Who'd done his typing? And not least, who was paying them? The National Front? The Croix de Feu? Or was it F.A.N.E?

But Vidal could no more ask again than ignore the sounds of Guillaume de Machaut that seeped from someone's walkman nearby. Notes from Heaven, lost amongst the arrivals and departures, and in a brief moment of stillness, its beauty tore at his heart.

"Some tart tried to pick me up, would you believe." Duvivier's voice destroyed it all, his hand still lingering on his disfigured cheek. "Obviously this didn't put her off."

"Obviously."

"Ought to get them off the streets. I equate them with dog shit."

"Indeed." Vidal watched as towns and cities to the east came and went on the huge screen. His Frankfurt train was going to be late. A signals problem near Verdun.

Merde.

It was important to be away from the Provençal. He made a move but, like the Breton, was held back.

"Talking of which," Duvivier murmured, "see that lot over there?" He pointed to a family huddled near a bookstall. "Yids."

The man's skullcap perched on a sea of thick hair, the fringes of his talith edging the jacket, white against black. His wife's head was disguised by a fleecy sheitel that reached her shoulders. "You'd think they'd be a bit more discreet, given the history," Duvivier said loudly, and as though she'd heard, the woman locked her husband's arm more tightly. But this encouraged him further. "Thou hast chosen us from all peoples; thou hast loved us and found pleasure in us. My God that's rich isn't it? – And hast exalted us above all tongues..."

Duvivier pulled up his collar and turned away as they looked round, their faces out of the light, shadowed by a sudden fear. The woman caught Vidal's eye thinking it was him. One second of centuries locked in the Ashkenazi's gaze, and the beautiful man from Lanvière broke away and ran with his bags of mammon knocking against his legs, down over the site of the first comic opera towards the church of St. Laurent.

***

Traffic in the Boulevard de Strasbourg had slowed around a long cortège heading for the west door. Behind the hearse glass, mounds of cream lilies and roses shivered like surreal desserts upon the coffin, untouched by the sun and destined to further sour the acrid cremation smoke hanging above the Père Lachaise.

Vidal followed, avoiding the two harpies with undesirably thick legs who reached out at him from the railings, past a solitary flower seller and a woman with a coated dog, and when the procession halted he slipped into the darkened nave and fell to his knees.

XXIV

In the unisex Toilettes of St. Anne's hostel, Nelly Augot skimmed her contact lenses off her eyes, splashed her face from the trickle of tap water, and replaced them. Then she cocked her head and grinned, allowing the gap between her teeth to fully show. It was enough to frighten horses. But not the *voyou* near the Champs de Mars. He'd wanted her alright – the sort who fancy their mothers and touch up little girls, she could tell. He would have bruised her, made her do things when quickies in alleyways and corners were all she wanted. Besides, something about him was scary, and not just his skin problem either.

She moved closer to the mirror, scrutinising the line of downy hairs above her top lip and the untrimmed slide of both eyebrows towards her hair. No tweezers, in fact nothing to improve things in the merciless beam of sunlight that showed up every preening mark on the speckled glass. She sprayed Dune all over and under her borrowed denim layers.

"Right, Yveline. Second time lucky," she told herself, slinging her bag over her shoulder and striding, through the foyer and its dangling Jesus, into the airless afternoon. She was aware of the receptionist's death stares and was tempted to go and sort her out, but her need of a bed was greater, and the only spare in the whole of the 16ième was hers.

Perspiration soon weighted her hair as she stood where the hordes had been. An old man in baggy overalls was painstakingly sweeping their leavings into a dustpan. He smiled up at her.

"Past it, sorry, love." He pocketed the bigger dimps then offered her one.

"Thanks." Rimmed by red lipstick, it reminded her of why she was there at all. On the game in a skirt too short and mules that strained the backs of her knees, and when he wasn't looking, she dropped it down a drain.

The American researcher in Room 30, who'd given her name as Romy Kirchner, had been more than generous, and over a bottle of Vittel, the redhead admitted she hadn't realised the extent of youth poverty in such a glorious country. And that was the invitation for Nelly to begin her life story and talk about the father she barely remembered.

Funny to think these clothes had started life in Boston, Nelly mused, feeling the coarse rub of seams on her skin as she reconnoitred for the best pitch for the rest of the afternoon.

She'd seen her mama do that, from ten floors up – no more than a coloured spindle and its shadow, like one of her little Guatemalan 'trouble dolls' testing out a length of pavement, getting the punters focussed before the final pull. Nelly never saw the men in close up. Once they'd reached the lift, she had to exit sharpish down the fire stairs. Every time, whatever the weather. Those were the terms if she wanted to eat, and on August 16th, she'd decided she preferred hunger.

She removed her waistcoat, keeping an eye on the kerb all the while, just like mama. Nonchalant and come-hitherish, except that no-one paid her any attention. Five hundred francs a go. Three hundred for hand relief although God knew she'd never even seen let alone touched one in her entire life, and eight hundred for a blow job. The going rate in the Avenue Renaud, and what was good enough for Micheline Augot was good enough for her virgin daughter. And what was His Holiness going to do about that?

Mental arithmetic promised a good whack for a week's work. Besides, there were more punters here than in Libourne. The reason she'd stayed. She'd have the return fare for herself and Colette within twenty-four hours. Nelly studied the party of Italians stranded by the lights, but not one reciprocated. Not even a glance.

"Gentlemen do not prefer pubes," she said wrily, primping her dark crinkly hair behind her ears, so she left the foreigners and teetered along the Boulevard des Forges in search of a chemist.

An hour and a half later, with thatch the colour of old brass and not quite dry, Nelly checked her purse. She was hot and confused, melting into her borrowed clothes with just twenty-five francs left to her name. Enough to take her down to Évry, to the Avenue Clemenceau and what was left of Chloë Doumiez's family.

XXV

Duvivier arrived back in the scented South in a bad humour. After Lyon, the hike in temperature had played havoc with his face and, even with the railway carriage's blind down, the sun had found him out.

As he struggled from the train, the quivering mirage along the track also seemed to reach him, stealing his sight. Almost blind, he moved with late holidaymakers towards the exit and the last bus to Cavalaire.

"My dear friend, how are you?"

Suddenly a warm hand was on his arm, guiding him out into the chequerboard patterns of light and shadow; and beyond, the bristling masts of pleasure vessels berthed for the night. "Have no fear, Father André, I've made all the arrangements."

"What arrangements?" Duvivier stopped, his eyes little more than pinpricks.

The Bishop of Beauregard, hatless in a grey suit, opened the boot of his Mercedes expectantly.

"I've written your sermon for the Family Eucharist at Ste Trinité tomorrow, and taken six charming children for the Confirmation class this morning." He slammed the boot shut when Duvivier didn't oblige, but instead clung to his holdall as though it was the Holy Grail. "That's six more souls from Les Pradels that we can save, but as for the other parishes, not good news."

"Why?"

"We've run out of priests. Simple as that."

The seventy-year-old bishop settled the bifocals further up his nose and started the engine, before turning his gaze to his companion. "So it's Deacons and sub-Deacons for the moment, but as you know, their duties are already burdensome. Your flock will be lucky to get one Solemn Mass a week."

"I'm sorry, your Lordship, but the condition of my liver is urgent."

"I'm sure it is. Docteur Brébisson has written, about your face as well. He confirms that a sojourn in the Pyrenees might also alleviate that problem."

Thank you, Doctor. Nine thousand francs from Déchaux's pocket can work miracles, n'est-ce-pas?

The bishop coughed, unsure how to continue. He could sense the big man's tension and needed to lighten things quickly.

"I must say, Father, we were all very taken with your performance at the Mass yesterday." A sly smile revealed just two teeth, and Duvivier thought of his father's dog Arsène, a half breed fattened up on fish oil, whose nose knew nothing else.

"I'm not St. Genesius you know."

"And I'm not laughing."

A tanned girl in a sarong crossed in front of the car, quickening away when she caught sight of them both.

"It seems that well over a million of our young people took part." The bishop's eyes narrowed, following her until she disappeared into a Bar Tabac. "Indeed a very moving experience, especially in such hard times."

"Especially."

Past the aerodrome and the Rade d'Hyères, its ferries still plying diagonal furrows towards the islands, the bishop, whose birth name was Henri Pereire, slipped in a tape and pulled down his visor, for although the homecoming sun now lay behind over the sea, the light on the road still dazzled.

"Wonderful," he breathed as Duvivier stiffened. He'd put in one of Vidal's tapes, and the boys of the Église de la Sainte Vierge in full glory filled the interior, drowning the rash of crickets in the roadside scrub.

Dammit.

A knot formed above the priest's groin. The notes soared clearer than anything outside, their breaths intimate as though sharing the same air. His fists tightened involuntarily and the driver noticed.

"You've had a long trip, Francke. Sleep if you wish." He clicked the central locking, but instead of feeling secure enough to doze, Duvivier felt doubly trapped. Why of all the music possible, had he chosen that? He turned the cassette cover over and saw Vidal's face in a dark oblong amongst the small print. Those eyes, luminous yet inscrutable. His diver. The Water Rat. His Action Man.

"Truly something for our sorry world to share. Something of beauty, don't you agree Father André?"

***

After Lavandou, decked out in flags for a karting event, the bishop steered on to the Corniche des Maures. The sea infinite and waiting beyond a blurred horizon.

"This kind of enterprise does the Church more good than a million Indulgences. Twenty unsullied little boys are quite irresistible, don't you think?" His passenger grunted as Pereire continued. "And my esteemed colleague Toussirot – if he's got his wits about him – will make Father Jean-Baptiste Musical Director for the entire Département." He braked behind a motorcyclist who took up the whole road, and instinctively, Duvivier ducked. "I'll speak with him tomorrow."

"But it's Moussac who's done all the work, so I heard," the priest added then regretted it.

The bishop changed down through the gears and turned to study his companion. "Moussac is dying."

"What?" Duvivier groaned. He saw the schedule, the carefully planned rehearsals all disintegrating like paper burnt at the edge of flames, curling to oblivion. And worst of all, he'd be blamed. "He can't be!"

"Leukaemia they think." Pereire ignored him. "With the Lord's Grace, three weeks, maybe four..."

Duvivier saw Pereire's mouth set into a hyphen. His face itself a death mask betraying nothing. This was an inside job, he could smell it.

This is sabotage.

"Father Jean-Baptiste's needed in the parish, your Lordship. As you've just said, the situation is dire. Most priests are over seventy and unlike the Haredim there's practically zero entry to the Seminaries." The driver looked at him, puzzled for a moment at his unexpected reference to Judaism. "Oh, and that survey in May from the Congregation of the Clergy, did you see it by any chance?"

"Of course."

"Well, according to that, twenty-five percent of us are suffering psychiatric disorders. That is good news, *hein?*"

The bishop glanced away.

"We'll have a sea change after His Holiness' visit. Mark my words. Instead of that gloomy statistic I'd say that seventy percent of our youth now feel a calling to the Church."

"Russian Orthodox maybe. Not us." Duvivier muttered. "And blame the Vatican II, say I."

The older man shifted in his seat.

"Besides he's got over two hundred parishioners. What about all of them?"

"You seem to know a lot about Father Jean-Baptiste, my friend, but then of course, I forgot, you were together at Villersourt during your *séjour de la honte...*" He gave a punctuating cough. "Tragic about Tessier, don't you think?"

"Our slates are clean, Monsignor. Whiter than white I should say."

Duvivier strained against his seat's clinging velour. His belt suddenly tight, compressing his breath, his very resourcefulness to survive.

"Would you say immaculate, though, Father André, as befits your calling?"

"Of course." Was too quick, too loud. He was losing.

"Let me put it like this. If I were to take your confession now, would you expect immediate Absolution, or have you anything else to tell me?" His voice quiet, yet full of a subtle menace enough to alter the vivid beauty outside and convert the tape's soprano solo into a wail from Hell.

"Don't be absurd," Duvivier growled. "You know what my dear mother meant to me, that there's never been another to touch her."

"Indeed we all knew that."

"So when that old *paysan*, Alexandre, called her a Jew, I had no choice. You'd have done the same. She was from Aachen, for God's sake! Kleinburgerlich Büber."

The bishop's eyebrows rose above his glasses. The car too began to climb, the petrol gauge showing red.

"It was *me* who put a word in with Montverger, remember? You'd still be festering in Villerscourt what with one thing and another, and your showing at Carpentras."

That one word plummeted into the sudden silence as sky and sea and the rising land cocooned him in the snare. The choristers on tape too, deserted, fading into the Amen. "Again I had to cover up, which is quite against my nature, you understand? And if His Holiness had had so much as a whiff of your zeal with a crowbar, it would have been my head for the guillotine. Finish. Kaput." His square hand stabbed the wheel, and for a split second, the car jerked, angling dangerously towards the edge.

"Holy Mary." Duvivier looked down. The waves pinkish now, like thin blood in the spreading sun, and he felt a chill reach his bones. Surreptitiously, his half-hidden eyes searched for a way out.

"From what I hear," his chauffeur began slowly, "you will need the whole of the Heavenly Host."

Enough.

The Provençal suddenly flung himself across the other man, and in that moment of distracted surprise, managed to open his own door lock.

"Are you *crazy*?" the bishop cried, veering out of control against loose stones lining the road. They rattled doom inside the car, as he tried to steer and keep Duvivier in his seat at the same time. On the rebound, the passenger door flung wide – nothing else in sight, and the descent until the bend was clear.

Duvivier braced his bulk around his bag and rolled free as the Merc spun back on its tracks. With a grating roar, the saloon lurched at the concrete base above the cliff and nosed through the barricade before plunging out of sight.

XXVI

17.22 hours, and despite the excluding silence surrounding the Église de la Sainte Vierge, Vidal willed the door to the Lady Chapel to open. He'd planned to light two candles, one for Colette, one for Bertrand, but the lock wouldn't surrender. Even the old wood and the stones were cold to the touch, for the wind had clawed at the sun too long in that exposed place.

He then tried the main door, recessed against the weather but again, his keys were redundant. For some reason the locks had been changed.

Fuck.

He listened hard, fancied for a moment in the swill of the breeze, he heard the choir ascend note by note until lost to the air. "Jews' breath," some said of that particular current from the alien east. He looked around, clearly alone save for the slanting headstones that littered the thin grass, and a party of crows in the ash tree.

Beyond this, lay the Rue Montbois and its line of shops closing for the day. An empty coach crawled by in slow motion then nothing. It was all too quiet. Something was up, and in that late August afternoon, he shivered.

Milk and bread.

Vidal picked up all his bags and followed the church path back down to the street. He might as well have been invisible, for neither the chief verger, in his doorway, nor the Peugeot mechanic, who'd once begged him to pray for his son, acknowledged him. So much for the performance at Longchamp. Pearls before swine, indeed.

The Supermarché Lion, no bigger than a room, was still open, although the charcuterie counter lay temptingly bright but empty under its glass and the only till was being cleared. He wasn't hungry now, and as his few provisions jerked along on the the rubber belt, the girl averted her eyes. Brigitte Caumartin, with Bardot's first name and little else, slapped his change down.

"What's the matter with our church, Brigitte? D'you know?" He tried engaging her in conversation as nonchalantly as he could.

"Been done over. While you were away." She closed the till with such vehemence he jumped. Then his Confirmation pupil left him, her hips huge and fruitful under her overall.

Probably no knickers. Poor bitch.

A man he didn't recognise stood by the door checking his watch and the moment the priest's heels had cleared the threshold, brought down the grille with such force that its din echoed long into the quiet.

Vidal, still with the sound in his ears walked the length of the shopping street, past the single storey telephone exchange and the École Maternelle, still boarded up for the summer holiday. He noticed fresh swastikas furred by paint drips on a side door, then on to his street, the Rue Fosse.

It was, as usual, lined with cars – the clapped-out remains of commuting lives rarely moved from their oily berths. Dusty windowsills, a litany of drabness only relieved by a glimpse of river trees beyond.

Number 145 was no exception, edged in umber, the shutters a different brown.

His Honda Deauville took up most of the hallway, dark as the shadows, waiting with his gear piled up on the seat. His hands moved over its solid curves. This was the real tart, and at 55,000 francs, a mere snippet out of his first pay packet.

Colette.

And it only took an instant for her name to deepen his emptiness.

He took the Monoprix bags up to his bedroom and locked them in the wardrobe amongst the hems of his *soutanes*. He looked for a moment at her photo that lay angled towards his bed, then hid it in a drawer of papers. Then he phoned his chief choir master at Charnevoux.

"Yes?" A girl's voice after a full minute.

"Father Jean-Baptiste calling. It's important I speak to Monsieur Moussac."

She paused, covered the mouthpiece. He thought she was asking permission from someone, and while waiting, toyed impatiently with his keys.

"He says he doesn't want to talk to anyone."

"Oh really? And who are you?"

"None of your business. I'm busy. Got to go..."

"Well be so good as to tell him I'll be at the choir practice tomorrow. OK?"

But the line was dead and a creeping anxiety took hold as he stared at the receiver.

What the Hell's up with Moussac? And what's she doing there? He's got no family...

In the half-light, he checked his watch then eyed his new bike. Still a full tank and only twenty minutes at the most to reach Charnevoux and, without bothering to change his clothes, he wheeled the machine out into the street.

A neighbour out with her mongrel and her neat shoes, looked the other way, but he knew from the curtain tremors opposite that his every move was being watched. Soon the bike's sweet engine was slipping up the gears through the sudden stench of a tomato processing plant, over the Meuse and into hamlet country populated by ginger cows.

***

Charnevoux, another place of ghosts. A Bar Tabac, a line of *poubelles*. That was it. Avenue Dornay. He secured the bike away from Moussac's small house, like his, practically on the street but white and cared for, with new shutters. The choirmaster's modest 2CV was up on the gravel. Its seats covered in sheet music. Outside lay chalky dog shit and a child's dummy. He rang the bell then stood aside as a blonde behind the glass opened the door and wedged it with her white trainer.

Just a girl, but uncannily like the young Colette he'd seen in photographs. The same cool eyes, the same skin, the golden layers of hair. He suddenly wanted to touch her breasts, her downy arm. A resurrection of desire flooded his body, and in that moment of weakness, that wide-eyed awakening, she shut the door in his face.

Shit.

He watched her white overall fade into the house's inner secrets. Housekeeper? Nurse? He had to find out.

Normally Moussac would have greeted him, even offered an *apéro*. The choirmaster had guessed about him and Colette, of course. Been there when they'd first met at her husband's burial, caught in the crossfire of their glances on a day itself wrapped in a chilling shroud of rain, and more rain.

On the Feast of St. Casimir he'd urged the wonderful *"Ange guardien, ami fidèle"* out of the church and into the cold March wind. No, unlike Bertrand, Moussac had never sat in judgement. Not even on the shame of Villerscourt.

Vidal stared for any trace of the man through the half-open shutters, but no luck. Instead, he ran to the end of the gravel and down a side alley where a row of prefabricated garages bordered the rear gardens. Most, except Moussac's were wedged by weeds. To his right, a screen of poplars along the River Thonne teased the sky.

No gate, so he vaulted over the fence and, using the shrubs as cover, crept close to the French windows which opened out on to a small terrace. Immediately, the smell of sickness reached him and the sound of coughing in a tortured sequence racked the quietude. Moussac was there in that room, he could tell.

"Jacques?"

"Who's that? Robert?"

"What the Hell's going on?"

"Hell is correct. But you must go. I mustn't see you. It will only make things worse."

Vidal crouched low in case that girl should reappear. The room faced north, its corners secretive, but he could just make out a Bechstein whose lid was closed and the draped bed end over a *pot de chambre.*

"Christ, Jacques, you were fine when I left to see my father."

"That was a lie, Robert. You were sent to Villerscourt and thanks to

Toussirot, I know the real reason why. Nothing to do with our choir..."

Vidal fell silent. So everybody knew his shame. That explained things.

Merci, Toussirot, you shrivelled old con.

The blonde girl came in, slopping fresh water and tried to close the windows but Vidal blocked her way.

"He's got to rest, can't you see?" She snarled a different mouth this time. A hardness that could never in all eternity have been Colette. He watched how she spilled some of the water and made no effort to wipe it up.

"Jacques, we've things to do," urged Vidal. "The Beata Viscera for Paris, the Alleluia Nativitas recording. Pérotin is waiting..." Already the familiar chords, the pulsing harmonies were playing in his mind.

"Not we, my friend. You. I'm done for."

Vidal charged inside the French windows and lay across Moussac's body as the girl disappeared.

"For God's sake, what's the matter?" he yelled. "Toussirot? Is he aware of any of this? Is anyone doing anything?"

"Oh, indeed. Much has already been done."

With a huge effort the fifty-nine-year-old turned over to face him and Vidal let out a cry seeing the sunken yellowed face that he hardly recognised. Not *his* eyes surely, once full of joy and purpose, now expressionless? A dribble of something vile slipped from the corner of his mouth and Vidal's stomach turned over.

"Oh, Sancta Maria," he whispered, taking his cold hand. "Sancta Maria."

"I would like Confession." Moussac moaned suddenly. "Now." He strained to change his position, and his assistant knelt alongside, his crucifix resting on the other man's fingers.

"Glorious Holy Spirit, give me the grace to know all my sins and to loathe them..." Moussac faltered. "I greet you, Marie, I greet you..."

Vidal gently wiped his chin. The stuff was like yoghurt. It was he who should be confessing, but he listened nevertheless and heard only the workings of his own mind. The doubts and disobediences. "Have you wished ill to those close to you?" he asked.

"I have no living relatives as you know but I have been a Judas to someone who is now very close."

Vidal moved nearer the rancid breath for every syllable.

What's he talking about?

"Your lover's son, he told me everything. He hated you, you know, but had no-one else to turn to."

"Go on." Vidal slowly, dreading what would come next.

"He also gave me a letter." Moussac's eyes closed as though the memory needed darkness. Vidal could hear his own heart loud and fearful. "I told him he should never have stolen from your house..."

"What do you mean, stolen?" Vidal shouted. "What letter?"

"A strange thing it was. No signature as I recall, just OPÉRATION JUDAS at the top, and a mobile phone number to contact. It was a personalised invitation to join the ACJ. To you, Robert."

Shit...

"That's a lie! The boy had a grudge. He stitched it up!"

"He was very agitated, that's all I can say."

"Why didn't you tell me?" Vidal shouted.

But Moussac lifted his hand, as pale and heavy as a piece of dead tree, his breathing threatening to break his chest. Vidal looked on powerless as a deep chord of loose bones played in the other's throat and his head moved from side to side like a metronome on the pillow.

"Dangerous, Robert, dangerous..."

"For God's sake."

"For my sins, I've been poisoned, bit by bit, and don't let them tell you anything else."

Vidal, with nothing to lose, gripped Moussac's neck. The pulse was dying, his mouth slack open.

"Where's that bloody letter? What have you done with it?"

"Toussirot... Toussi..."

My bishop...

The last syllable of that name lay trapped, unspoken on Moussac's tongue as the spirit left him.

Vidal crossed himself and shouted for the girl, but only a house of death answered, for Giselle Subradière was already halfway towards the Luxembourg border with her own hair freed in the wind.

***

Having dialled for an ambulance, Vidal got through to the Presbytère in Gerville where Philippe Toussirot, Dominican Bishop of Ramonville, was in the middle of a bath when the phone was brought to his pink, water-softened hand. He recoiled at Father Jean-Baptiste's tone and kept the receiver at arm's length.

"When exactly?"

"Nineteen hours. Today."

"Impossible."

"He's dead, my Lord. That is fact."

"But Doctor Foucaude was seeing him tomorrow, to arrange a Barium Meal test."

"Too late for that. It's irrelevant, anyhow. Nothing to do with cancer."

"What on earth do you mean, Father?"

"He said he'd been poisoned. Also, not so long ago, he gave you a letter. One addressed to me, at home."

"I don't know what you're talking about." Toussirot then paused, not from discomfiture but to think quickly and draw his pursuer away. "My friend has got it quite wrong. All very sad, but there it is. What has been vexing me is the vandalism at your church. First our silver is stolen, then the Blessed Virgin is despoiled. It's quite appalling. If I had a molecule of Paganism in my body, I'd say that place of God is cursed."

Vidal kept the phone at arm's length, letting him prattle on until he saw his watch.

"There's something else too, isn't there?"

Toussirot then fell silent. Let the plug out with his big toe.

"Look, if it'll help, I'll come on over. You stay there."

"No. Moussac told me everything, loud and clear. Someone wanted him out of the way."

"You're being quite hysterical and illogical, Father. And he may well have been delirious."

"It was his final confession, my Lord. He wouldn't lie."

"May I just remind you how much time and effort I put into damage limitation on your behalf, and also how reasonable my office has been over your requests for future absence?"

His tone different, unbending but Vidal hadn't finished.

"Who's the girl he had with him?"

"I've no idea."

"Well, she's gone. Vanished." He saw the SAMU estate car creep into the Avenue Dornay, a red light spinning on its roof. The Bishop was abandoned as he directed the driver to Number 9.

The neighbourhood began to stir with curiosity. Voyeurs hovered like dung beetles around the 2CV, and Vidal nimbly sidestepped those who asked questions. No time to go through any of Moussac's drawers, but a quick glimpse upstairs showed portions of the heavy country furniture gaping, already disembowelled.

"Damn."

A choirmaster was dead while his bishop lived. But who was lying?

He couldn't do everything. Besides, back in the makeshift bedroom, there was his old colleague staring a farewell, accusing him with his dead eyes.

***

Vidal got the name of Moussac's usual housekeeper from the Bar Tabac. She'd come in there once to ask if someone could wash her car – a Jeanne Laurent from Troismoulins – exact address unknown, but there were only six houses in the hamlet.

It was the wind that finally brought tears, but couldn't clear the pain suffusing his whole body, slowing his journey. Vidal murmured the Ave as the road opened out towards Troismoulins across low farmland razed of trees, but nothing was going to help now.

He had his questions ready but the only living inhabitant seemed to be a dog which railed against the double gates of the Maison de Mâitre. Vidal checked the name near the bell and moved on.

Dusk was now surreptitiously reducing everything to a dark oneness, and himself a vulnerable stranger. Each house the same, defying him. No longer the caring parish priest on a mission of mercy, here the mission of death rendered him dangerous and not one car slowed to help him out. Even the dog had disappeared. He, Father Jean-Baptiste was a pariah, and it hurt.

He decided then to lob the ball back into Toussirot's court, after all, the old cunt could handle it. Could float his way out of a bottomless cesspit if he cared and now was his chance. There was still the St. Sébastien concert to rehearse, and the Bishop would have to find a replacement. Urgently. Father Anselme was the only one he could think of. A lover of Conductus, but over seventy and ailing.

Merde twice over.

Vidal remounted his machine, the familiar and unfamiliar sharing his body. Anger and despair in equal parts as he circled round to make Lanvière by 22.00.

XXVII

The moon cast the town in a liverish glow and no matter where he looked, it was there, in Vidal's wing mirror, the windows over the chemist's shop, but worst of all the bile of God lay in his heart.

The same cars, the same eerie silence about his house. In three leaps he was in the bedroom and tipping out the drawer on to the bed. Colette's photo fell free of the rest, she was smiling up at him, offering him a sausage.

How had that little fucker of hers got in? There'd been no window opened or broken, no damage anywhere. And then as he sorted through Parish details of births, marriages, and deaths, the answer dawned. Either Colette had given him her key. Told him to have a snoop, see what he could find out about his other interests, or she herself had gone in and passed the letter to her adoring boy. Whatever, Moussac was right. The Opération Judas letter had gone.

Vidal searched again but knew it was fruitless. He felt unsteady, disorientated. There were too many other Judases already swimming in the pool. The pool of blood. And one of them wore a skirt. Then he realised he'd forgotten to get the church's new key off the dead man.

Crétin.

Moonlight intensified as he reached the square, while above the steps to the Apartments Cornay where he left the bike, street lamps struggled into life.

23.00 hours exactly. His boots mute on the mock marble. No sign of the Jew that Colette kept going on about. He'd told her not to keep calling on her and giving her things. That they'd had enough already, but after the way she'd looked at him, he'd let the matter rest. He wasn't going to push it.

As he reached the sixth floor he stopped and sniffed. A cigarette in the darkness, someone's breath, then the sudden rush of escape – invisible until a light somewhere came on.

Blackness again, too soon. He wasn't alone.

"Who's there?" His diving sense still his best ally. Breezeblock grated on his skin as he braced himself. A gush of air and someone was on him, a fist hard on his mouth. His head fell strangely soft against the wall.

He rebounded, forcing his assailant to the ground, then rode him until the cries became silence. Tessier all over again, except this creep was after something else. He felt in the pockets. Nothing but matches and a pack of Gitanes. Vidal took one, lit it, and saw a skinhead half his age, and a nostril ring bedded in blood. Saw too they were outside Colette's door.

"What you doing here, you arsehole?" His own head throbbing out a new rhythm. "You planning on nicking something?"

The youth tried to run but Vidal clamped his throat.

"Tell me, or in five seconds you'll be cold."

"Jus' obeyin' orders."

"Not good enough, Monsieur. That's insulting."

"'s true."

"Who then?"

"Dunno."

Vidal eased his grip.

"I happen to have a special friend who lives here. OK? and I take it very personally if some piece of scum starts interfering with the property."

"I wasn't doing nothing. Honest to God."

"God doesn't even know you exist, my young friend." The priest lit another match and hauled the boy up for a closer look. "But I know you from somewhere – Gilles Ferey – you came just the once if I remember, to my Confirmation class last year..."

"I'm starting again, honest..."

"Oh, really?" Vidal sneered, letting him go. "Well that's awfully decent of you, but I think Confession is more *à-propos*, don't you? Eleven o'clock sharp. Tomorrow."

"I might."

The youth was too quick, head-butting and galloping clear down the mausoleum stairs to the safety of the street. Vidal swore after him then felt his way to the door, his thoughts all questions and no answers.

The hum of a TV and a cat, near or far he couldn't tell, marking the night with fear. No other sound. Her key on his key ring next to those for the Church, was guilt in his hand. He slid the bolts behind him and drew the curtains, sealing in her perfume. Still eloquent – Je Reviens. He'd even bought her a bottle of it on her last birthday but it wasn't amongst the other things on her dressing table. His photo in an Art Deco frame stood behind baby lotion and a snap of Bertrand as a toddler with her in some park. He picked it up but when the serious eyes made contact, put it down again.

You poor bloody fools.

His mind on hold as he prowled the neat orderliness. Lingerie folded between pot pourri sachets and other drawers of mementoes caught up with coloured ribbons...

Nothing of any interest except that her parents looked remarkably composed the day before they'd gassed themselves. Nothing of his, not even in *Le Bébé's* room. That particular shrine repelled him and he quickly shut the door. He should pray for them, wish them everything he would wish himself but could not, and when he saw her flowers dried and drooping in chaos, left them untouched.

He tried Duvivier's number. No reply, not even an answerphone. Where the Hell was he? He checked his luminous watch again, removed his gloves and helped himself to a torch from under the sink and two finger scoops of paté from the fridge. Still fresh.

He let himself out. The cat's racket was even worse and liable to attract attention, so he followed the din back down to the ground floor and checked all four doors. Number 3, the only one not shut tight. It opened on his boot, but before he could defend himself a rush of stinking fur hurled itself at his chest, tearing through his clothes. Vidal squeezed the cat's neck until the thing went limp and fell away whimpering. He used both feet to finish the noise for ever then dropped it over the side.

This flat was different from Colette's, with the kitchen just a cubby hole off the one room. Likewise the sleeping area and bathroom with a shower that had rarely been used. Cheap soap, cheap everything, except there must have been something worth taking as darker oblongs showed up where pictures had recently been hung. Someone had got there first.

"Anyone here?"

A Mizrah on the wall that faced east. This must be the widow Levy's place.

You're nothing special, Madame. We're all exiles from the love of God...

But no sign of her. The place was deserted.

The rug rucked up under his boots as he tried all the cupboards. The best stuff had already gone, leaving dustless remains on the shelves and crumbs from packets of matzos and bourekas. No need to worry the lock on the one wardrobe – its doors fell open from the weight behind.

Vidal pulled the body out, no heavier than a bundle of rags, smothered by dingy clothes fallen from the hooks.

Dirty and foul smelling. Exactly. Der Ewige Jude...

She was still warm, her furred slippers part of her feet, but he couldn't bring himself to look at her face. He covered it with a cardigan that smelt of stale lavender, and arranged the wayward arms as though in death, she stood to attention.

Then he dribbled water on to his gloves and rubbed them clean like the surgeon in Metz had washed after the birth – his birth – before pulling the mask from his face to say he had done all he could.

Amélia Vidal, née Cordonnier.

The memories curdled as the water looped round the plug hole. And the blame of it all had never left him.

"You tore her womb, son" was all his father would say whenever he'd asked, and that was his only true inheritance. He'd violated so terribly that place of safety where the boxer's fists and diving legs had grown, where her sounds had been his sounds, her voice the softness he would never hear again and, as the waste pipe toyed with his leavings, Father Jean-Baptiste began to sob.

XXVIII

After the lunchless rendezvous at the Gare de l'Est, Michel Plagnol had lingered in the city, taking in Boucher's work – his favourites – and the Fragonards in the Cognacq-Jay, then a walk down to the tree lights along the Seine where the Bateaux Mouches' evening cruises were filling up with punters.

He'd bought a paper and sat for an hour just watching, absorbing the minutiae of loading and unloading, the staffing arrangements and most important of all, the pick-up place where he'd be waiting.

Then he'd dropped in on the Revue des Amazons in the Boulevard de Sebastopol with its worn velveteen seats and mini-binoculars. For two hundred francs the whole thing proved drab and disappointing. Thongs, spurred boots on lardy flesh and nipples hung with pearls and, to add insult to injury, the attentions of a tart, whom the good Lord must have put together during a bout of amnesia. No breasts, unlike Diana's budding delights so perfectly formed in oils.

He'd emerged unaroused and instead bought a porn magazine for later from a kiosk near the car park.

***

Now back in Drancy, on home ground, he waited until the area around the apartments was clear, then slipped in through the front door. The banister felt cold and damp as though someone's wet hand had got there first, and all the while, the blind woman's wailing eked out from under her door.

Give it a rest old Bellechasse, or there'll be no wafer next time...

Number 15a. And a few things to check over. He had to pick up a spare *soutane* and extra shirts. As for his almost-new white Laguna with a better silhouette than any woman, she was going to stay. Fact. Besides, the colour red in his book, was unlucky. Duvivier had a bloody nerve...

He felt the salami still in his throat. It lodged like one of the small weights his grandmother had used when baking, but he daren't cough in case that old crow Madame Suzelle was listening.

The carpet had been cleaned to perfection. He'd told his mother there'd been a party, and she'd dutifully obliged with her usual thorough cleaning routine on all fours with her little birdy arms moving backwards and forwards, her hips poking through her skirt.

He'd been a proper birth, through the usual place, not excised from her stomach like some tumour. So she'd said on the rare occasions they'd talked about such matters. But he'd wondered sometimes, looking at her, how God in his infinite wisdom had granted him safe passage into the world of light.

Air freshener and Cif in the air. Excellent. He sniffed deeply in all corners, looking for any tell-tale smears or scuffs, but she'd even been handy with a paintbrush. "May I with grace, grant her a special Benediction," he half prayed, keeping his ears on full alert.

He let himself out. The stairwell was empty, no doors breathing, no lights, but suddenly someone was behind. Someone reeking of stale perfume. Madame Suzelle.

"Well Father Jérôme, it's good to see you back. We all thought how inspired you looked for the Holy Father at Longchamp. Very, very nice." But she still kept her clammy hand on his, and lowered her voice in unnerving intimacy. "I've got to tell you, though; there've been some rum goings on here. To be honest I didn't know what to do..."

"Oh?" The *salope* wore too much make up. A mouth red and cracked like an old floor. But that didn't stop it working.

"Monsieur Cendrier said we should call the police. That you'd got immigrants shut up in there."

Plagnol put on his priestly face.

"And did you?"

"No. I said it was your property and none of our business."

He breathed relief and smiled.

"Thank you, Madame. I appreciate your courtesy. If I may say so," he kept a wary eye on the stairs in case the old busybody should appear, "Monsieur Cendrier is old and befuddled."

Plagnol recoiled from her puffed up skin, her thin, dyed hair and wanted to be away. "And I'd remind you that your *curé* is not just a man of words. God will judge us more truly on our actions. In my absence I provided shelter for, how shall I say, one of my more unfortunate fellows. He had no money, no home, as so many today. Better a Samaritan than a Levite, *hein*?"

She smiled, no teeth.

"You're right, Father, of course. When your heart is weighed against the feather you'll, surely to God, be spared from Damnation."

She'd followed him down the stairs still promising a happy and rewarding hereafter, but as he was about to leave, she grabbed him again. "I must tell you before you go. The other night there were two men fighting round your door, Father. I'd swear one was trying to break in, and the screaming was something awful. Monsieur Cendrier was round at his daughter's, so you can imagine I was scared out of my wits, but the really strange thing is, when I said I'd call the police..."

"Go on." Plagnol's pinkness had noticeably whitened.

"The younger one shouted that was exactly what he wanted. I couldn't make head nor tail of it."

"I'm not surprised." Plagnol's face lay pleated by soft furrows as he tried to think.

"Then there were these other two. About three minutes later. Bigger men." She went on. "Didn't like the look of them one bit, but the electricity had gone on the landing, it was difficult to see..."

Plagnol flicked the switch.

"Everything's all right now, Madame Suzelle. No problem. Probably addicts. They're everywhere, I'm afraid, these days. They may even have known him. That's the price one pays for doing a good deed, after all remember Our Saviour. He mingled with the unfortunates of this world."

"What we need is a proper concièrge." She said. "Someone to keep an eye on things." And then the old woman asked if he fancied a *pastis*.

"Most kind, Madame, but I must be away. I need to brief my replacement. Father Florian. He's always most accommodating. Far more so than myself, I might say."

"Will you be staying somewhere else then, Father?" She eyed his clothes and the carrier bags.

"My mother's not one hundred per cent. I thought I'd go and help her out for a while."

"I'm not surprised, all the cleaning she does. And she's got your old mamie. So she was telling me."

Plagnol wondered what else his garrulous mother had given away.

"Family is family, Madame, and if one can't look after one's own..."

"Well, look at me, Father. A lonely old widow. If it wasn't for your church..."

"The best family of all, I agree. By the way, we'll be having special prayers on Wednesday for St. Monica, rather appropriate I thought, to remember mothers everywhere."

"But I'm not a mother," she cried indignantly. "I never wanted kids."

"It'll do you good, nevertheless. Oh, and by the way, Madame, if anyone asks for a Charles Lautin, would you kindly say he's on holiday?"

"Oh, yes, Father."

How she enjoyed a little conspiracy, and the status it gave her, but he wished most fervently she wouldn't smile. He then made the sign of the cross as finally as he could and took his leave, still feeling her eyes on him as he turned the corner into the Boulevard François Premier where the beloved Laguna lay glistening like fresh snow under a street lamp.

He double checked that his maps, the updated travel CD and data were in order, wondering all the while who'd been interfering with the flat and why

Le Bébé had kept burbling how his mother had given him some key or other. That hadn't make any sense at all.

Plagnol slammed the boot and smiled on the thought that if the Kommandant ever suspected it had been Vidal and the Breton who'd called here, he'd break their legs. Plans or no plans.

***

Rosine Plagnol had made a special effort to welcome her only son. She wore a neat purple two-piece whose skirt drifted from her legs like meat off a bone, and in the kitchen fog of Number 300, Avenue St. Quentin, she stood over her *tarte au pigeon* with knife and spatula at the ready.

"Tomorrow perhaps." He eyed its plump greyness with distaste. Invalid food, easy on the palate. At only thirty-eight he wasn't there, yet.

He leaned back from the table, his belly bigger than than she'd ever seen it, distended by forces she couldn't fathom. My *cochon de Noël*, she thought, finally making an incision into the pie crust and putting two slices on separate plates.

"For Liliane and me, then." She folded two festive paper napkins alongside and mashed up one of the portions as she took it into the adjoining room.

The huge Toshiba TV pulsed underwater green, reflecting on the patient's face like a Fauve painting. It was some old Cousteau film she'd asked Rosine to record, but now she watched without interest. Liliane Argent lay inert under a pink cellular blanket, her head little more than a skull, her mouth without teeth a steadfast hole. Rosine pushed in the loaded teaspoon and wiped away the bits.

"Good, *hein*?"

Her mother's efforts at swallowing took all her concentration, but afterwards her gaze slid to the door.

"Yes, maman, Michel's with us for a while. But you know that, don't you? That'll be nice, won't it? Besides, he can pay a little something, which all helps." Instantly Liliane Argent became agitated and tried to move her hands as though she was part of the swirling deep on the screen, swimming for her life. "Oh, mother, don't." Rosine spooned in some more but it was spat out for the eighty-five-year-old hotelier from Meaux to shriek her despair.

"It's only for a week or so. Please be reasonable!"

But underneath she trembled too. The house wasn't even hers. She, the *ouvrier's* wife had no assets other than her son, and he now stood legs apart, flexing his fingers.

"Michel, it's impossible," she said. "I've only to mention your name..."

"What do you expect me to do? The poor old thing's had it. She'll soon be cradled in the arms of God. Requiescat in Pace." He pulled out his black rosary and felt for the smallest Ave. Then he knelt down, his bulk against the bed. With each solemn word he looked his maternal grandmother in the eye, till she could turn away no more.

The million francs from the sale of her Hôtel Victoire, safe with the bank, were drawing closer to home, and he finished the supplication so fervently that his mother tried to pull him away.

"That's enough, Michel. I know you mean well, but I can't be getting Doctor Salins in again."

"He'll come if I ask."

"That's not the point. I don't want him prying around, thinking I can't look after her."

"It's four-star here, what d'you mean? She's landed on her feet."

Rosine bent close against his greasy curls.

"We don't want her taken away. I mean, she might get you know, attached to someone elsewhere. Some care assistant or suchlike..."

"My dear maman, we have the Code Napoléon n'est-ce-pas? She wouldn't be allowed..."

Piranhas, like little, bloated leaves, darted by as the diver's shadow fell across the architecture of the underworld and something unrecognisable stalked the water ejecting a stream of bubbles. Rosine took her mother's hand while Plagnol watched with quiet satisfaction, every nuance of the old girl's fear. It was a good time to give his news. "I don't know how *au fait* you are with property prices, maman, but they're not exactly picking up, even in the suburbs."

"What are you trying to say, child?"

"I'm selling le Passage, then I can stay here and give you a hand."

Before Rosine could respond, her mother began to bang the sides of the bed with her ox knuckles, *clup clup clup,* until Plagnol pinned them down.

"It makes so much sense, dear sweet mamie," he purred. "A special Indulgence as I promised. I can be truly a good son and grandson, after all, since the *ouvrier* left us, it's not been easy."

"Which is why you went to the Seminary in the first place." Rosine fiddled with the pillow but her old mother tried to head butt the bed end. Failing that, she started to yell.

Her grandson backed away.

"I need cigars." He sighed, letting himself out and making for the Tabac two bocks away. "The old *vache* is giving me a migraine."

Too late he realised his Cognacq-Jay bags lay vulnerable on his bed and his mother, drawn to dirty washing like a fly to dung, wouldn't be able to resist. He didn't wait for the girl in the kiosk to give him change, nor did he notice her breasts, instead he loped back to the Avenue St. Quentin and arrived with his cheeks crimson.

He'd guessed right. Rosine Plagnol was in his room, arm in one of the bags, already busy with the booty. Guiltily she withdrew when she saw him.

"Out of bounds, maman. Sorry." His hand could have gone round her freckled old wrist twice. "Why don't you go and get my things ironed for tomorrow? Father Florian will be turning up with more demands. For a start, he wants extra pews for the disabled, and the Lady Chapel redecorated."

She flinched, not from what he did, but because his tone had changed. Not a big, soft, baby voice any more, and it scared her. Just like the mess in his flat which had been unlike anything she'd ever seen in her life. But what could she say? The cuckoo would probably suffocate her and throw her out of the nest. She'd be just another old woman scrounging round the flea markets and sleeping where she could.

Her mother was bawling again.

"Shut up, old bones!" her grandson shouted through to the makeshift bedroom, but that made the incumbent worse, her protests louder. Rosine pressed against the wallpaper for support. Her fingers tracing the anaglypta flowers. She stared at her son's bags, full of strange things. Things she'd never have associated with him.

Maybe they're someone else's. Maybe not. Oh, merde, what is going on?

The former member of Jeune Europe snatched them up without a glance, and took them down to the Laguna as she listened to his every sound, her heart throbbing in its ever-tightening cage.

At least this time he's not pestered me about his circumcision. I really am weary of telling him it was an infection that made me do it. Why else for God's sake? Why else?

And then, upon hearing those same boot beats return up the stairs, she stiffened, waiting until he'd reached her mother's mean accommodation. He paused before opening her room door and in readiness for his dress rehearsal, quietly locked it behind him.

XXIX

Émile Cacheux's greeting at Perpignan Station consisted of a brief stroke of his only son's new eyebrows and a smile that, out of consideration, was better left unborn.

The priest of St. Honoré retired hurt, to follow the head that had been burnt to a deep umber under the Corbières sun. Almost bald, it seemed that the convolutions of his father's brain now ridged its surface, and worse, dark hairs sprouted above his tee-shirt collar. Very Spanish. Very dirty. Éric Cacheux had also noticed both ears were full of red wax.

But the black Mondeo was a surprise. With only 350 kilometres on the clock, black leather seats and thick carpet, it still smelt of recent valeting. No trace of the vineyard here, unlike the van which was too foul to sit in.

"How's mother?" he asked tucking his belongings under his legs. "Is she still down in the dumps?"

"Never mind her. You were on TV," was said without a trace of paternal pride and Cacheux felt again the familiar chill of rejection he'd known since he could walk. "Mind you, I think His Holiness has got the wrong end of the bloody stick." He crossed himself with a practised hand.

The octogenarian nimbly joined the N9 for Narbonne into wind and more wind, buffeting in from the sea.

"I said, how's mother?"

After a pause and a sly glance in his direction, the propriétaire pointed inland.

"Madame Cacheux has found some new graves. God knows what for. Anyhow that's cheered her up a bit."

"Oh?"

"Don't ask me where. She's out from morning till night. I have to fend for myself most days."

Quel dommage. You hardly look starving.

Suddenly a Fiat topped by surfboards, overtook at speed, and Éric Cacheux stared at the men inside. Young gods with bleached hair and toffee-coloured skin.

"Cheeky sods." The old man floored the throttle and roared towards Vingrau, slewing off the roundabout, clipping the kerb. "Saw you gawping at the woofters. Serve you right."

"So you'd rather kill me this way?" He felt his neck burn even though the sun had gone.

"Got to protect you from yourself. Should have chopped your dick off first thing. That Montpeyrous seminary was the worst place on earth for you. I

111

often ask the Lord why He didn't prevent it."

"Your choice, Papa, as I recall."

"I'm not 'Papa.'"

Huge, dusty palm trees gave way to neolithic scrub, climbing in stony layers until topped by the Château d'Aguilar. The passenger knew his father's train of thought as well as any rosary, and anything he might say in self-defence would make things worse, especially for Mother.

But Émile Cacheux's thoughts became words. The same old mantra including no foreseeable grandchild for either the Cacheux line or the Château de Fourcat. The possibility of some vile disease and the disgrace of AIDS leading to public loathing. All this was followed by a monologue on Aloïs Brünner having been less than thorough in clearing queers from the soil of southern France.

Like the vine weevil on the leaf, this especially had lodged in his mind and now, although his father had finished with the usual disappointed drop of his wrists, he covered his ears with his hands while the car followed the Verdouble river deep into the hinterland. Éric Cacheux watched the sky turn purple over the sea, the still-bright terraces of the Domaine de Dufort Coopérative, and in the presence of such grandeur, such success, felt that same blight had also devoured his soul.

"Pater Sancte, sic transit gloria mundi..." he mouthed as the sunset spread over the mountains. And what would remain of it all? A soil of worms. No, even less.

"See how Dufort's beating us to it," his father muttered, gesturing to his left.

"Our vines look just as good," Cacheux lied.

"Ah, but they've got more workers. If the weather breaks, if we have hail..."

"Then I'll pray." His son too eager with what little he had, and Émile Cacheux duly laughed, for that was the order of things. His mockery always expected, always delivered. But there was one thing he didn't know, and the secrets, safe in their case against his son's lower legs, felt reassuring. "Alright. Mother and I will pray."

The car suddenly swerved on to the back road to St. Julien, veering over the loose stones. His father gripped the wheel, his jaw set like old Cressy's dog, deliberately finding potholes, pitching and lurching as though to further loosen his son's mind.

"That is the problem. And you try your damnedest to make it worse. You will never bloody understand that was why we sent you to that Seminary in the first place."

"We? Do please enlighten me." The same tone as for a parishioner whose confession was suspiciously brief and lacking in detail. Yet underneath, the anguish was beginning.

Émile Cacheux braked hard without warning. They were two dummies on a skid pan, both trapped in a dust cocoon. "Your mother and I, my son. Whatever else, whatever pathetic little ploys you used to try and win her over to your grubby ways, we were united in that one thing, and you can't divide us now."

Éric Cacheux pressed his nose against the glass as the vineyards once more came into view and his father restarted the engine.

"And I'm supposed to be grateful?"

"*We* were. It gave us time in which to forget."

The forty-year-old felt grief rising behind his eyes, remembering in a second, the interminable darkness of Montpeyrous; the interrupted sleep without even the smallest of comforts, for his mother had been forbidden to send him anything. She'd told him that later while they were picking figs outside the château, whispering like lovers in case the *propriétaire* should hear.

"*I* can't forget," he said.

"Good. Just as well and, knowing as you do that the Lord seest us, you should be cutting that kind of filth out."

The Mondeo was now past St. Julien, following a steep rubble track over the last curve of land before home. The priest gripped both sides of his seat, an anchor against the whirlwind of guilt and depression that suddenly engulfed him.

"I'm a virgin, for Christ's sake! I haven't done anything."

Except for Tessier whose cock tore me apart...

The echoes in his head seemed just then to be stronger than the Tramontaine that funnels through the Corbières, deafening his father's response and finally, when the car stopped, came the sound of Sophie Cacheux knocking on the glass.

***

She smelt warm and small in his arms. Stray colourless hairs from her chignon caught in his mouth already wet with tears as Émile Cacheux opened the boot and flung the new Vuitton suitcase to the ground.

"I told you Madame Cacheux, to stay inside."

"Éric's not well. Can't you try and understand?" She took her son's hand and he knew that if she held it for long enough and looked intently enough with her soft blue eyes he would tell her what he was carrying; all about Paris, in fact why he'd even gone at all.

Everyone else she knew in the Commune had been content enough to see the Pope on television, and these were decent and loyal enough Catholics. She knew instantly something had changed. Something was different.

"Let me take this." She made for the smaller case still where he'd left it by the car, but he snatched it away, almost pushing her over.

"It's private, maman," he whispered. "Very private."

She stared as he picked up the larger one, brushing it as if it were a treasured antique, before straightening his cuffs. Her handsome boy keeping her at bay, pretending now she was a ghost. Sophie Cacheux followed him into the cool tiled hall and watched as he climbed the stairs up to his room.

His *tanière*. White walls and rugs set out like a seven-card spread on floorboards which sighed under each step. He secured both bolts on the door then checked outside through the small circular window in case Heaven itself might be peering in. For that reason, he hesitated before turning on his light. It caught the tips of leaves near the window, the figs full and heavy like his own bald scrotum and the wires slung from one wall to the next, swaying in the rising wind. It also made him public.

He could hear his father slam the barn doors and mutter his abuse as he set the huge, mistrustful padlock. The man had been miserable for as long as he could remember, but now the forty-year-old's adrenaline quickened as he opened the various styrene cartons from the Entrepôt. Suddenly the years slipped away. He was a boy again and this was Christmas.

Parish matters and notices of Baptisms and Confirmations fell to the floor, usurped by more important things. Things that he was good at. A different kind of communication – for the world he lived in, not the hereafter he'd probably never know.

Spare phones, slim enough to escape any search if placed near the groin, and the list of codes and a couple of two-ways for close coverage if necessary.

Then he tried calling Duvivier at Les Pradels. Nothing doing. He sat back watching the sky spawn stars and the first slide of moon, puzzled as to why Melon hadn't answered at the appointed time. There was a sound from beyond the door. He held his breath and, like a fugitive, cleared the desk in a few deft movements and switched the room to darkness.

"Who is it?"

"Maman."

His suit like his conscience slipped from him, leaving his body bare and taut, fine marble veined around the joints, his buttocks tense. A quivering of pleasure above each thigh.

Slowly he pulled the first bolt, then the second, feeling the draught snake round his ankles. Red shoes, just for him, but in the half light at the top of the Château, he could still pretend they belonged to Vidal.

"Oh, my child."

A big newborn, he bent for her caress, her country hands familiar, more knowing than any man's while moonlight bleached his lips and turned his skin to albumen.

And in the aftermath of love, sitting close, it was the time for secrets. His not hers, from the City, which left her strangely distant and silent.

***

After supper, during which the *propriétaire* had guzzled his couscous and two carafes of last year's vintage, Sophie Cacheux left the room without explanation. She'd avoided her son's eyes throughout and now he called her name through the empty living quarters, even down into the cave where bats and scorpions were the only living things.

"Maman!"

Taking his torch instead of his gun, he secured his Breviary and rosary inside his *soutane* pocket and took the track east in the direction of Pech d'Oriole. Despite the meal, he still felt giddy and rested for a moment near the Château sign while Orion dominated the windy sky. He called again, afraid his father might hear, and set off walking between the ruts on higher ground, feeling the lumps of limestone through his shoes and using the beam to check for snakes.

Maman had been kind and gentle, and even though the night wind ripped his hair from his head and found his skin through his *soutane,* she was still there. Her scent, her words; oh, how she loved him, and how he'd always longed for time to turn around, for her breast to fill his mouth and feed him with herself. But now there was someone else, and during the breathless, joyful *petit mort,* he had told her of Robert Vidal. The man with the look of Christ himself.

Was that so terrible? That he was in love? He glanced up, but the sky held no answers, and the vines whispered only to themselves as he reached a fork in the track. Left for Pech d'Oriole and his church, right for 'Vilabou,' the Cressy place, and the biggest slum in the Commune. He stopped at the spindly iron cross embedded in a heap of stones, listening hard, not for natural noises of the night, but to gauge if any of the peasants were at home.

The stench of chicken shit suddenly reached him instead. Sweet rotting air from the pens and then the dog, a Fauve de Brétagne, hungry for blood, howled into the wind from its compound near the gate.

Cacheux had been there just once as a kid and never again. He had some vague memory of fooling about with the brothers in the small orchard. For a bet he'd had to drop his shorts then they'd called their father over from the barn to have a look. He'd never told his mother, it was too shameful. And he would hate that place for ever more.

Amongst the paradise of vines, the twelve Cressy hectares lay like an open sewer, with the two sons pissed as farts every day and night, and the old widow not much better. Even when Muriel Cressy had been alive, they'd never set foot inside the church of St. Honoré, not for the simplest Mass or worse, any baptism. Doomed to free fall down to Hell in their filthy rags, along with Jews, yuppie Cathars and anyone else arrogant enough to stay outside the Church of Rome.

Cacheux touched the cross and held his rosary for the moon's bright benediction and his prayers uniquely refined for the situation he was in. Not mess, although he could easily have used that word, but this new calling was of his own choice. There'd been no coercion, in fact the first letter in June had given him a week to decide. But he'd only needed an hour. One hour to feel needed and valued. Besides, the money on offer was more than his Deacon or Bishop would earn after ten years and, in Confession afterwards, he'd admitted a great honour to be truly in the service of God.

It wasn't enough for Pierre de la Palud to agree with Gregory IX that Jews attend Christian sermons – oh that the world could be made so simple and the grip of Zion be loosened so easily...

He turned his torch to the stars – two hundred and ninety-nine thousand kilometres per second to reach The Hunter's hand – and here, in the ancient silence, the openness of space, he could at last speak the truth and ask for a miracle. In his third year at Montpeyrous, he'd been flogged for a moral theology essay supporting Rousseau's claim in *Letters Written From the Mountain*, that miracles are the main obstacles to Christianity. And now, how he craved one more than ever.

"Pater noster, who sees me humble and bowed before you, I pray let me be worthy of my comrades in arms for my dedication and my skill for the glory of Thy name... and please Lord Jesus, let another of your servants, Father Jean-Baptiste love me as I love you and seek to remove all obstacles to the consummation of our devotion."

Suddenly, without warning, the torch was knocked from his grip. Chicken stink on the hand round his throat. Alphonse Cressy, a giant against the sky with beer fermented on his breath had heard every word.

"So this is God's travelling salesman. My, my, we were all riveted by your performance in the Bois de Boulogne, I must say... My old man made me watch to see what other bummers you might have picked up in gay Paree. And we weren't disappointed."

"If you would kindly let me go, Monsieur," Cacheux said as reasonably as he could, "I'm trying to reach my church."

"My church, he says. That's ripe from someone whose more bent than any old vine roots round here." He kicked the verge, shooting stones into the dark. "And anyhow, who are these comrades in arms, I'd like to know? What dirty little deeds are you using your skirts to disguise?"

He let go, but stayed close enough for spittle to land like fine rain, and close enough to seize Cacheux's cloth which he held like vermin found in the straw.

"And who, may I ask, is the lovely Father Jean-Baptiste?"

Where was reasonableness now?

"I don't have to take this, you peasant shit."

"It's you who likes the stuff round his dick. Christophe de la Bonté, my arse!" He laughed in Cacheux's face. The priest turned away, wishing he'd got his gun.

"As your humble parishioners, we have a right to know." Cressy persevered, pressing himself close.

"You've never come near the church."

"I ask again, Father. Who are the comrades in arms you spoke of? Tell me." Both hands now, as though his victim was a broiler with a second left to live.

"I made them up. It's stress." His voice thin with fear.

"I may not have your education, Father, but you continue to insult me and my family who..."

"Who what? Squat on the midden. Piss up the wall..."

Cressy tightened his grip.

"Risked their lives for France under Vichy." His voice oddly quiet and Cacheux could hear the bloody dog start up again. "In the morning, *mon ami*, someone will find you. Just another stiff with his eyes picked out. Tell me the names of your comrades."

Cacheux felt the wind up his nose, the blood tight in his head. He had to see the beautiful Vidal again, and his own mother. He had to live.

"At Montpeyrous, at the Seminary. I was lonely..."

"You're a liar, Cacheux. You crawled around like a viper with an empty gut. Everybody knows how it was for you there. You and Tessier."

Raymond Tessier. Cacheux's breath came in short desperate gasps. The Devil from Béziers with the dreaded silent footsteps.

The priest felt bile on the rise, his body giving out.

"I never touched him! He was damned."

"We can go and meet my dog, if you prefer." The younger Cressy's black eyes caught the moon as his filthy thumbs pressed in on the priest's pulsing carotid. "I don't feed him until morning, so he should be very interested in a piece of white meat."

Cacheux could hear the animal clawing at his cage, the wires singing like a Jew's harp into the night.

"Alive or dead, makes no difference. He's grateful for any small mercies."

A blackness blocked out the stars, and his voice seemed far away. Cacheux began to murmur his own last rites when a light wavered through the dark, casting both men black and gold.

Albert Cressy pushed his son away with such force that Cacheux heard the crash of dry grass and the scatter of stones. "That's not the way to do things, do you hear?"

Cacheux scrambled for his torch and almost fell. "Th... Thank you, Monsieur."

"I don't want your bloody thanks. You just bugger off and keep pretending to be holy. One thing though, Father..."

"Yes?"

"Just tell your miserable old *conard* of a father that the track you're standing on happens to be ours. Always has been."

Cacheux swallowed hard. The bruising stung.

"That's between you and him, monsieur." He flicked on the beam and saw Alphonse Cressy getting up, his mouth darkened by blood. "I'm afraid I can't intervene."

"Oh, yes, you can." The elder son began picking grit from his arms, wincing. "*We're* the heroes of the Corbières. If it wasn't for us, your precious vines would be ripening on corpses."

Cacheux listened, unsure whether to stay or make a dash for it, but he doubted if his legs could run as far as the church. "We can all over-dramatise." He tried his most priestly tone, but Alphonse lunged at him, only to be held by his father's steel arms.

"Say it, papa. Say how it was. How we had Jews up to here." He stabbed his forehead with a black finger. "And gyppos, you name it..."

"He's right. We kept twenty from Forca Réal in with the cows. When we had a few, that is. Winter 1943. Their tongues frozen, like so..." He stuck his out, pink, even in the dark. "Was it worth it, I ask? Were those wretched lives worth more than mine? The boy here not seven months and my wife poorly."

"I'm sure God in his wisdom gave you courage, monsieur."

Alphonse muttered obscenities but his father remained focussed, his lank grey hair still loyal to his head despite the sea wind rising.

"It wasn't courage, Father. No half-decent man needs that when he sees such terrible things. They'd escape that camp whatever the weather, some even had kids." But his hand span meant babies, the newborn.

"Camp? Where?"

"Fraisjean of course."

Cacheux bit his lip. Several of his flock worked there, mostly women.

"It's a meat processing place, surely?"

"What's the difference?"

A grim silence in which Cacheux thought of his mother.

"Are there graves?" Cacheux asked.

"Don't be so bloody stupid. There's nothing whatsoever. After doing their little make-believe course in crochet or woodwork, stuff like that, they'd be carted off. Tour de France to Drancy. Not many lasted here, mind." A sadness softened his voice, and fleetingly the priest remembered Plagnol's drab flat and the twenty-three-year-old who'd died looking into his eyes.

Suddenly Alphonse nudged his father, his expression eager like a child's. "You haven't finished yet. Shall I do it?"

Cacheux flinched, placing his torch over his heart.

"No. Let me." The old man rested on his rifle, and faced the priest, holding his gaze. "The last lot we saved – just three – two youngsters and a man, say fortyish, but to me and Muriel he looked more like eighty."

More restless howling, and in the distance, headlights of some *camionette* strobed amongst the vines. Cacheux strained to listen to the peasant's strong patois, part Languedoc, part elsewhere. "He brought me a gift, just a little frame for a photograph or suchlike. In iron – kind of fussy, but the sort of thing they like in Paris."

Alphonse shifted impatiently, and from his pocket pulled out a can of Krönenberg. He cracked the lid open with a sound like gunshot and the old man hit him in the chest partly from shock and partly because he didn't like being interrupted.

"So, where's all this leading, Monsieur?" Cacheux, chilled through to his bones. His church, St. Honoré now seemed too far away.

"Let *me* finish, papa." The overgrown son wheedled and passed him his can. "There's not much more to say."

The chicken farmer tipped the beer down his dry, old throat, Alphonse took his oil lamp and held it so that the priest resembled a figure from a Caravaggio he'd seen in one of his grandmother's books.

"The man was called Sorbey. Éric Sorbey." Albert Cressy burped.

"Éric?"

"Not a common name in 1944, least not round here. He was a Jew from Prats le Mollo. Told us his family was killed in the 'quake of '22, and after that he went to Prades as a metalworker. Oh, yes, he also played the violin."

"Clever chap." Cacheux saw the moon now visited by strands of cloud. He shivered, and instinctively felt for his rosary. These people were repellent. Their smell of ordure, their unwashed filth, they were animals themselves and yet he was transfixed as the man they described became more than words – he

119

actually began to live in his imagination. "Where's he now?"

Alphonse imitated gunfire and pointed towards the Pic Castellan, one of the highest and most bare of all the Corbières.

"And the others?"

"Ditto. Shot. We could do nothing. He wanted to take his chance, but the fucking Milice were like lice. Everywhere and hidden."

In the deep silence that followed, Albert Cressy drained his can and flung it into the scrub.

"After that, our farm went downhill. No-one was buying. They couldn't prove anything, just gossip, but your father..." He uttered the last word with difficulty. "Your father tried to get me killed. He was one of them. That is fact."

Cacheux looked from one to the other, their words like a winter sea rising up his body, numbing and slow.

"Then he took the road from us. Kicked us when we were down, the bastard. He greased a few palms, fiddled the Cadastre at the Mairie, no problem. Course, all that made my wife ill and she never recovered."

"I am truly sorry. But the sins of the fathers cannot be visited upon their children."

"That's not all, Monsieur le *curé*." Cressy interrupted. "Take the name Éric. Yours too, unless I'm mistaken."

"Don't be absurd!".

"I'm not. It's no coincidence. Your mother wanted the same for her only child."

"My *mother*?" Cacheux's torch clattered to the ground. His mouth fixed open.

"She's a Jew. But of course," his voice lowered even in that wild lonely place, "nobody else knows." He put a finger over his lips. "We have at least done the Cacheux family that favour."

The priest's thoughts spun back like a tape on rewind. Graves. Her never-ending searching... His trembling was nothing to do with the wind.

"Course, what she did for you was to leave you uncut, and a good job, too."

Cacheux stared, nonplussed suddenly recalling that hot day at Vilabou.

"And, funny thing, we still see her around, don't we, 'phonse? Poking about, still hunting for him. Some say she's a bit touched, but they'd never tell you – a man in your position and all that. But we're not impressed as you know. We're outside your stupid flock."

"Too right."

"But as one *voisin* to another, we'll keep *stumm*, unless..."

"What do you mean, unless?"

"We want our road back. No ifs, no buts. It's ours by rights, but your old man could block it, keep us in our place with no access. Do what he bloody well likes, whatever he bloody fancies."

"I'm sure it won't come to that." Cacheux could barely speak.

"You'll see that it won't, Father. We can rely on you." Alphonse picked up the torch and shone it into the priest's eyes. "After all, you have God on your side."

The wind now a tide in that dry exposed place with nothing to impede its run in from the sea, snatched Cacheux's *soutane* and lifted it behind him. He faced the force, leaving behind the two men and their spectres. Did he really have God on his side, or were they just liars and wreckers? It was easier for him to keep walking, to shift his confusion and the acid numbness in his stomach.

He was back in the Hôtel Marionnette seeing Plagnol's circumcised penis, and he wondered what sort of mother could hand her son such a passport to peril? But he'd been almost proud of it, The Pigface, strutting about, jiggling it in his hand like some soft toy. And then, like a meteor imploding inside his head, the implications of his own mother's legacy, hit him.

As if drunk, Cacheux followed the slope down between vines that led into an alleyway between a new barn conversion and his church. One hand tight around his rosary, the other on the torch whose bulb was fading fast until the first street lamp and the luxury of light.

Well don't think I'm going to do a Dan Burros and blow my brains out. I won't give anyone that pleasure, not round here at any rate. God made me leave my gun behind for a reason, didn't you, Lord? Speak to me...

***

Pech d'Oriole, once a cluster of cabanes, was now a small centre for tourist wine tastings. The purpose-built two-tone building painted with bottles of the Château de Fourcat and Domaine de Dufort wines was as big as the Romanesque church of St. Honoré itself. It also drew in more paying customers tired of the blowing sand along the barren coast and those looking for bargain second homes.

He noticed the Tuzons sitting on old wooden chairs outside, and smiled a *'Bonsoir'* as he headed for the Virgin's Arch. He quickened, fearful that they might see the black halo which now hung about his head.

"Father, not so fast," Old Tuzon got up and beckoned. "We want to thank you. Me and the wife."

The priest sighed. All he'd wanted was to check things for the morning, and have a few quiet moments to clear the Cressys' words from his mind.

"Our grandson's doing very well, after your prayers."

Florence Tuzon nodded agreement. "Christophe de la Bonté, you must have special gifts indeed. That's all I can say. Our little Marc is back in school and full of life again."

"That *is* good news." Cacheux brushed her shoulder with his hand. "However my Indulgences are no different from others the world over. It is God you must thank."

"We have done and still do." But the woman was peering intently into his eyes as though detecting the blight that had settled there. "How come you're so pale, Father? Pale as death. Come and share a bite of something with us. Nothing special, you understand, but it'll put some colour back in your cheeks." And before he could stop her, she'd reached up to his throat and straight away clucked alarm.

"Yvon, look, he's been hurt. Mother Mary, your neck, it's full of bruises!"

"I'm fine, really." Cacheux edged away. "And thank you for your kind ministrations, but I really must be getting on."

They both stared. Four eyes that had for seven decades watched the vines fighting for existence on the bare *terroir*, now saw God's representative look as though his was lost. Cacheux stumbled away under the lights to the Virgin's Arch, where she'd stood neatly recessed, Bible in hand, since the siege of Montségur. Her gaze led towards the Square and the small houses clustered around the Crucifix. Marble white amongst the plane trees, with blood some had claimed to see move, trailing from the stigmata to the sword's wound.

The last of the *pétanque* players had gone and also the moon captured by clouds drawn eastwards from the Pyrenees. The darkness deepened in the courtyard as he made his way towards the shallow steps before the door. Suddenly from up above, the bell shattered the silence, resonating the tenth hour far into the night. He shivered even though he was sheltered – its echo seemed to tremble the stone flags beneath him and rupture the very foundations set deep into the ground. He also clung to the Breviary in his other pocket. A small thing, worn to the shape of his hand, but at that moment, as each peal from the bell tower rocked his very being, it was all he had.

XXX

The channel breeze felt good, cleansing in its vigour as it bore the cross-tide in from the Atlantic together with huge vaporous clouds that had already soaked the English coast.

Dominique Mathieu stood above the shore, his breath blown back into his mouth. He was dwarfed by the pink granite rocks whose edges had long softened to resemble strange marshmallows. Miracles, he thought to himself, fixing on the mighty conglomerations that only God could have set in place. And God must know how he needed miracles after the events of the last few days.

As instructed, he'd left the Entrepôt and made his way across to the Pont de L'Alma with the new Samsung camera and fifty reels of film. Just another tripper taking photos of the trees where an electrician among the foliage, was repairing some of the lights. He also snapped the tourist traffic along the Avenue de New York; close-ups of hulls and prows and more particularly the berthing positioning of *Roquette IV* next to the safety barrier and finally the small boats of the *Brigade Fluvial* which almost unnoticed, trawl the length of the river.

He'd slept the sleep of the unjust through until seven, his black heart like a heavy onyx in his chest, keeping him there, unable to face the world and worse, the Baptism at midday. He'd let the phone ring four times, as he'd lain rigid, almost dead with fear – sure that it was Duvivier checking up. It was only when Madame Pinsolles from the flat below banged on his door to say Raôul Boura, the Bishop of Kervecamp wanted to speak to him, that he made it out of bed and into the daylight.

Boura instantly felt something was wrong with his favourite fellow Christian, but nevertheless kept up the jolly uncle tone, the kindly pleasantries, until the young priest of St. Jean had relaxed. But Mathieu, unshaven, his mouth as dry as a cuttlefish bone, knew he was no match for the well-disguised academic who'd trained in Rome. He strained to detect any doubt or distrust in his caller's voice, but it was disconcertingly normal.

"I felt you should know I've just been faxed a glowing testimonial from Father André of your recent efforts with Domus. It seems they can't do without you."

His pulse slowed down. He suddenly felt cold.

"That's reassuring. Thank you, but…"

"No buts. As far as I and Our Saviour are concerned, I'm sure any time spent with them is just as valuable as that spent in front of an altar."

"I feel honoured to be taking part, my Lord," he lied, recalling Duvivier's nasty little eyes. His bullying control. "The homeless problem's getting out of hand, causing begging, prostitution, drug-taking etcetera. But most people walk on the other side, saying 'there but for the Grace of God go I,' but that's not good enough for me."

Appalled by his ready falsehood, he silently thanked the same God that the miracles of technology kept him invisible.

"I realise that, my son. Now that I have the dates for your next release, I can arrange for old Father Cédric to take over again. He's frail, lord knows, but his eagerness has no bounds. Just as well, as you know, we're in crisis here, which I may say is not yet general knowledge. Only two oblates for Breil-Sorden this year – that fine Seminary may well have to close."

As he spoke, Mathieu stared at his precious collection of photographs ranged along the wall. Multiples of the youthful nun of Lisieux whose many eyes challenged his feckless soul and whose lips all seemed poised to admonish him.

"I'll pray to Saint Thérèse," he said. "She's intervened on everything I've asked so far." This sounded infantile in the extreme, and for the first time Boura hinted his irritation.

"With all due respect, Xavier-Marie, she can do nothing about man's inherent need to procreate. I'm afraid to say the world has greatly changed since she was last in it, flesh and blood like yourself is more precious to us than any gold or rubies. Our fabric is ageing and fraying like an old shroud. Soon the only Confessors will be octogenarians who've long forgotten the temptations of the flesh. I mean the..."

"I know exactly what you mean." Mathieu's gaze followed the light to the small harbour below. "We must be relevant and approachable."

"Exactly. One day, I can foresee you, Xavier-Marie, taking high office within the Church. Rest assured, I will personally recommend you when the time is right."

"That's most kind."

Mathieu's smile no more than a flicker, his free hand shaking.

"And it was good to see one of our very own priests supporting His Holiness at Longchamp. Most reverential. I'd no idea you'd gone to Paris. Father André never said."

Mathieu was caught off guard.

Why so oblique? Is he trying to catch me out? Help me Thérèse.

"I had to see the homeless situation there for myself. Then came the Vigil and the Mass..."

"Well, it's the sort of thing our flock here responds to. Active service. Do as

I do, not do as I say."

"I actually found the whole experience very moving."

"That was obvious, Father. So moving in fact you looked as though you were attending a Requiem Mass."

"It was."

"I beg your pardon, Xavier-Marie?"

"I said, to some it was."

Boura paused.

"If I understand things correctly, His Holiness was giving a message of hope to the poor, the dispossessed, to the youth of the world and, of course, there was his special plea for religious tolerance. Especially since the Algerian massacre."

"Precisely, your Lordship." He sensed the other man's puzzlement and knew he'd implied enough. Enough to salve a little of his ailing conscience. Just a little.

Mathieu winced at the recollection. Duvivier's pitted face suddenly overlaid the visionary from Lisieux, cancelling her luminous gaze with two bore holes as the Bishop of Kervecamp remounted his hobby horse.

"After all, 1997 has been designated European Year Against Racism, so it was more than appropriate His Holiness addressed that issue. The two are indeed inseparable now that borders are opening up and we have much greater freedom of movement to find work etcetera." Then suddenly he laughed in a way Mathieu couldn't fathom.

"I've recorded you on video, you know. You and your fellows – a mixed bunch of Dominicans if ever there was. And wasn't that Father André with you? You see, we've actually never met. Only corresponded. Spoken over the telephone…"

"Yes. And very supportive he was, too." Mathieu spluttered. His pretence evaporating like the summer mist when the sun climbs over the Île de Bréhat.

The bishop clearly hadn't finished.

"Had you met the others before the Celebration?"

A trap. Watch out.

"No. And to be honest, my Lord, I didn't much care for them. Ships that pass in the night, you know how it is on those occasions."

"Well I have to say again you looked none too pleased with things, in fact…"

"Yes?"

"One or two from St. Jean de la Motte wondered what was going on."

"I was just a bit emotional, that's all. I'm very sorry."

"No need to be sorry. But I'll show the film to you sometime, then you can see for yourself."

A tight, tense pause followed.

"Now, Father, speaking from experience, and I hope you won't take this the wrong way, but it might restore your position within St. Jean de la Motte Mauron if perhaps you were to hold a small parish meeting..."

Restore? What's he talking about?

"Oh?"

"Just a small one, as I say, to explain how it was. Why you seemed so distressed, so unlike the young man we've all got to know and, dare I say it, depend upon."

"I see."

"Give it a thought, anyhow, and may God in his infinite wisdom, be with you." The bishop then left him with a deeper unease than before.

A meeting? Forcing me to relive that hideous weekend? I'll have to be ill. Something to tide me over till it's all forgotten.

He turned away from the sea through the small park where screams from kids on the Crazy Golf course shattered his concentration. The Church would be empty. Ninian the evangelist from the north of England wasn't on the list of Saints to be celebrated, so he could go and think himself out of the hole Boura had dug for him, besides lighting overdue candles for Colette and Bertrand in peace.

The sun between clouds was hot on his head, his mind a maelstrom of unconnected thoughts. The *fleuriste* was due in at ten, the baptism of David Berthier at noon, a Mass for St. Augustine with the Deacon on the 28th and then... Then, by the 30th, Duvivier wants the shots of the boats and another trip overnight for the final images.

Merde. He almost collided with someone by the park gates. Dressed in jeans and a sweatshirt, mercifully no-one recognised him, and after a quick apology, he ran through the covered market towards the twin spires of St. Jean de la Motte Mauron.

Six steps, deep in shadow. A homecoming so needed, yet so strangely empty. His love, Thérèse, hadn't kept Bertrand from the water or healed Colette's distress. Neither had she moved Vidal to befriend her, nor to destroy the plans. That man had his own ambitions, it was obvious, but whether he was as diabolical as Duvivier and Plagnol was another matter.

Mathieu cursed himself for having replied to Duvivier's advert in the first place. But he'd been tempted by the prospect of doing good and finding love at the same time.

Now as he pushed open the church's heavy main door, he felt the biggest Lonely Heart on the planet, and pretty Simone Haubrey with the long, gold-blonde hair, was probably laughing all the way to the bank. His cheque, for the introduction with her, safe in her designer handbag.

After the opening creak, the sheer magnitude of the interior always made him gasp. Everything massive, over-sized late Renaissance, copied from The Basilica Torino. Hushed and chilled by sea air. Dark without candles. He went over towards the Lady chapel to collect a taper, when something hard pressed into his ribs. Someone was there, buried by the dense shadow. The hairs on his neck bristled with fear.

Duvivier? Plagnol? Is it my turn to be hunted...?

"Got you. You're dead."

"Holy Jesus."

Two figures emerged from the darkness. Two boys no more than twelve, brandishing guns. Mathieu tried to stop them running away, and cornered them by the tomb of an eighteenth-century Bishop of Kervekamp lying in blissful repose.

Laurence and Stéphane Petrus, choirboys, straight off the beach in matching gaudy shorts, stood in front of him, their brown legs quaking. Sand in their hair.

"What the Hell do you think you're playing at, you stupid little shits? You gave me the fright of my life!" He held each one by the scruff of the neck and knocked their heads together. The sound of it echoed dully in the silence, as the sand fell and their toys crashed down on the stones. The twins cried out, so he repeated the punishment and again, despite their yells for mercy, until his rage was extinguished. Father Xavier-Marie then heaved at the latch and threw them both out, sobbing into the morning.

***

He slumped into the first chair he could find. Old and spindly, it barely took his weight as he rocked backwards and forwards, head in his hands.

Meanwhile, at the altar end, beneath the arching angels, old Aouregan Tasset was lighting candles. Slowly like a growing soul, each one came into being, honeying the walls and gilding the altar cloth, while the sun, now right behind the St. Jean window, beamed the saint's robed body into the gloom. Violet and vermilion, white and cerulean, fixed like a kaleidoscope at rest. But none of this reached Mathieu who was locked in his own torment.

Like the plague, the violence of Paris had insinuated itself into his very core. He was trapped, and nothing in earth or Heaven could free him. Not even dear sweet Thérèse.

"Are you alright, Father?" The aged acolyte from Tregastel stood over him, smelling of smoke. "Can I fetch you anything?"

Mathieu suddenly stood up, sweeping the thin hair from his face. His watch showed 10.15 p.m. "I'm fine, Aouro. Just a little contretemps, that's all. Are we OK for the Berthiers?"

"We are." But the eighty-year-old didn't think the young *curé* looked up to much more than a good sleep. "Bonnefort's been practising the choir while you were gone and..."

Damn.

He'd forgotten Madame Berthier had asked for the choir. Alarm for a moment, thinking of the Petrus boys. Two of its shining lights...

"Don't worry," said Aouregan. "They all sounded wonderful."

"I'm sure. I'm sure, but why not let Bonnefort do it? The whole thing I mean. Instead of Father Cédric."

The old man hired in from the Gueribois monastery wasn't used to disruption and stared at the priest with tired transparent eyes.

"He's not well himself, Father. Stomach problems, in the night." He rubbed his own with a long white hand.

"He could have told me."

"Said he tried, but no-one answered."

"Really?"

And as Mathieu tried to avoid the inevitable, the *fleuriste* bustled in carrying two bunches of red gladioli. Coffins, he thought. He hated those flowers. Death's more glamorous partners. Even their smell was hideous. She kissed him on both cheeks, then stood back, her strong country face missing nothing of his demeanour.

"Well, Father Xavier-Marie, if I may say so, you seemed pretty fed up in Paris and now you look even worse."

"Thank you, Madame; I appreciate your concern." But his irony was wasted and she tip tapped away down the nave.

"I'd better go and get things ready, too." Aouregan was glad of the long walk back to his simple duties, and Mathieu watched until the frail figure disappeared.

Alone, near the great font of Megalithic rock, he peered in, seeing in close up the myriad gouge marks from unknown hands. Diagonals, cross-hatched, following the curve, the only testament to those faraway lives. And now unable even to speak to his mother, Angélique, or his public-spirited father, and unfit in the eyes of God to cleanse a new infant of sin, he let his tears of shame drop one by one, silently, into the sacred vessel.

XXXI

"Laboureurs et vignerons,
Devant Dieu courbons nos fronts!
C'est lui qui dont la main, nous donne les fruits
Que mûrit l'automne..."

Colette could hear the chapel choir above the storm which despite their supplications had already flattened some of the St. Émilion vines and now reached deep into the bowels of the Refuge. Like a silver thread, the voices persisted through the fierce spasms of thunder that forced her to crouch next to the thin mattress, rather than lie vulnerably on it. At least that way she could see the door.

Something in her had died as the key had turned, not once but twice, abandoning her to the dark airless humidity. This was no *chai* – a ground floor wine storage area – for there weren't any casks, and in Bordeaux, because of the terrain and the high water table, caves as such couldn't be excavated. She'd remembered that from school, where the little library book, *Wine Regions of France* had been a favoured companion.

So what was this, reeking of damp and wet underfoot? Although cold, she was sweating all over and her robes felt leaden and imprisoning. She stood up to grope around the walls for any kind of opening, a grille, a vent – anything.

She had to have air.

Colette ripped off her veil. For the first time her hands touched her head. A hideous alien thing, beginning to bristle short spiky hairs.

"You evil bitches!" she yelled and kicked at the door until her voice gave out, as thunder again racked the building. She also tore the underskirt and the outer dress from her body and, although she had no recollection of being robed in that way, other images were slowly returning. They'd tried to make her a stranger, even to herself, but she was going to hang on. To cling to the boy waving from the summer bank, his face trapped in sunlight. The boy whose birthday had gone.

No body hair either. Under arm or down below where the dark-skinned man had once caressed her. She was bald as a seven-year-old; naked save for a pair of black institutional boots.

"Witches!" Colette struck the door again and stood against it, listening. Her senses sharper now despite the shivering.

The singing had stopped and the procession from the chapel was beginning overhead, as desperately, she moved along the wet wall to her right, the one not yet explored but which she reasoned must follow the way out of the Refuge.

129

Her fingers traced over shallow carvings, initials of others who'd been there, holed up like the Templars at Chinon. Pathetic remnants of a line here, a cross there, but on some, this cross was different with Greek gammas at each end.

Swastikas? Here of all places? I'm going mad...

She moved away from the strange testimonies, along the same cold stone, the same crumbling mortar, and yet... Suddenly, something came away, loose and heavy in her hand.

Deo gratias!

This stone was generally smoother, obviously shaped to fit that particular place. She laid it down as though it was the Holy Grail and carefully removed another, and a third, until a definite cavity opened up.

The smell grew more potent with each withdrawal. All too easy – someone had been there before, but not quite far enough into the massive thickness. Colette imagined tantalising daylight, a quick slither through to the grounds and freedom to hold her son in her arms. She cried out in frustration and for a moment pulled back. The whole thing was useless and would only take up the last of her precious energy. Besides, she could forget grass and sky, what lay beyond was probably more of the same, all underground.

The thunder made her cling to the wall waiting for the aftermath to pass. Better to try and think things through, she thought, try and plan a strategy while she could, before that needle hit her arm again.

She would apologise. Confess to having lied. That all the priests were the most Holy of men concerned only for God's kingdom on earth. That might get some of her things back – her rosary, her own clothes, her bag with the photograph of her son. And now, what was he trying to tell her?

Talk to me, for Jesus' sake! Tell me where you are!

The hole in the wall gradually grew in size. Like a painstaking surgical procedure, each obstacle was eased away, but still it led nowhere. A mocking hollow womb of dreams that stank in her face. The same as the killing tunnel at Drancy, just yards from a different life, a better death.

She'd lost track of time. After all, the darkness was constant, and with no watch or other means of marking it, seconds, minutes and hours meant nothing. The only thing that mattered was to get out. Her feet were sodden in the silt that slopped around her ankles. Two lead weights, but protection at least against rats. She listened. Water from somewhere. Both her hands felt around the opening and shuddered as a trickle of ice covered her fingers.

"Oh, Holy Mother."

Colette began to cram the discarded stones back into the space, but the pressure from deep behind, forced them back to the edge to fall on her shoes.

She screamed to the God of false hope as the flow increased, bringing lumps of mortar and stone flints stinging against her skin. It had all been too easy, too convenient. Obviously whoever was imprisoned there was meant to find this temptation, and she'd been a fool.

She struggled over to her robes, now almost too heavy to lift, but she managed to drag them to the door and pile them up. She stood on top, gaining some height, but as the flood swilled past the second layer of stones, they subsided, taking her down into the rising current.

"Sancta Maria, Mater Dei, ora pro nobis peccatoribus nunc et in hora mortis nostrae..."

Even her words were drowned as she hammered in vain on the door, growing more numb and feeble with every breath. Death was now gently at her knees. The rush of water from the wall was more subtle, quietly enveloping. Her clothes splayed out and lifted away leaving her anchored to the floor. Whatever else, she had to lose the boots, but they were laced up too tight for a quick pull to release them. She'd lose her balance if she bent down, and worse, her face would be under water. Had they known that to drown was her greatest fear? Had she given that one away as well?

So the comforting Sister Agnès, the sublime Marie-Ange and the Percheron peasant had planned a silent end. A mute immersion.

Not bloody likely!

She inhaled till her lungs could take no more and yelled while her whole freezing body shook with rage. They'd picked the wrong one this time. She, Sister Barbara, was going to get out, whatever it took. Another breath, another barrage against the lock, as sweet Bertrand hovered in her mind, willing her on, making her remember the smile that Agnès had shared with the hostel receptionist. He'd been there alright. He was telling her...

Suddenly the water was different. Thickened with brown solids that nudged her before bobbing away leaving a distinctly sulphurous smell. This was a sewer, and each centimetre gained by the filth was a centimetre frozen. Both breasts now unknown save for their stinging nipples, her arms useless as the foul liquid reached her throat.

With the door next to her back, she stood on tiptoe, but that too was pointless, for her mouth was covered. Her last prayer silent. She held her nose, eyes tight like the triplets, her head just some frozen thing. Colette angled her body into the current and lay floating, spluttering and spewing from wherever she could. Her hands worked like fins to keep herself from sinking as suddenly her eyes opened to a light from above, whose beam fell on her belly.

Someone was up there watching, but she was too weak to cry out and just before unconsciousness, a loud gargle issued from the wall behind – the water sucking her towards the opening.

To Hell and back – an obscene birth in reverse. Frantically her arms flayed on either side to move her free of the suction. She took in more filth and dribbled it out, but at least she was clear, feeling the icy flow begin to drain away. She tried to stand but toppled and, again, gasped for breath in the fetid residue. With the beam still following her every move, she managed to reach her robes.

She hadn't confessed any more, nor given these Devil's daughters the satisfaction of submission. It was as though her son had reached out to her, willing her to live, and she had. She had survived.

***

"Well now, did our dear Novitiate relish her baptism?"

Colette recognised the Sister Superior's mocking tone that seemed to emanate from way beyond the ceiling. She also heard the tinny echo of her little bell. "But we are none the wiser, are we not?"

"I told you the truth and that's all you're getting!" Colette's teeth jarred against each other. She could barely speak.

"I'm afraid Sister Barbara that..." But her words were completely buried by new thunder. Thunder that tore from the Heavens as though to demolish the place. Colette's heart raced in her chest as she moved to the door, and in shivering delirium she grabbed the slat where normally a handle would have been.

It opened inwards almost knocking her over. One of the triplets in matching red Wellingtons carried a cloak, none too clean and smelling of stables.

"Here, take this!" She thrust it at Colette who instantly covered her nakedness. "There's a note in the pocket," she hissed, her simple dough face puckered into a frown. Suddenly the beam was on her this time, but only Colette could see it.

"Victorine. What are you doing?" The Sister Superior's voice swelled into the terrible calm but the girl was single-mindedly finishing her errand.

"Don't worry, they won't hurt me," she said. "I'm too important to them. I'll come again tomorrow." She then turned and ran up the steps.

"Tomorrow? Here? Dear God, I can't last another day..." Colette's thawing stomach lurched on nothing and when she tried to walk her feet gave way – nerves and tissue welded to ice.

"You will both be punished for this," came the Sister Superior's voice again as the light probed the cell then lingered on Colette's bare head. "That is my promise."

She had to hide, so, having subsided on to the wet-shit floor, she wriggled to the nearest corner, just like Bertrand used to do before he was able to stand.

That way the beam couldn't quite reach her as she burrowed for the letter in the deep slit pocket. Her fingers were so cold they almost missed it.

At that moment it was the most precious thing and, as she extracted it, the permutations of possible senders reeled through her mind. Chloë? Nelly? But best of all, Bertrand? In the darkness she felt over each Braille dot that made up the words, her excitement fading as each fearsome word was complete: *Chloë is dead. I will help you escape.*

"Holy Mary, Mother of God." Colette stuffed it in her mouth then swallowed it. She crossed herself and murmured a little prayer for the girl and her dead baby, aware that she was barely alive herself. Her toes still rigid, her body convulsed by new spasms.

That same chilling sneer reached her ears. "She's not paying you any attention, I can tell you."

"Somebody will be. You'll see."

The light cut out. Coletté could hear the run of rat-like feet overhead. Then nothing, just the suck of waste saturating the earth floor. Colette covered her mouth. Already she was beginning to itch and her stomach heaved in fits and starts. She had to try and get something to Nelly's mama, or even to Medex and she prayed that brave Victorine would keep her promise.

***

She noticed other sounds had replaced the storm as it rolled eastwards over the Dordogne. Faint shouts and activity in the Chapel as the organ released a fugue into the night. Something was wrong, she could tell. Too much movement, too much clamour. She felt a cold draught on her scalp, then shrieks and cries as someone stumbled into her space. The door crashed shut and was fiercely locked.

The figure stood sobbing, and Colette could just make out the shorter veil, the same blood colour of her dress.

"Victorine?"

The girl fell into her arms, trying to catch her breath, and with a final effort managed to speak.

"The Percheron's been hit by lightning, and they're saying because you're Sister Barbara, you could have saved her."

Colette felt a new tide of madness envelope her that was more terrifying than anything else. Unstoppable, insatiable. Now she really knew what she was up against.

"Victorine, we've got to get out." But the eighteen-year-old tucked herself further into Colette's cloak, moaning her sisters' names.

"We'll try and help them as well, but you've got to listen. If you're let out of here before me, I want you to memorise an address, OK? Make sure every word's gone in, like so." She tapped her own head. "Micheline Augot, Flat 41, 85, Avenue Renaud, St. Denis, and don't worry about a post code. You got that? Right, now say it back."

Victorine obliged, less falteringly each time, so that at midnight on the second stroke when Sister Agnès silently reclaimed her, she was word perfect.

XXXII

Sunday August 24th

The storms which had inundated the eastern areas had reached as far as Le Mans, but left the Paris basin unrefreshed and the fumes in the Capital undiluted.

Nelly Augot's eyes couldn't take the contacts any more so she dropped them down the lavatory and watched as her disguise sank slowly into the stained bowl. Her chest was sore from coughing and she couldn't afford anything for it. Not the best shape to be in for a knight in shining armour, she thought, returning to her cramped room that overlooked the tiny Cimitière Raphaël. She slammed the window shut and the afternoon sun blazed its exclusion through the smeared glass.

No-one had answered at the Doumiez's flat in Évry. In fact, it had been boarded up and the letterbox jammed open with hypermarket offers that she'd dumped in a bin. She'd tried neighbours to no avail and even stopped people in the Avenue Clemenceau below. What else could she do? It could be tricky calling the police. Maybe there were secrets that weren't for her to pry into.

She tipped out the contents of her purse on to the table, scratched with the hearts and arrows of other lovers. She should be so lucky. Apart from a Pole outside the Musée des Lunettes, she'd managed to pull three, all faceless and anonymous.

Whatever it took. For 200 francs a go she'd let them suck and fumble, but the old boy in the Boulevard St. Hippolyte never made it. He'd been due for prostate tests, so he said, and his dick had been as soft as a wind funnel in a breeze. So she'd let him have a go at her tits instead. The other two, and she winced at the memory, had been quick and jerky and none too clever with their hands. The black from Toulon had come the moment he touched her, and made her bleed. The other, who'd introduced himself as a Charentais, had said he was quite happy with his wife of ten years but could never resist *"une poule."* Especially one with nice sturdy legs and a meaty *derrière*.

Sometimes she still felt the smell of it on her. The same that hung about her mama. She felt sick with disgust that she did those things, and especially as she'd have to phone to see if Colette had been in touch.

She coughed again, hot and ill as she counted out 600 francs and what was left of her dole. It had taken three days working the strip between the Avenues Georges Mandel and Raymond Pointcaré. Three long boiling days when, if she'd been a blonde on stilts, she'd have made both their Bordeaux fares in as many hours.

Nelly saw the stubs of graves above the undergrowth outside, and although she had no particular God to pray to, nevertheless put her hands together and prayed that Colette, who was the mother she'd always longed for, was alright and holding on. Blast the Doumiez's! Why couldn't they have just been there for their kid?

She couldn't afford to go again; besides, she couldn't be responsible for the whole bloody world. Nelly quickly primped her hair into some kind of order and straightened her bedspread that looked even more dingy grey in the sunlight. "Roger," the soft toy dog she'd rescued from a skip in the Rue Calenta perched on guard on the bolster. Something at least to cuddle without having to have another dick between her legs...

**

The hostel was quiet, with most of its occupants out either hustling or shoplifting. Only a few had part-time work, but she hadn't met one who professed to see Christ as their kindred spirit. not even after the Pope's Mass when the press had proclaimed a new surge towards the Catholic Church.

"Doesn't buy you bread, does it?" Max Bellino, the stray from Clermont Ferrand in the next room had laughed, but like her and all the others, had sported a cheap crucifix just to get a bed. He'd just joined Les Flammes. Something to do, and at least it entitled him to soup and a roll every day, even though the R.G.P.P. would probably be starting a nice fat file on him.

She saw the week's dust and leavings drifted against the stairs, and the resin Jesus in a slow self-absorbed dance from his wire. For some reason as she passed beneath him, she crossed herself. For Colette and Chloë and a ticket for the Paris-Montparnasse TGV at 6.55 in the morning.

Claude Lefêbvre ignored her as usual. The sleek groomed head stayed posed in front of her p.c. Nelly considered using the payphone, but she wasn't the only one who reckoned the cool bitch listened in and passed things on.

"Hi," Nelly said, deliberately before stepping out again into the hot, thick air. "Mama?" She repeated while the phone in the St. Denis apartment was still ringing. "Mama?"

Perhaps she's on the job. Perhaps...

"Nelly? That you?"

Micheline Augot seemed more drugged than drowsy, her words slurred together in a way that frightened her caller.

"You sound bad," said Nelly, but couldn't mention her own cough, or the rough loss of her virginity behind the Rue Didier. Give, give, give... All she was used to. There was a pause as though her mother was hauling herself out of bed.

"Five o'clock," she muttered. "Jesus Christ..."

"Mama, have you had a letter or anything from someone called Colette?" Nelly thought she was going to faint in the choking cubicle.

"A letter? Dear God..." Then came the noise of something falling off the bedside table.

"Never mind that, mama, I need to know. C..O..L..E..T..T..E.." And as she spelled out each letter, her last image of the poor woman from Lanvière came to mind. "She's in big trouble."

"You watch what you get into my girl. She's not a dyke, is she?"

"Stop it!"

"Well let me think..."

Nelly pressed her ear against the greasy handset and heard her mama shuffling papers.

"I did get something yesterday afternoon."

"Yesterday afternoon. Oh, mama."

"I have other things to do, you know."

"Quickly. Read it. Now."

Outside the booth, a woman in a dark suit impatiently checked her watch.

"Wait a minute..."

That minute was the closest thing to eternity. The heat boiling her bones, seizing up her lungs. Micheline Augot coughed over the words when they finally came...

"Chloë dead. Ask hostel about Bertrand Bataille again. My son. God bless. Colette." She paused. "Lord knows what that's all about..." Her mama wittered on as the waiting woman stood closer and knocked on the glass.

"Piss off," shouted Nelly.

"Is that meant for me, my girl?" Micheline snapped, but Nelly had nothing else to say. She put the phone down, slid the door open and stuck her tongue out at the Parisian who called her a tart.

"Exactly. Got it in one." And, in that moment, was proud of what she'd done, and knew what she had to do next.

She slung her bag round her neck and, for the first time since meeting her friend Colette, plucked up the courage to call in at the Gendarmerie near the Place de Mexico.

XXXIII

Monday August 25th

The two churchmen in Room 108 of the Hôpital Malâtre stood dark against the daylight whitened blind. René Martin, Deacon of Les Bourreux, wore his new biretta low over his eyes like a hooded snake. He took both Duvivier's hands and held them as he spoke.

"Thank you, Father André for your kind intercessions on behalf of our dear departed. I know God in his great goodness will reward you." He looked drained, not just from his own intensive prayers but the fact that Pereire's death would now plunge him into the nest of vipers vying for the office.

"I could do nothing less." Duvivier disengaged himself and as he reclaimed the bunch of lilies he'd bought for the bedside, the stamens brushed his chin, leaving indelible sienna smears. He left the over-large Get Well card showing the Gelderland crucifixion where it was, glowing indecently with more life than the body next to it. Bones that seemed mountainous under the sheet. That mischievous mouth closed tight.

Death had finally rendered harmless the man who'd known too much and who'd been too ready to interfere, who hunted small boys like St. Eustace along the banks of the Tiber...

"Worrying times." Martin patted the bed for the last time as Duvivier noticed the nurse's economical waist and her breasts tight under the uniform. He could afford a secret smile – there was to be no further investigation of the accident. A tragic loss of concentration, nothing more, nothing less, and as Henri Pereire had been notorious for his solitary jaunts around the area, the Examining Magistrate wasn't looking for anyone else in connection with his death.

Besides, no-one had yet come forward to refute this thesis.

The young nurse avoided his eyes while Martin struggled to give instructions from the Legate in Paris for removal and disposal of the body. Then Duvivier led him smartly out of the building – the place with its reek of mortality and its memories already silting up his mind.

...I remember she was taller than Pereire. They had to pull back the pillow so she didn't look as though she was about to rear up and condemn me to a deeper part of Hell. One hand I couldn't touch because of the bandages, but the other, with her ring, was free and the only thing she ever let me have. A gift in Death, stiff and cold.

But at least it was her hand, and without her knowledge, I could touch the new freckles, follow the lie of that pale land to each painted nail. Red again. Red on white. Blood under the dressings darkening and dying... Oh, mother, why?

When you could have had me...?

He was aware of René Martin squinting at him in the sun.

"This is where I must leave you, Father André. I have a trip to the capital tomorrow. The Papal Nuncio is curious. Things to be sorted, you know..."

"Indeed," said Duvivier noticing how those two eyebrows knit together in ambition and how soon the tears had dried.

"In all probability the Requiem will be held in Fayence."

"I'd have thought Ste Trinité would be more central. Better roads, more hostelries..."

"Birthplace, my good man. After all, there's no other family, no other claims."

"Pity."

"Your church is enviable, Father André, both historically and ecclesiastically, but I'm sure you'd be the first to admit it's looking somewhat jaded. Lacklustre's the word. Especially the grounds. Couple of goats would do the trick."

Duvivier stayed silent, watching the smirk of satisfaction creep over Martin's face. Suddenly, two black Safranes drew up into reserved spaces.

"Aha. We have company." The Deacon feigned surprise. He straightened his cape, removed his biretta and smoothed down what remained of his hair. Duvivier saw dandruff but wasn't going to help him out. He had other plans, besides, his secret journey back to Cavalaire had unnerved him, orienteering without a compass, just the moon and the wind for company.

"I must go."

The lilies hid his face before he turned away, but René Martin with his diaconate future firmly on his mind, hurried over to meet the Archdeacon and Pereire's 'Familia.' All men and all in mourning. Enemies and their shadows sharp as swords in the sun.

***

Duvivier bit his teeth into his lower lip as he picked up a cab in the Square de la Lettre de Tassigny.

"Ste Trinité. My church," he barked at the driver. "Make it snappy."

The young man cast a furtive glance at his fare as he pulled away, deliberately allowing a coach to overtake.

"Lovely flowers, Father. For your place?"

"They are."

"Nice touch that."

"Like the cost of this trip, if you don't shift it."

The driver stared through his rear-view mirror. Something in those pinprick eyes kindled danger. He stepped on the gas and took the next set of lights on red noting no change of expression.

139

"And when we get there, you're to give me five minutes."

"Sorry but I've got to be in La Croix by six."

Duvivier leaned forwards.

"Your problem, not mine. I've hired you. Simple."

The Toledo veered away from the sea, past endless rows of boutiques and tourist kiosks towards the northern hills. After the Camping de l'Horizon, the gradient increased, and suddenly, from the depths of his pocket, Duvivier's mobile beeped into life. He tried to stifle it but Vidal's scrambled voice persisted.

"Not now, Father," the Provençal snapped, seeing the driver's growing curiosity.

"Look here, I've been trying to get through since I got back. God knows what's going on.... Moussac's dead, murdered, and Toussirot..."

"Later. It's tricky."

Übertolpen.

He'd kept his anger under control, but was now in danger of losing it. This saloon was in the wrong gear, straying across the road.

"Here?" asked the imbecile at the wheel.

"Yes."

***

His presbytery and the church loomed up on the left, its wrought-iron bell tower resembling a giant insect curled up against the sky. Black and malevolent, dotted by crows. Duvivier felt the driver watch him as he climbed out and passed under the archway, so he took his time through to where weeds devoured the angels and other saintly figurines marking the local graves. Brother Hubert next to his mother, both mottled by laurel, and the one empty plot alongside.

The cab driver kept the engine running giving impatient little revs, and when that didn't work, switched on Django Rheinhart and whistled him into the deepening gloom.

The door of the Portal to The Virgin was already open. That wasn't unusual, for old Javel and his unmarried daughter were always around fiddling about doing something or other. Checking the offertory boxes, sweeping and dusting, but because outside had grown so wild, that wasn't now on his agenda. Nevertheless, the priest sensed something was amiss. He ran his hand over the seated Virgin and Child as though her sandstone lips would somehow speak to protect him. But she was merely a copy, and not a very good one at that, planted there long before his time.

Duvivier blinked in the sudden darkness. That bleak hour before the lighting of candles when the House of God seemed full of spirits. All Souls, every day, unbidden, despite visitors with pushchairs and conscience money from the beach sybarites clattering into the void. He strode up the nave, crossed himself by the altar and headed for the sacristy.

"Hervé? Renate?" His shoes pattered like a dog's on the ancient tiles and dust hung blue-green in the light shaft from the west window where the sun struggled to regain the sky. The life-size alabaster of his namesake clasping a fish gave him the same quizzical look as the day he was first installed, and Duvivier called again as he pushed open the small door.

The sacristy smelt different. Something was up. Smoke not incense, and from a cigar he recognised. A Belgian Panatella...

"Well, well Francke, quite a flood of raw sewage under the old bridge since we last met." Georges Déchaux stood killing the stub on the floor leaving a mark like a bullet hole. He'd slipped one of Duvivier's spare *soutanes* over his own clothes and twirled round like a girl. "And how do I look? D'you think I could have been like you with a bit more practice, you know, with an Elevation here and a Sanctus there?" A wicked twinkle lit his eyes. The eyes of a puppeteer in full control, except for the fudge-coloured growth on his nose. "My God, how I used to envy your power. With just one word from the Almighty, you could really spoil someone's whole life. Never mind someone's day. Especially mine. But it certainly fired me up to go one better." His smile big, his handshake bigger without this time the usual symbolic pitting of his thumb.

Duvivier glanced at the door.

"Oh, don't worry. I've sent both your minions off shopping. More candles and a bloody lawnmower for a start. If my memory serves me, Garden Centres are open till eight round here." The atheist's smile vanished. "There's too much of a mess outside, my friend. Attracts the wrong kind of attention. Just keep things dull and ordinary, like it used to be. There's a good chap."

For once the priest was stuck for words.

"And if you're about to ask why I didn't wait for you inside your luxurious presbytery, the reason is obvious. I find your museum collection nauseous. Always have."

"Are you referring to my dear late mother by any chance?"

"Of course. Your dear late *suicide*. Let's be accurate."

Duvivier stared and shivered. "We could have had some supper, a glass of something," he tried weakly. "I've a nice dry white."

"I'm afraid I don't find clinical photography conducive to such things, besides," he paused, "this isn't a social call."

"Oh?"

The NATO général from Reims hauled the *soutane* over his head and slicked down his eyebrows. "I want some answers, Monsieur *le curé*. First, *Le Bébé*. It was not your remit to chop him, at least not until we'd found his maman."

Duvivier sat down on the one chair amongst all the stools, shaking beneath his black disguise.

"You continue to foul things up, my friend. I'm sure had Madame Bataille known her precious son was merely being kept as a precaution, she'd have behaved herself and not gone running off telling tales."

"You're talking in riddles."

"Am I? I do beg your pardon." The général again ground his cigar stub on the tiles, this time leaving a black circular graze. Duvivier looked on, helpless. "What did you do to frighten her off I wonder? A quick grope or worse?" He placed a finger hard into the priest's knee. "Come on, confess to uncle Georges. Out in the open. Face to face. That's the thing these days, isn't it?"

"I swear to God I didn't do anything. She was hysterical from the moment we got to the Hôtel Marionnette when she found out there was nothing doing with Number 2. Besides, you'd told me and the others not to tell a soul..."

Duvivier tried to leave, but the army man pinned him down by the shoulders, his shadow cast by the high west window. "Save your breath my friend, for secondly, and just as worrying, we have the matter of Henri Pereire, which, through your good offices has become a major incident."

"He was on to me, I'm telling you. Christ knows I was just hoping for a peaceful journey back. I never asked him to pick me up, he was just there at the station, waiting."

Déchaux sat down on a stool used by the shorter choirboys to reach their surplices, and lit another cigar. His movements slow and considered, designed to cause the most uncertainty.

"Pereire knew something I'm sure of that," he inhaled deeply, calming himself down, "but they're not going to prod about too much, so we don't tempt Providence. Like yourself, he has a murky underbelly, which we all know about, but what interests me is, who was throwing titbits to the big fish?"

"God knows."

Duvivier relieved, crossed his heart, yet still felt those cool, brown eyes work into his. "He said Moussac had cancer."

"Our friend was probably lying. Testing you." He bent down to tie a shoe lace. City brogues with stitching detail. "But I didn't tell you to feed him to the eels." When he looked up, blood had pinked his normally white face. The mole on his nose even more prominent.

"He'd locked me in the car. He had a gun."

"They never found one. Besides, Francke, this sort of thing, this sort of recklessness just opens up unnecessary cans of worms."

Duvivier's fists clenched in his pockets. His pitted cheek beginning to burn again.

"When the only worms we're interested in will be wriggling nicely in the Seine on the third of October. But what I really came to see you about, Father André, is the widow. We know exactly where she is."

They heard the taxi make a screeching turn outside and blast off into the evening. Duvivier remembered his forgotten lilies, then suddenly jumped. His mobile once again, louder in the vaulted room, this time, more insistent. He checked Déchaux for his next move.

"Answer it."

Duvivier held the phone close as though it was a lover whose secrets he couldn't share.

"Yes. I'm on my own." He covered the mouthpiece and when the warbling became a voice, signalled to Déchaux. "It's just Number 2. Keeping in touch."

The général sat down again, scraping his stool on the terracotta floor. Duvivier kept his eyes on his every move and the next chore for the Javels.

"Moussac? Yes, it's shocking..." Then he held the phone in such a way for Déchaux to hear the other priest's lamentation on the loss of his musical collaborator. "But there's plenty more can fiddle with the organ, I'd have thought." Duvivier's nerves mercifully winning. "Take the girl I've got here, Renate. Self taught. When everyone's singing no-one can hear the odd bum notes..." He forced a smile for the général's benefit, but the man wasn't interested.

"That's insulting, and you know it."

"Apologies."

"All I know right now is there's to be an autopsy and Toussirot's smelling like a piece of shit." Vidal shouted into the sacristy.

Déchaux got up. Vidal still in full flow. "Tell me, why was Moussac poisoned? And what did that turd Toussirot do with my letter?"

The général blew out smoke like a sperm whale. He took the mobile, punched OFF, and handed it back to a startled Duvivier.

"What letter is he talking about?"

"Nothing. The sooner the better he starts diving again then he'll forget about things that aren't important."

Déchaux toyed with his gold lighter and brought the flame close to the Provençal's sleeve. "I said no more questions, remember? And as far as any autopsy's concerned, our dear Lord Bishop of Ramonville is dealing with it, and our very important friend, Dr. Brébisson sips from his hand like a kitten. Isn't that nice?"

Duvivier shivered. He was simply a pawn in a game whose rules changed on the whims of the wind. He suddenly needed the toilet.

"Our handsome friend has too much temperament, I'm afraid. Mountain people." Déchaux pocketed his lighter. "And on occasions, too much sentimentality, which is far more dangerous. Our purpose is not best served by that particular weakness, and I wouldn't discuss anything with him. Now, as to why I'm here." He fastened each leather button on his Paul Smith jacket with great care, for Monday's sun had sunk low behind the Col de Canébas, and a chill from the empty church seeped through into the room. "Madame Bataille has latched on to a women's Holy Order. Hiding amongst skirts, just like *Le Bébé*. I'm afraid any more detail is strictly Classified. I'm dealing with it."

"How did you find that out?"

Déchaux tapped his nose avoiding the wart.

"She's been squealing. They warned me." The général consulted his Rolex. "Our little team should be on the way by now and our irritant taken care of. Nothing to Number 2, OK? Oh, and by the way, Francke." His tone hardened. "Next time a woman of a certain age, *comme votre maman* comes along, try and resist the temptation to how shall I say, impress?"

Those three little words slotted like bromide in a sandwich, made Duvivier pale, and nerves suddenly reach his bowels.

"Comme votre maman. What do you mean, like your mother?"

Déchaux's eyes narrowed like those of a hunting hawk poised to strike, but his intended victim had already turned for the door and the sanctuary of the transept.

"Your lust will do for us all, unless you curb it, Father André. It's already given you un *casier judicaire* which at the time of your brother's demise caused me no small embarrassment. Fortunately for you, it was my vote to keep you out of gaol that counted in the end. Don't forget."

The Provençal tried to wrestle the grip from his shoulder, but the brown square hand, always efficient and trained to fight, stayed put.

"Out there, how sweetly they lie together, your dear mother and your sibling. In death as in life, inseparable." He smiled. "I think you get my drift, Father. And now I must away before my, I'm sorry, *your* minions return."

Duvivier fumbled for the key to the small outer door as Déchaux pressed close, the smell of the hair restorer *Brunaugment* suddenly obvious.

"Now, Kommandant, on the fourth time of asking, is there Any Other Business?"

"Nein, Hauptsturmbannführer." Duvivier clicked his heels and gave a brief salute. "Number 2 is seeing Ayache on September 4th. The rest are on line. Just

144

waiting for prints from 5, that's all." Omitting that Cacheux was too busy fantasising to help with any forward planning and The Pigface was gaining grammes not losing them.

"Nice and straightforward. Good oh. I'll be in touch." Déchaux pulled up his jacket collar. "By the way," he turned unexpectedly, "I've arranged with le commandant Malaigue – not his real name of course – to give you all some upgraded drills, on a date to be arranged." He smiled. "And guess what? Someone's made us some straw dummies in striped uniforms complete with yellow stars. What do you think?"

"Kussel used to do that."

"Oh, Francke, you're such a spoilsport." Then he picked his way back among the nettles to where a black Toyota Celica had drawn up by the side gate. Through its tinted glass Duvivier could just make out a swatch of blonde hair beneath a chauffeur's cap as the woman's gloved hands turned the wheel and bore him away.

Déchaux was messing him about, keeping secrets, and worse, leaning too much on his past, on his one true act of passion. The priest felt his pitted cheek, hot even though the air had cooled and thunderous clouds had seen off the sunset. His pulse lurched beneath his punishment, anarchy and chaos in unison. The young Doctor Brébisson had announced that with God on his side, he'd got ten years left unless he went for major maxillofacial surgery.

Not an option, for he loathed hospitals. So every day, like now, he'd check the border for escapees. Eleven pot holes at the last count, but there was no logical progression, no plan he could intercept. The only constant was knowing God was most certainly on his side, even though The Almighty moved in mysterious ways, usually during the disadvantage of sleep.

Duvivier's lips tightened as he found the lichen path round to the first graveyard where the family stones stood still pristine after twenty-seven years. The lettering clear despite the poor light.

HUBERT BÜBER DUVIVIER   MADELEINE IRMA BÜBER
1er. août 1955 - 20 août 1967   6 février 1925 - 20 août 1970
UN FRÈRE BIEN AIMÉ.   LA MAMAN DE MON COEUR.

Those were his words behind the mason's hand, and his money for the best that money could buy. He wouldn't have used those lilies anyhow – they were Pereire's, already soiled. Maybe that driver was taking them home to his wife, but it didn't matter.

Duvivier knelt on the weedy oblong set aside for his father that felt soft and alive under his robe. He cleared the grasses away from her slab and repositioned the knick-knacks and plastic roses that had blown askew from their holder. He could have had photographs like the others, whose old soft focus faces stared out enigmatically at the future, but that would have been too public. Too intrusive.

His fingers moved slowly as though this would somehow magnetise her back to life through the deep dry earth. He kissed the Jesus heart, repeating his confession to her through ever numbing lips. "...que j'ai grandement pêché en pensées, en paroles, et en actions par ma faute, ma faute, ma très grande faute. C'est pourquoi je prie..."

Close now, his crucifix trailing where her own heart might be, and in his ramblings, her first son imagined her ears reopening, her hair growing anew from the skull like a lion's, to frame her beauty. He smelt once more her scent, the sweetness of her being, smothering the stench snaking upwards from two metres below.

"...toujours Vierge, saint Michel Archange, saint Jean-Baptiste, les Apôtres, saint Pierre et Saint Paul. Oh, maman, you should have loved me! You should have loved me, and given me your name, not his!"

At that moment, the force that had once expelled him from her body seemed now to pull him down for a final homecoming. He tore at the lungwort and Black Nightshade, splicing his fingers, staining his palms and as he finished the act of Contrition, tried to raise the tomb itself, oblivious to the mobile ringing again in his pocket.

***

The Javels spotted him as they came through the main gate, then quickened into the Church.

"He's on the turn, as God's my witness," Hervé Javel wheezed.

"You're right." His daughter once inside the porch retied her hair and caught the stray pieces in two clips. "People are beginning to notice. Would *you* go to him for confession now?"

"Never." He laid down the two boxes of candles. White for the chapels, red for the altar, then checked the weight of the collection boxes. "He won't be getting the Bishop's job, that's for sure."

"If there's any justice."

"We're alright, then." He grinned.

"By the way, papa, who do you think that smoothie with the weird nose was?" she asked.

"Looked a right *bourgeois* to me. I'm sure I remember him from somewhere. I'm trying to think. That's the trouble with getting old. Did you see his shoes though?"

"Bloody cheek that's all I can say, telling us to get a mower. I'm the domestic and you're for things ecclesiastical, or whatever. He'd have had you grave digging if there'd been any more room in the ground."

"Too right." Her father returned to the main door and peered round. "Bet you five to one our mother's boy'll have dug her up by Christmas."

"Oh, God." Renate crossed herself. You and me, three wise monkeys, OK? See no evil, etcetera."

"OK." The seventy-five-year-old in dungarees and a lumberjack shirt rearranged the photocopied sheets of the church's history then signalled to his daughter. "Time to exit."

And, as the clouds deepened over La Croix Valmer, plunging Les Pradels into premature darkness, the two crept back to their Bedford van and made for Cavalaire. They left Duvivier prostrate on his mother's black marble, his breathing rough and irregular until the cold crystalline limestone lowered his fever. After a few minutes he felt composed enough to stand and brush down his clothes. He then went to see if the Javels had returned.

The ancient cedar branches brushed his forehead and he leapt sideways half expecting his pale-faced persecutor to spring from the shadows.

"Damn you, Déchaux," he muttered as a pair of ravens lifted towards the bell tower, croaking their contempt. "And damn you, Javel and your ugly, barren daughter. Where the Hell are you?"

He hung around light-headed, pacing between the Coronation of the Virgin and the main door before locking up. Ste Trinité felt awesomely empty without their footsteps, and during the past ten years he'd come to rely on them both for everything, including her lamb couscous every Wednesday night and the weekly washing of socks.

Duvivier looked back to where he'd embraced his mother and knew what he must do to prepare things for the rest of his next life. 7.13 p.m. exactly. Six kilometres to 'Le Souterrain.' He could smell the place already and the idiot dog, Arsène, would be halfway down the track waiting to take his leg off.

He shook the edge of his robe again and tucked his crucifix inside, then, having checked the hall light in the Presbytery, made his way on foot up the Route de Montjean towards his own unfinished business.

**

Away from the sea's influence and into the dry rugged hills, Duvivier was sheltered from that same south-easterly that had buffeted him senseless on his journey back from Cavalaire.

His cape shielded him from the worst of the wind as headlights came and went, and all the while he counted the number of steps away from Madeleine Büber's body, each one more difficult than the last, his lungs tight in the remembering.

A horsebox, a VW camper van, with a Dutch number plate, and youngsters crammed into old 306's going down to the beach bars. Then the silence of

Eternity before the hum of his father's generator and the one light of 'Le Souterrain.'

The priest fingered the bungalow's post box at the end of the track – sometimes rewarding when Victor Duvivier forgot, but not tonight. No stars either, just a vague interlocking of clouds big with rain.

"Arsène!"

The white terrier was usually there, hurling himself skywards then worrying round his heels. Duvivier looked and listened with the practised ear of a night fisherman as he walked the last stretch down to the single storey dwelling whose walls sunk deep into the beginnings of the Col du Canadel.

Still no dog. "Arsène!" He clapped his hands and yodelled, a ploy that never failed, but only the crickets in the scrub replied.

Then something soft against his foot. White, in what little light there was, and lying across the path, lay the terrier, its ribs etched through the skin. Duvivier knelt down and stroked its head. Still warm, the eyes scrolled upwards to some Heaven, the paws draped in fresh blood from a wound to the heart.

He cradled the lifeless creature to the door, triggering the security light. He kicked against the new wood until his father stirred, grumbling from his armchair. His replica eyes passed from his son to the dog. A Pietà of sorts, white on black, except the wrong one was alive.

Victor Duvivier let out a cry like a foghorn through a winter mist then vanished into the back of the house. He returned holding out a hunting knife, straight and deadly as he sleep walked past his son who'd hidden behind a clump of bougainvillea.

With fingers sticking together, the priest laid the dog down, and followed his father at a safe distance.

Almost night. Nothing but the trickery of a moving sky and a plane from Hyères winking red, heading east.

"Probably old Barras going for rabbits. An accident," he ventured.

"Barras, my backside. He won't dare come round here after what I did last time. No, I know who did this." He stopped. "And it's all down to you, son."

Francke Duvivier froze as the old man turned to face him, bigger in every respect, not shrunken as most do with age. The knife end toyed with his crucifix.

"I had a visitor."

"A visitor? When?"

The fisherman checked his watch.

"Half an hour ago, if that. I'd just let the dog out." For a moment his voice faltered but he kept the fine steel point firm on his son's chest. "White face with a growth on his nose. Smart shoes, brown leather jacket. Parisian, definitely. Must have left his car up the end."

Déchaux...

"What the Hell's that to do with me?"

"Said I had certain duties as a father. Fucking cheek. As if I've ever been able to keep you in check." Hatred beamed from his hiding eyes, anchovies sour on his breath.

"What's that supposed to mean?"

"Never you mind. Any more let-downs and he'd be back. That's what he said." Victor Duvivier tapped the Jesus with his knife. "So maybe you'd better be asking your friend for some helpful advice. God knows what you're up to."

"Did he give his name?"

"What do you think." His father's mouth trembled. "I loved that little dog, for goodness sake."

"Whoever he was, he's wrong. Got us mixed up with someone else. You know what goes on round here, trafficking, stolen goods. Last place God made and all that. I tell you, it's nothing to do with me."

But Déchaux's inscrutable face and his shadow were stretching further over his life.

"Smells to me like the Croix de Feu's still burning. You're in it, aren't you?"

"Don't be ridiculous! I've far too much to do."

"I remember you couldn't wait to get your grubby little hands on my uniform, and my Knight's Cross. You still got that, by the way?"

The French volunteer of the Third Reich found the button which secured his son's cape and severed it with one neat twist. "Now Hubert always said you were mad. To your mother he was the calm after the storm."

Francke Duvivier hit the knife from his father's hand and seized his neck.

"Leave her out of this! She hated your stinking guts when you were in the Charlemagne Division. Strutting here and there, bringing all those creeps home..."

"And you, you could never keep your nose out. It was just a game, but that was too subtle for you."

The priest suddenly laughed, but it came out wrong and his grim roar faded into the hills. "I went to bloody Villerscourt, remember?"

"You were the laughing stock. And the Javels, well they split their sides."

Francke Duvivier stared at the man, who must have possessed his mother at least twice, and had blackmailed his surviving son for a final place by her side. And who'd sold his business to his brother-in-law and paid a top lawyer to alter his will so he wouldn't inherit. And in that face which swelled from his strengthening grasp, he saw the past he had to lose. He'd never wanted the stinking boats, the breeze-block shed or the unworkable land.

"Can't you see, I just want to lie next to Mother?"

"And our Hubert?" Victor Duvivier gurgled. "You've got the Devil's nerve after what you did. That's *my* plot and son or no son, Father André, you can rot somewhere else."

His words strangled to a whisper. His fishing arms limp, no longer fighting, as the priest heaped him up on to his shoulder and carried him across No Man's Land between the Duvivier hectares and the Pic de Redon.

"Je m'accuse de tous ces péchés, de tous ceux que je dois oublier, de ceux de ma vie passée. J'en demande Pardon à Dieu et vous, mon père, la pénitence at l'absolution si vous..."

The end of his confession was taken up by the wind as stones became boulders on the rising ground and the rash of bedstraw clung to his hem, holding him to the place of sin.

XXXIV

At exactly 06.55 hours the TGV Atlantique slipped away from the Gare Montparnasse as dawn grew into a bright opacity that stifled Nelly Augot's eyes and disguised the gulls looping westward towards the Seine.

She squinted out at the blur of office windows, saw white shirts busy behind each porthole, and felt more than a pang of jealousy for those with a salaried ordered life.

Over the Porte Briançon and out into suburbs, gathering speed through Massy and Palaiseau with three hours twenty minutes for her to go over and over the plan as though it was all she'd ever do with her life. This one mission of mercy.

The Gendarmerie had been useless, and after she'd finished her story about the nuns and poor desperate Chloë being dead, they'd quizzed her about her mama's associates and after more questions on how long she'd been at the hostel, and what was she doing to survive, finally accused her of being on something.

"Fuck the lot of them."

But the rest of Colette's message was all she could think of now. *Ask hostel about Bertrand Bataille again. My son... God bless...* and again and again as the wheels beneath her added their own counterpoint.

With a seat to herself, she spread out her belongings. A rucksack specially cleaned for the occasion, a Galeries Lafayette carrier bag with map, torch, rope, all concealed in a pretty toiletries bag, while snug in the pocket reserved for soap lay her 9mm automatic.

"Just the job for a lady," Max Bellino had laughed bad teeth after she'd begged him to borrow it for three days. Then he'd unzipped himself and made her gobble his dick and other things until she'd gagged. "One suck for every hour of the loan." That was the deal. She squirmed at the memory, and licked round her mouth. Tried a fresh Hollywood gum but still couldn't get rid of him and wondered, as houses outside became sparse and new, if her mama liked doing that to a man. Or what the Miller's Wife would have made of it all.

Nelly extracted her battered Chaucer and pretended to read, to be once again the intense and interesting student, but suddenly she felt a current of danger, a warning almost, as two young women approached down the gangway looking for reserved seats.

Both tall, the older one although probably not more than thirty, wearing a black headscarf, crisp red suit and matching wild red mouth. Her companion in a silver tracksuit, her dark hair cropped close, bore no make-up. Nelly stared hard. There was something about the sporty one she particularly recognised as they finally sat down on the other side. Neither wore any kind of ring.

She set off for the WC keeping the plastic bag close to her legs as the train passed through Voves station and endless two-tone fields that stretched away to the sky. She was an appropriate couple of minutes, then the long walk back past businessmen and singles out job hunting, not visiting.

The red suit studied the window but her partner's eyes were fixed ahead as Nelly reached her.

That's it! The hostel's cool receptionist bitch.

What was she doing on the train? And why so different, with her bobbed hair razored up her neck?

"Hi, I'm Nelly Augot, remember?" she said. "Room 35 at St, Anne's hostel?"

But the tracksuit feigned a search for something in her overnight bag while the other woman still pretended to be hypnotised by the view.

"This is crazy! I'd know you anywhere. Claude Lefêbvre."

"I'm afraid you're mistaken. Now if you don't mind..." The woman recrossed her legs and flicked through the latest copy of *Paris Match* as though the girl from St. Denis didn't exist. But Nelly Augot, who'd had to fight to stay on at the Lycée to do her Bac, and funded herself through University, was not to be denied.

"You can tell me now, did a Bertrand Bataille ever stay at your place?" A quick glance between the two other travellers was enough to tell Nelly they knew something. "You *have* heard of him, haven't you? So stop treating me like an idiot."

"Leave us alone. We don't know what you're on about. Far as we're concerned, you're a complete stranger, and if you don't lay off, I'll call the guard."

"Well, that's charming." Nelly noticed other heads turning their way. "Why are you lying? What have you got to hide?" she raised her voice. "Look here, someone very special to me is searching for him. Bertrand Bataille."

"Piss off."

"Piss off yourself. If it wasn't for *chômeurs* like me you'd be out of a bloody job."

"Say what you like."

"Bloody snob. But I tell you something Mademoiselle Lefêbvre – I'm going to get to the bottom of this even if..."

"It kills you?" The unmade face turned, sneering, sending a shiver through Nelly's body. She sat down again, trembling, and turned to the *Pardoner's Tale* with no intention of reading it. Staple fodder of her second year, and no more relevant to her life than how to grow Bonsai. She kept a wary eye on Lefêbvre while the train sped through the Loir et Cher with the sun showing yellow in the clearing sky and furred ribbons of trees becoming just memory – until the occupants of seats 54 and 55 abruptly got up and left the compartment.

Nelly followed. They were at the bar ordering spritzers, their baggage alongside. A neat red case and the holdall.

Gripping the seats, she neared them but, in doing so, accidentally clipped an elderly man's head, dislodging his hat.

"Allez." His reaction was enough to attract unwanted attention. Nelly tried to hide, but too late. The two young women, wineglasses at their lips had seen her, and glared in unison. Then the red suit began to slide from her stool, her hand feeling in her pocket. Romy Kirchner, the fake Bostonian, who'd lent her the clothes. The one who knew everything.

Nelly didn't wait for the rest. She sprinted back to the far end of the train, to the *Fourgon à bagages* and subsided next to the door under the curious gaze of a family playing a card game.

Dear Colette, I'm doing my best, God knows. Stay safe for me. I couldn't bear it if anything happened to you...

Then she put her hands together and prayed.

As if to answer her, the train careered ever faster through the vineyards of the Dronne, and when at 10.15 it rested at Libourne she stepped on to the platform, her bare eyes heavy with sun, the two hunters were nowhere to be seen.

XXXV

"Well, Father Jean-Baptiste, it's good to see you again." Madame Noiret beamed as she opened the door of the Coiffeuse de l'Aube before Vidal had finished shaking his umbrella. And now he stood in a widening puddle, the object of mother and daughter's undisguised admiration.

"Jacqueline, a towel. Vite." The tiny, black-haired woman clapped her hands then lifted the new trench coat from his shoulders. She noticed the label. A priest who was clearly doing well, who was a week earlier than usual for her attentions.

"Thank you. Most kind."

Jacqueline returned, her mouth as usual agape, her enormous eyes like marbles whose sealed twists of blue never left her face. He rubbed his hair into a damp confusion and sat down in his customary place, directly underneath his father François' apartment.

Killing two birds with one stone. Useful stuff, hein?

The girl was behind him in the mirror. Sixteen years old but not grown in the normal way. Instead of hiding her daughter in the back room, Madame Noiret allowed her to wash heads, set curlers and occasionally apply blue rinses to the *retraitées*. But today, she and the *propriétaire* were going to see to the most beautiful head of all.

"How's your papa, then?" she asked, her fingers raking his hair back under the mini-hose's warm spray.

Colette had been the last woman to touch him. The last woman to betray him. That much he knew.

"Not seen much of him, I have to say. Usually he comes down Mondays and Wednesdays for his cigarettes and some shopping, but not this week. Have you noticed him, Jacqueline?"

The girl nodded, neither yes nor no. He watched her reflection in the misty mirror.

"I've tried phoning," Vidal lied. "But he must have been out or asleep."

"Well, you're a busy man now, from what we hear," said Madame Noiret, taking over.

"What have you heard, then?" The priest inclined his head to let water out of his left ear.

"Now that poor old Moussac's with the Almighty, you're going to be seeing to all the choirs and another recording. Quite a star. Everyone says."

"Dead man's shoes, Madame Noiret. Is that what you're really thinking?"

"Oh, I didn't mean that, Father, believe me, not at all."

"Well, let me tell you, it's a rare honour. To me, music is the only real way

154

to catch the ear of God. Now does that sound heretical to you?"

"Not at all."

The hairdresser's hand wavered and she let out a nervous laugh as her comb ploughed a temporary side parting.

His eyes are on guard, flecked dark like some creature of the night...

They were suddenly too penetrating for that small salon done out in *vert sorbet* with its delicate white wrought-iron work.

She excused herself, pretending to need new scissors. Usually there'd be Madame Zafara, and Julie Lemaille who sang Piaf in the Bar Rivoli and liked her roots done before she looked a cheat. But today for some reason, they'd deserted, just when she needed them.

The rain doesn't help, mind you; but I'm not afraid. Goodness, no. Though there is something different about him, more tense than usual. Better watch what I say and keep Jacqueline busy...

Madame Noiret looked through the plastic striped curtain into the salon and saw with relief her daughter sorting hairpins. She crossed herself and returned bearing the same scissors which he noticed. His soft black hair fell in sharp patches on to his shoulders as she cut along the comb edge.

"Not so much this time," she remarked.

"No indeed."

His hair was unusually fine for a man, and later, she would save a piece and mount it on scotch with the day's date. How could she be blamed for wanting a memento? Others did the same for less good reason. But by secreting it in her mock Fabergé egg, she knew she was elevating these bits of the priest from Lanvière to relics.

"Well, Madame, what else have you gleaned from the redoubtable locals of Eberswïhr?" the lover of Pérotin suddenly asked without moving his eyes.

"I'm sure I don't know what you mean, Father Jean-Baptiste. People here are just trying to keep a spoon to their lips."

"I'm not a halfwit. Now please enlighten me." He swivelled round, because to face her in the mirror wasn't enough. For a moment she stopped cutting and let a segment of hair fall to the floor.

"It's not my place. I'm just a hairdresser."

"But you're a woman, Madame Noiret, and I've always found women to be very keen observers of our human condition."

From the Confessional or from your bed?

"So, what else do you know?"

She backed away, looking for Jacqueline. Suddenly the handsome *'renard'* had become a darkly menacing wolf, and she was a child again, lost in the penumbral Forêt des Singes, deep in the deepest Vosges with the echo of her parents' voices faltering, victim to the night.

"It's nothing really. Just that my brother's sister-in-law has started working at Medex."

"Medex?"

"Yes. As a Laboratory assistant, part time. Not very well paid, but it is a second income, and in this day and age, she's grateful of course."

"And?" His pupils contracted to slits. No more reflection and Madame Noiret was beginning to regret her garrulousness.

"As I said, it's none of my business, but Amélie – that's her name – says that your friend has gone missing." She'd said the word 'friend' delicately, feeling her way, and watched as she gave that friend a name. "Colette Bataille. A lovely lady. Her son too, an only child. Maybe they just wanted to start a new life somewhere. He had no job, no prospects, what was to stop them? But her..."

"Yes?"

"She was very well thought of. Apparently the Directeur Général wanted to take her with him to New York for a meeting. Expanding, they are... despite the dreadful Natolyn business. There. Finished."

She held a hand mirror so he could see all round his head, and waited for approval like a *garçon* in a bar with a newly-opened bottle. But she could tell he wasn't interested. "Amélie also told me he's got on to the police. Yesterday. That's the last I heard." She peeled the towel from his shoulders, then busied herself with the trolley. "We'll just have to pray."

"My dear Madame Noiret, with all my heart I wish I could be as forthcoming as you. However," he stood up and brushed off his sleeves, "your guess is as good as mine. Madame Bataille was, I mean, is, a great supporter of Ste Trinité, especially with the Masses for the old and infirm and our plans for the Millième Anniversaire."

Especially between the sheets is what you mean.

"As you say, we can only pray. Now, is it the usual?"

"One hundred, Father."

He gave her a two-hundred note.

"Give the change to Jacqueline."

The girl had come in with the broom and begun to sweep round them both in slow motion.

"Say thank you to Father Jean-Baptiste," said the hairdresser.

But her daughter frowned instead. She'd sensed her mother's fear and wanted the man to go.

"Jacqueline..."

"What's a hundred francs? The Mammon of Unrighteousness," he patted her head, making her flinch. Then unexpectedly he took her mother's hand as it left the till. "Please keep an eye on papa for me, Madame Noiret. I'm off to Rome for the next few weeks."

"Oh, I've always wanted to go there, haven't I, Jacqueline? The Vatican, the Coliseum..."

His touch was unsettling, his skin warm as new bread, so she reclaimed her hand, pretending to sort coins instead.

"It's not a holiday, I can assure you, Madame. I'll be studying in detail the Christifideles Laici and the Sacerdotalis Caelibatus amongst other things." He checked to see if she knew what he was talking about, but her face looked up as blank as that of her daughter. "Quite fortuitous, actually, while La Sainte Vierge's closed for repairs."

"Mary no head," Jacqueline said suddenly.

"Hush, child." Madame Noiret whispered.

"She's right. So much for those who press for our churches to be left open. That is another matter I'll be discussing, and," he lowered his voice, "how I can hopefully become a better padre, or rather, a more holy one."

"That's impossible, surely?"

"Thank you. You're most kind." His smile came and went. "And by the way, Father Anselme will be taking the Eucharist and choir rehearsals at Monzeppe. If there's any problem with papa, Madame, do let Bishop Toussirot know. Thank you again."

The dutiful son, the hard-working *curé*, but all the same she was relieved when his raincoat was back on his arm.

"My number. Don't hesitate." He gave her his card – discreet, laminated, with a black cross down the side. Address and home phone number only.

"I won't. But there's something you should know."

"Oh?"

"I was going to tell you straight away, Father, but trying to find the right moment wasn't easy."

She noticed Jacqueline had gone.

Those eyes again. My God, they're burning into my soul...

"It was last week. Youngsters, you know how headstrong they can be, well there's a group of them here, Les Flammes. Anticipating the elections probably, opposing the F.N. and Extrême Droite..."

"And?" Vidal closed up his umbrella and secured it, avoiding her eyes.

"They want Chêvenement to deal with the *sans-papiers* problem."

"Ah, yes. The *sans-papiers*. Of course."

"And the growing number of attacks on Jews."

"So what's all this to do with papa?"

"They tried to make him answer the door. Apparently they wore Devil's masks with flames not horns. Made a terrible noise."

"When?"

"Last Thursday. They probably knew I was closed."

"It makes no sense." But a dark line divided his forehead, adding years.

"Exactly, Father. But you'll soon see what they've done."

Vidal slammed the door, his pulse quickening. Felt the wind around his shorn head before leaping up the stairs to the apartment's foyer.

FASCIST PIG! JEW HATER! VICHY PAWN!

Revulsion spelt out in red aerosol, one word on another covering the walls. His heart stopped. His stomach suddenly leaden as he took it all in. All the rotten secrets leaked out into the light of day. And to the police.

Merde.

They'd been the plain-clothed strangers at Moussac's funeral, he was sure of that.

"Papa! It's me, Robert!" He called out.

"Leave me be," came the growl from inside.

"I'm here to help."

"You make things worse. *Go.*"

Vidal knew there was no other way in. No fire exit, just the small square landing and the one blue door. He looked round to see if Madame Noiret had followed him. All clear.

"I'm coming in."

"Damn you."

Vidal stepped back to lunge sideways at the door. No joy. It hurt and he had diving and other important things to think about. "Stupid man, I'm all you've got."

"I thought everyone had God."

"You know what I mean."

"So? I'd rather go without."

His son scoured the thin blue paint and the slicks of metal showing through it. No point in trying for another key, there were bolts on the other side.

"You need to get out of here."

"I pay my taxes. I'm, staying and I'm fighting."

"What for? Tell me?"

"La Patrie. To keep the shit out of France."

Vidal checked the stairs again. Saw a woman's legs go into the Coiffeuse. Rain powered against the Velux overhead and he thought he heard thunder.

Doom aka Publicity. How wonderful. The neo-Nazi has a son – ah, yes. Let's take a closer look, just as Opération Judas gets into gear and the second generous payment *will be sitting in the pocket on September30th.*

The wetness from his mac had reached his skin. He shivered. 11.06 a.m. Then he took a deep breath. "I said, I'm coming in, whether you like it or not."

The Browning's silencer fitted snugly, and the first shot took the lock with a sound like a cough. He waited, heard the bolts released, one by one. He scanned the room. It was more like the inside of a tent with a formica table, three metal chairs and a TV skewed on a pile of books. The bed was a mountain of blankets under a display of Hitler's 100th anniversary souvenirs.

François Vidal stared at the pistol, clearly shocked.

"Where did you get that thing from? Priests and guns, Jesus wept."

"My own protection, OK?"

"You'll have to repair that lock." His father, shrunken in just a month. His face pickled in bitterness.

"I'll see to it and that crap on the wall."

With a backward kick the door was shut. Vidal lowered his voice.

"You're coming with me."

"No."

"It's for your own good. I've two bedrooms. It's a quiet neighbourhood, nobody would guess."

"You don't understand. You deserted when you went into the bloody church. Someone's got to keep things going."

"You're a fool, papa. Behave yourself."

"Everyone must know. How can I be silent when the whole fucking show's in the fat greasy hands of the Yids. They've crawled in everywhere and all we get is to lick their arses. The Protocols are the truth I tell you. The tip of the bloody iceberg."

Vidal felt a tremor creep up his spine at his own echo.

"Now I tell *you* something," the priest's voice hardening to brittle. "I'm making a go of my life, with the music, my choirs. Some people, important people, believe in me. I don't want any *cacas* in the nest. *Compris?*" He pocketed the pistol.

The sixty-six-year-old looked nearer eighty running his hand through his hair, making it stand up on end. Grey to white above his ears.

"You have a short memory, son. That's all I can say. Have you forgotten how the Cordonniers still live like pigs? Your own flesh and blood. Your maman's mother and father use leaves to wipe themselves. Their light is string in goose fat, and Jesus Christ only knows what they put in their bellies. All because that begging whining pair of Rosenbaums turned up. Two months of lying low courtesy of the *Mas des Cailles,* then buggering off when it suited them. Thank you very much."

"The Milice took everything?"

"Everything except our fucking walls. And when your mama died..." the pearl of a tear grew in his eye corner, "I gave mamie and papy what she'd left for me, and you, of course. Listen, son," his voice hardened, "when you next have a collection for the poor and needy, send them the money. Charity begins at home, *hein*?"

Vidal listened. Just to hear the words, *Mas des Cailles* was enough.

Hidden from the road by the breast of land and edged by oaks – my tree, my Paradise – its arms still outstretched. Still waiting, guarding the hectares of Henaménil in the forêt de Parroy. The wood store, high as the stable wall, and that room done out in pink roses as big as heads, where maman was born, overlooking the Lac des Cygnes. She must have seen it often as a child, where my boat, La Princesse had keeled over, just like that. I remember now, reaching down trying to touch it as it sank, then because I couldn't imagine living without it, I dived in but there was nothing. Nothing but the dead cold. I must have been nine, ten? Anyhow it was the last time I ever went there. I could never go again after that. Soon, there'll be another boat. Another Acte de Dieu. Quel dommage...

"I have to go to Rome tomorrow. Jus Canonicum etcetera," he said. "You must decide now, papa. You stay and I am disgraced, or you come with me and I continue my vocation. In the name of God, do you want me to join the *chômeurs*? Be another statistic for the *cocos*? What else could I turn my hand to?"

"You're still young. You have your strength. Why not use it with me?" The same brown eyes had suddenly widened alive with possibilities. The unruly eyebrows risen halfway up his forehead. "Fight with me, Robert. *Pourquoi non?* We won't have to run anywhere. More than half the country wants Jews out, Arabs out. Jobs for the French, *Égalité* for the French and *Fraternité* for us who are fighting the next war. The real one. The climate is right, I'm telling you."

"Fine words, papa. But it's life or death for me. Now get your coat, a few things. Five minutes, no more." Words hard as the edge of rock. His gun now pointing as François Vidal scuttled round the room collecting this and that into carrier bags. The photo of 'Bijou' didn't fit so his son kicked a holdall from near the bed into the middle of the floor.

"Try that."

11.40 hours, with the taxi due at any minute, the train in thirty. Vidal went to the landing and froze at the conspiracy of voices down below. Madame Noiret and a middle-aged man were looking at him up the stairs.

"Papa's coming with me for a change of scene, Madame. I'll sort it with old Léonce about the damage to the door. Looks like someone tried to break in."

He saw her hands cover her face, the driver check his watch. "Pretty bad, eh? No place for a *retraité*." He ushered his father out. Ricard and cheap aftershave reached his nose, reminding him of Plagnol. He'd scribbled a note and now passed it to her.

I'll organise repair to the lock, erase graffiti, and see the police. Leave it to me.

She stared after him, then folded the paper into her overall pocket.

***

Through Eberswïhr's sloping streets to the station, neither father nor son spoke, giving the rain sole monopoly on power and despair.

XXXVI

Tuesday August 26th

Nelly awoke tired after a night of dreams and apparitions that stalked her semi-conscious until the alarm at seven. Those two strange women on the train, enlarged, mocking. Butchers' carcasses dotted with flies, and worse, Colette and Chloë shrouded, tied up below the chin, suspended like them, from black, iron hooks…

***

Having arrived at Libourne, instead of going straight to the Refuge as originally planned, she'd decided it was best to reconnaître the surroundings at different times of the day. This loss of nerve was costing an extra 150 francs on a room over the Bar des Chênes, but she'd convinced herself it would be the best option for an early start after a good breakfast.

Not so.

The day was made sullen by thick unbroken cloud that muffled the incoming Bordeaux traffic. Muffled her brain.

Merde. Is there no justice?

She knelt down and prayed in her own way to whoever was out there, that she wanted to feel strong and capable for what she had to do. No rosary or crucifix either. She'd thrown that cheap one out with the garbage. Just her words, her hazy eyes and the stuff she'd brought with her.

One and a half kilometres along the Avenue des Vignes, with traffic nose to tail, huge things and *convois exceptionnels*. The whole bloody world on the move filling up supermarket shelves for those with the money to pay. She wished she'd persevered with her contact lenses, for in this different, powerful light, everything seemed more blurred than ever; her priority once she'd got Colette to safety.

Nelly flexed her arms, her fingers. Tightened her calves with each step, and after the Cinq Routes roundabout retied her black scarf, checking her neat little gun was safe in her cleavage. She had reached the Refuge's lodge.

Here goes.

"Nelly Augot," she said to the cooped-up nun with a huge nose. "The Sister Superior is expecting me."

The gatekeeper repeated the name into her mobile.

"Nine o six. Correct." Then pointed towards a line of cypresses, whose short shadows were pointing her way. It was a gloomy, nerve-wracking walk past the saintly statuary inlaid amongst the trees – Mary, Anne, Cathérine, Barbara – all vapid. All *douleureuse*. No bird song either, she noticed as she reached an archway triple-glazed and security grilled at the front of the low building, only last second rehearsals as she pressed the bell and again as the iron door opened inwards.

Two things she recognised from Paris. The smell, and Sister Marie-Ange herself, although paler if that were possible, and her waist gone to nothing. African violet eyes immediately latched on to the Jesus heart Nelly had pinned to her sober grey pinafore dress.

Here goes, again...

"My conscience has been in torment since I was last with the Pauvres Soeurs," she began.

"Your conscience or your soul, Mademoiselle?"

"I mean my soul, pardon."

My God she's quick. Now don't panic. Just keep to the script. Whatever.

"Sister Superior, you were kind enough to give me shelter in the Bois de Boulogne, and instead of showing gratitude and making myself useful to your good cause, I deserted..."

"We didn't expect you to be useful. Just to be still for a while to prepare for His Holiness and listen to the voice of God."

"The truth is, I guessed you were having some kind of trouble with Madame Bataille, but I just wasn't ready to take on her problems as well."

"She has many, that is true. Not least that she persists in her heresies."

"Please let me help. I know I can."

Not so fast. Don't mention her again. That was enough. Nor Chloë either, for pity's sake.

"You can help more effectively by praying for us, for we have just lost our beloved Sister Cecilia to the wrath of God."

"Oh? I am sorry." With as much feeling as she could muster.

That's alright, then. One less evil bitch to deal with. I wonder if this one can tell what I'm thinking. I bet she can. She's so bloody weird...

"What happened?"

"Lightning. Our Creator's hand works in terrible and mysterious ways. Clearly we're not working hard enough to make His kingdom the only one. Now, Mademoiselle, would you like something to drink? Paris is hardly the next Département."

"Thanks. A coffee."

Sister Marie-Ange led the way into a large light room off the vestibule. No chairs, nothing really to hold on to. Just a lectern bearing a thick New Testament by the window and the same desk she'd seen at the Résidence, placed in the centre. One of the triplets brought a tray, curtsied keeping her face down-turned, and left.

"Victorine, too, is a problem for us," the Sister Superior stared after her.

163

"She's been in disgrace."

"Oh, dear. Why?"

I'm forgetting my lines. Jesus Christ, help me. Get a grip. Get a grip.

"The matter is closed now. She received full Absolution after Matins yesterday and we can only pray her penance has been effective. All three of those poor girls, so young, so, how shall I say, impressionable."

Nelly studied her cup inlaid with gold lustre, and the teaspoon weighted at the end by a miniature St. Peter.

Whoever had helped Colette, had risked their life, that was for sure. This is shite coffee, probably made in a bedpan...

Suddenly, the Sister Superior bent down and picked up her rucksack.

Fuck this for a game of soldiers...

"Follow me, Nelly." And the student kept her distance. Hearing her first name like that, was unnerving. Several other Pauvres Soeurs were busy polishing skirting boards, and though they kept their faces hidden, she could tell neither Colette nor Chloë was among them.

On into the Chapel – colder, brighter, decked out in modern stained glass. Abstract stuff. New pews but no hassocks, no comfort, while the body-sized altar was emblazoned by huge red hearts. On top, besides the usual Eucharistic paraphernalia, stood a carving of a Virgin and Child. The only antique there, and painfully out of place. Both expressions lost to dark wood grain scars which, over the centuries had invaded their painted flesh.

Nelly's eyes never left her belongings as she knelt alongside the nun and saw the white hand clamped possessively over the opening to her rucksack.

"Dear Holy Mother, look upon our new friend with your great love and favour all her intentions with your good guidance so that her piety may be increased daily and through the words and prayers of our Order, she may attain everlasting salvation. Amen."

As her voice dwindled, Sister Marie-Ange undid the rucksack's ties.

No...

Ten o'clock bells, deafeningly prolonged, filled everywhere, while panic lurched in Nelly's throat.

"My punishments, Sister Superior," as one by one the means of escape were brought out, "flagellation, blood-letting. I don't deserve any better."

With awful precision the nun returned everything to its place, including a robe Nelly had stolen from the Résidence in Paris.

"We'll keep these things from you. That's for the best." And as Marie-Ange reset her hands for prayer, Nelly felt the first rush of terror through her body.

"Sainte Vierge, your daughter here in front of me is too full of self loathing and her spirit is therefore too imprisoned to fully serve you. Grant her freedom from this affliction and make her sound in body and mind for our great purpose on Earth."

So that was it. They were going to brand her a nutter. Keep her out of the way, do God knows what, just like poor Victorine and her sisters. Help me, Holy Mother, help me.

The nun crossed herself and beckoned for Nelly to accompany her into the Confessional. New wood again, but intricately carved into trefoils and curlicues by some local artisan. Inside, however, that same urine smell and a slightly damp cushion which the student of English avoided.

She could hear the Sister Superior settling herself invisibly behind the screen, but felt her breath the moment it left her mouth. "Nelly Augot, we know you are sincere in your intentions to rejoin our Order, but as with all our novice supplicants, you must immediately seek Absolution for all your thoughts and deeds which render you impure. What is the *prima peccata* you wish me to hear?"

Each syllable she spoke gave Nelly precious time. Her escape plan *kaput*, but there was still a chance...

"Materially, I am poor, Sister Superior. My mama is a streetwalker and my father died five years ago, but I have in all honesty done my best."

"In what way?" the other woman sneered.

"I got my Bac, paid for myself through University – waitressing, cleaning at Mercure, anything to buy books you understand, and God knows I needed enough of those."

"Six Aves for your lapse of respect."

"I'm so sorry. Where was I? Oh yes, then I joined the Justice pour les Jeunes. I was actually secretary for a year till I had too many Assignments, stuff like that. But I'm still a member."

"Trotskyites? Communists?" The tone changed and Nelly felt a tremor of fear despite warming to her cause.

"Not at all. That's just hysteria. The young have a right to either train part-time or at least be offered some kind of security. After all, we are the future."

"And what now, Mademoiselle? Why exactly are you seeking us out again? What is your shame, your need for redemption?"

Nelly had it all ready, and silently slipped off her shoes. With pauses and enough elaborate detail she gave witness to her mama's life, then her own days on the capital's streets, and when Sister Marie-Ange finally began the litany of penance, the novice was already past the altar and out into the warm drizzle. She felt inside her pinafore dress below her left breast, where Bellino's automatic was still safe.

XXXVII

Wednesday October 1ˢᵗ

"Your portrait, sir?" The *beur* squinted up at Duvivier as he flicked desultorily through a sheaf of Montmartre watercolours outside the Atelier Louis Lamet. The priest ignored him, and because a party of Japanese were closing in, anticipating the outcome, Mathieu offered himself instead.

"Very good, sir. Thank you," said the man. "You have a strong jaw. Nice eyes."

"Idiot," whispered Vidal, trying to pull him away, but already the swift charcoal had begun its journey, and the practised thumb blended in the tones. "Voilà." Then came a buzz of fixative, turning the paper a temporary yellow.

"Truly amazing." Mathieu skewed himself round to look, and a ripple of applause leaked from the onlookers clustered in the shadow of the Sacré Coeur.

"How much?"

The native of Beni-Messous smiled. "Nothing, sir. You seem a good person."

"Oh, come on. We're all brothers. I don't need favours."

"With two massacres in my country in one month, my family and I at last feel safe here. This is my gift."

"It's his party trick, can't you see?" Vidal hissed, and for a second the *noir* caught his eye.

Mathieu unpeeled a fifty. A blurred St. Éxupery, and pressed it into the artist's pink palm.

"Please. My mother'll really like it," he said. "I'll get it framed for her."

My lies are slipping from me like a haemorrhage. Help me.

A tap on his shoulder made him turn. Vidal was scowling.

"Bin it. You heard. Could get into the wrong hands." But Plagnol, who'd watched the Algerian roll it up with great care and insert it into a cardboard tube, got there first and knocked Mathieu playfully on the head.

His laughter made him too conspicuous.

"For the first time, I've got something he wants." Plagnol roared anew beneath his baseball cap, and people began to edge away. Despite the Basilica's shade, it was too hot for a fight, but Mathieu took him on. Got his thumb and locked it back against his wrist until the drawing fell to the ground.

Vidal looked for Duvivier, but he was still browsing. Modigliani, Cassat, Sisley... the colours of the Seine furred and feathered, and skies the same blue of the south. The very last things on his mind...

The Kommandant's losing it, too.

Vidal stared at his every move.

Dangerous.

Then he squeezed Plagnol's arm.

"Don't you know the one about the crazy man who laughs too much?"

Plagnol turned from pink to red.

"What d'you mean?"

"Loufouque. He's always the next to die. Watch out."

Cacheux sidled up to show off a leather wallet he'd just bought, embossed with a camel. He sniffed it and passed it over.

"What does that smell remind you of, Father Jean-Baptiste?"

"That noir's arsehole."

"How droll we are." But all the same, he was wary, seeing his small advances rebuffed with increasing brusqueness. Cruelty even, which was not a little intoxicating. "I have a terrible need," he'd confessed to his mother before leaving the Château de Fourcat. "And my soul won't rest until it has drunk from his. Robert Vidal is my light and my life. What life I have."

Now he watched as the object of his desire checked his Rolex and tried to distract Duvivier away from yet more souvenirs.

XXXVIII

The eve of Rosh Hashanah had become a sultry combination of sweat and diesel emissions as an Indian Summer sun lay over Paris. Tourists still visiting the French capital to see where one month ago, the late Princess of Wales and her lover had crashed in the Pont de l'Alma tunnel, moved in slow motion, too enervated to bargain for things made in hide and cheap glass that dangled amongst cruising wasps and flies. Dogs lay comatose in doorways. Preparation indeed for the Solemn Days, Mathieu murmured his own private prayer, fingering the rosary inside his pocket.

Suddenly a bellicose roar added to the Savoyard's eleven peals. Plagnol was twisting a new umbrella over his head, standing legs apart, singing.

"Je cherche fortune

Autour du Chat Noir

Au clair de la lune

A Montmartre le soir,

Et je sais qui a visité *Le Bébé*..."

Vidal came up close. "You're dead meat if you let that one out again. Understand?" He pushed him towards the steps down to the Square Willette and stayed as they processed in the direction of the Palais Royal on the Rue Seveste. Duvivier kept his distance, in that same solitary world as when he'd met them at the Opéra, and when Vidal drew alongside and tried to discuss The Pigface's bizarre behaviour, he was ignored.

***

The Palais Royal, purveyor of 'Chinese and Thai Cuisine' was seriously empty. The five priests took a table near the window hung with a silk dragon that moved on their breath. The one candle smelt of tom cats and Cacheux nipped its flame between his thumb and finger and smiled at Vidal as its rancid aftermath hung in the air.

It had been Vidal's idea to book the place, working on the principle that the Landsturm needed calories but nothing which might slow down reflexes. Three-weeks' instruction with Gulf war veteran Dan Ayache at his diving school in the Rue Bunüel, had given him a new impetus, while drills in the Forêt de Fontainebleau had streamlined his body into a sleek machine. He was in control, and not just of himself. Of Colette? Fat chance. He'd been forbidden to make contact with her at Lanvière. Forbidden most things except water and steel.

He gazed at Duvivier. The man looked pale, paying no attention to the Asian who dispensed the huge, tasselled menus with an overdone decorum. Nor did he want to eat.

"Come on squire. A few prawn balls will set you up," Plagnol joked.

Duvivier glared. The holes in his cheek dark against the rest.

"OK. Please yourself." Running a fat finger down the wine list.

"No alcohol. No apéros." Vidal snapped it shut, and when the waiter returned, summarised the order and asked for Evian instead.

***

12.08 hours.

He drummed his nails on the tablecloth until the meal arrived.

"Our boat leaves at 15.00, but we're seeing Jalibert first at 14.00. Mangez." He raised his glass, effervescent against Duvivier's douleur. "To a good show."

Mathieu kept his eyes lowered as he forced the food down his throat, until a sudden cough showered Cacheux with rice.

"Thanks, you." The priest from St. Honoré stood up, moved nearer Vidal and brushed down his fresh, white suit, paying particular attention to his flies.

Keep away from me, cocksucker.

Vidal elbowed him away. Again, nothing from Father André which made the next rung of the ladder feel even safer under his feet.

After the unsatisfactory meal, they took a short walk to Abbesses, the nearest metro, where fresh notices of guaranteed seats for pregnant women, the infirm and those soldiers mutilated in the war, covered the walls.

"Save some for us, then," Plagnol laughed, the first to sit down. Sweating in the heat, his lips set in what was to be a lasting smile.

"You on something or what?" Cacheux still fixed his gaze on Vidal.

"Let's just say, the Lord's been good to me."

"What's that supposed to mean?"

Plagnol leant closer. Cacheux recoiled at his breath. "On September 8th last, two blessings."

"So?"

"The birth of Our Blessed Virgin and..." he paused, his piggy eyes alight. "the sudden and unforeseen departure of my beloved *mamie*. In her sleep, it was. Peaceful and beautiful to behold. My name was the last word she uttered..."

Cacheux stared, seeing a saliva line eke from the man's mouth.

"So I am to be rich. Can't you see? Mother already fancies a Maison de Maître in Aubervilliers. Less than one kilometre from my Notre-Dame. Liliane Argent had the right name, that's for sure." He laughed to himself as the vineyard owner's son fell silent. The thick, used air of the city not so different from that day before last week's storm. So dense, he'd had to snort like a horse to clear his lungs, and when the black sky came, it was as though the Devil himself rode the wind and hurled down hailstones the size of *boules,* razing all the vines, scarring the soil so nothing remained. Nothing for the only son, who was sending home his new money, only a hopeless yearning for the man two seats away.

"A lovely interment, I have to say," Plagnol continued, grinning. "Though it meant a lot of extra work I could have done without."

Cacheux saw those knees, trembling fat muscle under his trousers.

Cochon fou.

***

As their train drew away from Trinité, six Moroccans arranged themselves opposite. Vidal got up and came over to sit next to Cacheux, giving them a berating glance as he did so. Cacheux wanted to touch the new suede of his coat, let his hands roam, but this wasn't the time or the place. The diver meant business.

"At de l'Alma we *stroll,*" he said. "Touristes, remember? Rubbernecks, like everyone else." He felt Cacheux's desire burn into his back.

Dead meat by All Souls, my friend. You make Hades come too soon.

***

13.15 hours
And hotter still by the Seine. Worse than August.

Hell isn't only Jews and perverts, it's the lack of air and the choking shit that'll make corpses of us all by the evening.

Vidal glowered at the Breton who'd been heaving since they'd left the restaurant. "Give it a rest, OK?"

"I can't help it."

Dear sweet Thérèse, don't fail me.

Even with a handkerchief over his nose and mouth, Mathieu knew the damage to his lungs had already been done.

"Try, for God's sake!"

Vidal then let Duvivier catch up. The man, who hadn't spoken since they'd met outside the Ibis in the Rue Orsel, was suffocated, not by the temperature but by the events of the previous week. He gripped his file case like a drunk at the deck rail and studied the ground as he walked.

"We have an invalid. Bad news, eh?" said Vidal.

"What do you think?"

Their boots in unison. Occupying forces en route to the Rue Salacroux, until Mathieu's retching slowed them up.

Stroll.

"He'll draw too much attention."

"Too bad. We need some final shots. In case anything's changed."

"OK. So I isolate him."

"Whatever."

"Now tell me. What's up?"

"I can't."

Déchaux has a dagger in my back. And like God, worse than God, is playing cat and mouse. He means to be everywhere...

"You never told me what Toussirot did with my letter."

"How the fuck do I know?"

Past the Théatre des Champs-Elysées, up a side street off the Rue Masclé made sombre by opposing rows of houses built at the same time as those on the Île de St. Louis, whose balconies almost touched overhead. Vidal noted the neighbours. A paediatrician, a chiropractor, lawyers and an art gallery showing socks cast in bronze.

Jalibert et Fils were on the third floor of Number 26.

Without eye contact, Vidal told Cacheux to buy a paper and hang around, and Mathieu to back him up discreetly. From somewhere close by, a shofar sounded. Somewhere in the 8ième were serious Jews. "T'kiah.. t'ruah... kiah..." Smooth and pure before the disintegration.

Exactly.

Vidal followed the repetition with his lips, making sure the queer was in situ, then he allowed the other two to take the stairs in front.

Duvivier suddenly stopped and turned to him, causing Plagnol to stumble.

"Tell Number 4 to make contact if they see a black Toyota Celica. Female chauffeur. Bottle blonde. Get the plate."

"What the Hell do you mean?" An old fear returned. The one thing he couldn't control.

"Just tell him."

XXXIX

Although the suave Yves Jalibert was obviously used to callers, with his greeting hand slipping in and out of the others with ease, Vidal detected tension in his eyes and wondered what was up. He looked round for any signs of a laundry. He'd been expecting damp sheets, steam and women in white, *à la Zola*. In fact the place was so low key, so anonymous, it could have been used for anything.

Definitely *un mercenaire*.

"Come this way, do."

Duvivier had evinced a slight smile of recognition, but that was all. Even Plagnol sensing the formality, sat in silence while Jalibert, immaculate in a dark suit and a discreet *fleur de lys* pin in his button hole, unrolled a length of paper onto a nearby table and secured it with outspread hands. His fingertips less than steady.

"Who drew this for you?" asked Vidal, seeing a detailed cross section drawing of a *Bateau-Mouche* bearing the name *Roquette IV*. He could still taste prawns in his mouth and wanted somewhere to spit.

"I did it myself, Monsieur. Before I took in washing, I was a fully trained architect. No real work though unless you were a Jew or a Freemason. And the rest as my friend here can tell us, is history. By the way," he looked first at Plagnol, then Vidal, "I don't know who you or the others are. Thibaut's the only name I have. Better that way."

Indeed.

"Now, some bad news from yesterday. They've rescheduled the lunch for tomorrow..."

So, I was right.

"Tomorrow?" Vidal challenged. "No Jew has fun on the first day of Rosh Hashanah."

"These will, believe me. And the power boat race still happens on the 4th. Thibaut, I couldn't reach you at all. Nor could Marcel."

A silence lasting too long.

"I was busy," Duvivier lied to break it. "My apologies."

"Who's Marcel?" asked Vidal. His mind on fire.

"My son." Jalibert seemed a touch offended.

"Where is he, then?"

The entrepreneur glanced at his Gucci watch. Two eyebrows greyer than his head, drew together. "Should be here by now."

Merde. I don't like this one bit.

"We press on."

"No we don't," snapped Vidal. "We wait."

Another silence, thicker than the fug outside as Jalibert perched on a stool, continually changed legs. A wasp who'd crawled through an air vent, died noisily on the sill as Plagnol farted. Just then, two bleeps from Duvivier's phone. For a moment he forgot its whereabouts, his hands like blind moles under his duffel coat.

"I'll take it." Vidal kept his promise. "Yes?"

Cacheux spoke fast. Vidal mentally registered the number prefixed 51. Reims. A black Celica, mud up the sills, had come down the street twice. The Breton had recognised the chauffeur, mainly by her blonde hair. Cacheux was impressive in his detail, and Duvivier paled when he saw what Vidal had jotted down. He straightened up as though on guard. The cunt had said he'd be in Bosnia...

"Stay put and don't let the Breton roam too far. Give us five more minutes." He'd not used their code names. The less the laundry man knew, the better.

"So what time does my performance start, Monsieur?" he asked him.

"Six-thirty."

Plagnol whistled.

"It'll be daylight." Vidal again communed with his watch.

"Thing is, security's been tightened up. There are now two more guards. Old Hermans had an incident last Friday, that's why."

"Please explain."

"Bloody students. Tried to fix some flag or other on the prow. They managed to rough him up quite a bit, threatened to push him overboard or else a quick cremation. That seems to be the trademark."

"How kind." Vidal wondered briefly about Les Flammes and hoped his father was still keeping his nose clean.

"Indeed, just the ticket." Duvivier sighed as though the world's weight lay behind his eyes.

Vidal stood up. "Can't do it. Simple as that."

"You'll have to." The Provençal felt Déchaux's greedy breath on his neck. "Just pray for a splendid misty morning, that's all."

Jalibert coughed, *sotto voce*.

"There are no more, how shall I put it, Jewish jollifications on the water until..." He scoured his desk diary... "Hanukkah. December 27th. *Le Canard's* putting on a special gourmet boat for publishers et al. We're doing the linen again. They seem to like us." He joined Vidal at the window and stood sideways looking out.

"Let's go for it, then." Plagnol fished a sweet out of his pocket. The second payment not safe in the bank until 1700 hours. "What's an hour, anyhow?"

"Life or death, Pigface. Just a small matter."

The priest from Drancy seemed embarrassed that Jalibert now knew his nickname, and Vidal regretted having revealed it.

Then, urgent footsteps and Jalibert senior slid like a lizard behind the door, his Smith & Wesson ready – black with a wood grip and red dot sight.

Classy, like the rest of him. At least he tries.

Four knocks.

Three other guns ready as the door edged open. He sighed relief.

"Ah, Marcel. *Bienvenue.*"

An energy surge accompanied the young redhead into the room. Short, compact, as casual as his father was formal, but the kisses were businesslike.

Cacheux might like this one. Obviously the delivery boy. At least it would keep him off my back.

Marcel shook Vidal's hand first, smiled at Duvivier and Plagnol, then went straight over to the plan. He peeled off his trainers and used them to keep the map ends down. "Roquette IV. Nice little boat. Been in service six years, no previous problems." He looked up. "Your recce day, *hein?*"

Vidal nodded, still unsure of him.

"Well, it's busy out there and getting worse. On board, just get to your tables and sit down. No pissing about, you might get noticed."

Not the delivery boy after all.

"Look at the views by all means, but don't order anything out of the ordinary, and don't talk too loud. Even the breeze has ears, though there won't be much of that today, mind. Just meld."

Meld. Fat chance with the Breton croaking like a donkey and The Pigface into serial combustion.

"Get the feel of it all, but everything you need to know is right here."

Five heads studied the boat's elevations. Above and below. Air and water. Two sections of intricate seductive detail with the guards' likely movements in red. "Got this as well." The son extracted a folded sheet of A4. A tidal chart expertly copied by hand in the style of a medical illustration. He laid it over his father's dissection of the boat.

"Did you do this?" Vidal asked.

Leonardo, eat your heart out.

"Took me a while, but at least it's accurate. Handy size, too."

"Very impressive." Plagnol's index finger settled on the Pont de l'Alma.

"And here's the key." Marcel passed Vidal a ring box in the shape of a heart. "Two turns left. One to the right." When I leave after my first visit, I'll cancel the alarm."

"How come you know the code?"

"I stuck my finger up Herman's ass. He liked that."

Just the job, then, for Christophe de la Bonté.

"We've been extremely thorough, I can assure you." Jalibert senior smiled. "After all, this isn't our first – *comment s'appelle?* – adventure. Nor our last."

His coolness chilled the room. Vidal sensed water again. He'd already been tested in different swells and cross currents, with propellers and other foreign bodies. Had his oxygen cut off deeper than under the Pont de l'Alma with no trace of the bends. He was more than ready.

"Eight kilometres per hour is the norm," added the tooled-up Jalibert. "Not exactly a speedboat, but it gives the punters plenty of time. And you, of course. Can be slippery underneath, specially the ropes. They seem to pick up all the shit that's going. Might need gloves."

"Got them."

"We also have a photographer." Duvivier finally spoke.

"Just the sights, remember. You're tourists."

"For God's sake." Plagnol interrupted. "What if I happen to see a nice ass or better still, a breast? The Lord knows, I cannot resist such treasures."

Young Jalibert looked at Vidal and mouthed, "ground him."

***

"OK you've got our number," said the redhead. "Any change let us know. Remember the emergency engine door shuts 'clunk.' No need to lock. Get the Hell out. Then you'll see our vans. Three of them. If there's only two, then hide. Don't attempt to make the Pont des Invalides. One last thing." He extracted a wallet from his jeans and handed Vidal the tickets for *Roquette IV*.

Forged but good. Van Megeren has an heir, I see.

"Bon voyage and happy hunting."

"Do we meet again?" Vidal asked, holding them up to the light.

"I hope not. And those are strictly kosher by the way. Listen." He pulled down the sash window as the door to the balcony was sealed. The unbroken wail from the Synagogue on the Boulevard Mardilly snaked into the room. A primordial, hypnotic sound, untramelled by flies or the burr of traffic.

"They're at it again. Must be swamp fever in the Marais." Jalibert senior laughed. "Makes one feel quite at home, doesn't it?" And for the first time, Duvivier allowed himself a smile.

"And God rises from his throne of judgement and sits down on a throne of mercy."

"While the ever so humble servants beg for life," Vidal added, slipping the key and tickets into his coat. "Now that's what I call irresistible."

XL

How many days and nights had passed since she'd first been caught? Too many. And where was Colette? Where? Was she alive or dead? And what about her son?

The midday Angelus pealed out from the Refuge bell tower, causing the coven of crows who'd settled on its warm brick, to scatter into the sky.

Nelly knew that she stank. The stolen robe from the Résidence had been half the weight and size of this one, and with just the threadbare towel and sliver of cheap soap thrown in on her first morning of imprisonment, no wonder her inner thighs were chapped and sore. No wonder too, she'd lost weight; felt bones she never knew she had. The food, if you could call it that, had been left on her filthy floor each morning at, she'd judged, the same time. Why, on this last occasion, in her airless, windowless prison, she'd been ready. Also the precious gun she'd kept hidden between her buttocks.

Deo Gratias.

She was outside in the windy heat, and running as if her heart would burst. First, into the parking area behind the chapel that protruded beyond the main building. No cars, not even a bicycle. Whoever was here, was here for good. But there was a coach. Brand new, and the incongruity of it surprised her. Green and cream with strawberry-coloured seats, its bulk cast a useful shadow while she changed behind the trash bins.

"Vacances Mémorables," she read along its gleaming side. "That's the sickest thing I've ever seen." Then she put her hands together and squeezed her eyes shut to murmur what she remembered of the prayer.

"Domini nuntiavit Mariae; et concepit de Spiritu Sanctu..." As though being blind would somehow make her smaller – part of the detritus that spilled out around the *poubelles* and heaped up against the kitchen wall. Cooking smells escaped from somewhere. Horse mince filled out with cheap pasta – like she'd had for the 'hospitality' meal in the Bois de Boulogne.

Ugh.

But the red bits – the haemoglobin still strung with tendons – had given her the trots. Trots and a stone floor. A partnership contrived in Hell. No wonder they'd not bothered to come and clean.

Nelly finally stood up, adjusted her veil, then rehearsed with her gun. Every move in exact sequence, seven times for luck, only pausing when voices suddenly permeated the windless heat.

She stopped breathing. There was one she recognised beyond all doubt. Claude Lefêbvre. Again.

Jesus wept.

She peered out of her sanctuary at the immaculate lawn studded with white markers topped by single red hearts. Graves. She shivered despite the melting heat, and thought of poor dead Chloë. Of her friend Colette, and, fleetingly, of her own mother.

Beyond, lay a patch of newly rotavated soil, darkly brown after the brief drizzle, being hoed by three nuns whose robes were patched in sweat, their faces reddened by the sun. Suddenly and without warning, two of the group picked up their implements and walked away.

"See you at Vespers," the remaining one called out in that same high-pitched voice, the same inflection as she'd heard on the train. Perfectly at home in the place.

What the fuck's going on?

But danger touched every nerve as Nelly kept to the wall then began to stalk across the damp grass, her shadow trawling behind. Claude Lefêbvre was now less than a metre away, desultorily poking at the earth. She wasn't preparing any ground for crops, she'd come to kill her. Or her and Colette.

This was no movie, this was real, and a surge of courage suddenly filled Nelly's body. She was ready.

"Don't bloody move till I say so."

The nun swung round, her veil revealing eyes of ice on fire. Her hoe fell to the ground.

"Now. Over there. *Vite.*" Nelly pushed her towards a clump of poplars and scrub with a hut roof showing above. This was out of the sun at least, and out of sight of the Refuge. Supposing Lefêbvre too was armed? Supposing the other one was waiting...

Mon Dieu.

But she wasn't going to give her that chance.

"Your mate? She here as well?"

"No."

"Liar."

"She went on to Bordeaux."

"So what are you up to? Bitch from Hell." She'd pinned Lefêbvre against the shed. Her enemy taller, stronger in every way. "Where's Colette Bataille? You tell me, or I'll blow your head off."

"What the fuck are you talking about?"

"Why else are you here? Don't tell me you've suddenly come to join a Holy Order. Pull the other one." Nelly moved the gun up between her adversary's shoulders. "You show me where they're keeping Colette Bataille or the word 'morning' will mean nothing to you."

Overhead the sun had beamed away the last of the usurping clouds and now reigned supreme over the wrecked vineyards as they processed back past the coach towards the chapel. Two minutes in which Nelly reminded Lefêbvre of Bertrand, at the same time desperate to get her bearings.

At the archway to the cellars, the taller girl stopped, resting a hand on a pile of Breviaries left out for latecomers. The other was raised too quickly for Nelly to duck and the blow rocked her off balance. Her 9 milli spun down the steps into total darkness. Blindly she followed its echo, slithering and tripping on her oversize robe, bumping and jarring her bottom. Someone else had now joined Lefêbvre, a blur against the ceiling. Nelly reached the door and hammered with every molecule of strength, dizzy and faint.

"Who's that?"

Even though the female voice seemed to come from a long way off and sounded weak, Nelly knew instantly it was Colette.

"You've got to open this door!"

I'm going to die.

"I can't! I'm locked in."

By some miracle, Nelly's foot nudged the gun towards her. Slimy, stinking but priceless, it was now back in her hand. She pointed it up the stairs, but Georges Déchaux hadn't got big in the DRM or anywhere else on lack of foresight.

Both his women were prepared. Poachers turned gamekeepers, they approached their prey.

"Drop it." Kirchner spat at her.

"Fuck you." And as the chapel choir soared in praise to the organ crescendo, Nelly fired. First at her then Lefêbvre, before doubling up in the wet shit, still hearing their screams. Ready to vomit.

***

Silence. Then Victorine approached barefoot, her skin wheatmeal even in the dark. She held out a key and a bag weighted by stale bread and a carton of milk.

"Sod the grub," said Nelly. "Let's get Colette out of here."

"I'm trying." The blind triplet felt for the lock hole with her finger. Each second an agony. Suddenly the door creaked open and the stench hit her.

"Jesus."

But for Nelly, nothing mattered now except her friend. A fleeting embrace. The start of tears, for both women were unrecognisable to each other.

"Did you try the hostel? Have you found Bertrand?" gasped Colette.

"Tell you later." Nelly grabbed her hand, cold as a corpse and, as the choir and a posse of novices filed out of the chapel and into the Refectory, helped haul her leaden robe up the steps.

"We'll see you in Heaven." Colette touched Victorine's cheek and saw grief where her eyes should have been. "Victorine. If you hadn't helped me..."

"So it was *you* sent that message?" Nelly whispered to the triplet. "Brave girl."

"It was nothing. But now, I must get back, or else..." Victorine locked the door then pushed past them both, her whole body shaking.

She's terrified, poor little thing. Holy Mary, where are you?

"Come with us," Nelly urged her.

"I can't."

"Well at least be careful. There are two more evil women out there and they'll be even more dangerous now."

"You shot them. I heard."

"What?" Colette faced her.

"No choice, I'm afraid. But they'll live."

"My God..."

Victorine tapped Nelly's arm. "You need to turn right into the chapel, at the back. There's a door into the stores. It's got a window that's always open, I know, because sometimes after Compline I have to sort stuff out. "

Then she was gone. The diligent servant with the key, caught up with the lame nun who was joined by Sister Agnès holding a white lily.

"What two women did you mean?" Colette asked Nelly. She shook with cold and fear as they crouched by the corner ready to move.

"Sssh! Never mind." For in the seemingly empty chapel a murmur of voices meant someone was still in Confession.

Merde.

"Quick!"

The door was wedged but they pushed against it, hard and silently until it moved against baskets of new candles and tea chests of doubtful origins. Boxes stamped Moscow and Berlin, cartons of printed matter from Brussels. A full house.

"That's bloody odd."

Nelly set to and stacked them up against the door, while Colette stood gulping in fresh air and staring at freedom.

"Hey, look at this." Nelly peered at a scrap of paper listing fifteen pairs of gardening gloves and eighty black shirts in varying sizes. 4,500 francs including carrier. The supplier's name at the top torn away. "What do you make of that? Nuns don't wear black shirts, surely?" Nelly frowned.

"Schutzstaffel."

"Pardon?"

"Nothing. I think I am going mad after all." Colette turned it over, her eyes

179

still smarting. "It's got an address in Paris, in the fifth. FAO the Abbé de Lagrange Vivray. That name's familiar from somewhere."

"Too right. I told you about him. He's the one running the whole shebang. What a find. So he's not shacked up here with all the women, then. Must be too old or queer." She tucked it in her bra.

"I've got to see him," Colette said out loud.

"We, remember?"

"Oh, God, it's been so long. I couldn't have lasted another hour in there."

"You don't have to. Everything's OK now."

"You're an angel, Nelly. I won't ever be able to pay you back."

"I don't expect you to. I just love you."

For a moment, Colette seemed stunned. No-one had ever said that to her before. Not even the priest. Not even Bertrand. She began to cry again, tears down her raw, white face.

"Besides, when we get out of all this, I want you to be my mum. So there."

"Oh, Nelly. Just look at me."

"And me. It's been three weeks at least."

"I pong to high Heaven."

"Join the club."

"Look!"

High up on the wall, a gauze square with PSS in the corner, moved in front of a small window.

"I'll never reach that." Nelly sighed, as Colette helped her drag over things on which to stand.

"Course you will."

Suddenly, Colette stopped.

"Can you hear something?"

"Shhh."

Shouting not singing from the chapel, and the drum of boots on the tiles coming closer.

"Go!" Colette yelled.

Nelly stripped off her hated robe and threw it out of the window. Then Colette, finding new strength, pushed her friend's feet clear of the top box and heaved her through. Colette too, dropped out into the sun as the store room door was being pounded like the recent thunder. "Tie it like this." Colette made a rough sarong from the robe, then they ran like schoolgirls over the grass, following the sun south towards Libourne, as the bell from the Refuge tolled the half hour. More trees. Another miracle, at least until the bloody wall loomed up.

Oh, Jesus.

It was over two metres high, new brick. No hand or feet holds and its top edges studded with glass chips. That much Nelly could see. She turned to Colette.

"Pretend we're apes, right? Not hard to imagine. You ready?" She was already halfway up the full grown Butternut, her sturdy thighs gripping the trunk. "This was the only way. Sorry."

She reached a fork in the main branches, tested her weight on the one spreading towards the wall, then retied her robe into giant knots around her hips. Colette held her breath in horror as the girl crawled along keeping her balance as that branch creaked and bowed. When Nelly reached the end, she swung herself over into a bank of nettles. Colette winced at her cries as she began to crawl, seeing the end of the bough sag so much below the edge of the pieces of glass.

Oh darling Bertrand, help me, please!

She managed to twist herself over to the other side. Just, but not enough, and smelt the sickly sweetness of her own blood as it coursed down her arm.

"Run!"

The two ragged figures careered in the direction of the river Isle, through an uncut meadow of late Lammas grass, Colette tipping the spears with red until respite came in the form of an abandoned tractor listing on its buckled wheels.

"They're coming!" Her breath too fast, too shallow, her carotid pumping up like a bullfrog. Nelly held her until she was calm then tore off some of her own sleeve to bind the wound.

Jesus, how she trusts me. I can't see a single, fucking thing...

"No-one's around," she said. "Only us. Take a look."

Colette raised herself to scan the field, her eyes raw and exposed without eyelashes. Then seeing nothing amiss, she leaned back in the tractor's shadow letting a host of Common Blue butterflies settle on her boots.

Whose souls are these, I wonder? Such beauty after where I've been...

"Oh, Nelly, what a place that was. I thought I was going to die there and never see my lovely boy again."

"Don't think about it now. You're free."

"What'll they do to Victorine?"

"She'll be OK. She's done her Penance, though God knows what that was."

For a moment, Colette fell silent, then both put her hands together for the Prayer for the Dead. When she'd finished, she looked haunted. "That hostel. I *know* Bertrand went there."

Nelly spat on her hem and used it to soothe the nettle stings. Then she wiped away some of the filth from Colette's face, starting with her nose. "Colette, I must tell you something, but you've got to help me as well. It's about those two women. One of them worked at St. Anne's. I couldn't stand her, and the others used to say she tampered with their mail, listened while they phoned. Reckoned the line was tapped, too, though I never used it. "

Colette's eyes widened, but the way Nelly spoke made her stomach turn over.

"Is she called Antoinette?"

"No. Why?"

"Sister Agnès called her that."

Nelly frowned, trying to think as Colette continued. "We went there looking for Bertrand. I could have sworn they knew each other."

"Maybe. Anything's possible. Oh, God, all this is doing my head in." She looked up at the sky for release. "They're both hard bitches, probably got false IDs anyhow. I bet Lefêbvre put my dog Roger down the bog the minute I left." Nelly paused as if to remember her faithful, almost real hound. "And the other one's no better."

"Who was she?" Colette's lips felt sore and swollen in the heat.

"Romy Kirchner. So she said. I cadged some clothes from her. Actually thought I'd got genuine U.S. of A. gear."

"You borrowed clothes? Nelly, why on earth did you need to do that?"

"Secret. Anyhow, something really scary's going on. They followed me here, hoping I'd lead them to you."

"Me? What have *I* done? Colette suddenly felt her throat dry as desert sand, her insides contract as though for a terrible birth.

"Think. You must."

"I am... was, just an ordinary working mother doing an ordinary job. It's never been easy, specially with Bertrand unemployed for so long after University..."

The sun glowered directly overhead, burning but not healing her blood. Triggering her pulse out of control before Nelly started cleaning her forehead in small curving strokes.

That's nice. That's better.

"Concentrate."

Colette frowned, closed her eyes, surrendering to the crude, hypnotic light. She was back in that hostel foyer with the nun. The colluding smiles returned, repeating, enlarging to grotesque lips and teeth – red on white, pale on pale...

"What did you tell Agnès?" Nelly was trying to wipe her ears, following the convolutions with a thorough finger. "Think."

But Colette was shaking with fear and anger. She pushed the girl away and stood up. "We've got to see the police. I must find my son."

"Been there, done it. They just said I was bonkers." Nelly leant closer.

"Colette, just why are you so important to these freaks? For God's sake, what have you done? What have you said?"

"Robert Vidal..." The words felt like lead on Colette's tongue.

"Who?"

"A man I was once in love with. A priest. At my church in Lanvière."

"I'm listening."

And when Colette had finished, Nelly's face had tightened in alarm.

"So you're saying this man's a neo-Nazi, and you gave this man's key to Bertrand so he could poke around?" She asked, incredulous. "I don't believe you did something so bloody stupid."

"He didn't find anything. I made him swear on the Bible about that."

"How do you know? People think they can read their kids inside out, but kids are sometimes bloody clever. Supposing he did find something? Serious stuff? It's possible. It would certainly explain a few things, for God's sake. Just imagine, your dear Bertrand could have caused quite a bit of aggro in his own way. He didn't want you and this Robert to be an item, did he?" She was about to add, "and who can blame him?"

Colette coloured and sat bolt upright. "You're talking about my only child! How dare you!" But her expression told a different story. While her fists clenched and unclenched, the terrible possibilities dawned.

"I think," Nelly stood up picking her words as carefully as the things she'd shifted from the stubble on Colette's head, "your son got himself into far more shitty water than you've just been in."

"What on earth do you mean?"

"I just have this awful feeling. Oh, Colette." She buried her head in her hands. "Specially after what you told Agnès and those beasts in there. I think they were prepared to kill you."

Still are, if we're not careful, with Lefêbvre and Kirchner retired hurt – they'll be even more dangerous.

"Me? What about *him*?" Colette's cry higher than the corn buntings that wheeled upwards from the wires into the sun. "I just want to see him again."

"Course you do. And you will," Nelly lied badly. "I'm just playing Devil's Advocate, that's all. You've also got to remember the Secret Services are probably on to us. Going to the police again will be like stroking that same Devil's backside."

"That's not true!"

"Look. Let's be honest. Our options now are pretty nil. The main thing is to find somewhere safe to hide. Then like you said, we see that Abbott. Seems he's the choreographer of all this shit."

Colette sprang up, her robe falling away as she began to lope, dizzy and terrified away from the words which like a skilled chisel, had chipped away at the vision of her saintly son and created for her an impossible burden of guilt.

"Colette! For God's sake!" Without her glasses, Nelly stumbled over the rough ground, but like a naked fugitive from Bosch's 'Purgatory,' her friend disappeared beyond a line of alders, as a single gunshot tore through the air.

***

Nelly Augot's progress back towards the copse where Colette had collapsed in fright and exhaustion, took longer than expected.

The poplars along the high uneven bank made strange configurations against the sky, alive with the palaver of migrating hordes from the north, and where the vineyards ended, great tracts of untended land bristled with the rusting skeletons of another age. It was an upturned plough she leaned on to draw breath and get her bearings. To listen with all her antennae for signs of new danger.

After that shot, she'd hidden with Colette amongst the brambles and let the afternoon take its course before leaving her to try the small town of Guizac for a replacement pair of glasses, some cheap clothes and food for the journey back to the capital. Leftover money and her ID were still intact as she'd sewn a pocket into her knickers before leaving Paris. The one practical thing to foil muggers and greedy pimps, that her mama had actually shown her.

No sound except the distant upheavals in the trees and the sighs of milkers foraging on ground to the east.

"Colette?" she whispered. "Can you hear me?" Her heart on overtime as she searched for the familiar clump of hazel and turned full circle before realising it lay behind. "Shit."

She struggled over old furrows, her two bags bumping on the hard earth. One from a charity shop tucked away behind an *auto-école*, the other from Rallye that had still been open at six. Two miracles, and the third was that Colette looked rested and alert when she eventually found her.

Thank you, God.

"Voilà."

"You deserve a medal, you really do."

"Don't speak too soon. We'll look like nothing on bloody earth in this gear. Still, we can always join a circus. The rest was all kid's stuff I'm afraid. Hey, do you like my glasses? Two francs fifty. Not bad, *hein*?"

"They're red."

"Better red than dead."

Colette gave her a hug. Then saw her own boots, millstones at the end of each leg, still damp and stinking

"I can't wear these any more." She thought of her neat row of pastel sling-

184

backs waiting in the wardrobe at Lanvière.

"You must, in case we have to make a run for it. Anyhow, boots are trendy." Then Nelly coughed, embarrassed that she'd found some court shoes for herself. She took her friend's hand.

"Colette? Can I ask you a big favour?"

"Of course. Anything."

"I'd like to come back to Lanvière with you, if that's OK. I wouldn't be a nuisance, honestly. I'd protect you.."

"You don't even have to ask. Silly girl. That'd be wonderful, and good for me while I wait for..." Colette stopped short. Tears already welling up. "But what about your mama? Surely she must want to see you again?"

After a brief silence, Nelly took a breath.

"She's a prostitute." The word spoken with such clarity, made Colette gasp. "Open all day, we never clothe. You know the sort of thing. Enough said."

"Oh, Nelly. You've not mentioned this before."

"Bit of a conversation killer really. See, after my papa died she couldn't get a job, even though she tried everything. So in the end... I try not to think about it too much... She's done her best, I suppose. But it's why she rarely answers the phone. Always on the job..."

"Weren't *you* ever tempted?" Colette asked cautiously. "After all, it's cash in hand, isn't it? I remember Bertrand telling me some of the girls in his year at university used to do the same."

"No. Never." Nelly said too quickly. "Not after what I've seen, *merci.*"

"You poor thing. You must miss your papa terribly. I do think girls especially, need a father."

"I never really knew him." Nelly said matter-of-factly. "Even after nineteen years, he was still a stranger. It's weird."

"I can imagine." Colette felt the same tears, the same uncertainty grip her, and as the afternoon advanced, concealing all the components of that flat uncultivated land even from themselves, the two fugitives warmed by dead men's clothes, began their hike to the station at Cubzénaut.

It was only then Colette realised in a rush of shameful despair that she'd forgotten Bertrand's birthday. September 6th had been weeks ago.

XLI

Mathieu had started smoking again and lit up his sixth Gauloises since boarding the *Roquette IV*. Despite his foul throat and raw diaphragm, he still craved the same comfort as on the day of his Ordination. After all, St. Thérèse hadn't made the boat disappear or struck any of their sinful number down. So what else was there? And now the packet lay soft, half-empty in his jeans pocket alongside his rosary.

"Came off the nipple too early, obviously." Plagnol stared down at the dark green water as the *Bateau-Mouche* plied her way past the Trocadéro. "Me, I could never get enough, so Mother says. She kept me going till I had a good set of teeth. Bless her."

I bet she did, you greedy, amoral pig.

Mathieu eyed his companion's profile below the baseball cap and secretly resolved to give this creature special mention when seeking Absolution at the end of it all. One lapse in twenty-four years and nothing to do with Free Will. He'd been duped by Satan himself. Easy pickings, and, oh, the shame of it.

There were more tables than usual near the stern's lifebelts, casting a cross-hatch of shadows on the small deck space so he took a few shots. Also of a black Celica tailing the boat along the Porte de Passy. With the smell of new paint still strong in the clinging heat, he edged round the crowd of diners darkened by glass. Saw Duvivier and Vidal sitting close together over a pastis with Cacheux ever attentive, like a white paper sculpture in his sharp new suit.

Four exposures left.

Good word, that. One for each of them, which is only fair.

Mathieu then made his way down to the *toilettes*, borne by waves of conversations and sudden laughter. There, he plucked out the roll of Fuji Colour from the camera and hid it tight inside his briefs next to his folded, forbidden portrait.

XLII

As *Roquette IV* slid between the narrow confines of the Allée des Cygnes and the Porte Georges Pompidou, people moved to its deck's rails to see Barnard's modernist Maison de Radio France rear up in the hazy sunlight.

Vidal finished his second Ricard and let his glass rock back and fore in his hand, gripping tighter as tension took hold. It was time to act. Time to focus, for Duvivier had received a message from Toussirot cancelling the choir's trip to St. Sébastien, due to Father Anselme's angina. The Bishop hadn't had the guts to tell him personally. Bad move. Not just for him.

"Nature calls." He suddenly scraped back his chair still aware of Cacheux directly behind. "Éxcusez-moi." He smiled for the benefit of others close by, but really wanted to knee the clinging creep in his balls.

Duvivier simply stared at his beer mat, focussed only on what he'd recently revealed to Vidal. But sharing his problems hadn't halved them, rather increased his anxiety as to how the man from Lanvière might abuse his vulnerability. Hadn't he already had a preview with the Jaliberts? Quite an impressive performance by any standards.

Well, so be it. Déchaux can screw him instead.

The one name he'd withheld on pain of death, but his own crucifixion was to be a silent and secret affair.

He was now so deep in that man's dark pocket there was only one method of repayment, and Duvivier shivered despite the clinging heat. Déchaux had connived with the malleable coroner at the Judicial Enquiry to write the word Suicide on his father's death certificate, helped by the addition of binder twine and a Whitebeam tree. But he'd threatened to relieve the priest of his legacy by his namesake's day, if anything further went awry. Everything to lose, he'd said. And that didn't just mean francs. The burial plot next to his mother as well.

In the name of Jesus, what is life if I can't end it there?

From his eye corner he saw the white suit move to follow Vidal. Down the little faux marble steps, too well lit, too public, but Cacheux stayed close, and the moment his *amour fou* chose a cubicle, he was on him.

The lavatory still smelt of Gauloises, and to Cacheux's surprise, his living icon, tense and silent, let him bring down his zip and begin to stroke with a connoisseur's care.

"Anges de Dieu..."

Tessier all over again. What is it about angels? But this one's a living corpse. Blind to the snare...

Vidal let him cup his balls then letting both thumbs stray along to the frenulum, stretching him, drawing the blood along until he finally clasped the pulsing shaft with a moist, pale hand.

"Now see what God in his goodness has given me," murmured Cacheux.

"My turn now."

Cacheux's prick was jutting from his suit, jerking its desire. "It's for you, Robert. Take it. I've waited my whole life for this..." His pleading dissolved into different tears, his face a crumple of longing.

Vidal obliged, kneeling so his boots were wedged between the lavatory bowl and the partition. No gaps, perfectly private, and as a prelude to his confession, he closed his eyes. His aniseed tongue then toyed with the queer's purpling helmet beneath its foreskin, tasting anchovies, making it bob and throb, taking the queer to his limits while his own cock stayed inert in Cacheux's grasp. The symphony of gasps and groans suddenly quickened when his mouth was on it, gliding from end to end, cushioning his teeth with his wet lips.

No pubic hair. Instead, the waxed *mons veneris* resembled a mound of duck breast, and the scrotum below, two bald damsons. Crystallised, ready.

"God help me," moaned the queer, but the predator from Lanvière was waiting for the exact moment when Cacheux's prayer for mercy would reach its most urgent height. When as anticipated, that cry became a cry for all eternity, the wolf was ready.

XLIII

Guy Baralet prised open the blinds of his office window at the top of the Medex building in Lanvière, and peered down at the Rue Marchessant.

His wife was late.

The sun's brightness made him scan rather than linger on the scene below. Five floats decked out with fruit and vegetables and a little girl dressed as The Green Spirit perched on the middle lorry. Ten years to the day since his daughter Céline had done the same. But she was different now from most of Lanvière's young. She had a job. She was a perfect dentist in Nancy, making perfect teeth. Rebuilding with the latest porcelain and acrylics so her wealthy patients could smile again.

If only our kind and clever child could do the same for me. But I mustn't ask too much...

He fiddled with his blotter till it lay parallel to the desk edge, and for the third time restacked his pens into the ceramic pot she'd made at school, then rang for Marie-Claude.

"Yes, sir?"

"Would you see if my wife's downstairs? Tell her I'm waiting."

This temp wasn't prone to smiling either. Smart to a fault, never a crease or hair out of place, but she wasn't Colette, and he still hadn't got used to her at his cherished secretary's desk. The moment his right-hand superwoman returned, this one would get short shrift. Unemployment or no unemployment.

13.58. Come on, Lise.

She was never late. Couldn't afford to be, as funerals don't wait for flowers to grow. Besides, with her business Fleur de Lise, she was known for her unfailing reliability.

You promised.

Since Colette had vanished, only he would lock the office, there being too much at stake in the Files Strong-room for him to trust anyone else, let alone the replacement secretary. He'd even put New York on hold until she showed up. Her audio and shorthand were his lifeline and he wasn't prepared to swim alone with unknown quantities.

The bell from La Sainte Vierge was also late. Its two o'clock chimes mingled with cheers from the local crowd as the procession moved off towards the Place 11 Novembre. Even though he'd never set foot in the place, he'd just been touched by Bishop Toussirot for 10,000 francs to restore the decapitated Virgin.

The cheque lay unsigned in his drawer. Also, Colette had asked him to help with the purchase of new copies of Pérotin's Quadrupla for the choir. That was different, and how could he refuse? Although he'd thought it a rather odd request at the time.

The books had been delivered just before poor Moussac's funeral, and a moving letter of thanks from Father Jean-Baptiste had arrived ending with an invitation to come and hear his choir. No, thank you; he'd replied in his own handwriting. *My family and my work is my religion, besides, incense is like the breath of the dying. Forgive me.*

The temp reappeared.

"Monsieur? Your wife isn't there."

"Are you sure?"

The girl looked put out.

"OK," he said. "Thanks. Any calls that come in for me here, transfer to reception. Just in case."

Within thirty seconds, Colette's diary was safe in his inside pocket, his office locked and triple checked.

Lise, for God's sake...

The lift was crammed with employees coming down from lunch in the canteen, so he half ran half slid to the bottom of the shallow stairs.

"In a hurry?" asked one of the guys from Research.

"Seen my wife anywhere?"

"I'd know if I had," he smiled. "Anything wrong?"

"I bloody hope not." As the receptionist stared up from behind her glass partition, in the car park Barelet searched for the familiar red Punto.

Rien.

His Safrane's interior was like a furnace until the air conditioning sighed into action and he noticed with dismay that a boiled sweet had liquefied next to his cigar. He could hear the carnival lorries moving closer. He'd have been better off walking or even picking her up from the shop.

Hindsight is the Devil's tease...

His fingers drummed against the warm steel as he followed a posse of schoolchildren turning cartwheels into the Rue Montbois. Saw too, the freckles on his hand conspiring towards old age, but not with Medex. Not now. Natolyn had just taken some bad press after a date-rape trial in St. Die. Besides, the company had let him down over Colette and maybe he should reword his insouciant reply to the priest and look into the deals for early retirement.

No-one had been willing to go to the police. Not even the bloody caretaker. So a week ago, he'd gone solo to the Gendarmerie, seen Noblet, the young agent, and asked for a daily update to be faxed to his office. What had he been sent? Nothing. It was a sick farce.

Suddenly he spotted the Punto parked in front of the Telephone Exchange, its legend FLEURS DE LISE along the doors, bright gold in the sun. His wife was in the driver's seat, motionless, head bowed.

What the Hell's going on?

"Lise?" He yelled, crashing his gear into third and swerved across into the slip road. When her reached her, he leant in and embraced her. The scent of freesias, from inside the van, was overpowering. "Mon ange? Tell me."

"It's been awful. I knew something was wrong the minute I started unloading the wreaths for tomorrow. I was rushing, trying to get to you before the procession started..."

"And? Come on..."

"These two skinheads, about eighteen, nineteen, were hanging around by the shop, and when I drove off they followed."

"Bastards."

"I was terrified they were after money, as Madame Duforge and the restaurant had just paid me."

"What make of car? Did you get any of its number?" Baralet felt his hands begin to sweat, the back of his neck to tingle. A warning he'd learnt to trust.

"Citroën. Saxo, I think. Blue. But I just wanted to get away, give them the slip. Christ..." She violently shook her head as though that would somehow lose it all. "I went everywhere. To Stenay, to Montmédy... Thank God I'd enough petrol. They didn't though. I passed them on my way back. Serve them bloody right. They looked pathetic, half up the verge."

Not so pathetic. They know her shop, they know her car, and Medex.

He suddenly held her tighter and felt her heartbeat on his. Then he detached her car's mobile phone but just as quickly replaced it.

"What's the matter?"

"Look, Lise, I think we're being tapped. Left right and centre. How else would they know we were going to the Gendarmerie? I tell you, this whole thing's beginning to bloody stink."

He didn't normally swear. Didn't normally perspire. But she had to tell him the rest. "I've noticed one of them before, but didn't think anything of it."

"Where?"

"I was delivering a bouquet to old Madame Blainville from her daughter in Lyons. Apartments Cornay in the Rue de l'Église..."

"Colette lives there."

"Well, this thin youth was on the first landing, I remember. Smoking." She paused, hearing the procession throb over the roundabout and down the Rue Montbois. "He looked pretty evil. Just sort of stared at me."

"Oh Lise. Someone's trying to stop us finding Colette. I mean for God's sake, I told the world I was worried about the way she'd not come back from that Mass. That I was going to get it investigated. What an idiot I've been."

Although his wife stayed silent, her eyes spoke with fresh tears.

"No you haven't, but there's our daughter as well."

"She's a big girl now, and we have to move. Come on, I'll drive."

***

At three o'clock, an hour later than arranged, the Managing Director of Medex Pharmaceuticals and his wife sat down with Lieutenant Audugard in the Gendarmerie and told him their phones were no longer private and their lives were in danger. They also threatened him with his Superior, the Préfet de Police unless the hunt for mother and son was made urgently and conspicuously public and their line was cleared.

Finally, Guy Baralet also left him her diary, in which the last entry dated August 20th was the most interesting of all and nothing to do with the office.

Robert. Out of Villerscourt. 10 a.m. tomorrow – Paris. R-V TBC.

XLIV

Thursday October 2nd. 03.59 hrs.

"One must know three things if one is to write an Organum; how to begin, how to proceed and how to conclude."

How apt, I must say.

Father Jean-Baptiste carefully laid shaving cream on his cheeks, and while he waited for his skin to soften for the razor, used his mobile to dial home in the Rue Fosse.

04.06, and François Vidal, his father, spat his annoyance at the interruption. His son smiled under the foam and ended the call without a word, leaving his lodger sleepless and wondering who the Hell that had been.

The diver finished shaving and slapped water over his face. The Seine would be colder, filthier than this. Ayache had already tried him in oil and shit, at different depths testing the radio and re-breather, and been more than pleased. Vidal shut his eyes, something he'd not done all night, and rehearsed each minutiae in his mind. Then finally prayed that the old *clochard* would be in his usual dossing place on the Port de la Conférence and had read the script.

The priest from La Sainte Vierge arranged all his gear on the bed. Neoprene suit and undersuit, torch, twin hose regulator, knife, and specially silenced compressor. Then, forgetting he was naked, checked the southern sky from the window where smog blanketed the city as far as his eye could see. Nothing of the Louvre, the Pompidou, or Notre-Dame. Even St. Sébastien was veiled for the day. But not in his heart.

Excellent. Merci.

He would deal with Toussirot when this was all over.

First, his eyes. He squeezed in Opticlaire and blinked until his sight returned.

Merciful Guardian Angels, may I live so Perotinus lives... Deo gratias...

He hummed through the tenor part of Viderunt Omnes as he pulled on his black jock strap, then suddenly stopped, remembering the queer's repugnant display on the boat.

A pity he still lives.

04.16 a.m.

The dawn although still persisting in its mystery, failed to muffle the first Shofar blast from the neighbouring Marais.

Rosh Hashanah with a vengeance. The cry of war. If that's what they want, so be it. Now the broken sounds. But we mustn't be fooled into thinking they represent la condition humaine. In the shit called humanity, some are more equal than others. How simple, how literal it all is. And limited to one purpose only, despite what the Torah says. A pity the great masters Leoninus and Perotinus have passed them by, so the gutter is where they stay. To my mind. And like Nebuchadnezzar I ask if their God can save them...

The *curé* from the Meuse zipped up the dry-suit leaving the hood to lie flat under the black tee and matching jeans. Anonymous and easy to shift, part of the shadows by the Bridge of the Soul, under the gaze of the old Zouave sculpture who only yesterday had stood in water up to his chest.

He placed everything in readiness by the door and made a cup of coffee with the things provided. All scaled down, even the cellophaned cookies – camping size for the tourists and commercial travellers in perpetual motion. He was different in every way from them, with almost too much time, the *cartes de visites* of other more tangential thoughts arriving like uninvited guests.

Plagnol was due at 5.24 with just a bag each and the Semtex. Nothing obvious, then the casual drop by the plane tree with the litter bin. Father Jean-Baptiste found his rosary, and used each bead as an *aide-mémoire* until he was satisfied; until he could plan no more, while the backdrop of wailing notes from the Synagogue in the Avenue Chény permeated his brain.

Father forgive me.

Then he lay on the bed in a strangely altered state, as though Hypoxia had taken hold. The pristine room, the hospital curtains, and glimpse of white bowls and receptacles for bodily fluids and solids in the en suite. The bed like a slab and one reason he'd not slept. And now he knew. It was in reality, a birthing bed, a place of hard labour, and above, to the left, hung all the accoutrements for invasive inducement.

A saline drip with its forcing bag, a black sphygmomanometer looped around itself, and a pewter dish for the collection of blood.

He curled up, aware of his pulse quickening as his body slackened under the rubber casing, sweating, slippery, but trying not to be born.

An infant can survive in water as its lungs involuntarily contract, so here I am. Oh, Mother, I have sinned against you. I have broken the Sixth Commandment into a thousand pieces, so what now do I have to lose?

And as though to absolve him, the dream of St. Dominic's mother filled him like a rising sea, and he swam untrammelled in her bloated womb as she cried for his birth. Her longing filled his ears with echoes, deep, deep below the disturbance of boats where only the sturgeon lays its spawn and trawls the bed for worms.

Thus the priest from the Meuse flatlands slept like a baby until a knock on the door at 05.00 hrs brought him to his senses.

05.22 hrs. He dialled his home in the Rue Fosse again, this time from the car. But instead of his father's reassuring rage, there was no reply.

XLV

Day 1 of the Ten Days of Repentance. Thou shalt not kill. But I say Deo Gratias for small mercies. My jeans etc. sink without trace, unlike Father Xavier-Marie's rosary, which, although he tried to reclaim it, for all we know has already reached the Île St. Germain.

It's quiet. Almost too quiet, but still dark enough, which is all that matters. Our Father is with me. And my mother. I can feel it but, what the Hell's this?

Merde. Father André said no dogs, and true, we'd never seen one here, but this one's staring hunger and hope, so at least I'm safe.

His nose is on my leg as I crawl the last metre to the gap of water, his smell curdled by the mist. I've only four minutes, but being a dog, he is unaware of such constraints and places himself underneath, obviously valuing his life more than mine. That is the pity of it and, like Tessier he is easy.

I slide into darkness, without a signal, of course. Colder than the lake at Les Cailles, but the current isn't too unhelpful. Marcel was right though. Visibility nil, and the water's thick like isinglass with the oil and scum worse near the ropes. So my fingers take over...

Twelve seconds till the fucking beam comes round, and I'm counting. Voilà. Two turns left, one to the right. Now the plastic – so discreet in so many ways, but it's not appropriate now to think apocalyptically. That's their problem.

The little womb door closes, like the laundry men said it would, which is comforting in a comfortless world, don't you think? And where, I ask myself, would we be without friends?

I can hear air bubbling through the exhaust valve as I drop to 3.75 metres to avoid the boat's stern. Now, two hundred and thirty strokes upriver to the Pont des Invalides, past the old soldier then on to the steps. My breathing's good. Pulse normal.

It's black under here, blacker than Hell, but I'm not alone. Something brushes my leg. It can't be the dog, the current's wrong, but whatever it is, it's big. It's human. My size. Jesus help me. I get out quick, thinking of Le Bébé. Mon Dieu. No, it can't be...

I kick my rubber skin off into the flow, then I wait for the blood to return to my hands. Christ, that was close. I see the filthy tramp exactly where he should be. Thank God for creatures of habit. I want to tell him what I've seen but there is still Task Five to accomplish.

His grizzled mouth jerks on some dream and suddenly his snores grind to silence as I finish ahead of schedule and steal his clothes. They cling to me, stinking wet, but no matter, it's all give and take, for with a quiet push, he slips obligingly into his first decent bath.

***

No fishermen, not yet. But another dog who shits where my friend had his bed. I like that. Come to think of it, Colette always said I had a nice sense of humour when I wasn't laughing at Jews. It does come in useful sometimes I can tell you.

Colette…? That's strange. For a moment when I surfaced I thought I saw her, but maybe it's just the cast of the new light.

And talking of lights, they've just come on in the Bateaux Mouches. The cleaners are in. Then the laundry vans, Jalibert et Fils. Lined up neatly, taking care. Three of them, thank God for that. One must trust them utterly, although I still have a problem with the boy, Marcel.

The mist lasts as long as I need it. God again on my side, not theirs, and Mother Seine bears all her sons away as traffic builds up along the Cours-la-Reine – stops and starts, the whispers of other lives. A breeze, cold and fresh. I've got dog shit on my shoe which The Pigface won't like. Good. Start as I mean to go on…

06.36. Notre-Dame's in the clear now and in just over six hours all my Jews will be snuffling into their sauce nivernois, slipping the caviare down their throats. Then the honey sweetmeats, for a happy and prosperous New Year. Ignoring the heart of my soul, and deaf to the chants of Our Lady's choir. Reddening the water.

A girl gives me ten francs. She smells of the kind of flowers brought in for Toussaint. Something I can never forget. There's concern in her eyes, but I'm afraid it's misplaced.

"Jean-Baptiste?"

I confess I'd not heard the car. I was expecting the Laguna but get the queer instead, in something red. A Xantia. What's going on? Where's Plagnol? Merde alors. Cacheux's white as a wafer. For a moment as I climb in, he watches the girl's legs, her scarf blown against her mouth as she crosses the bridge. Then he says with his eyes she doesn't matter. As if I bloody well care.

"Where's Plagnol?" That does matter.

"Sniffing round some pouffiasse near the Place du Canada."

I knew it. Crétin. Worse. A man whose olfactory parameters are limited to cunt is a liability. Proven.

I try not to look Cacheux in the eye when I thank him, and although it hurts to say so, the queer has probably saved my life.

"All part of the service."

I get in.

The polythene skin covering my seat sighs as I sit down. He's come well prepared, and because he has the advantage, he takes it. His hand's on my knee and stays there. He lights a Silk Cut and passes it to me, but as I'm still trembling it falls into my lap.

"You OK?"

"So so."

"I'm still sore, you know." He retrieves the cigarette for me, taking longer than necessary. *Draws hard then kills it. His left hand rests on his fly.* "Would you like to see?"

I feel vomit rising.

He drives past the end of the Quai D'Orsay towards the Place de la Résistance, trapped too long in the shadows of stuff from Spain. He bites his lip till it's blue.

One eye in the rear view mirror and his deep frown has changed him. For the first time, fear leaches into my stomach. Wrong place, wrong time. Maybe.

The white Laguna, like a whale, suddenly lies close up, nudging us. Cacheux's heel's on the floor but the cobbles are winning.

Merde.

The lights are in our favour over the river again, weaving a web into the Place de la Concorde, wide and grey. But I'm too numb to fart.

"Fuck it." *He slots in a CD. Songs of the Auvergne. Not him at all. Something's definitely up. He pushes me off the wheel with half a word. A crack of glass before his head butts the window. His blood, the dog's blood – all the same. Babylon and catastrophe. I pull up, stroke his cheek, which he'll be sure to misinterpret, then try to exit, but Plagnol's already there. His pig face peering in, too busy smiling to notice that same black Toyota and its blonde driver as it sweeps past.*

"Use this!" *Cacheux's quick with his shirt at least, but the wound has a life of its own. It's disconcerting to see the queer's blood so much deeper than mine, whatever that means. Have I been sold short? I wonder, taking over, making him lie on the back seat. We can't risk being seen. When I look up, that Celica's gone and my phone is ringing.*

It's 6.59. "Melon to the Wine Merchant…"

I take the message and pretend no problems, when in reality we have an emergency. There's a tunnel south west of the Port de la Tournelle. That's where we rendezvous afterwards. Meanwhile, I'm beginning to suspect there are too many worm holes in these Elysian Fields.

Hélas.

XLVI

At the moment when the Breton cast his mother's rosary into the water and watched its refusal to sink, Nelly Augot accompanied by Colette, pulled on the bell rope outside 50, Rue de St. Aubin in the 5ième.

Five storeys of oxidised stone reared upwards to the yellow sky, its overall austerity unaffected by a row of filigree balconies on the third floor and upper dormer windows jutting from a steep mansard roof. Colette still felt a wreck, despite four hours' sleep in Cubzénaut station's new waiting room and a wash under her clothes with hot water.

"I speak first. OK?" But Nelly looked pale behind her charity-shop glasses and Colette saw her hand tremble as she pulled the bell rope again. "Come on Monsieur Père Supérieur. Get your bloody skates on."

After several minutes an old woman wearing a white servant's cap and matching apron kept the door on its chain. She'd seen enough street dossers and *marginaux* to know better than to open up. Colette knew exactly what she must be thinking. Their clothes from Beau Monde in Guizac made an esoteric collection – Nelly in leggings and a red sweatshirt appliqued with sheep. She herself sporting a rust-coloured beret and maternity trousers. But nothing had prepared her for the painful memories they brought. Hadn't she worn exactly the same all those years ago with Bertrand nestled safe inside her? Now the waist was bunched and tied with an elastic band under an equally baggy blouse. But none of this mattered. The first priority was here.

"In your best Parisian, now. Go on." she whispered to Nelly. Then realised the woman in front of them was profoundly deaf.

"Madame, we've an appointment with the Abbot of Lagrange Vivray."

"You have?" The old housekeeper's voice, after her lip-reading, was inordinately loud and deep. "But it's his birthday."

"Well then, we can come and give the old *con* our *félicitations*."

"Nelly!"

However, the woman was still curious enough to undo the chain, and skewed her head towards them, her hearing aid glistening in her right ear like a huge wax abscess.

"Our appointment with him is for midday, as we know he goes to St. Nicholas after lunch," Nelly lied convincingly.

"Your names?" Two watery eyes looked the visitors up and down.

Hesitation. "What now?"

"I'm giving mine," whispered Colette.

"OK."

The old girl showed no reaction except to wipe an eye with her cuff.

"I'm Madame Gramme. You'd better come in."

"Excellent. *Merci.*"

The housekeeper led them into a gloomy hallway tiled in a muted Art Deco design and smelling faintly of pork simmering somewhere in the house's nether regions. "Watch the steps," she said, opening another door to sudden darkness in which she took a candle from a holder on the wall and lit it.

"No way. I'm not going down there." Colette hung back, fear gripping her legs.

"Look, we can't let him wriggle out of this, not after everything you've been through." Nelly tried to take her hand, but Colette pulled away, crying out as the Great Bell from Notre-Dame boomed out midday, reviving all her terrors.

"Just remember."

"I am."

"Come on, then."

The stairs ended on stone flags with gaps so wide Nelly almost keeled over in her unfamiliar shoes while their guide was nimble and sure-footed in the wavering light.

Suddenly she stopped for there was nowhere else to go.

"Your Lordship!" She knocked at a studded door that was part of the blackness. "Your three o'clock appointment's here."

Colette's stomach tightened.

"Entrez."

Madame Gramme disappeared, leaving them an expanse of Persian carpet that stretched away to the far wall. Crimson and ultramarine wool glowed in the candlelight. Of the Abbot there was no sign, until Nelly went over to an embroidered screen and stood on tiptoe to see over the top. Colette joined her and gasped.

"Do come closer so I may see you." An old man's voice rang out. But Christian Désespoir was upside down, his blood-filled head cradled by a foam pad. His thin grey pony tail curled on the floor alongside. Colette stared transfixed by the man's velveteen suit, replica of an eighteenth century hunting costume. By his sinewy agility.

"Happy Birthday, by the way." Her voice flinty hard, ignored Nelly's gesture to leave well alone.

"That's most awfully kind," he replied. "But first may I have the honour of knowing who shares my celebration? And who lied about having made an appointment?"

Colette calmed herself. She was here for others, not herself.

"Madame Bataille and Mademoiselle Augot. We do have an urgent matter to discuss, your Lordship. It was the only way."

He closed his eyes, then his legs quivered with indecision. Finally, his body curved over, still supported by two large white hands, knuckles rising like sunken rocks until he could stand.

"Ah. That's better. Blood to the head, so important as one gets older, don't you think?"

The Abbot de Lagrange Vivray rearranged his jacket that had hung off him like the split cupule of a beech nut. His cheeks a startling pink in the cadaverous face, and eyes so deep like Duvivier's, that Colette could only guess his thoughts. "Eighty-three today, blessed by the Lord's bountiful Grace." He crossed himself and went over to a wide window with, it appeared, no view.

Colette stared at it too.

An aquarium with no fish. How bloody weird.

She and Nelly peered at some tunnel's ancient brick wall and the dark almost black beyond. Something was moving inside it, probably rats.

"Ugh!" Nelly grimaced.

"But fascinating, don't you think, ladies? We can see in, but alas, nothing can see out." He took the biggest chair for himself and pointed to two smaller ones, each with a drawer under the seat. "Where others favour a vista from a normal window, I have pure history."

"History?" Nelly ventured.

"Indeed. This unique tunnel leads to the Seine. S..e..i..n..e. Fluctuet nec mergitur. Which reminds me," he poured out three glasses of Château La Voile and raised his own to a sinister smile. "Your very good health."

The Graves wine looked too much like blood and Colette demurred, seeing her mission evaporate.

"In 1794 this very section was stuffed with the corpses of our noble French," he continued. "But mark my words, it'll come again. This time, from over there." He pointed north towards The Marais over the Île de St. Louis. Three kilometres as the crow flies to the Unknown Jewish Martyr in the Avenue Geoffroy l'Asnier. So you see, I like to have an outlook on this singular piece of the world. To witness new history being made."

Colette and Nelly exchanged glances, and for something to do, Nelly put the wineglass to her lips and drank.

"I think my papa hid somewhere down here during the riots in May '68." She said suddenly, and Colette reached over to take her hand. But already the Abbot's skin had crinkled into fragile folds across his forehead.

"A child of Marx, *oui*?"

"You could say that. He was proud of what the protesters did. Down with the status quo, long live the revolution."

Colette squeezed Nelly's arm. This wasn't the place or the time, and her time was running out. She took a deep breath.

"Your Lordship. Since August 24th we've just endured the most degrading and terrifying time of our lives with the Pauvres Soeurs down in Libourne. Look what they've done to us. And we're not the only ones. But I had special treatment." She showed him her bare eyelids, then whipped off her beret to reveal her shorn head. He looked at her, unblinking. "Tell me why, and what will you do to punish them?"

His expression changed again. Now reptilian and dangerous, all the blood gone from his face. "You've made an absurd mistake, Madame Bataille. All religious orders have certain traditions. All for good reasons."

Nelly's snigger made him look her way.

"Are you calling me a liar?" Colette began to shake.

"I am saying you are deluded, and to me, an untutored eye, your blemishes seem – how shall I put it – like self-mutilation."

Their anger was drowned by a telephone's sudden ring and the birthing stutter of a fax. Both women looked round for the source, but beyond the candlelight, the room was secretively obscure. Then the Abbot opened the double doors of a large Louis XVI cabinet on to an array of the latest technology. PC, modems, sound boxes, the works.

Website, Internet. He's got the whole world in his wicked hands...

"So there *is* electricity," whispered Colette.

"Excuse me a moment," he called. "Help yourselves to more refreshment, do."

Désespoir studied the faxed letter then twisted it into a taper for the candle flame to devour.

Well, well. Our Georges is nothing if not thorough, though he does tend to forget I am now in my eighty-fourth year. He really should climb off my back.

He shut the cabinet and carried the same candle over to Colette.

"So why exactly are you both here, pestering an old man. What do you expect me to do?"

He held it too close; the flame breathed hot on her cheek. She had nothing to lose, and like Jéhanne d'Arc, the vision of her purpose sustained her.

"I've seen proof that you own The Pauvres Soeurs des Souffrances and you manage everything there. I was Number 45, unfortunately. Is that significant to you?" She raised her voice. "Well, it was to them. They had to have that magic total, of course they didn't bank on poor sweet Chloë Doumiez's state of mind."

"She died," Nelly said simply.

"But she wasn't meant to. They didn't take into account her despair. She was just another innocent, another sucker to keep the whole sick show going, whatever is going on down there. And I was treated worse than a dog. At least dogs aren't given truth drugs. Look!" She showed the Abbot the purple souvenirs on her inner arm, but he was studying the label on the wine bottle.

"I used to work for Medex, and the Natolyn they shoved in me was their latest product. I should know. So I've come to inform you," she looked over at Nelly who'd slumped as though dozing in the chair, "that when I get home I'll be taking legal advice. Abduction is dangerous too, Seigneur."

Désespoir turned his back on her to face the tunnel again as she continued. "There I was, looking for my son in the Bois de Boulogne just before the Pope's Mass, when along comes the caring, concerned Saint Agnès." Her sarcasm made him start. "She lures me and Nelly into what we thought was an ordinary hostel, but my friend here got out early. She was lucky, while I was drugged and taken to your special Hell hole..."

"What a loyal friend you have," he sneered. "Who needs enemies?"

Colette bit her lip. Let it go.

"Now I want all my things back. My money, 900 francs, two credit cards and a photo of my boy. I also had a car. A turquoise Peugeot 306. God knows what's happened to that."

Christian Désespoir turned round to smile first at Nelly and then Colette. It stretched his dry lips but left his eyes untouched.

"But we're sure that St. Anne's hostel has something to do with all this." Colette was undeterred. "Who's that Antoinette woman that your Agnès obviously knew? And why were those swastikas daubed in the Refuge's cellar? Someone's harmless doodling? Hardly. So what the Hell's going on?" she shouted. "Because Hell is where I've been."

"My dear, Madame, you're in danger of committing a slander. I have not the faintest idea what you're talking about. Distressing as all this sounds..."

"Distressing? My God!" Colette glared up at him. "If it wasn't for Nelly here, I'd have died."

"Ah, Nelly. Such a charming name," yet he spoke as if it was shit on his shoe. "Such a pity, too. Oh dear..."

"What do you mean?"

"I think, Madame, your companion is feeling unwell. Perhaps it's the air, or lack of it. Shall I call Madame Gramme?"

Colette saw her friend now sprawled motionless in her chair. A smile of red wine augmented her mouth. Her glass was empty.

Merde...

"Wake up! Wake up!" She looked at Désespoir who was still smiling. "What have you done?"

"Tiring of your accusations, Madame. Your friend is merely sleepy."

But the pulse was low, both eyes open, unseeing behind her comical glasses. Colette remembered Nelly's gun, and on the pretext of loosening the waist of her leggings, felt for it while his gaze followed her every move. Suddenly, it was in her hand. Something she'd never done before. Now it pointed at his head. He didn't flinch.

"Let us out of here so she can get to hospital."

"Now wait a moment..."

But she'd already grabbed Nelly around the chest and backed towards the door. Her friend's weapon still dangerously poised. "Turn the bloody lights on for a start. You're as evil as the rest of them."

"Madame, you'll regret these words. You came to me, remember, under a gross misapprehension, when in fact it is your actions which are evil, and worse. Heretical."

That word again. He knows. Gentle Mother Mary, when is this going to end?

"You spoke of priests – our Brothers in God – who are fornicators and murderers who use the Lord's church on earth as a cover for their aberrations. Madame, what in Heaven's name do you expect us to do?"

Us?

His own weapon came from nowhere. Bigger than hers in every way. And unlike her, he probably knew how to use it. His hand steady. Yes, he knew alright.

"Our women injured by your friend here, have just informed me you'd be armed."

Our women? They must have sent that fax. Oh, Jesus.

To save her own life, Colette propped Nelly up in front of her. The most cowardly thing she'd ever done and, in that split second, prayed for forgiveness.

"So you'd rather kill both of us? See where that'll get you." Her voice had shrivelled with fear.

"It may have escaped your notice that I have considerably less far, chronologically, to go than you, but it's not that which pre-occupies me. You are troublesome, Madame Bataille, just like your son, I'm sorry to say. And more's the pity you didn't properly savour your wine. At least Mademoiselle Augot has co-operated."

"So you've drugged her?"

Another sick, sick smile.

"And you've just called my son troublesome. Why?"

"Because it's true."

A wave of panic suddenly swamped Colette's every nerve, every muscle.

This was the Devil himself, with velvet wrinkles under each knee. "Hand over the gun," he snapped, taking aim again. "Now."

"Do it," breathed Nelly. "Just do it."

Damn you.

She did.

"Thank you, Madame. That's one less worry to deal with."

Colette helped Nelly regain her balance, then tried to think.

"This bastard's got a phone. I could try Guy Baralet's number, but I've forgotten it. What about your mama?"

"We can't rely on her."

"I'll have to."

"What are you doing, pray?" Désespoir's pistol still at her eye level.

"Keep away from me."

She pushed sideways against his desk, loaded with books and papers.

He watched as she dialled the prostitute in St. Denis.

No reply. Not even an answerphone.

Dammit.

"I told you..." Nelly sagged against her, draining what little strength she had, as Colette felt the forces of darkness engulf them both again. She was Eve once more, seeking the shadow of trees while a black-winged angel chased her from the Garden; out of Paradise and into everlasting torment. Childless and withering to dust.

The Abbot's smile returned to partner Schumann's *Kinderszenen* flowing into the room. Nelly began to moan and heave in turn.

"If she dies..." said Colette. "Then…"

"She won't. This is a temporary lapse. You'll see…"

"Uuuurrggh!" Nelly couldn't help herself.

"Oh dear. My precious carpet." He fished inside his collar and pressed his panic button. Immediately, sounds of rabbit feet nearing the door. Then Madame Gramme appeared, wiping her hands.

"Yes, your Lordship?"

"A bowl, towel and carpet cleaner, please."

"Very well."

"Madame!" Colette yelled after her. "Help us, please."

She tried to reach her while the door was still ajar, but like the Gates of Hell, it slammed shut in her face. Nelly's eyes flickered. Drenched in sweat, she trembled like something wild, newborn, but Colette held her tight while the Abbot settled himself back in his chair and prepared his pipe. Once his thin, white fingers had pushed the last wayward strand of tobacco into the polished, wooden nest, he began his story like the summer snake peeling off

205

its slough.

How his name – in true mediaeval fashion – was eponymous with a hamlet near St. Èmilion, and how as *'un haut fonctionnaire'* in Bordeaux in 1943, his paperwork had earned him the title *'Le Génie des Documents.'* How, after the Abbey he'd founded at Vivray in 1952 had succumbed to the lack of faith and commitment shown by the country's young men, he'd turned to susceptible women. The Pauvres Soeurs des Souffrances were a small cog in the wheel to save France from its Zionist stranglehold.

Just then, Nelly lurched from Colette's grasp sending another spray of vomit over the floor as the front door bell chime filled the room and the housekeeper scuttled in to whisper in his ear.

"Where's the bowl etcetera?" he demanded.

"I've been too busy watching out..."

"What for?"

Their eyes met. Tense, fearful. Not needing words.

"Take them both to the scullery. Vite, Madame."

This time she nodded.

How could they protest? The old witch had a gun too, deep in her apron pocket, and as the bell chimed again, in frantic impatience, Nelly and Colette found themselves in a cold room next to the kitchen, where, apart from a large white sink and a frayed old towel, wall-to-wall tins of everything under the sun had been arranged in size order, as if a siege was expected. With icy water thrown at her face, Nelly began to revive, and the vomiting stopped.

"Why didn't you help when I begged you?" Colette challenged the housekeeper. "She could have choked on her own sick." Then realised she'd probably gone to fetch her gun. As scared as they were.

"Too busy."

"Here?"

"You've no idea. Always entertaining is the Abbot. Has to keep up appearances with those who matter. And as he can't cook, it's down to me."

Meanwhile, Christian Désespoir had picked up his phone on the third ring, staring warily at the lounge door as he did so.

"Many happy returns, my good friend," said the man who'd just faxed him. The man he hated most. "Are we alone?"

A trick question. Be careful.

"Apart from Madame Gamme, both troublemakers are out of sight, out of mind. They arrived here forty minutes ago."

"Excellent. Just checking. Backs up what I've seen. And as a thank you, I can reveal you're about to receive an even better birthday gift. The most perfect ever."

"When?"

"Soon. Just listen, and I'll call you again."

XLVII

At 13.32 hours, not everyone heard the booming blast and terrified shrieks coming from the Seine. Certainly not the three women in the scullery of 50, Rue St. Aubin where the sound of running water had grumbled and spurted its way from the antediluvian tap.

The din of death was borne on an easterly breeze which, during the morning, had cleared the haze over the city, giving the thirty-eight revellers on *Roquette IV* a perfect view of the city. Then sirens like sopranos singing from Hell suddenly tainted the early afternoon, shredding autumn's fragile beauty into shrouds, while ten minutes later, helicopters of the Terrorist Police added the bass to the symphony of despair.

The phone again as promised. Désespoir's hand shook on the receiver.

"Happy New Year." His caller shouted above a background tinkling of glasses and laughter a-plenty.

"I hope it will be."

"Oh, come on Christian. Lighten up, do."

"I'll try."

"Good. Right, places to go. People to see. You know how it is, dear friend."

"Indeed." The Abbot looked at the wine in his glass. The same red porphyry that now bathed the pleasure boat. "Tell me, Georges. That other friend – on your face..."

"What of it?"

"I know someone who can treat it. A very good man in Auxerre."

"My dear Christian, we've had enough surgery for one day, don't you think? By the way, I found some Tintin get-well cards for Claude and Romy – *ma souris rouge*. What do you think? A good idea?"

"Quite charming."

"Well, I'm glad to say both our girls are almost back to active service. A few more days of physio, then we move in... Oh, by the way, my friend..."

"Yes?"

"Keep our *Verräteren* – our traitors – secure until the 16th, when all the fuss will have died down. Understood? You'll be getting instructions."

"Good."

Yet the Abbot felt an old stomach ulcer reassert itself, and tension constrict his throat. Normally, on another less important day, he and the général would have both eaten well in the dining room, courtesy of Madame Gramme, on a large oval table decked out in Breton lace. Dark foods – at the général's request, unlike the recent banquet on the *Bateau-Mouche*. olives and cèpes with the earth still on their skins, pork studded in prunes, and for dessert, a roulade

208

of chocolate and blackberries.

But with this NATO official there was always the maggot in the apple, he thought, surveying the rat-infested tunnel in the aftermath. One can give too much and it becomes demeaning. However good his, Désespoir's organisation, it was never enough. Besides, the main interest, the Refuge in Libourne had become too burdensome, Marie-Ange too zealous, deflecting from the real purpose. And God knew he was weary of it all.

He and Madame Gramme could perhaps slip away to a cottage in the Quercy, a favourite region, for he'd remained unmarried except to the host of Guardian Angels above, and she a widow who'd known only his roof over her head for the last twenty-four years. Désespoir finished the général's wine, retied his grey pony tail and allowed a thin smile to cross his face.

Something was beginning to rot in the state of Denmark.

Déchaux had seemed more than a little perturbed that the Eberswïhr police had arrested Robert Vidal's father. They were sniffing dogs who couldn't be bought. That was disappointment number two, and if the Général was perturbed, it was time to reassess. Time to cut his losses. He rang for Madame Gamme who brought in both nuisance bitches and closed the door behind them.

"Come here ladies, please," he said. "Both of you. There's something you should see."

***

"Why?" complained Nelly with her hair still damp, pressing her nose on that unusual glass oblong behind which seemed to be an ancient, poorly-lit brick tunnel, alive it seemed, with scampering rats. "What are we supposed to be looking for, apart from vermin?"

"Patience, please," said Désespoir, before explaining that when the Foundation of the Brothers in God had first occupied the house some hundred years before, this section of tunnel had been set aside as a cell for 'the contemplation of sins.'

"Why aren't you in it, then?"

"That is disrespectful, Mademoiselle. But on this occasion, I'll let it pass."

The old Abbot returned to his vantage point. The one-way mirror now bristling with erratic torchlight from the confining space beyond the glass.
Nelly, feeling groggy, crouched below her chair, as if convinced that whoever was in that tunnel would be able to see her. "Get down," she said to Colette, who obeyed.

"Ah, at last." Désespoir leaned towards the glass as five figures, the fourth with a bloodied bandage round his head, stooped almost double, filed past. "Our patience is rewarded. Here come our very brave friends."

Colette's mouth fell open.

It's them. What in Hell's name have they been doing?

Robert Vidal came first, checking behind him all the time. A shaven head like hers, the whites of his eyes like those of some hunted animal. Next, Duvivier, the Breton, Plagnol and Cacheux. She continued to watch as they stumbled like the blind until they'd passed from sight.

"I smell a problem." Désespoir smiled to himself. "Tut tut. Too clever by half I shouldn't wonder. As you know, ladies, life at its most important moments is a lonely business – they didn't need five. Too many cooks, said I. But there we are."

"Too many cooks for what?"

No reply, just a small, strange noise from his throat.

Colette's mind was on fire. Why were Robert and the other priests in that tunnel? Where were they going, and what had they done to seem so agitated? Of course, she'd pretended not to recognise the bedraggled quintet, but Nelly must have realised something was up. Perhaps when they were both free again, back in Lanvière, they could talk.

No. *Must* talk.

XLVIII

Unbeknown to the priest from Ste Trinité, Colette was now watching her former lover move with a frantic purpose on all fours despite the tunnel's confined space, the sweating bricks that condensed the stench of centuries in his nostrils.

Neither could he see her turn away, wiping her eyes with her sleeve.

***

Below the Rue St. Aubin in this cramped tomb, there was no sky, no birdsong, yet always some bird or other persevered in the trees by his church. Vidal remembered this with such searing clarity, the pain of it drove him on, until a moment later, Cacheux piled into his rear.

"Pardon, Father."

"Watch it, or I'll finish you off."

The white suit duly hung back, his head like the weight of the world, its pulse the pulse of millions.

"How much further?"

"Till I say so."

He was longing for some widening, some offshoot of the tunnel where they could spread out rather than lie vulnerably in a line.

"You stupid shit," he shouted back to Plagnol. "This is all your bloody fault." And he noticed the priest of Notre-Dame-de-la-Consolation had actually stopped laughing.

Vidal could also hear Duvivier breathing badly – the man looked like he'd shat himself when they'd met up near the Ibis, and nothing would make him talk about the black Toyota. Whose it was and why they'd been shot at.

"Mother of God."

"She's busy. Try again later." Mathieu muttered, feeling a strange delirium grip him.

"Fuck."

"Precisely."

"I can't go on," Cacheux announced, his voice small in the dark.

"You have to." Mathieu nudged him along, his once pristine whites as filthy as the rest of them. Rendered the same by the nature of their sin, but sixteen hours in the stench was no penance. That was for the rest of his life, and he who could no longer be the priest of St. Jean de Motte Mauron saw how vile was the company in that Godless place.

The distance between Vidal and the others increased as the Breton attended to Cacheux, and Plagnol who'd earlier felt Duvivier's fists and were still smarting, before stopping to relieve himself.

"This way. Move it." Vidal's words rolled through the tunnel with a force of a high tide. They'd reached a bifurcation which, according to his compass, led south-east, on the one hand, and west, on the other. Either way could mean more space. He chose west. Here, brick became stone, the mortar damp and unstable under his fingers. He checked his watch for the hundredth time. Then Duvivier.

"Pray if you must. God knows, we need to," he muttered.

Mathieu stared, puzzled.

"I won't be. Thank you."

"Please yourself, squire."

"I intend to."

"We move off at 16.30. It'll take at least an hour to get back. By the way, which car? The traitor's Laguna?"

Duvivier slumped sideways, his legs stiff as splints. Doom in his tiny eyes, doom on his lips. "Yes, but we'll torch it down in the vineyards. There's enough heat round here at the moment."

"What you getting at?" Vidal unscrewed a half bottle of Evian and gargled it down his throat.

"I mean I had a call."

"And?" the Lanvière priest's face obscured by the label's image of glacial peaks and a cerulean sky.

"Eberswïhr have arrested your papa. 4.18 this morning. Good, isn't it? Another little cross for us to bear."

Vidal let the bottle slip from his grasp and watched as the only pure thing in that stinking place trickled away into the mud.

XLIX

LES MORTS. (SEPT VICTIMES RESTENT ENCORE DISPARUES)

Simon Heckel	26	Raymond Aubry	41	Patrick Roth	60
Lucien Schwab	50	Olivier Bailbe	45	Julius Weber	61
Sarah Wassover	49	Eugene Fuchs	47	Julie Schnabel	54
Jean-Marie Rube	47	Henri Tobiasz	52	Karl Joseph	51
Fritz Chomensk	61	Marc Kraemer	63	David Bosom	38
Émile Rauch	30	Charles Beckman	48	Ricard Jermann	46
Martin Altman	32	Harry Klemper	39	Abram Wolkowitz	68
Franz Mittelberg	46	Michel Lammel	49	Paul Green	45
Sarah Gluck	52	Daniel Hoverstadt	35	Felix Zimmerman	63
Georges Kaufman	39	Jules Broder	40	Jan Lappidus	49
Micha Weinberg	57				

PAS ENCORE TROUVÉS

André Lipman	41	David Wolpert	42	Nat Moulx	52
Pierre Escher	54	Olivier Grunfeld	48	Serge Moise	51
Tony Mendelsöhn	53				

LES EMPLOYÉS

Geneviève Baudet	20	Francis Gallieni	43 (capitaine)
Laurence Chabon	24	Jean-Paul Lantiez	25 (securité)
Annik Caby	19	Louise Ernée	27
Josette Grouiller	23	José de Romero	46 (securité)
Bruno Rey	52		
Christelle Frenois	36		

L

The tunnel's meagre light had deteriorated, and without candles, that gloomy coffin space was empty even of rats.

Now all Colette and Nelly were contemplating was how to exit. Their fear and humiliations past and present, had clearly given the Abbot more than a frisson of pleasure. His voice now reached them from behind.

"Is Mademoiselle Augot feeling better after that little interlude? I do hope so."

"I'm OK." Then under her breath, "no thanks to you, slimy old creep. And where's my gun?"

Colette stared at her with a mixture of admiration and alarm, remembering his gun. Remembering hers...

"Exactly. Quite right to ask, my dear," he purred. "But I was simply ob..."

"Obeying orders?" Colette found the courage to interrupt. "The past fifty years in this country have been founded on that pathetic excuse."

"Madame, I was about to send out for the antidote as I wasn't prepared to have a corpse for Madame Gramme to deal with, but you beat me to it, remember?"

"That's so kind. So who rang your doorbell? Was it him?"

"No. Just a neighbour wishing me a happy birthday," said Désespoir, helping himself to another glass of wine, this time from an already opened Bordeaux. His pistol still too handy. His mouth eerily lined by a dark redness.

Suddenly, without warning, came the strangest sound she'd ever heard.

"Sssh! Listen!" She took Nelly's arm as shofars and more sirens – this time, en masse – the broken sounds of shevorim and t'ruah filtered up the ancient tunnel, permeating the very stones of the former Seminary. The Paris Jews still holding to the voice of Jacob proclaiming God's kingdom from every synagogue north, south, east and west of the Seine. Yet another blood river like the Rhine and the Don, risen too close to its banks... "What in God's name is going on out there?"

"Oh, there's usually something every day. If it's not some festival or other it's troublemakers. Too many people, not enough work. The same everywhere. I thought you'd find it interesting."

"Sounds more than that to me." Colette strained to listen, and the awareness that something terrible had happened, gradually dawned. She looked at Nelly who tapped her watch.

Bertrand. And time's running out. Go on...

"My son was troublesome, you said." Colette reminded him yet again. "Why the past tense?" She'd sensed his wavering, his confusion, and like the fly trap around the hovering prey, she would choose her moment. The Abbot procrastinated, waiting until the housekeeper had cleared away the empty wine bottle and the wine glasses.

"My sister," he declared the moment she'd gone.

"My son," snapped Colette.

"Ah, yes. Where was I?"

He stood by the plate glass window where already a fine mist of condensation was clouding the view. "We've got four hours. I need to be on the road before dark. That is essential as I am not a night driver, you understand."

Colette and Nelly stared at each other.

What's the old dickhead going on about?

"I want to know about my Bertrand. Now."

Christian Désespoir pulled two dining chairs away from the table and with a nervous flick of the hand, told them both to sit down.

"I am an old man, and I can with a pure heart and an easy conscience say I have loved my country all my life. Almost too much, some would say."

Where the Hell's this leading? Bertrand, darling, make him tell me...

Colette crossed herself so quickly she might have been dusting something off her chest. Her eyes suddenly tired, the lids itching with the growth of new lashes.

"I now need to spend the rest of my days talking to God," he continued, avoiding their disbelief. "What days He'll be good enough to grant me."

"You have sinned," Nelly said suddenly, in a voice Colette didn't recognise. "More than anyone else I've ever known. What about Chloë Doumiez and the triplets? What's happened to them? And poor Bertrand?"

The pistol. He's still got it. And Nelly's gun. Be careful.

The founder of the Brothers in God and the Pauvres Soeurs suddenly looked as old as the earth itself. He sank into his chair, clasping both hands under his chin.

"You're right again, of course, and I'm afraid, Madame Bataille, I'm very much afraid.. " His aqueous eyes met hers. Colette's breath leapt from her lungs but found no escape. Her heart was alive with too much trepidation. "Your son is dead, of course. And even though I'm not the one to say it, may his soul rest in peace."

The silence became a chasm into which her very being plunged. Her belief, doubtful all along, vanished with those words, beyond recall. Forever. While the Abbot of Lagrange Vivray weary of his supporting role in the Great Scheme of Things, the Unfinished Business, recounted with clinical precision, what he knew.

Nelly held her, cradled Colette's shorn head, her thin limp body, and tried every way she could to lessen the reality. To weave impossible scenarios of hope as light as thistledown, only to be broken on a breath.

"My baby! My baby! Where is he?"

But everything she and Bertrand had said and done from her handing him over the priest's keys and his strange smile at her request, to his final wave as he'd ridden away on his mission, recurred with such grim clarity, it rendered her silent.

I knew it. I knew it. It's all my fault. Dear Mary, Mother of God.

"Madame, as you can see, I have not been blessed with the wherewithal to give birth, but I can understand. And because I understand, I cannot oblige you."

Nelly turned to tap the Abbott's velvet arm. Still unsteady, but deadly serious, spiced with a coquettishness learnt from her mother on the streets. "Père Supérieur, you have to confess, and whatever you say will stay a secret. That's a promise."

"I do have need, you are right. And to go over to St. Nicholas' church now would be too dangerous."

"I'll listen instead." She looked up at him, her lips moving on silent words...

'I had a git like you inside me not so long ago, with a piece of old rope for a dick. You're no better.'

"Do sit down and make yourselves comfortable."

With the tunnel now clear behind him, and a fresh candle lit and thriving, the former inhabitant of Désespoir village began the saga of his transgressions. When he'd finished, he handed his speechless audience five hundred francs each, which they promptly threw to the floor. He ignored the gesture, urging them instead to leave immediately but stay hidden.

"My gun," Nelly said.

"Please believe me, Mademoiselle, at the moment, my need for it is greater than yours. Until your lover whom we've just seen, decides you also know too much."

Before Colette could protest, the eighty-three-year-old excused himself and, bending low to turn his bony buttocks in the air, elegantly eased himself into another headstand.

LI

Friday October 3rd

News of the massacre was everywhere Colette and Nelly turned. On radio and TV; the front of every newspaper and on everyone's horrified lips from the Mediterranean to the Channel coast. Images of *Roquette IV's* fragments floating along a reddened Seine and of traumatised emergency personnel would linger long in their minds. As for the victims' photographs taken in happier times, those carefree smiles possessed an almost grotesque poignancy. Only Sarah Wassover, mother of two teenage boys and director of a bed linen company in Amiens, had survived – albeit with terrible injuries – only to die during the rush to hospital. Seven other diners were still missing, presumed drowned.

The latest hourly report from the Paris police confirmed that the search for five white Caucasian men, who'd been spotted behaving suspiciously on the boat the day before, was in full swing. Whoever they were, had been well-prepared and ruthless. Heads would roll. Reprisals sure to follow. Meanwhile, every synagogue in the land was offering prayers for the dead and bereaved. Families, who would never be the same again, and for those survivors of the WWII round-ups, this tragedy would only restore their worst nightmares.

Colette had taken it all in, sick to her stomach that no-one had listened to her warnings. And at 10.08 a.m. the next morning, she and Nelly Augot both stood on the threshold of Number 6 Apartments Cornay in the company of two officers from the Eberswïhr Gendarmerie. Sub-lieutenant Olivier Sedan and the unfortunately named Captain Jules Prêtre. Both tall, out of uniform in smart Le Coq Sportif casuals as though a golf course might be their next port of call.

Stranger already to the apartment's grey ordinariness, and unwilling to step where Bertrand's room lay waiting like the black chasm she'd already imagined, Colette was still crying, unable to rationalise anything, including the state of Dolina Levy's flat. Her windows blanked out with whitewash for privacy had been scored with swastikas and equally shameful messages. Mitzvah, her pretty tortoiseshell cat had been found speared by the boundary railings; his neck broken. His mouth stretched wide with terror. It was as if the evil that had fouled the Seine had reached here. Her sanctuary.

Colette prayed hard for all the dead, and the widow's soul to rest in peace, but she couldn't ask that for Bertrand. Until he appeared, there was still hope, despite what Désespoir had said. And it was hope that finally spurred her on to the welcome mat and into their home, to switch on the television and radio for any news.

"With so many dead from that bomb, it seems selfish to focus on Bertrand."

She said, blowing her nose, eyeing the clear-up taking place on the capital's river of death.

"You're his mother," Nelly reminded her, taking a look round. "I'd be the same."

The police from Eberswïhr had already been in two days before – Sedan had already admitted that – but also that it was obvious to them that someone else had got there first.

"Not the same freak who killed poor Madame Levy?" Colette turned to him with fresh fear.

"More than likely, but don't you go worrying about that now. We've taken prints, and," his tone became frighteningly confidential, "we're DNA testing semen found in your underwear drawer."

Colette and Nelly gasped in unison. There was worse to come. They knew it.

"Bloody sicko!" Nelly looked shaken like the vulnerable little girl she'd once been.

"I'm sorry, ladies, not very pleasant, and I'm afraid we've had to take certain items away for the time being. But, of course, where we could, we've made replacements. Just one thing," he looked at Prêtre for concurrence. "This place was also bugged. Very cleverly indeed, I might add. Whoever did it knew a thing or two and had the time to do it. Still," he patted her shoulder, "you should find everything back to normal."

"Bugged? Normal?" The words were grotesque.

"Surely after what's happened to Colette's poor old neighbour, you're not going to leave us on our own?" asked Nelly, paler then ever behind her party glasses.

"Us?" Sedan looked quizzically from one to the other. They didn't look the sort, besides it was Madame Bataille who'd notoriously seduced the *curé* from the straight and narrow.

"Even Robert Vidal might be a threat."

"As from now," he consulted his watch, rather than respond to that one, "you'll have a guard outside, twenty-four hours a day until we feel you're in no more danger. And I've arranged for Doctor Blanco to call at four o'clock and check you over."

"We're fine," Nelly protested.

"Better to be on the safe side."

"Of course," Colette said bleakly.

Sedan signalled to Prêtre to join him at the table and sat down. "Now then, you've told us about Libourne, the Abbé de Lagrange Vivray and what you witnessed in that tunnel, but we need anything else you can recollect, however small and inconsequential it may seem to you. If we're to help our Paris colleagues make arrests. If we're to find your boy."

If, not when. He's now twenty-four...

Silence as Colette dried her eyes.

"Nothing's been inconsequential I can assure you We've both told you everything."

She then went over to the sink and filled the kettle. Such a wonderfully simple thing to grip its handle, feel the familiar weight of it in a comfortless world, but when she offered the two men coffee, they declined.

"We think you ought to know that a Monsieur François Vidal formerly of Eberswïhr has been detained on matters relating to his son," said Prêtre.

Colette stopped. Her coffee tilting recklessly in its cup.

"Did you know he was living with him?" asked Sedan.

Her thoughts raced in time with all the other events, now out of control.

"I'd no idea. I know nothing about him. Father Jean-Baptiste never mentioned his parents except to say that his mother died in childbirth."

"A pity he didn't," the sub-lieutenant mumbled, screwing on the top to his pen. "Well, we're talking about a serious and committed neo-Nazi here. A very unsavoury type indeed. But we only have forty-eight hours to hold him. Some pretty colourful stuff outside his old flat, mind. Obviously not very popular with some of the natives. We could get them for that, but there's too much on right now."

"Who?"

"Les Flammes. Call themselves anti-fascists, you name it..."

"I remember now," Nelly interrupted. "Just before I set off for Libourne, I met some *roux* who said he belonged to them." She wasn't going to mention Bellino and he certainly wasn't going to get his gun back. He was history. "Degree in Medicine if you please, from René Déscartes, and jobless like me. He tried to get me to join them rigging flags on the Vedettes de Pont Neuf and the *Bateaux-Mouches...*"

"*Bateaux-Mouches?*" Sedan queried, jotting it down.

"Yeah, crap like that. Kindergarten stuff; oh, and the Pompidou. So he said. Anything to draw attention to the growing problem. Then François Vidal's name came up, and someone else, Guillaume Farges, I think. Public enemies, he called them."

"Got him as well. Yesterday." Prêtre announced as Colette's stomach shifted into pain mode. Her lover's shadow indestructible, blacker than the Devil himself. "So we'll see what they've got to say for themselves." The younger man was using too many clichés in an effort to keep the tone light. "He might do us all a favour and tell us where we can find his son. On the other hand, he might be as bloody minded as old Toussirot. They know the law, see. Clever like that. And you can't touch them. The Bishop knew Robert Vidal had gone up for the Mass but swore he didn't know anything else. Funny thing, my wife's a believer. Me, I'd like to see a little more honesty among God's representatives before I commit myself."

Colette interrupted. "Have you tried the Hôtel Marionnette in the Rue Goncourt? The management there may have overheard something."

"All hotels have now been contacted. It's odd his choir's performance at Saint Sébastien was cancelled. Bit of a music freak, isn't he?"

Colette nodded in shame.

"Apparently Father Anselme had chest pains last minute. Told us he'd been very honoured to be asked to stand in, but he's old, so there we are."

"Official covering up all round," Sedan sighed, "and there's not a lot we can do. However, we've done a run through of all the parishes, with the help of the R.G., of course."

"The R.G?" Nelly pulled a face.

"I can assure you, Mademoiselle, they're not all rotten apples."

"Just a few, then."

Colette frowned as Sedan continued.

"Some of their priests are unwell, some are practically walking corpses, but there are one or two with – how shall we say – irregular absences. And, Colette, may I call you that? The names match the ones you gave. Thank you. We're indebted."

"You've also got the Abbott's address, the Hostel and the Refuge, so something's bound to turn up," she said softly.

Both men exchanged glances. Sedan smiled.

"Indeed. We are moderately optimistic. And of course, Monsieur Baralet's been most zealous on your behalf. Oh, by the way," he fished in his back pocket and pulled out a pink envelope, still warm, moulded from his buttock. "For you. He didn't want to send it, just in case..."

"Oh?"

"Fan mail." Nelly peered over to see it.

GET WELL COLETTE, AND WE HOPE TO SEE YOU BACK SOON.

OUR KINDEST WISHES, GUY AND LISE BARALET.

Colette placed it next to the withered flowers.

"Unlike Lanvière, we took him seriously when he reported you missing, but at Eberswïhr we pride ourselves on a quick response. It's the only way these days. Now then," the Captain lowered his voice, "this is strictly *entre nous*." He looked first at Colette then Nelly." The Préfet's gone to Paris today to liaise with Interpol. They're not talking Muslim or Ultra-Orthodox, they're talking

Hakenkreuz, and closer to home than you think."

Colette closed her eyes.

"Bloody Interpol are dodgy, too." Nelly said, unimpressed.

"Now we really are in fantasy land. I'm afraid most students still harbour these rather immature notions. It's just not helpful, especially in your case." Prêtre's tone suddenly stern. "One other important thing, Colette. Your guard will be in disguise. An odd job man round the place – bit of this, bit of that, you know the sort of thing. Didier Molinari. 'Didi.' to you. Best if you don't mention this to anyone. He's trained and armed. OK?"

"Thank you."

"And your car, in case you're wondering..." Prêtre leafed through a small hide-covered notebook. "Found in the 17th, near the Square des Bagatelles. Whoever took it was obviously surprised. Looked like there was a plan to burn it."

"What about my son's baby blanket? Pathetic, she knew, when there'd been others of his age who'd just died, but Prêtre coughed tactfully and made a note.

"Not sure about that, I'm afraid, but the vehicle is salvageable. Be back tomorrow." Sedan touched her arm solicitously. "Someone's had it in for you in a big way, and not only you." He looked at his superior. "Shall we tell them about the girls?"

"What girls? Chloë? Victorine?"

"No. These two were found near the Gare de Lyon. Quite smart, knew their rights and all that. They're now under surveillance at the Salpêtrière. Both shot in the leg, somewhere, somehow. Both expertly bandaged up."

Nelly looked at Colette, her eyes widening as Sedan continued.

"One of the nurses got suspicious about their phone calls and managed to listen in. False IDs for a start. Romy Kirchner and Claude Lefêbvre whose real names are Christine Souchier and Antoinette Ruffiac. Do any of these mean anything?"

And that was the sluice gate opening on the current of loss and pain that Colette and Nelly allowed to run, to fill the small apartment of faded flowers and a stranger's evil seed, until they could speak no more. Just as they finished, with Nelly holding Colette's hand like some precious object of devotion, the telephone rang. Sedan picked it up. He set Record, unsure what to expect.

"Madame Bataille? Sure. Hold on." He set the tape and winked at his companion as Nelly turned down the TV. Then he passed the receiver to Colette for the priest's three hurried words.

"I love you."

Then silence.

"Where the Hell did that come from?" Sedan asked, seeing Colette white and hard, her lips pursed in silence.

"Better ask Madame."

After all, she's the best bait we've got.

LII

At four o'clock precisely, with Vidal's message still haunting her, Colette unlocked the door of her apartment to Doctor Didier Blanco. Of similar age to Guy Baralet, but unlike her former boss, any remnant of youthful good looks had been subsumed into recent widowhood and a medical practice swelled by the malaise of unemployment and asylum seekers from Algeria and the east. Crumbs had also lodged in both wings of his moustache.

Although he'd not seen Colette for two years since her last '*frottis,*' the native of Norvillers couldn't disguise his shock at her appearance.

"Madame Bataille, do we have somewhere private?" He cast around, keeping himself busy putting his case and file on the table. Anything rather than focus on the woman who'd always lent a certain style to the streets of Lanvière.

"Yes, my bedroom, there. The door next to Bertrand's."

Nelly had tactfully debunked to the boxroom sorting out her few things.

"Fine. My nurse will be along in a minute."

"Nurse? Oh God, no..."

His weak brown eyes widened in surprise. "Madame, I'm not permitted to carry out any, how shall I say, an intimate examination without her. Even as your humble family doctor, I do have regulations."

"Nelly, my friend's here. Won't she do?" Colette stared and he wished then he'd simply come to take her pulse.

"I'm afraid not. Ideally after your ordeal you should have gone straight to hospital, but your situation is to say the least, unusual."

Thank you for telling me that, Doctor. You can now add perception to your list of attributes.

"The sooner we start, the sooner we finish. Are you eating normally, by the way?" he asked, extracting her medical card as the doorbell rang again.

"Yes," she lied.

Because every day's a death day until he's home.

"Bowels?"

"Good." Another lie.

"Ah, here she is. Sister Patrice."

"Sister? No. No way."

"Please, Madame Bataille, I can do nothing without her. She's the best agency nurse I've got."

Colette reluctantly let in a slender young woman in a white overall who smiled as though she was a long lost friend. Not a single golden blonde hair strayed from her neat chignon and, as Colette studied her badge, the infirmière Patrice Sassoule slipped her long fingers into a pair of surgical gloves and followed the Doctor into the bedroom.

After weighing and blood pressure, the nurse spread out a paper sheet on the bedspread.

"Be so good as to step out of your things and lie down. Just some basic procedures to go through, nothing you've not already had before..." He peered through a gap in the curtain as his patient prepared herself, keeping a wary eye on the young nurse.

She lay back in the room that she and Bertrand had decorated in *vert anis* and pink. He'd sneered, saying it was just like the Ibis he'd stayed in for the Futuroscope trip, but to her it represented a calm sanctum at the end of a working day, and more so with its print of the 'Virgin of the Rocks' facing the bed.

Now she wanted to tear it down. Mary and her infant like everything else, no longer any comfort.

"Blood pressure, normal. Excellent." Then Dr Blanco paused. He'd started examining her arms, his hands surprisingly cool and light. He looked closer, moving his glasses up his nose. his moustache touching her skin. She stiffened then bent her elbows protectively over each basilic vein as he frowned.

"They gave me Natolyn. At least four shots, maybe more. Bastards."

"Natolyn, eh?" he nodded to his nurse. "What makes you so sure?"

"I saw the box. I should know."

"Indeed. I'd not forgotten. You work for Medex."

"Used to."

"Well, whoever did this was obviously experienced. A very neat job, I'd say."

"A neat job?" Colette reared up. "They were trying to bloody kill me!"

The nurse eased her back down on to the paper, her beatific smile still shaping her face, her teeth large and even as she tightened a band on the upper arm.

"Right. Let's see what else we can glean. Just a little prick now."

"Thank you Madame. Just relax for a moment." Doctor Blanco then leant over to let his fingers lift the edge of her slip and travel her ribs and abdomen. Below her navel he stopped, before backtracking to the right and the left. It felt to Colette like the sign of the Cross, but too deliberate, fearful almost.

"When is your next period due?"

"Next week. Why? Is anything wrong?" She tried to glimpse his face beyond the nurse.

"Er...no, Madame. Everything seems *en bonne forme.*"

But Hélas, I cannot tell her, the way things are at present...

For his hands had told a different story.

"You're not telling me the truth, are you, Doctor Blanco? What's the matter?"

"My dear Madame Bataille, if you'd forgive me, but I did this very same thing twenty four years ago. I remember you came to me in great distress believing you were pregnant. That it was some kind of punishment for being unmarried."

"What the Hell's that got to with now?" she shouted. "Anyhow, it's none of *her* business!" Colette glared at the nurse who instantly blushed.

"Madame, Sister Sassoule works with me, and is therefore entrusted with my patients' confidences. Some people are quite relieved and more eager to talk when there's a woman present. Now we're just going to take a smear to reassure ourselves." He coughed discreetly. "Please just let your knees fall apart."

**

Ten minutes later, having promised to send her the results with a hospital appointment if necessary, and refusing any refreshment, the Doctor and his nurse left the apartment. He let the young woman go on ahead while he rested his notepad on a balcony edge to record details still fresh in his mind. His pen was slippery with perspiration, his words wayward on the page.

Nothing in writing for her at the moment. Poor woman. I fear cauterization of the fallopians has been expertly done. Keyhole, through the abdomen, and not a mark to be seen. It's obvious these Sisters of Suffering are not only adept in matters of the soul. But why?

Then he wrote POLICE in block capitals, and was so anxious to reach his car phone as quickly as possible, he didn't notice the attractive and efficient Patrice Sassoule had disappeared.

LIII

If Cacheux had been fit enough to drive, it would have been the Xantia not the Laguna reaching the hamlet of St. Julien at twenty past four in the morning. No longer white but two-tone black and grey from the journey, it suddenly stalled outside the garage of Leclerc et Fils. One pump, a defunct jet wash, and total silence.

Inside the sweating car, the latest news bulletin on the *Bateau-Mouche* bombing ended and Duvivier pulled his hat down over his ears before slinking low in the passenger seat as Plagnol's foot pumped the gas.

To no avail.

"Fuck this thing." Cacheux signed a cross on his own forehead then tried his door handle. The shit from the tunnel had made him a leper even to himself. The stuff was in his nails, up his nose. Everywhere, and his head was making him dizzy.

"No you don't!" Vidal held him fast, and like a first-date lover, Cacheux made no effort to free himself.

"We can walk from here," he said. "Two kilometres, that's all."

Duvivier turned round, keeping his lips together. "My friend, this may be your cherished abode, but my first impressions are unfortunate. This is at best *un trou aux rats*."

Cacheux began to protest.

"What should we have done, then? Drancy?" Vidal countered. "And had The Pigface's skinny maman peck all over us?" He was pleased to see Plagnol's neck redden. "Move!"

The carburettor whimpered the first of several false promises.

"We're getting somewhere." The Pigface's thigh pumping up and down as though on a leg toner in the gym, not coaxing a top-of-the-range saloon.

"Good oh." Vidal stared gloomily out of the window at the one-horse place with Dégustation lit by a single flickering bulb. The rest, scrubland and vineyards flattened by the recent storms, lay in semi-darkness as far as the eye could see. Easy pickings for the wild boar before the start of *La Chasse*. Not for much else.

"You'll have to push." Plagnol breathless.

"Your penance for taking a pot shot at me," said Cacheux.

"For God's sake. It wasn't me."

"Could have ruined everything," snapped Duvivier, nevertheless thinking thoughts he shouldn't. Thinking black Celica…

Vidal didn't believe The Pigface, but it was too late now to go looking for the bullet. He scanned the desolate scene for other signs of life but there was no-one else around, just a light dry wind off the sea and the smell of soil, as the Renault finally spluttered into life and took off down the street.

"Run!" Vidal yelled, and eight weary legs chased the tail lights past the few shuttered houses and a stone trough with its dripping tap. Deserted, like an open grave, Vidal thought, getting in last.

"Told you to lose this damned thing all along," Duvivier snapped again. "It's too bloody visible."

"Won't matter where we're going." Cacheux gripped Plagnol's seat in front and saw close up the driver's hair shine with neglect. "Now, next left."

The road suddenly narrowed to a track and tarmac became stones as it climbed nearer the lightening sky. *Réserve de Chasse* signs stood on either side, and by the first gateway, a placard with the faded letters, Domaine de Fourcat. Its vines crushed by a recent storm.

"In here." Cacheux craned forwards in readiness for his lie. "Like I said, the *genitori* aren't in residence. Feel free."

"Dream on." Mathieu murmured, trying to distance himself from the one he despised most. Vidal was too close, his presence stifling. No more *'Bijou.'* No more even meeting him a quarter of the way for a conversation. He had finished with it all.

Duvivier, showing the inconsistencies of power, continued to ignore him, his hidden eyes roaming from one window to the next.

"Château de Fourcat, king of the Corbières." Cacheux announced, the sole inheritor of three hundred hectares of the grenache grape and a trout farm beyond the garden. "Romans, Saxons, Moors, it's seen the bloody lot."

"Don't tell me, no Jews?"

"Not bloody likely."

"OK, spare us the history, Father," said Vidal. "More importantly, where do we kip?"

"Outside somewhere. I don't trust the place," Duvivier had decided.

The car shuddered round to the back of the château where a mountain of old vine roots writhed in the labouring light. Plagnol yawned like a hippopotamus and parked under the furthest lean-to, covered by fig trees.

"Take your gear, your bags. Everybody out." Cacheux was aping Vidal's more authoritative tone. "Remember we're *paysans*. Vineyard workers from Maisons, just tidying up for Monsieur Cacheux senior. Émile's his name in case you're asked. My maman's called Sophie."

Vidal let the native show the way, crouching against the dark spur of land.

The sound of a faraway dog heightened the tension as nose to tail they crept over the slipping stones until an opening led down to a small cabane overrun with weeds. Its tiles lay in chaos, and inside reeked of dung, so they used its northerly wall as a windbreak and fell in a heap of exhaustion amongst the fescues and yellow rattle.

The vast tie-and-dye sky grew lighter with every second, rendering the night shift and the land they'd commandeered as one. Cacheux's mobile suddenly delivered a polyphony of voices.

"Abort." Duvivier rolled his bulk to face the heavens. It was probably meant for him, but he wasn't in the mood. "Sleep. Four hours minimum, thanks to the fucking truckers lording it over their compatriots. And then, *mes amis*, the icing on the cake, we move Heaven and earth to find the tart."

Such disobedience was therapeutic and a snore soon germinated in his throat.

"Should have given Limoges a wide berth." Vidal tried to deny the lurch in his stomach. "But as ever, I'm a lone voice." He placed his worker's hat over his face, not just to exclude the beginnings of day but more important now, to wonder in secret why Colette wasn't answering. Not even giving him the chance to warn her. But unlike his contribution for the Feast for the Guardian Angels, he wasn't going to let her drift away. It was bad enough missing the sweet innocent irony of his twelve trebles reaching the highest gilded star as *Roquette IV* had fouled the Seine. And worse that their God hadn't been given the chance to hear Pérotin's clausulas above the cries of his Jews. Toussirot had put paid to all that, and now no-one was going to stand in his way.

The choirmaster listened hard. Heard the sleeping breaths then checked his watch, a neon disc in Plagnol's shadow. Three hours fifty-one minutes to go, and from beneath his hat rim, one lizard eye saw the Breton keeping his distance, trying to stay awake. Vidal missed nothing as Dominique Mathieu changed from one elbow to the other as if rehearsing how best to stand. Never mind they'd all be back with their parishes until the Presentation of The Virgin, researching their third target in Alsace – this man was restless.

All at once, without warning, Mathieu drew out his Samsung. The flash of new film seized on the crumpled bodies, the startled eyes, once, twice, three times, and before Vidal could wrench his leg from under Plagnol's weight, the newly-fit priest from Perros Guirec was gone.

LIV

06.04 hours on the Feast of Gedaliah, and a call from Déchaux competing with a rush of late swallows heading east. With a shaking hand, Duvivier groped for his phone. The Judas from Perros Guirec was his problem and his alone, and he wasn't going to share it.

"Melon, my friend. Some news." The général got in first, his communications technology making Reims seem as if it was the next vineyard.

The Provençal crept away from the others who'd returned too easily to sleep, and the way their faces caught the first sun, reminded him of his mistake at father's funeral. He too had let its rays kiss his cheek. Wrong place, wrong time, marked out as the next to die, and the fright of it altered his voice.

"What news?" He could hear his heart.

"Mossad's getting very agitated. Looks like they're setting up near the Parc des Vosges... You still there?"

"I am. What about the yellow stars in Essecotte?"

"All as planned. But keep your heads down. Double pay, remember? I'll be away again for a few days. Banja Luka to be precise. Mission of mercy, you know the sort of thing. A horse actually."

A pale one, I hope.

"On Wednesday and yesterday, Antoinette Ruffiac was seen driving you in Paris," Duvivier accused recklessly. "Yet you'd planned to be in Bosnia."

Silence.

Merde. He might just as well have swallowed a cyanide pill.

"Number 3? Still with you?" Déchaux barked instead.

"Er... yes."

"Too bad. Get rid or I will."

Duvivier's stomach lapsed into his groin. He saw The Pigface get up and pee against the cabane. His piss an amber arc catching the early sun.

"And his fucking car. Don't forget."

"I won't."

"And by the way, my friend..."

What now you murderous jackal?

"Madame Bataille's given us the slip. Apparently she's safely installed herself *chez-elle* with some female she met at Libourne. A nutter with a gun."

"That's impossible."

"I don't think so. She shot both my best girls in the legs while she was there, so leave her to us. They were too careless. Managed to get picked up by the flics as they were about to board a train back home, if you please. That's the trouble with today's skirt. Too much spoon-feeding keeps *das kind auf der*

Kinderzimmer, hein?"

"I quite agree."

"Still, I've just sprung them from the Salpêtrière. They're at home with me now. Safe and sound."

I bet they are, poor cows.

"At least they've not been singing, which is more than others I could name. Number 2's papa's not been too clever either. A little humility wouldn't come amiss, so he'll be crapping in a bucket for the foreseeable future. Keep all this under your hat, by the way. There's my good man."

Duvivier remained speechless until he suddenly remembered Cacheux. His tentative cough was by way of introduction.

"Someone had a go at Number 4 yesterday, in the Champs-Elysées. Not very nice." He wasn't going to mention the Celica, just needed the reaction.

"You mean, his cock?"

Another silence.

"Maybe, my friend, it was a reminder from me to stay alert..."

The line went dead. Duvivier stared at the phone.

Sick bastard. Besides, a 'merci' for such a successful outcome would have been better appreciated.

***

No birds either. No sound in that high wild place, except his heart pumping the impotence of the bought and sold. He saw The Pigface settling down to more sleep and felt the whispering shrimp net's mesh embrace him; hold him fast.

Duvivier scoured the tracks between the beaten vines, but Dominique Mathieu had well and truly vanished. His eyes slitted against the sun that eased into the sky beyond the Roc de l'Aigle, and he imagined a poplar with rogue branches on one of the lower ridges, gradually become a figure. A Revenant, swaying to the southerly breeze. Black, worm-fouled, beckoning his follower to a grave somewhere in those Godforsaken hills. As Kommandant in the pecking order, he, Francke Victor Duvivier, *célibataire,* but lover of his country, knew he was next.

He clenched his fists to stop them trembling and felt someone behind him. It was Vidal with sleep on his breath, his open shirt showing brown flesh and smooth, dark hairs.

"I'll catch Mathieu, the little runt," he said.

"What's the point?"

Déchaux will get there first. That is fact.

"Look here, Robert. You've got to help me."

"Why?"

"I've seen too many signs and portents. More than any man of God can bear..."

Vidal buttoned up his shirt, reset his cap on his head and studied the man who was visibly faltering. "Remember our friend St. Bernard and our sweet anorexic of Sienna?"

"Can't you just say yes?"

"The path of the sinful soul to divine union starts with servile fear..."

Then Duvivier took it up. "Timor autem servilis est. Cum per timorem gehennae coninet se homo a peccato... I know, I know. But it's not Death I fear."

I have at last the plot next to my loved one, but at what price? And how soon shall I know it?

"What then?" Vidal careful to keep his voice cold and distant.

For that way lies the greater dividend. In the confessional, it is the pauses, the sudden silences, like music almost, that like a bare floor, make for a cleaner birth.

The coward beside him was shaking, looking enviously to where Cacheux and Plagnol lay spreadeagled among the weeds.

"Someone who will make me his Nevella."

"You won't tell me?"

"I can't."

"So what am I supposed to do?"

They walked back in silence to rejoin the others and Vidal noticed Cacheux's eyes on his groin.

"You're getting too morbid in your old age, Francke," he said to Duvivier. "Chill out a bit. We're not finished yet. The best as you know, is yet to come."

Duvivier stopped, shaded his eyes gone to nothing under his hand and let Vidal continue. "Don't forget, to Jews we are heretics. Our bread is defiled by its manufacture, our baptismal waters impure. And worse, they shit on the notion of Our Lord's Divinity saying how can one born from a woman be without sin?" His voice refuelling to quiet rage as Cacheux and Plagnol scrambled to their feet, fearing strangers, while a tear, quite detached from this polemic, formed on Duvivier's cheek.

Ecce enim in peccatis conceptus sum et in iniquitatem conceput me mater mea...

Cacheux suddenly shouted something and pointed towards Vilabou where a green *camionette* was nudging its way through the broken vines.

"The Cressy's!" he yelled. "Come on!"

Using the cabane to block the peasants' view of them, the four ran down over the feckless stones and roots half-buried by the slide of mud, until the single tall chimney of the Château de Fourcat appeared.

"This way." Cacheux's bandage uncurled from his head as his dirty white suit made a detour to the far side where the main barn adjoined. Proud to lead on this, his home ground especially as he knew Vidal was behind. But the doors were already open, the padlock dangling. His father's black Mondeo lay alongside a Citroën van in the shadows, both dusty and unused.

Vidal eyed the sleek saloon. "Whose is that?"

"Mine."

The Cressy's were gaining, their old engine roaring.

"They're armed!" Plagnol hollered, trying to reach Duvivier and cling on and, as the Renault van came into full view, three rifles bristled from its sides.

The Devil take you...

Cacheux had the key ready on his rosary and held the plain, wooden front door open. New blood leaked from his head wound on to his hand as he locked up, and Vidal was close, too close.

No. not now. Not ever.

Vidal took over as the Renault outside puttered to a halt followed by the ominous slam of doors. "Vite." He sped up the marble staircase into a vast salon lit from above by two Velux windows.

"Papa!" Cacheux yelled behind him. "Are you there?" He hoped by his tone to keep his mother away wherever she was. To frighten her into staying away.

A shot thundered out from below, then six fists pounded the outer door.

"Take no notice. Les *impétueux* have had too much sun, too much booze. We'll be safe here," he boasted.

"What do these half-wits want, then?" Vidal began prowling, looking for the Mondeo's real owner.

"Their right of way re-established over our land for a start. You'd think they'd have enough gloating to do after our bloody harvest. Pagan turds."

"Ssh. Listen!" Duvivier's big head was cocked. "What are they saying?" Fisherman's ears tuned to the songs and the sighs of the sea. The shouts grew louder, more pronounced as the pummelling subsided. "Something about your mother. They've got her."

Cacheux heard it too, and gasped. When he crossed himself, his fingers stuck together with blood. He looked to Vidal, but the man had found a phone and was dialling.

"Better go see." Duvivier said without interest. "You never know."

"Come with me," Cacheux pleaded.

"I'd rather not, thank you. Can't you see I'm already bearing the world on these shoulders?"

"Michel?" To the Pigface who'd just slotted a sugared almond into his mouth. "Two grand for you, OK?"

And Plagnol duly followed, keeping his worker's hat over his heart as the priest from St. Honoré took a deep breath to steady his voice, then unlocked and opened the main door. "What do you mean, you've got my mother?" he shouted at the van.

"Come and see."

Sweet Jesus.

"Maman?" he called out. "Maman?"

The sunlight fell on him and the raw bullet graze above his left ear..

"Our Father has nearly been in Heaven, I see." Albert Cressy grinned bad teeth and with one hand pushed his rifle behind his seat. The other two still poked threateningly from the dark interior. So dark, Cacheux couldn't quite make out if his twin sons were with him or not.

"Where is she?"

Cressy looked Plagnol up and down with obvious distaste.

"This one of your friends in arms?"

He hasn't forgotten. Mon Dieu.

"As you say, just a friend." He leant forwards to test the darkness. "Maman?"

"Not so fast. Let's have a name first of all."

Cacheux looked round, but Plagnol was already smiling, holding out his hand. The jovial parish priest all over again, willing to shake with anybody. For a price. The younger twin, Alphonse Cressy suddenly got out, opened the boot and whispered a command.

Cacheux saw the dog first. No muzzle. A ton of hunger, wet leather jaws peeled back ready for Plagnol's leg. His scream shot down the sunlit morning as he fell to the ground, writhing in delirium. Albert Cressy held the Drancy man down while Sophie Cacheux, moaning and cursing, was helped from the car.

"And let me tell you, you scum in priest's clothing, we too have friends in arms. Friends who saved the *decent* heart of France."

Girard Cressy dragged the bleeding Plagnol, too shocked to retaliate, into the old woman's place. Then as Vidal and Duvivier ran out from the door, the man of the Maquis reversed the van and hurtled out into the scrub, spraying the helpless watchers with a rain of dried silt.

Vidal took aim and caught a tyre. Tried again into the dust cloud, but Cacheux in a desperate effort to restrain him, brought his arm down.

"You don't know bloody anything!"

Vidal turned to look at him and swung the Zastava against his cheek, making Cacheux cry out. "What do we need to know, you tart?"

"Leave it." Duvivier searched for his lighter and loped over to where the Laguna lay secreted under the fig trees. "If The Pigface squeals, we're stuffed."

Cacheux tried to hold on to his mother, but she elbowed him away and stumbled into the château, where, from a top window, his father, Émile Cacheux looked down.

The Laguna took four minutes to blow up, taking the trees, spraying the hard figs skywards and making the old Mas tremble. Its smoke drifted over, carrying burnt fragments into their hair.

"We don't wait for Marheshvan. We go now. To Essecotte." Vidal's face was hard with purpose. His jaw pulsing to its own deep rhythm. He pulled Cacheux towards him until their noses almost touched. "Get your things."

"I'm not going."

"Do I need to correct my hearing?"

"I'm staying here. My parents need me." Cacheux's tone faltered. In the silence he heard Vidal reset his pistol.

"That won't make any difference. Look, my father can see you." His eyes fixed on the two faces of Monsieur and Madame staring out, conjoined, shrunken and pale like old mushrooms.

Vidal pointed the muzzle upwards, moved it from side to side seeing how they followed it. This neat baton, more powerful than anything he'd waved inside church or even at Colette, was stronger than any prayer. He had nothing to lose.

Plus ça change...

Duvivier gripped his wrist and wrenched it sideways. The pistol still in place.

"*We'll* just go."

"Are you mad? They've seen us. They'll talk."

"We'll have to trust them."

I know someone who won't. Adieu chair morte.

Neither looked back, so the priest from St. Honoré's tears went unnoticed and, as they crouched among the torn crops parallel to the road to St. Julien, the Kommandant felt at least one of his burdens had been lifted. They'd still got cash and phones. Besides, with just one left of the *Landsturm,* things would be nice and simple. And focussed.

"I phoned home again," Vidal lied, as the backs of houses came into view. "No reply. I could try Eberswïhr. See what's going on."

Mad wolf.

"I wouldn't if I were you."

Vidal spun round. "You know something?"

"No more than what I've told you already."

***

They reached Leclerc et Fils. A misnomer, for the only living soul, apart from a sleepy dog, was a dark-haired woman perched in the tiny reception area. Her green eyes took in the two paysans, the one with the sensual eyes and mouth, the other repellent without one redeeming feature while she prattled on about the loss of the Domaine de Fourcat's vines.

"That's why we need a car," Vidal explained, noting her knees at the end of her skirt. "To get us to Domaine de Lantour. Just west of Perpignan. Plenty of work there."

"I know it. They've been one of the lucky ones." She tapped into her desktop, then dialled a nine-figure number as Duvivier nudged him.

What the Hell can she be checking in this dump? There's either a car or there isn't...

Duvivier also sniffed danger. The same as off Cap Lardier with a sea swell beginning. He told the woman they'd changed their minds and pushed his way out of the office.

***

Vidal caught him up by a half-finished villa where they lay breathless in a forest of dead sunflowers, and when the Provençal had recovered, he crawled away on the pretext of taking a squat, and phoned Déchaux just before he left his office. Without giving the général a chance to interject, told him to have a car, five new IDs and sets of the *bleu de travail* at Tautavel by midday. They weren't going to hang around. Nor could he admit the team was down to two.

"Who did you phone?" said Vidal, when he returned. It was time the crater face came clean.

"I'm not permitted to say."

"You'd better."

The sunflowers' woody stems cracked and buckled under his weight as he lunged at Duvivier.

"No secrets, remember?" He pinned him down under a hail of dead seeds. "Is this some other God Almighty I don't know about?"

A knee on the older man's chest, crushing his diaphragm.

"If I tell you, I'm dead," gasped Duvivier.

"You're dead anyway."

His patella found the hollow and the soft lung tissue beneath his breast bone. Duvivier moaned before the last of the air gave out. "Déchaux... Général..." the Provençal spluttered.

"Never heard of him. What does he do?"

"He's a horse lover."

Vidal pressed down again, enjoying himself, sensing victory over the bungler.

"Do me a favour."

"And a peacekeeper in Bosnia."

"That's hilarious. Anything else?"

Duvivier's breath was a succession of painful grunts. His mouth contorted with the effort. "SRM. Part-time, I think."

Vidal eased off, realising why the Tronchet warehouse had served them so well. The diving school and the rest. The Société du Renseignement Militaire probably had more pots of gold than Midas.

And the king has long arms.

"Does he pay us, this Général?"

A nod.

"Double for Essecotte."

Vidal suddenly jumped up, watching the older man struggle to his feet. "Well pal, we'd better go and earn our keep."

And then, I'll go and find Colette.

LV

After three sleepless nights at the Hôtel Fleuris in Tours, Vidal and Duvivier with new IDs as artisan plumbers and clothes to match, sat outside the Café Dauphine opposite the Cathédrale St. Gatien and the Musée de Beaux-Arts. When a police car cruised by, checking the pavements, they studied the menu with sudden intensity.

"My father knows when to keep his mouth shut, so it's not a problem." Vidal tasted the hot dark coffee, felt it travel through his body, warming him against the sour Atlantic wind.

But Baralet's diary is, my friend. So watch out.

"Well, you know him better than I do," Duvivier mumbled. "What's he got on you?"

"Nothing." Vidal put his cup down and frowned into it.

"Well, our *Bébé* Bataille found something not to his advantage, *hein*?"

Vidal replied by pressing a dark finger on to the Provençal's hand, which was small, white as dough. "And so have I. I can't ever trust you again." He said suddenly, summoning the *garçon* over. "You were never going to say about the letter he stole from me, or about our Friend in High Places, were you?"

"If you'd been in my boots for the past two months, you'd feel differently. The waters of Acheron are already licking my knees."

Amen to that.

Vidal watched as the Café Dauphin filled up with the grey brigade looking for a late lunch after taking in the early Italian Masters and *The Flight into Egypt*, while the speciality steak hachés dribbled their blood into the flames.

Duvivier leaned forwards, confidentiality tightening his mouth.

"There've been too many *anicroches*. Our Hauptsturmbannführer likes his Operations simple. Cut and dried. Which is why I don't need to volunteer our cock-ups."

"The queer, The Pigface, the Judas...?"

"Of course. But because I walk the tightrope, we move on. The only way is west. To the King David Hotel. As agreed."

The *garçon* kept the bill under his thumb, but as he set the new coffees down, it fluttered to the floor. "Éxcusez-moi." He bent down and noticed how clean were the workers' shoes and the legs of their *bleu de travail*. "New job?" he ventured as Vidal counted out centimes.

"You could say that."

"My father started today, too. Twenty floors up. Éspace de Loisirs. You know it?"

"Course. Big place."

The boy stared for a moment. There was something odd, about the older one, especially, he thought. His eyes, and that terrible skin.

"He tried to get me on it, but the thing is, I like meeting people."

"So I see."

The boy's expression changed when he saw no tip was forthcoming. He flounced away scowling.

"Cheeky sod," said Vidal. "I could lose him his precious job."

"Not now, Robert, eh?"

And when the pest had gone, the two edged in closer, shutting out the world that was beginning to encroach. Their hands almost touching, their coffee breaths intermingling.

"Would you say, all things considered, that our Faith has made us more whole than we were before?" Vidal suddenly asked, licking his spoon.

"Only the woman with an issue of blood could answer that, my friend." And before either could finish, two more police cars swung into the square, sirens clamouring, and stopped in front of the Cathédrale.

LVI

Twenty-two-year-old Leila Fraenkel deliberately kept her bedroom window open, letting the westerly wind from along the Loire blow her long hair back from her face. Three full days to the start of Yom Kippur. Three more days of small indulgences before the fast – so she took another waffle from the pack; felt its sweetness, honey and icing sugar, melt on her tongue.

She opened her boyfriend's letter again. Singapore, September 3rd. The flimsy airmail seemed to represent the rest of him, and she soon gave up trying to extract the most meaning, the most possibilities from his easy words. Water from a stone, she thought bitterly, screwing it up and throwing it in the bin.

"But God matched you and Ben the moment you both were born," her mother would insist whenever mail or a call from him came through. But these had become ever rarer, and the last few times Leila had tried the Compasun office where he worked, the receptionist, always chatty, nevertheless apologised for his absence and seemed genuinely sorry.

"That's it, then." Leila finished the waffle, realising that ending the relationship would be like pulling teeth. For when Pauline Fraenkel had threatened like a good Jewish mother, to fly out and confront him, the generation gap that had simmered for years, exploded.

"I want to live my own life, mama. Just because papa was the first boy you met... It's not like that for me. I have been five years in Paris, remember?"

"I do. Only too well."

"What's that supposed to mean?"

"When you're my age, you'll understand that memory lengthens like an evening shadow, bearing with it all the mistakes, the heartbreak of the past..."

And then she'd not spoken for a week, smiling to the hotel guests in her best silk pleated skirts, but coldly sweeping by when her only child appeared. Leila went into the bathroom to wash her hands, but no water came. Instead, just a hollow gurgle from the gold tap. Even the toilet had no flush.

Damn and blast.

She sprayed perfume on herself instead.

The members of the Touraine Cultural Committee would be arriving soon. All of them over sixty. All of them either musical or artistic, or both, but none had been deterred from their mission by yesterday's terrible tragedy in Paris.

Leila was grateful for their fortitude, especially as she'd spent time and money framing her latest paintings for the Treasurer, an American woman now living in Tours who was interested in promoting her. Working for a patron with contacts was better than working in the hotel, and success and involvement might help her forget the useless, long-distance love affair. Besides, she missed the Art School, her friends, the whole Parisian thing...

She brushed her hair again and checked her blouse buttons. Pink and pale pink. Happy, happy. Then she took the lift down to reception.

"Got a little problem with my bathroom." She gave Simon Müller, trainee manager, a wry little flirty smile. "No water."

"I'll tell Monsieur Fraenkel right away, and we'll do a check on the others as well, though there've been no complaints so far."

"Thanks," then she hesitated. "Oh, by the way. Simon?"

"Yes?"

"I know you've got other more important things to worry about, but, from a male perspective, what do you think I should do about about... you know... Ben?"

Her huge dark eyes that in a certain light seemed edged with gold, fixed him like a specimen on a pin. He was clearly embarrassed, but it had been his dutiful nature that had appealed to the Fraenkels in the first place and now it prevailed again.

"You both seemed to get on brilliantly whenever he stayed here, but it's like, well..."

"Go on."

"He's not bothered any more."

Her heart plummeted in her chest.

"It's that obvious?"

He nodded.

"I know what I'd do if I was him. Stop messing you about. "

"Oh Simon."

Then, as if by looking at this younger man, barely out of technical college, her lover's memory was sharpened and honed so as to be almost unbearable. The quiff like a little black wave on his forehead. His laughing mouth...

"Are you alright?"

"No, not really."

But he'd turned to straighten his tie. People were coming in. "By the way, I won't forget about the water."

"Thanks."

Next moment she saw her mother, and could tell by the swing of her skirt that something was up. Pauline Fraenkel's strong, immaculately made up face was seized with fear. In her hand a cassette tape. Plain, with no cover, no details of contents. She passed it over to her daughter without a word.

"Just play it. Came with the afternoon post. At first, I thought it might have been another bomb."

Leila shivered.

"Does papa know?"

"Not yet. I wanted you to hear it first."

Her daughter took it upstairs, grateful that at last her mother was willing to share something with her other than Ben Lokolieff. The thing felt dirty, strangely heavy. She held it with trembling fingertips. What on earth was going on?

She was aware of the expected company milling around in the foyer below, and that her patron had spotted her and called her name. But somehow this felt more important. No sign of her father.

Comme d'habitude.

From under her bed she pulled out her old ghetto blaster, with INXS still in place. She held her breath as she traded the simple joys of teenage bedroom dancing for something strange, darker. And dangerous.

"So who's left?"...

"Fill him up. When wine goes in the secret comes out, n'est-ce-pas? And what's yours my friend. What are you hiding from us?"

"I loathe all Jews. They're the black worms of our planet... I see them as a plague on all our earthly lives."

"He's lying. Lose him before it's too late."

"I disagree. Our new friend's quite delightful."

"Fill him up again. I'm fascinated."

"I have never knowingly lied in my life. The Black Death will come again. I have seen it in dreams. I also believe the notion of roasting a sheep's head as opposed to the rest of it, is to promote the illusion that they are superior. That they think they are the head of things and the rest of us are arseholes..."

"Better and better..."

Even before the tape had finished, Leila extracted it using a tissue. She'd already thought of fingerprints.

Too late. Mine, mama's and God knows who else's must be on it...

She flew down the stairs, gripping the foul thing as though it had symbiotically become a part of her – an extension to her hand. A key to the door of Hell and all the chambers it had spawned.

"Papa!"

Michèle in reception pointed to the salon, her dark eyebrows raised.

The chandeliers were lit even though it was afternoon and still light. Four of Leila's paintings took up one wall, deliberately for Della Schwarz to see her latest work. Close-ups of food for Rosh Hashanah, yellows and greens for the New Year.

A pianist in the corner beyond the suits and smart dresses, persevered with a Chopin Étude – a sound so light and delicately cadenced it was almost lost among the earnest talk and sudden laughter. But when he saw the hotelier's normally sober daughter charged through the gathering, he stopped playing altogether.

"Papa! You must get the police. Now," she shouted. "It's us who are in danger now." She thrust the cassette at him, but Mordecai Fraenkel seemed nonplussed, aware, as a sensitive host that his guests looked disorientated, even frightened. "I'm going to try and find the packaging," she said. "See what the postmark was."

"My dear Leila, I haven't the faintest idea what you're talking about. This is all very embarrassing. You know these good people are dipping deep into their pockets to save our Synagogue..."

"I do know, but I don't want to die for it."

He watched her weave back through the room, her dark hair flying. He saw too, his wife's distracted expression despite Gidéon Zupert's attentions. The last time he'd seen her like that, was after news of what had really befallen her aunt Agathe and her twin sons near the yellow Vistula. This was serious.

Fraenkel quickly excused himself to his immediate guests and made his way over to her, his frown deepening with each step. "Tell me what's wrong."

"Not here." She led him out into the foyer, to a corner next to the main display cabinet. Porcelain titbits and *animaux boîtes* twinkling under the lights. A cocooned and tempting world now easy to ignore.

"Pipi, I don't think you and Leila understand. I've worked hard to get all this organised." He checked his watch. "I can't really leave these good people. They're our guests."

"I'm sure they'd understand." She said wrily. "I think someone's been considerate enough to send us a warning. Oh, Mordy. It's frightening. Four or five men talking such filth..."

"Filth?"

Leila emerged from the study. In one hand the tape covered in a pink tissue, in the other a padded envelope.

"Reims. Posted yesterday. 2 p.m."

Reims?

Through the cabinet glass she saw the receptionist staring as she answered the phone, so Leila turned her back on her. "Take them, Papa, and call the police. Please. For all of us."

"Kvetching. Kvetching... OK. OK. Let's hear the thing first. It's too easy to be emotive. Knee-jerk may not be the best response in this instance..."

Mother and daughter looked at each other in despair and Simon Muller who was too polite to ask what was wrong, coughed before he spoke.

"Monsieur 'Dame, Mademoiselle here asked me to mention there's a problem with the water supply to her en suite..."

"I forgot to tell you," Leila said quickly, colouring. "What with all this..."

"I've already seen to it," the receptionist announced from her desk. "Kitchen had reported a blip with the waste disposal as well, so I took the liberty of getting the firm from St. Cyr. They're due here at sixteen thirty."

"Thank you, Michèle. Much appreciated." The hotelier smiled back at her. Another of his top class recruits proving indispensable.

Once inside the study, he listened to the recording with his eyes closed, hands becoming fists as the conversation in the Hôtel Marionnette unfolded. A chill descended on the room, normally warm and welcoming. Death fixing their paled faces, planning their destiny.

Fraenkel leapt to the phone and asked for 'his friend' at the Angenay Gendarmerie.

"Tell him to come over *now*," Pauline urged pulling on his sleeve, but he covered the receiver.

"He can't. Got a meeting with the Examining Magistrate."

"I'll take it, then," Leila's voice high with anxiety. "I can be there in ten minutes."

"You're needed here, my good girl, with our guests. We keep calm, that's the most important thing."

"Exactly what Uncle Auguste said when the first tank turned the corner into the Herengraacht." Pauline scoffed, but there was no smile, instead that family's spectres haunted her eyes. "Come on." She took Leila's arm. "Tell Mademoiselle Schwarz her protégé will be back before the meeting."

The two women left by the main revolving door and, for a split second, Leila noticed that Michèle Bauer-Lutyens had left her post.

***

At four thirty precisely, while the Touraine Cultural Committee were ensconced round the occasional tables in the salon, with sweet muscat and honey cakes for refreshment, the pair of plumbers from St. Cyr rang the bell at the *entrée de service* and were shown to their stations.

LVII

Dominique Mathieu spent half an hour in the toilettes at Tours Centre Gare shaving the stubble that in twenty-four hours had turned his jaws brown. Something was triggering the follicles into overdrive – probably guilt and fear. Whatever, twenty-four hours was all it had taken, and nerves now gave him a damaging hand. His clean shirt collar was soon marked by blots of dark drying blood.

But this is the least of my punishments.

"In a hurry, eh?" A salesman stood alongside snicking his nostril hairs with a miniature pair of scissors. "Can't keep a girl waiting."

"You're right." Mathieu didn't want to talk at all, but silence might arouse suspicion.

"Where's she, then?"

"Oh, some hotel. Near the river." And before Mathieu could cultivate more lies his companion clapped him on the shoulder.

"Aye, aye. One of those, eh? Here. Try this." He passed him a Calvin Klein body spray.

Eternity. Yes, yes please...

"Works bloody wonders. Just a whiff and wow, you have a pair of legs open at the ready."

"Thanks."

He tried to avoid the other man's eyes, for his own imagined photofit lay already reflected by the mirror. Him and the others set out in a line of hatred in *Le Monde, Figaro, Paris Soir*. Deadly half-tones with gloomy lowering gazes.

He'd sent the complete, traitorous Kodak film off to his father with a note of sorrow and regret begging him to act. Anonymously, if need be. And urgently. Also to clear out his flat and contact Raôul Boura for a prayer. His mother Angélique was not to know.

"Well, good luck, then." The salesman zipped up his case, and Mathieu watched him swagger through the door. When his soles had tap-tapped him away up the steps, he crammed a beret on his head and unfolded a Michelin of Tours and its historic environs.

Ah. The Forêt d'Essecotte. I remember Duvivier mentioning it for later... Something useful at least from the swine... Could be 20 kilometres from here... but how on earth to get there...?

His finger traced the journey with increasing despair. He couldn't use a taxi and the railway went either south-west, the wrong side of the Loir, or north-east, towards Orléans and Paris. Nor could he hitch, having to stay as anonymous as possible.

After a final dab at his cuts, Dominique Mathieu moved swiftly, driven from behind by the rising wind that suddenly seemed autumnal, and the desire to make some amends for his weakness, his shocking collaboration.

Loose leaves from the plane trees along the Champ Malgagne spun like bats and fastened themselves on his body. His face even, blinding him for an instant before he found what he was looking for.

A Peugeot bike. No lock. Ready and waiting. A miracle when he needed it most, except he'd resolved he would no longer be recognising such things. Tyres hard, and a narrow saddle he could just about live with.

Thank you, whoever you are. You don't know what this means to me.

Early evening traffic sang its own repetitive dirge as he diverted through Luynes on the D76 and found the road to Essecotte. Colder, sharper than Marseilles, where his tiny attic room in the Pension Bienvenue near the Gare St. Charles had been almost suffocating. He sneezed twice. Then he saw the sign.

Le Manoir King David. Tout confort. Restaurant gourmand.

Hunger and thirst had silently devoured him to the point where his stomach began to hurt. He thought of a steak Béarnaise and melting frites, until he remembered why he was there.

All at once, the sound of a speeding car behind him made him pull over, his heart wild with fear, made his near-side pedal catch on a clump of weed.

Damn you. Damn.

A silver Clio veered past. A fleeting glance showed two dark-haired women. The younger one driving was stunning. He stared after her, noting the Paris number plate and a Euro Disney sticker on the boot.

She's obviously lived away and come back home. For what? Doesn't she realise?

Mathieu had instinctively known they were from the hotel, and too beautiful to die. He pedalled harder, vainly attempting to catch them up as the road through the Gatine Plateau levelled, brushed on either side by heathers and huge russet ferns.

Soon he was on a driveway lined by young poplars and soft with chippings that skewed his tyres and threw him off balance.

Just then, behind him, the keening whine of a gear too low coming closer, like the scream of an eagle nearing its prey. Headlights, even though it wasn't yet dusk, and two men inside, their faces urgent and troubled. Faces he recognised.

Duvivier and Vidal. Someone help me. Help me...

A plumber's van. A Bedford Rascal. Something et Fils. He couldn't quite make it out. Mathieu's mouth fell open. His breath on hold and fingers trembling on the handlebars.

Father forgive them, for they know not what they do...

A chipping flew up and scorched his cheek. Then, they were gone.

17.23 hrs.

He stood up to ride, all his weight on the pedals, labouring against the tricky surface. One push forward, two slides back, until he saw the grey blur of parked cars and the hotel lights beyond. Mathieu flung the bike down and charged between the Mercs and Audis towards the main entrance.

He glimpsed *Shalom* scripted in gold above a star of David, but there was no-one in reception, just a hum of voices to the left. The runaway pushed open the gilded double doors and immediately, forty-five startled faces turned his way. He looked for the beautiful girl he'd just seen, to no avail.

"Get out!" he yelled at the top of his voice. "Everyone get out! For God's sake!"

As if in slow motion, pens were lowered, papers put to one side before the Cultural Committee got to its collective feet. Black suits, navy suits, dark, demure dresses, all very calm without a word, reliving as one, old *cauchemars*, showered from above by a million faceted crystals.

"This place will be next. I know it!" His voice unrecognisable from the tape, and never so huge in St. Jean de la Motte Mauron, had now found a cause. "Come on, *vite!*"

There came the splintering of glass from the far corner as the fire alarm, half siren half shofar, echoed through the building above the terror of fleeing cars. Leila Fraenkel had used her shoe to break the glass, but her hand was bleeding.

"Mama! Papa! Move! We have to believe him," she shrieked, and Mathieu saw her properly, for the first time. Her shining hair, her exquisite face.

I love you already, whoever you are.

But her father sat still with his sheaf of papers resolutely in place. Central Synagogue. Devis de Travaux. Roof beams, re-felting, re-tiling, the new Jerusalem.

His eyes sunk behind his glasses, caught hers.

"My father always said to me, stay with your dream whatever storms beset you. And dear daughter, I know you understand all about that."

"Monsieur!" Mathieu tried to pull him from his seat. "There is a device that could go off at any time. Are you mad?"

Both men stared at each other. Tears began from each for the other, but neither tears nor words were enough.

"I built this place up from a ruin. Just as I want to rebuild the Synagogue. And I will. God knows I will. Remember, my name represents the Chesed. Charity and forgiveness..." He slumped back in his chair as Pauline Fraenkel was frantically trying to prise her daughter's paintings from the wall. But they'd been mirror-plated and there was no screwdriver to release them. She tried her nails and broke them all as Mathieu dragged Leila out into the drive.

"Mama! Leave them," she cried. "It doesn't matter. Oh, papa..."

Mathieu let her cling to him, feeling her body next to his. Her mouth in his hair for comfort, any comfort and, as the blast shot the hotel in two and a massive tower of flame licked the darkening sky above, he slipped his folded-up charcoal portrait into her hand.

LVIII

As Nelly cleared away the lunch things and stacked them by the sink, she noticed Didier Molinari move across the window. Although the glass had recently borne the brunt of the easterly rain, and her charity shop spectacles were still on her nose, he was clear enough for her to recognise.

A tap on the door. Not the usual four, but three. She frowned, wishing Bellino's gun was still in her pocket. Why she kept the chain on since she'd arrived at Colette's apartment four days ago, like she'd been told, but would really have liked to allow the guard in just to gaze at his dark good looks. No matter he wore decorator's overalls under a sou'wester with an uncool cap on his curls.

"Car's just been delivered," he said. "Could you tell Madame Bataille? I'll be waiting by the steps, just in case."

Then he was gone.

Tell Madame Bataille... She was the one he'd always noticed. She the one he liked. C'est ma vie...

"Who was that?" Colette was in Bertrand's room putting on clean sheets and replacing fresh pyjamas inside his panda on the pillow.

"Your other fan club says your car's back."

"Oh, Nelly, stop it!" She slammed the bedroom door, said sorry to her son for her carelessness; then, having stuffed the hospital letter in her pocket, slipped her mac over her shoulders.

"I'll lead." Nelly offered.

"Fine." But Colette's voice betrayed a nervousness grown more severe since the King David Hotel bombing. Although news of this atrocity had segued into that of the wrecked *Bateau-Mouche*, it was photographs of the handsome hotelier and his wife who'd perished, that took up whole front pages of the local and national press. Colette at first had wanted to try and contact their artist daughter, Leila to tell her she wasn't alone, but Nelly would have none of it and told her to hang on for Bertrand instead. But she nevertheless felt evil draw closer, like cloud shadows on the land, and knew that before long, that same darkness she'd endured would embrace her again.

This was the first time she'd left the flat since returning to Lanvière, and, even with Nelly in front, the solid rain found her face, obliterating all sounds from the street below. She felt doubly scared and vulnerable.

"Where's the bloody guard? What's going on?" She hung back, looking along the damp concrete landings and pillars wide enough to conceal a body.

"He's around somewhere," Nelly, with hope in her voice. "Come on."

Colette spotted Dolina Levy's door already half covered by an *À Vendre* sign and touched it in sorrow.

Someone's not wasted much time. Poor woman...

Then she realised Nelly had disappeared round the corner.

"Nelly? Wait!"

A shriek suddenly filled the air.

Colette ran, her legs leaden with fear and saw two men blocking the way. The Molinari lookalike and another. Four silhouetted black hands...

"Stupid bitches," the shorter one's voice softened by his hood. "Go for their gobs." Gilles Ferey snatched a chunky, metal key-ring from his pocket.

"Two gobs, two bullets. Great."

Colette leapt on Nelly and brought her down facing the wet floor. Cats' piss and new rain, their breaths urgent gasps. Her wig adrift of her head.

So this is it. All over again... Goodbye Bertrand... Nelly....

Then a scuffle. Someone else was there. Colette recognised agent Sedan's voice yelling for help and the thud of booted feet against the wall. The blast from the key ring gun and a hail of other shots, echoed through the apartment block.

"Oh, Jesus." She kept Nelly's head close, twin heart beats racing under the cries and groans of death nearby. They froze as warm blood dried and last words evaporated. No last rites, no consoling, and only when sub-lieutenant Sedan touched her arm did she turn to look at the terrible landscape of carnage, of bodies still stirring in slow, slow motion.

He was dying too. It was written on his face and the rest of him.

"Help," was a whisper in the rain that only Colette could discern with her ear next to his mouth as Nelly scrambled to her feet and charged back up to the flat.

"I'm here. You'll be alright," Colette murmured to him.

"I've had it. You'd better get out."

She cradled him as he paled – the last woman he would ever hold. Bald, pink-eyed, better than nothing and the best she could do. For a tiny, terrible moment she pretended it was Bertrand's little breath on her cheek. But then the man stiffened, his blue eyes blanked on nothing and Colette cried out, letting him fall from her grasp.

***

The SAMU car whined into the Rue St. Léger followed by a war of feet on the concrete steps. Someone vomited during Colette's little prayer so there was no time to finish it. No time for the niceties of life. There were already too many dead.

LIX

If Abraham was prepared to offer up his son as sacrifice, well, I've gone seventy-one better, and I must say it would be nice to see some gratitude, even dare I say, a small reward? Are you listening up there?

In the schooling ring at 'L'Havre de Paix,' its owner, Georges Déchaux drew on his panatella and tightened the lunging rein bringing his latest acquisition to an abrupt halt. Seventeen hands, and perfectly formed, the rescued Lippizaner whose last owner, Colonel Anton Kopeck had been killed in a mortar attack, stood ghost-white against the blackening sky. His vastus muscle trembled in his flank as Déchaux marched towards him in the outdoor school.

"Cnaba, Cnaba," he smiled. He'd renamed him 'Glory' in the language of its birthplace and already the stallion knew his voice, both ears on full alert as he approached. "You're truly a horse of Heaven." The général unwrapped a portion of *tarte aux pommes* and offered it up to the whiskered lips that daintily took it.

Warm against warm, Cnaba then sniffed the left-over cigar, the skin cream, the hair restorer before sighing against his new owner's neck.

For the first time, for a small moment, his *Havre de Paix* – meaning safe haven – seemed to match its name.

· "Too much has gone wrong, my friend," he began. "Better that the Landsturm had been a herd of pigs with Plagnol as Hauptsturmbannführer. They've let me down. Badly. Six weeks too soon with Marheshvan nowhere in sight. Damn every one of them, and Line and Ferey – local bunglers. Waste of bloody skin, don't you think?" Déchaux used his handkerchief to pick an insect from the corner of the horse's dark blue eye. "Let's hope pretty Nina Zeresche keeps her head on her shoulders at Eberswïhr. And what about those other girls, my beauty, who, without myself and Sister Marie-Ange, would have been walking the streets?" He lowered his voice. "Lefêbvre was the worst. Duping me by sending the Breton's tape to the Jews in Essecotte. I should have finished off her and Kirchner at the Salpêtrière. However, better late than never, don't you agree?" He looked over to where a pile of new cavaletti lay near the schooling ring's fence, covering a length of heavy sand. Deep and freshly impacted.

Excellent. A nice quiet grave. Adieu, Claude, ma jolie lesbienne...

Cnaba teased the man's mole, and he smiled, for unlike the critical youngster in Ghirlandajo's *Vieillard*, the animal seemed to be finding some pleasure in it.

When the général slackened the rein and flicked the lunging whip near his thigh, the horse began a collected trot, widening the circle, his tail high over his rump and nostrils glowing like carnelians. Then a change of leg at the canter followed by a cabriole from a sudden stop, and a whinny of ambition.

"That's my boy." Déchaux stared in wonderment while the sky succumbed to the quiet dark and the girls' bedroom windows in his farmhouse flickered on and off like morse. Recalled from duty, they were, with the exception of Ruffiac, restless and demanding. All his *'poules'* come home to roost.

He lit another cigar as he led his charge back through the gate across a chalky field once full of brood mares he'd brought up from Provence, to the stables that lined the eastern wall. One of those detained upstairs – his *'souris rouge,'* – had made a nameplate from a pizza base with the letters CNABA scripted in felt pen. But he'd been insulted enough already, and had jammed her mouth with it instead. Cnaba, his special creature would have silver instead. Maybe the best porcelain. He would have to decide which.

It was like old times watching the stallion walk sweetly into his stall, to be knee deep in fresh straw. After just a day, the Russian-bred was settled, and now as his fine enquiring head was turned his way, the mother-loving Father André's preachings from Revelations came to mind...

Behold a Pale Horse, and he that sat on him was Death...

Déchaux shivered and hastily filled the metal feeder with a mix of bran and the best oats from a dealer in Foucourt. Even though he was on official sick leave, lying low, he still had five hours work ahead to save himself.

Revenons à nos moutons.

Old Désespoir and his peculiar wife had disappeared, and their home village was already under surveillance, but from his conversation with the lovely Sister Superior at the Refuge, they were known to be near Saintes and heading south to Libourne.

Soon these rats will be wearing the biggest smile of all.

The Banja Lukan exile picked at his feed, as if mindful of his new owner's audible thoughts and nuances of tone. His mouth peppered by grain, his huge ultramarine eyes fixed on him with disconcerting depth.

"And now, my Seian Horse." The man stroked the pink muzzle, soft and pliant as Ruffiac's breasts had been. "Tell me, what is poor Georges to do with himself?" He paused, waiting politely just like his Confessor at Ste Trinité had always done... "I see. You are absolutely right, of course..."

Almost five hours left until Duvivier's visit for a business chat and then, with a sextet of girls to choose from, with one more still to come, who could ask for a better nightcap? The général set the alarm and secured the end stable door.

***

The sky over the chalk downlands south of Reims was almost dark, not naturally from subtle dusk, but by the swathe of onyx cloud that had stealthily advanced from the north-east. From its coal slags and war fields. A kind of grim Gethsemane that silently clasped everything to its dark heart, and as the général discarded his riding boots and unlocked the side door to the farmhouse, the telephone in his office was ringing.

LX

When her employer, Guy Baralet called at Number 6, Apartments Cornay with a spray of pink chrysanthemums, he looked a worried man. It was Colette who responded first, having used the spy hole and recognising his voice on the Intercom. His weary smile echoed her own, prelude to a long embrace, while Nelly hung back.

Colette then introduced her. "Guy, this is Nelly Augot. She actually saved my life."

The ex-student greeted him warmly. Another good-looking man, until she saw his wedding ring. Baralet was trying not to stare at his former secretary. The new wig that Jacqueline Noiret had helped her choose, her bruised and swollen feet, but he couldn't bring himself to ask for a glimpse of her eyes. Those sunglasses were giving nothing away.

Colette had felt good to be dressing for a man again, and that hadn't included Didier Blanco. She'd had two hours since Guy Baralet's call to get ready. Checking her make-up, doing her nails...

"You look wonderful," he lied badly.

"Thank you."

"We've all missed you terribly, Colette, and I have to say, that although I've never been back inside a church since I was a nipper, I have been praying. Lise as well."

"You're both too kind." She found a matching vase under the sink and he saw how with one deft movement his gift was arranged and placed on the table.

"Flowers of gold. Lise was telling me. For a golden lady."

Colette blushed.

"Do thank her. They make all the difference."

He took her hands. "We know what you've both been through, and neither of us could bear it. And your dear Bertrand? Still no news?"

I am shameful. How can I tell her that the Seine near the Pont Neuf was being dredged, and those seven dead passengers found from the boat were all over forty and from the Oise? Forgive me.

"No, not yet." She gripped him even more tightly. "But I am praying."

"And what about our *curé*?" He studied her carefully. "Seems he has some questions to answer."

"What on?"

"Tell him." Nelly urged, setting out cups for coffee. "You must."

" OK. He's tried to get in touch. And been taped."

"Not the only one, from what I heard this morning."

"Meaning?"

"Leila Fraenkel claimed to have recognised Dominique Mathieu's voice on the hate tape sent to the King David's Hotel. He's one of the five priests still being hunted. A Breton. It's been officially matched up, but all very hush-hush at the moment."

Colette felt as though a stone had settled in her stomach.

"Young, good-looking, he must have been deranged," Nelly went on.

"No, he wasn't. He was the only one with any heart."

Baralet raised his considerable eyebrows.

"Some heart," Nelly said wrily as Colette blinked away stinging tears.

"What about Leila Fraenkel, then? I could go and tell her what he was really like."

"I wouldn't. Anyhow, she's been tucked away somewhere. Out of sight out of mind for the time being." The businessman's frown stayed put. He coughed, as if unsure how to start. "Look Colette. I know this isn't what you want to hear," he began softly, "and as the whole thing's still being investigated. Prêtre's not saying much, but closer to home, our man of God's in pretty deep, too. Up to here, in fact." He pointed to his forehead, then suddenly checked the window in case he'd been followed. "I'd keep well clear, if I were you. If he makes contact again, tell Captain Prêtre straight away. Myself as well. I've arranged a new line, nothing to do with Medex. Strictly private." He passed her a small card.

"Good grief, how much did that cost?"

"Doesn't matter."

She blushed again. Guy Baralet released his hands to pat her shoulder.

"Thanks to you and Nelly, they're now sniffing right at the top. This is one hell of a bottomless cesspit. If you thought The Beast that Brecht referred to had died in 1945, you're wrong. It's merely been dozing..."

Perspiration crawled under Colette's wig as Baralet went on.

"Someone's trying to warn me off as well. Swastikas, you name it, all over our new walls. Then Les Flammes have just put their spoke in, so it's a right bloody mess at the moment. Just had a quote today for nearly half a million to put the damage right. But," he took his coffee and managed a smile for Nelly. "it's you both I'm worried about, and I don't know if it's been made clear to you how much danger you're both in. Look," he drained his cup, "why don't you come and stay with us at *'La Passerelle'*? Our daughter's away, so we've got two extra rooms, all mod cons..."

But Colette was staring at her son's bedroom door.

Until I have news of Bertrand, I'm not leaving. This is his place and I'll be here for him, always. Besides, this is where Robert would expect to find me...

"I can't thank you and Lise enough, but..."

"But what?" Nelly impatiently rinsed her cup.

"I need to wait for my son."

For the first time, Nelly sighed impatience. And Baralet noticed.

For God's sake, Colette. For everyone's sake, just tell him you gave Vidal's key to Bertrand. This is hideous.

"We've all had a bellyful of this, I know," Nelly went on, "but worrying every twenty-four hours of every bloody day that you're the Bull's Eye is fucking unbearable. Sorry." She turned to the woman whose resolve was now so unnerving. "I've got no choice. And thank you, Monsieur. I'd like to take you up on that if I may. I've had enough."

The managing director looked bemused. This wasn't going to plan.

But if she goes, maybe Colette will follow...

"Look, I can fix you up with your old job, or part-time even," he said to Colette. Just a few hours of your help is worth a hundred of Mademoiselle Hiron's, your replacement."

"Thank you."

But why, oh why, couldn't you have done that for Bertrand? Lord knows he asked for work enough times.

"Is she still there?"

"No. She just upped and left this morning. No note, no forwarding address. Even the agency couldn't trace her."

"That's odd." Colette frowned.

"Anyhow, I missed you what with all the Natolyn brouhaha. Not proven, thank God, but the good news is Medoxin's on target and were getting ready for its launch."

"Don't tempt me."

"We could still do New York. It's up to you."

"Go on," Nelly almost shouted. "I've never even had a bloody job. Let alone the luxury of turning one down."

Baralet put a finger to his lips. Colette was interested.

There's my desk, the way I like to do things. Even my jar of déca, and...

She suddenly turned to Baralet.

"My Diary? Is it still there?"

Nelly saw him turn an instant grey.

"Yes, of course. Don't worry."

Oh, Hélas.

"Are you sure?"

"Why? What's it got in it? All your lovers' names?" Nelly quipped, but

Colette wasn't smiling.

"How could your desk diary be of interest to anyone else?" Baralet asked as casually as he could. Then remembered with a jolt that he'd once caught the temp, Mademoiselle Hiron, looking at it.

"Exactly." Nelly had pulled out a Nike holdall and was cramming it with her few possessions.

"So there's no persuading you?" Guy Baralet looked suddenly older, the lines of concern deeper around his eyes.

"No. It's better this way. I'm not afraid," she lied. "Besides, Eberswïhr have put two more guards on here."

And someone else I'm waiting for.

"I know to my cost. They quizzed me long enough. I've never been frisked before, either." He managed a small smile.

"I just want to say I'm grateful for all you've done," she said. "And I'm flattered you want me back, but just think if your daughter had vanished and you'd been told she was dead, with no evidence, nothing to show, what would you and Lise do? Go away on holiday? Visit relations, or would you stay, just in case?"

"I understand. But you take every care now. Ring if there's anything you need, however small."

"Yeah, and I'll get your shopping. Just phone me your list," Nelly said, zipping up her bag with finality. They kissed goodbye with Nelly's hot new tears burning her cheek. "You've got to understand, Colette, I've had no shut-eye at all since we got back, and I feel so bloody scared, so half-alive especially since Didi and Sedan got killed. That was it, really. But I don't want to leave you..."

"You mustn't feel guilty. I'll be alright." Colette touched her still anarchic hair. "You've been the best friend I could have had, and I'll never forget what you did, coming down to Libourne. Just let me know if you hear any news of Victorine and her sisters, or if the Doumiez family manage to trace you."

"I will. Oh, and by the way, next week I'll try *Le Canard enchainé* for any freelancing work, then I'm going to Cologne to meet up with other *chômeurs*, you know, from I. G. Metall and D.G.B. You never know, I might even see Ber..."

"No. Don't say it. Here, have this." Colette instead, handed her a square of folded bank notes specially withdrawn from her account with Crédit Agricole.

"I can't."

"Yes, you can, and you must." She smiled. "For new glasses."

And then, very quickly, she was alone. Just as she had been a lifetime ago on that hot August day. Alone with her hospital appointment looming and the beautiful flowers that gave no happiness. Just fears and memories distilling into pure terror. So that when one of the replacement guards turned up with the latest edition of *France Est*, he thought she looked on the point of collapse.

"Come on, it might never happen," Jean Guillon had tried to make light of it. "But it has for these poor buggers."

She couldn't begin to alter his perception of things and didn't try, but when she saw the latest headline, she felt the blood drain from her face:

TRAGÉDIE AU REFUGE DES PAUVRES SOEURS DES SOUFFRANCES.

Her heart stopped, for underneath the main photo of the Abbé de Lagrange Vivray taken at his Paris desk and captioned, 'The Founder,' were others. Quickly, she hid them under her hand. No way was she ever going to look into those cruel eyes again. But one face persisted between her spread fingers. More male than female, Leisel Falco. Driver/instructor, and former Olympic clay pigeon shot. Colette noticed her shirt. The same as listed on the invoice. Panic thudded in her chest as she propped herself up against the kitchen wall to study the Refuge's ground plan and, having folded the row of faces out of sight, checked the smaller print for any more clues. But the reportage was predictably elegiac, with no hint of the horrors she'd experienced. No mention either of Falco's youthful involvement with the Aryan Nations, or the training schedule for National Socialism's secret infiltrators.

She felt cheated and betrayed, and if she hadn't been so vulnerable, would have contacted the editor immediately to put things right. The report stated that the mass gassing had centred around the altar, marked with an X, and collective suicide seemed to have been the *prima facie* motive.

Colette stared in amazement.

Suicide? That's crazy. They loved themselves too much for that. Thought they were the saviours of the bloody world. Besides, who in the name of God could have organised it? Got everyone to agree to die. No, it just doesn't ring true, but the Press would prefer it, of course, as it would make them all martyrs.. And there's nothing like a martyr in times of trouble.

She thought of the heroic Victorine and her identical sisters as she turned up the sound on both radio and TV. Solemn music on TV2 with stills of the poplars, the new bell tower, the statuary along the drive. All frighteningly familiar but now deserted. A place of tragic ghosts.

Forgetting for a moment her own predicament, Colette prayed for the innocents there, that their souls might find permanent communion with the saints. Then she removed her wig, cut it into pieces, and buried it in the waste bin.

Now, after Désespoir's death together with that of Madame Gamme, she increasingly believed his verdict on Bertrand to be a fabrication. The utterances of a senile misogynist who'd gorged on her suffering like a dawn hyena.

We'll show him, won't we? Please, dear Bertrand, let it be a lie...

Then the phone rang, and her hand hovered trembling over it like a water diviner trying to gauge its whereabouts.

"Madame Bataille?"

"Who are you?"

"Lieutenant-Colonel Yannick Wintzer. Eberswihr. Your car's ready. We've garaged it for you, would you like to come down?" His accent more German than Lorraine.

"How come you've got a garage key?"

"Monsieur Saulx was most kind. "

"Mmm." She'd never seen her landlord. All her affairs were arranged through a solicitor in Bouillon. "OK. And by the way?"

"Yes?"

"I don't think the Pauvres Soeurs would ever have killed themselves in a million years. It's ridiculous."

"Sorry, Madame, but I'm not able to say anything further at the moment. There are several factors being taken into account, and we'll keep you informed as appropriate."

"Just one other thing." She could tell he was busy and trying to stay civil, but at work she'd been good at pushing things just that little bit further, to say what she wanted. Particularly with men. And now she expressed her sorrow at the murder of agent Sedan who'd risked his life on her behalf, leaving a widow with a teenage son. A man of rare kindness, she said, feeling the start of fresh tears.

"I agree. One of our best. He'll be hard to replace." She could hear him shuffle papers. "But with Guillon and Trignac you have excellent protection. However, like most things, our resources are finite."

"What do you mean?" Panic crept through her body.

"I would urge you to reconsider Monsieur Baralet's kind offer." The words sunk like stones in her heart. "We gather Mademoiselle Augot has already gone with him."

"She hasn't a son to wait for. Besides, his bed's here. All his things."

"I have to be honest, Madame, we can only guarantee 24-hour surveillance for a further six days. Our men are needed in so many places, we have a growing problem as I'm sure you're aware."

"Of course I'm aware." *The Beast... OPÉRATION JUDAS... l'Armée Contre Juifs... Yes, I do know, but not until Bertrand is home.* "But what's more important than keeping a mother safe for her child? I pay my taxes, I've not claimed any benefits. He needs me here."

"Look, you've been through enough, I know, but we do have a 'safe house' available now. Three rooms, etcetera. It's actually in our Headquarters. I'd give it serious thought. Oh, and Guillon will drop your keys through in three minutes."

Then he was gone.

Just before she replaced the receiver, she heard the faintest sound, like a cherry stone dropped into water. Someone else had been listening.

Merde.

Colette felt that familiar trap tightening around her. That cellar again, the dark stench of death, and without Nelly, without anyone, she knew only loneliness would be her future. The flowers looked obscene in their abundance. All her possessions cheap and worthless.

And why should Bertrand come back to this? How can I expect it? I still haven't bought him his birthday present.

The Peugeot key duly clattered into the newly installed letter cage. Its Futuroscope key ring missing. She fixed a scarf round her head then let herself out, past the ochre stains where all three men had died, past Madame Neufour from Number 10, who'd tried complaining about all the commotion. Down to where two more men were rebuilding the communal gardens' walls. They looked up briefly, took in her good legs and her out-of-place sunglasses, following her every move to the lock-ups and the only door with a hurriedly-cleaned swastika.

Salauds.

The boot first, almost jamming the key, then she raised it slowly, peering in, little by little. A void. Nothing. Like the rest of her life, the blanket had gone.

So is Bertrand I know it now. Not even an echo or a shadow. What kind of God have we got?

Her trembling hands trawled the empty space as though by some miracle their need would be answered, but her prayers were worn thin with despair. She slammed the boot shut. Its hollow finality still echoing in her head as she opened the driver's door.

The interior smelt different, newly valeted, with all the seats shrouded in white polythene. Depersonalised, not hers any more. She could pretend it was a hire job, that neither her son or her lover had ever sat alongside her. Even the glove-box sweets had vanished as the eye of Science had scoured every crevice for clues.

***

She reversed too fast. The *ouvriers* stared and Trignac checked his watch. Her sunglasses bounced to the floor.

11.52 hours, and the beginnings of rain as she veered past the locked church, through the town and alongside Medex, its show piece, disfigured by slogans as far as the top floor. Over the Meuse and over the speed limit, short-cutting along the Forêt des Woëvres, towards the left fork in the road signed Eberswïhr.

In the town's back streets she stopped to ask the way, but the woman shielding two baguettes was too alarmed to speak.

Centre Ville. Voilà. Merci, whoever you are.

The Préfecture de Police was a grimy, gothic block fronted by a large notice board filled with posters. She parked in the only free space reserved for disabled then ran towards the entrance, sunglasses forgotten.

Suddenly she stopped, her breath on hold. One of the clerks was busy securing the Public Information case with a screwdriver. It was full of photographs, edge to edge, a monochrome gallery of the wanted.

Recherché par la Police.
ARMÉE CONTRE JUIFS

His face came first. Robert Vidal, staring from behind the glass. His lips parted as though about to call her name. She could barely bring herself to look, but his hunted, haunted eyes still seemed to follow her as she saw the others in their priests' black, lined up next to the late Désespoir. Mathieu the last, finally one of them. Then a man she didn't recognise, in a different uniform. As pale as the background of some spring ceremonial in Paris. His strange nose and smirking mouth filled her with a choking nausea.

Next, five women, all under forty years old whose expressions had hardened to hatred above their robes of the Pauvres Soeurs. Whose pseudonyms and changes in appearance had confused the police for too long. However, Colette gasped when she recognised the name of Marie-Claude Huron who'd cunningly infiltrated Medex. Cried out upon seeing Patrice Sassoule, the now darker-haired nurse who'd so intimately viewed her. This native of Reims had also been known as Giselle Subradière and Simone Haubrey.

And weren't Claude Lefêbvre and Romy Kirchner the ones Nelly had shot at in Libourne? They were next to Michèle Bauer-Lutyens... Where on earth could they all be?

She left the clerk giving the glass a final wipe over, as her heels jarred on the steps.

"Yes Madame?" An attractive brunette in civilian clothes, called out from the switchboard.

"I must see Lieutenant-Colonel Wintzer. It's urgent."

260

"Name please?" She then wrote it down, pointed towards the stairs. "Number 8. First on the right." She then rang to warn him.

Wintzer gulped down the rest of his coffee and wiped his mouth with his hand. Every day brought new surprises, and this was one he could have done without.

"Good to see you've changed your mind, Madame." He pulled out a regulation chair, trying to avoid her eyes.

"I haven't."

"Oh?"

She declined the seat. "I need to tell you something."

The forty-three-year-old, freshly transferred by personal request from the Lanvière Gendarmerie, leant forwards. The first edition proof of *France Est* with Romy Kirchner's story inside, lay hidden in his lap.

"I'm without a priest, as you know," Colette began. "Everything's been transferred to St. Marc and the Apostles at Monzeppe. It's too far. There's only you."

"What do you mean exactly?" Wintzer seemed genuinely puzzled.

"You must hear my confession."

The air in the office grew cold. He shivered as he silently switched on the tape. "Do you mind?" he asked, but she wasn't listening.

The moment was drawing closer, as inevitably as the tidal surge down the Canal de l'Est – permanent umbilical of the Meuse – and, like that lunar tide, the dates and times of her latest witness hurtled along too quickly for him to intercept until her final words had ended.

***

"So you see, Inspector. My Bertrand should never have been born. What kind of mother knowingly risks her son's life? Tell me."

She swayed unsteadily, back in that hall again with the Percheron, Sister Agnès and the Sister Superior. But this was no interrogation. And at the end, she had nothing left to say.

"Sit down, Madame Bataille." He fidgeted with his watch. "I'm only sorry Mireille Bech isn't here to assist."

"Who's she?"

"Part of our Community Policing Programme. A retired officer, but very good at giving comfort and support".

"Comfort and support? What for? What's going on?"

"I'm afraid I've bad news." He finally extended a hand to reach hers, but she desisted.

"Just get on with it, please."

Again, a glance at his watch. Then a small cough.

"At eleven o'clock exactly, just after I'd called you, we received a message from the River Police at the Port de la Bourdonnais..." He paused, unable to look her in the eye. "Your son's body was found together with one of the Roquette's security staff very close to the boat's remains."

***

Wintzer took advantage of her frozen silence to continue. "I tried to call, but obviously you were on your way here. I'm afraid, Madame, you will have to go to the Hôpital St. Camillus, in the eighth..." He extracted the tape and got up as Kirchner's revenge slipped to the floor under his desk. "It appears your son was followed to Paris in the first place, then the St. Anne's hostel tipped off our so-called men of God... I'm so very sorry."

This time she let him take her hand, but in her numbness hardly felt it. "Are you ready?" he said.

How do they know it's him? It's bound to be someone else. Please make it be someone else. Just because Jesus died in front of his mother doesn't mean I have to suffer as well. Why are you doing this to me?

"Colette? Are you ready?" he asked again, gently.

She followed him in a trance as he knocked on another door, whereupon two more uniformed police emerged. The stairs down were difficult, but she kept the outer door in her sights, facing north-west. Facing the Capital with just numbness, no pain, no pain. Almost surreal, until she saw the young woman on the switchboard hurriedly making a connection to somewhere.

"Who's that?" Colette asked, loud enough for all to hear.

"Mademoiselle Zeresche. A trainee. Why?"

"I have to say something."

Deep black water... my baby, my baby...

"What is it, Madame?"

"Our phone line at my flat. You know, the special one. I'm sure it's tapped. After your last call I heard something odd."

At this, the young brunette tried to duck under the sectioned counter, but the two officers were on her as she kicked and wrestled with them to retrieve her gun.

***

Thirty minutes later, with the rain coursing like a blown veil off the windscreen, the unmarked Peugeot with its driver and three passengers sped south towards Verdun to join the A4, the fastest route to the Metropolis.

As urban sprawl supplanted fields of grazing livestock, and traffic thickened, news from the Rue St. Aubin came over Yannick Wintzer's radio. A handwritten suicide note and impromptu will had been found in Christian Désespoir's study. Undated, but judging by its condition, had been recently composed. The reporter kept his voice under control as he began…

"…The Armée Contre Juifs used my initiative for Les Pauvres Soeurs in Libourne like a parasite, to grow even bigger than its reluctant host. It still grows, nourished by the Unfinished Business of Jews in Europe. Général Georges Déchaux has threatened myself and my wife – Madame Gamme – with our lives every day since August 1995 when the Refuge first opened. The fists of this arch-criminal and his friends in the Police and Secret Services have been linked together for too long, while we too, sinned in the eyes of God.

"Because of my transgressions, we wish to leave what remains of our estate to the furtherance of racial tolerance in this country I have loved since my childhood in the Mayenne. I was twelve when the enemy first appeared with those black serpents on their arms. Now they are among us again."

LXI

Robert Vidal sat alone outside the Bar du Pont in Châteauroux, having tried the pay phone to try and reach Colette.

In his own clothes, jeans, black leather jacket and lumberjack shirt he could have passed for anyone. Everyman, except that his burdens were growing by the minute, to match his loneliness and isolation. He needed Colette's voice, her just being there, and this need gnawed at his soul, obliterating his choir, the ritual demands of his religion, and the fact that his father had vanished from police custody, now rendering himself to all intents and purposes, an orphan.

What if François should start singing?

There's nothing I can do.

He sucked the bitter *citron pressé* through the straw, flinching at the sourness on his tongue. In five minutes, he'd try her again, before his journey. By 20.00 hours he'd be in Lanvière, feeling her body against his, her scent more than incense could ever be...

DEATH TO THE NEO-NAZIS! Join LES FLAMMES!

A long-haired student sandwiched between the words in red, stopped at his table and held out his cap. Vidal obliged with ten francs, alarmed by the tremor in his hand.

Stupid shits. Go and do something useful.

"Thank you, Monsieur."

Vidal watched him pester the rest of the clientèle until *le patron* saw him off with a wave of the menu. He then finished his drink. Duvivier had been summoned urgently and without explanation by the général, and left an hour before, strained and jittery. He couldn't pretend for much longer that only two of the first cell remained. That the ACJ's third project in Strasbourg, during Hanukkah, was in doubt.

His problem, not mine. I'm through with it all. I want a life. Or rather, a death...

Suddenly, as a coda to his reverie, a blue van veered into the kerb, throwing dust and gravel in its wake. A dirt fleck landed in his glass.

The driver chucked a slab of newspapers to the ground. "Journaux!" he called.

Instantly Vidal saw half of a headline DOGS OF WAR, then half of himself and the others. His lungs numb while he gave a sign of the cross so rapidly that no-one noticed *le patron* pick up the pile and take it into the bar.

The priest left a generous tip then hurried in the direction of a lorry park on the edge of an industrial estate next to the River Indre. He phoned Colette again. No reply. He broke into a trot going against all the advice for someone on the run with a newly public face.

Meld. He reminded himself. *Fucking impossible.*

Everything was here for the weekend for DIY and gardening punters. Huge white hangars spilled their stock out on to their forecourts. Barbecues in reconstituted stone as big as crematoria, and picnic chairs stacked to impossible heights spotted with migrant bird slime. Vidal too, passed through it all towards the juggernauts.

Fredo Rattino, Norbert Dentresangle, Spedition, Eddie Stobart with a UK number plate all slumbered in warm, diesel rows with their curtains drawn. *Rétameur, tailleur, soldat, matelot... which one to choose?...*

Taking a deep breath, he knocked on the cab window of Jaime Bonnêtre, Fruit et Légumes. Paris plate. Hopefully going north.

The daisy-patterned curtain on the driver's side, stirred and a young face looked out. A woman, no more than twenty-five, sleep still round her mouth.

"Yes?"

Too late to try another. She's seen me now, and would remember....

"A 20 North?" His Midi accent good.

"I might be."

"I need Paris, then Reims."

"Now, shall I tell you Monsieur, what I need?"

"OK." His pulse quickened.

"I need rough scum like you like a dose of the claps. Clear off."

But Vidal was already on the door and he pulled it open. Once she'd seen the pistol she edged over so he could perch alongside. Then he drew his pretty little curtain over and noticed her fingers.

No ring.

"Move it, Mademoiselle."

"Madame, if you don't mind."

"I don't."

She pursed her lips, pushed her hair back and jerked the gear stick into reverse, before edging round to the exit. He didn't like the way she kept sneaking glances at him from the corner of her eye, so he stubbed the Zastava against her thigh, skinny as a chopstick.

"Act normally, or I'll get busy."

She flashed, raised her hand as she overtook a Gröningen cheese truck.

"Don't do that again."

"He's a mate of mine."

"I said, don't." He settled back and pulled the day's *France Soir* from the crowded glove box as she reached 110 heading for Viérzon. She must have just bought it. The ink was still soft.

Mother of God.

'LE MALIN.'

He was looking at himself again. The same shot Toussirot had taken before the Mary Magdalene concert in July. The flash trapped in his right eye.

Toussirot the sly cunt...

"Step on it," whispered the choirmaster as she held the middle lane, alongside caravans petrol tankers and the frequent but unescorted *convoi exceptionnel.*

"Don't worry, I know who you are," she said suddenly. "You're that priest from Lanvière." Her blue eyes met his, and he could see she was genuinely unafraid. Something was making her secure, or else she was mad. But the knife-edge he stood on was honing to such a deadly nothingness, that for the first time since he'd gone to Plagnol's flat with the Breton, he was unsure what to do.

No new ID, no home to go to, his own bed a relic of the past. Just the third payment in the Banca del Corte that morning, from a man he'd never met.

"Best if you don't speak if you've nothing intelligent to say," he said quietly. But saw how his hand was shaking, the pistol like a road drill against her leg.

"Get that thing off me or.. "

"Or what?"

The driver's jaw stuck out resolutely. While she had the wheel, she held the power. He wasn't stupid.

"I can cause an incident, Father. Easy as pie. The *flics* would take less than three minutes to get here from Vaudebois. You wouldn't have a prayer."

The cheeky bitch. My last lap. The only way to Colette. I've no choice. She's right. What prayers can I say now?

He withdrew the Browning and buried it in his pocket alongside the rosary, whose beads were now simply beads. A dead weight he no longer needed. "Would you like these instead?" He pulled them out. Black and scarred, the Aves and Pater Paternosters dangling in his lap. Her laugh was hard and scornful.

"Oh, put them away, for God's sake. I'm a Pantheist."

Vidal lowered his window just enough to cram them through the gap and heard their death rattle under the wheels.

"Tell you something I did like..." She set the wipers to intermittent and sent washer spray over the view.

"What's that?"

"I heard your latest tape. The one that came out last July. Pérotin. I was impressed." But Vidal felt no pride, just sweat leach under his collar, and his neck begin to burn. "Got it for my papa's birthday. He is, was, I mean, a big fan of yours."

Was. That says it all. My choir, my boys. He remembered Charles, the ten-year-old with the voice of liquid silver, and Kevin who could hold a note longer than anyone. And Moussac, murdered, his mouth full of yellow pus...

"I think you'd better stop," he said suddenly. "The next Services will do."

"You're crazy."

"Correct, Madame."

She turned to look at him.

"Where exactly do you want to go? I don't have to pick up until midday tomorrow."

"No tricks?"

"No tricks."

"Melun. Thanks."

***

Silence as the shaved fields gave way to the Legoland of dealerships and wholesalers – Peugeot, Renault, Citroën, and a string of cheap out of town hotels.

"I'll need to fill up before Orléans."

"That's OK." But he had other words ready, swelling, boiling in his mouth. and he was with a stranger, just as he in his time had been stranger to a multitude of guilty tongues in the dark vertical coffins at the l'Église de la St. Vierge. Each one with their own secretive windows, whose intricate carvings had been softened by a million sighs. And now it was necessary that in this open, makeshift confessional, she listen.

"I still care for a woman who lives there."

"Oh, yeah?"

"Yes. And it's her grief that's destroying me. You see... I'm sorry I don't even know your name..."

"Joëlle."

But he didn't seem to notice.

"You see, she had a son who once begged to sing in my choir, but because of our – you know – liaison, and not because his voice had broken as I'd made out, it was impossible. But that's nothing to what happened later."

The young woman slowed down to cruise, the rain thickening on the windscreen, and from far away, the growl of thunder almost devoured his words.

"He was tall for his age. So tall, he almost had to stoop. I suppose that made him seem older, and he'd always been teased about it at school, even at University, so that made her more protective. Nothing was too much trouble –

she wanted the world for him, and when the world didn't respond, he changed. Surly and secretive, you know. Teenager thing, except he was twenty-three. He hated me. I used to see him with that look during the Sunday Mass. I knew he'd do anything to land me in it, and he did. He wanted his mother all to himself. He spread the word. Why I ended up in a boot camp..."

"Why didn't you tell her?"

"How could I? She doted on him. He was the first proper man she'd ever had round the place. Her eyes, her ears."

"Wasn't she ever married?"

"Once, when the boy was nine. But he'd got some kind of wasting disease and died in '86. She'd not had much luck..." Vidal tailed off as his driver signalled right and turned off into the Aire des Beaux Champs. Petrol, diesel and a boutique. Almost deserted.

"So when she suspected me of..."

"Of?" Huge eyes on his. He hesitated. "Go on."

"I'm going to say it. I've always had a problem with Jews. No, this isn't some self-pitying confession, God knows I've heard enough of those. It's how it really was, after the war. Starting with my grandparents. They lost everything on account of the Rosenbaum's turning up, demanding shelter. Then my father gets the push from this Jewish firm where he'd worked all his life. No reason given, just on a whim. Finito. But apart from all that, it's the expectations of faith that hold the key, and the more I studied the Scriptures, the more I resented the supreme arrogance of their rejection of Christ who was the only true prophet – the Dominus Mundi – whose nailed hands held our pasts our futures. The Jews still wait for the Messiah, whoever that may be."

"What about Buddhists and Hindus etcetera?"

"They didn't crucify Him."

"Ah."

She switched off the engine and got out her purse.

"So the woman I love..."

"Love is it now?" She looked up, her eyes narrowing.

"Well, it used to be, before all this. As I was saying, she gives her son the key to my house to see if he could find anything of interest. A stick to beat me with. She used to say to me, "you never say anything kind about poor old Dolina Levy," a Jew living in the same block of flats. Or I'd get, "Why don't you give some of the church collection to help her out. God won't mind.""

"Well, he wouldn't, would he?" she said.

But Vidal wasn't listening.

"Anyhow, the snooper son strikes lucky."

"And?"

"He finds my letter of introduction to Opération Judas."

"What's that?" Joëlle frowned.

"In a moment, if you don't mind. Where was I? Ah, yes... So he passes it on without a qualm to my bishop, without realising the consequences for himself or his mother. And because he'd discovered too much, he was, you know, taken care of."

"I bet she's feeling good. Is he still OK?"

"His mother thinks he might be."

"Maybe she's right..."

"No, no. They put him in the Seine. Fully dressed."

"Holy shit." The driver gasped, her fingers locked round her door handle. "Who's 'they?'"

"The Armée Contre Juifs. The first cell."

"My God." She stared at the man alongside. Someone quite different was there now. Someone who'd just sent an arrow of fear through her system.

"Didn't you try and help him, I mean, after all, as he was your lover's son?"

"No."

"Ugh!"

She slammed the door shut, trapping him in a vacuum of dread. It wasn't just Duvivier who'd been a reckless simpleton. He'd told a total stranger far too much and, instead of feeling a certain blessed release, the partial confession had served only to fur his lungs, and finally numb his tongue.

Nothing to lose. Time to go.

He knew what the girl must be thinking. Maybe she'd chance a quick call to the *flics*, or tell the cashier in his booth.

I should have finished her off while I could. Merde... merde...

He peered round his curtain. Saw in the wing mirror the driver behind getting restless. And her. Where was she? She was neither by the Caisse, nor as far as he could tell, near the shop.

***

16.00 hrs.

He slid over into her seat. No key, but a scour of the various compartments, for this and that, yielded a spare attached to a circle of dirty string.

Why am I still deserving of miracles?

Unlike the Honda, this was a dinosaur. Slow and churlish past the pumps, then a tight circle back to the Paris sign. With his heel on the floor, the Mercedes joined the dual carriageway and took the first exit.

No Péage, thank God. No need to stop...

He picked up the mobile, tried Duvivier and let it ring, but no answer.

Selfish freak show.

He crossed himself again as the empty hulk roared through straggling villages and open farmland, under universal grey in the gathering storm. The thunder closer, with lightning to the west, briefly bleaching the sky.

Colette again. His fingers automatically settled on her number. Was it her voice or interference? He'd never had that before. But his heart leapt at the small sound.

"Colette?" he shouted.

"Yessss? Who's that?"

"Number 2. I'm coming. Be ready. That's all I ask. I'll be at La Sainte Vierge on Friday night – to allow for any hold-ups. Then we can fly to..." He listened hard and thought he detected breathing, magnified into his ear. Then *rien*.

The phone followed his rosary on to the road as rain and spray lashed his face and the first sign for Montargis loomed up out of the rain.

East, east... Give me wings...

But who was listening? There was only the piston of his heart needing more than could ever be given, as one hundred and ten kilometres due north in the Hôpital St. Camillus, Colette Bataille drew back the sheet and saw at last, the bloated, purple face of her dead son.

LXII

Thursday October 9ᵗʰ

The curtains in Dominique Mathieu's small bedroom high above the Orléans Centre Gare, moved with each breath of the rising wind as the staccato rain began to fall.

He turned away, pulling the hostel's sheet tight over his head while night trains slid in and out of the deserted platforms below.

Oh, that I was a corpse already. How much longer will it be?

However, as though in defiance, his pulse thudded even harder against the pillow, young and strong. Seventy years too many away from a natural end.

Leila... Leila...

Mathieu smelt his hands that she'd held in the dark, the aftermath, while the hotel's cremation had added a million evil stars to the watching sky, but there was nothing left of her. Just his own scent of shame and self-loathing.

His palm clamped over his mouth. Warm, not cold. Keeping oxygen at bay.

So, I must try harder, much harder. My Consolamentum is too slow in coming. Mon Épuration...

She'd recognised his voice from the tape that Duvivier had sworn to destroy after Rosh Hashanah, and then torn the drawing into shreds in front of him.

He's the real Judas. He has cost me my happiness. Oh, Saint Thérèse, where are you now? On your eternal sick bed, coughing and retching. What earthly use is that to me, or to anyone? Belief and Faith are no more than twin aberrations of the brain – I know that now.

Better that Father had never given his seed. He's as wicked as Duvivier and the rest. Worse because he never told me he was one of the rocks of shit that built the FN, and when I trusted him to help, he did nothing. Nothing. And maman, did she know? If so, why wasn't I smothered at birth... Maman? Maman?...

Now the young priest's palm pressed harder. Skin on skin. Watertight. Airtight, until his lungs heaved with neglect and his losing mind slipped away, following Angélique Mathieu's rosary through the layered dark as it finally met the graveyard of the Seine.

LXIII

19.03 hours, with the vast two-tone sky lighting up the farm that jutted like a bright gem from the rollered plains around Prunonnes. The storm was gathering momentum overhead, its deep disturbance reaching the stable block's solitary occupant who trance-like, patrolled his loose box driven by a distant memory of freedom.

Duvivier, one hour early, heard its hooves against the door, an eerily hollow sound in the excluding silence, as he left the hire car by the already opened gates and warily followed the gravel drive towards the house. He'd found a damp copy of *France Est* in the toilettes near Château-Thierry, and left without doing up his flies.

Meanwhile, the 'red mouse' had been squeaking big time. She'd not enjoyed having the initials GVD carved into her face, and seeing her friend lose her nails.

How kind. How kind...

His watch showed 19.07. He'd give it three minutes, no more. He was sweating his own salty rain, basted by a burning ear and hatred as the blind buildings grew before him, their inky shadows defining the many new extensions on either side. The wealth discreet but tangible. Nothing but the best materials.

Duvivier took in the solid oak door, craftsman bevelled and polished, and not entirely shut. The new marble slabs and the plaque prohibiting hawkers and circulars spelt out in bas-relief bronze. He then realised that none of the detention-camp security lights had responded to his presence. Perched along the roof, designed to swivel and cover the surrounding hectares, their beams were defunct. Immobilised, like his heart, but not his memory. That this man, Georges Véry Déchaux, once partaker of the Eucharist at Ste Trinité, could deny him his rightful place next to his mother, was the only reason he needed. But something made him hold back.

A death in the pot of Gilgal?

He crouched his bulk down, listening. His breath rough and uneven.

Un mausolée. That's what he's brought me to. The bastard. Does he now want me to join it?

Duvivier sat back on his heels, found his torch and fitted the silencer to his automatic.

Fuck. That bloody horse again...

He crawled right up to the front door and pushed it with his fingertip. Warm fetid air hit him first. Then the smell. His empty stomach lurched as the beam probed the hallway and up the open slatted stairs.

He tried the lights. Nothing. Just a tap dripping somewhere, and the squeak of his boots on the new parquet. Then a sudden slip on an island of blood.

Mon Dieu.

Its trail led through to the rear, past a kitchen, all granite and chrome, as the abattoir stench intensified. One door left, and the Provençal sealed his lips as he kicked it open.

Computers, modems a switchboard and filing cabinets marked ACJ – all lines of communication dismembered and knotted, stained by the dead.

No prayers. I can't, so don't ask me... Oh Jesus...

The drip he'd heard wasn't a tap but something else, worse than he'd ever seen in all his years of carnage on the seas, and beyond his imagining. It came from the throats of seven corpses, stacked like a log pile on the central desk.

Shechita.

The young women – apart from the redhead – were indistinguishable half-hidden under the only man. In death as in life, the Master and most of his pawns, for where was the blonde-wigged chauffeur – the busy informant from the hostel who, with Kirchner had been shot at in Libourne? He dared not think, instead beamed in on that balding head, the startled eyes and the distinctive brown lump on the end of the nose.

He took a deep breath, aimed and shot at the général's dead heart, then puked on to his own feet. Dizzily he waded towards them like a marsh fisherman under too much sun, to pluck the little scroll that had fallen from Déchaux's chest. The words were almost impossible to read so he wiped the blood off on to his tormentor's nearest leg.

TEREFAH. TO BE CAST TO THE DOGS.

Then replaced it.

Non merci. I have better things to do with my mouth, mon Général.

Duvivier set the torch between his teeth – once more the Domini Canis he'd always dreamt of being, with his torch to light the polluted world.

***

He charged outside to where banks of wisteria and honeysuckle smothered the adjoining car port. He walked towards it, trying to recognise the car parked inside and barely distinguishable from the dark. The black Celica.

Voilà. Not much use to you now, my friend.

He kicked its alloys for good measure, before reaching the stable block where he shot the bolts and let the Lippizaner loose, catching the hot lather off its white flanks as the captive careered away from the eye of the storm.

The priest then lifted his gun.

This is for me, for Arsène and my mother who will soon have her lost son closer than he's ever been...

The beautiful ghost snorted, faltered and fell. Its legs cast in a dance of agony. Duvivier stood still, strangely exalted, allowing the huge drops of rain come from over the Ardennes, to soften his skin and drain the unclean blood away.

LXIV

Friday October 10th

"I beg you, God, I have erred, been iniquitous and wilfully sinned before You, I and my household. I beg You with Your Name, God, forgive please the errors, iniquities, and..."

The Avinu Malkenu had started, and Robert Vidal, one-time priest of the Église de la Sainte Vierge, stood in the porch of the new Synagogue in Eberswïhr, listening to the Kohen Gadol's words for Friday evening's Yom Kippur eke out into the night. Words that suddenly and without warning, so profoundly touched his heart that he drew his soaking clothes around him and tightened his eyes shut to contain the tears, as the voice grew in strength.

"...and been iniquitous and wilfully sinned before You, I and my household..."

I and my household, the Cordonniers and my father, they are the black worms on this earth, born and raised in Hell, so how then, dear God, am I supposed to still honour them and give them comfort?

"As it is written in the torah of Moshe, Your servant, from Your glorious expression; For on this day He shall atone for you to cleanse you; from all your sins before God..."

Vidal ran down the steps, lifted by this unconditional promise of hope. The Latin rote of guilt, even the brief consolation of music now subsumed by the might of a higher Universal Truth. That he still could be saved.

My penance began with being born, and I'm so weary of it. Mother will understand. Oh, joy. Oh, joy.

Rainwater puddles sprayed him as he tore along the deserted Avenue Etray, followed by the ram horn's disintegrating notes, towards the roundabout for Reims and Lanvière. A new future driving him on. He'd see Colette. Make amends for poor Bertrand, and with that pure new soul of his, find somewhere deep in *la France profonde* to pursue a life of contemplation.

Ish for Man, Ishah for Woman. Faith and Truth. We can do it. We can do it...

The homing pigeon with a gun, hid behind a row of billboards until an army convoy heading for Reims finally disappeared. He was *sans papiers*, like all the rest but buoyed up by a heady freedom. A fresh purpose with the only person who'd ever really loved him.

He'd driven the Bonnêtre lorry throughout Wednesday night and ditched it yesterday outside Révigny, sensing another tail. No way would anyone be following him to Lanvière. Even now he kept looking back, ears tuned to the slightest change. To the whisper of the grassy verge or the starlings scavenging near a distant farm. Maybe the young woman driver had talked,

275

maybe she hadn't. It didn't matter any more.

The storm was on his side as he dodged into dripping shadows whenever a vehicle swept by along the remorselessly straight road.

Merci, Napoléon. You built for war, not peace.

Like the Kommandant in Prunonnes, impatience had made him too early, and at 20.30 hours exactly, Vidal reached his home town. As he passed the small park of broken swings, he hunted in his back pocket for Dégrelle's soggy little book and flung it into the night sky where it hung like a dead bird on a nearby branch.

Medex still played host to its scaffolding. Still the smell of stone paint as he sloped past, in the shadows, collar up, hands deep on the only protection he had. Down an unlit passageway less than 500 metres from the Rue Fosse. he noticed Gendarmes, one on each corner and a vehicle halfway down.

The smell of burning reached him then a fire engine's siren drawing closer through the town, finally dwindling at his house. No time to stop and investigate.

He daren't risk it. Not now. Not even for his precious Deauville.

His energy suddenly sapped, his lungs heavy as he struggled over the wall at the end of the alleyway, bordering the footpath to the church. He regretted ditching the mobile. At least he could have tried her again.

Make her be here... make her be here...

Water had made the track slippery, and three times he fell and scrambled up again as it led to no more than a silty stream round to the northerly end of the graveyard. Treacherous and invisible without the first lamp near the oldest of the tombs. No light. It had been smashed to bits.

Fuck.

Vidal cut across the unkempt grass keeping to the wall.

Colette... Colette...

Familiar stones under his hands, cold as always, even though they'd once clasped the most wonderful music on earth. They were now repellent and repelling to his happier heart, and he kicked them as he went.

One for sorrow, one for sorrow, one for sorrow...

The bells for nine o'clock, twenty seconds late and losing every hour, tolled bleakly overhead. His clothes now moulded like the Neoprene suit as he hovered by the main door. So near the wilted flowers, the severed Virgin, and yet so far.

Keys?

Somewhere... Somewhere...

He'd forgotten Moussac had never given them to him and he'd never had the new ones. He searched every pocket, every lining and recess, ever more agitated until... There, against his heart, through cotton, through leather, lay something folded, changed by the rain. Her face. His only real sanctuary.

Suddenly he jumped at the rush of sound as the ash-tree crows fled upwards.

"Father Jean-Baptiste?"

The autumn night grew cold to match her voice, different, strained, and its chill gripped him. "Colette? Where are you?"

Je Reviens. I can smell the scent. Oh help me... Where is she?

He could just make out her umbrella. Domed black against the black tree, but the simulacrum underneath was all too visible. Bald as an egg, creating a perfect but alien oval of her whole face. And her eyes that had wept too much now stared unflinching at the desperate resurrection of the *recherché* photograph now probably everywhere.

Where've you been that I couldn't help you? Colette, what have you done?

"I bury my son on Monday. *Le Bébé*, remember? That's what you called him, wasn't it? According to the media."

"Oh, Colette..." He stretched out his hand but she drew back, using her umbrella as a shield.

"Don't touch me. Not now. I couldn't bear it."

"I just want to say two things. Please, you must hear me..." his voice diminished to a whisper. "First, I'm a changed man, God knows... Give me another chance Colette.. I've thought of nothing but you since..."

"What's the second, then?" her tone enough to turn the air to winter.

"I want to make it up to you. We could have another child, it wouldn't be too late. You and me somewhere peaceful..." Vidal took a deep breath as though to sustain his memory of the Temple service... "For on this day He shall atone for you to cleanse you; from all your sins before God... Isn't that wonderful, Colette. Just think of it... A fresh start. With just one soul saved, I save the whole world..."

"Whose soul? Yours or mine?"

"Does it matter?"

But the unborn, the grandchildren she'd never have, swelled into her mind. She puckered her mouth, sucked in her cheeks and spat at his feet.

That was the signal.

Silently a group of figures, barely distinguishable from the murky night, stepped forward, united in their intent. That same smell of burning reached him, and Devils' masks surmounted by flames which licked the dying leaves above. At least twenty stood there. All young. Mostly male.

"Hands up."

A voice he recognised.

Marcel Jalibert... Yet another Judas.

The Parisian took the Browning, tossed it back to one of the others, then booted Vidal on the shin. Once, twice, before slugging him in the chest.

"For the dead who can't speak!"

Vidal managed to raise his arms as Jalibert stepped forward and frisked him with expert hands. Vidal groaned her name. Heard the other man load the rifle, saw its muzzle glint in the darkness, and could smell already his own death.

"You're bloody fools," he muttered witheringly. "I've friends in high places."

"Who? God Almighty?" Jalibert sneered, moving the barrel from side to side.

"You wait."

"No. *You* wait, you Nazi scum. We'll get the lot of you. Priests, my arse. Pretty rich, isn't it? And you used Madame Bataille here to take you to the Pope's Mass, to put on a show, to set things up. You'll rot soon enough..."

Silence as the masked eyes stared and smoke trails hung in the dark. His church, too; livid against the end of night.

"Still, she's just promised to be a good friend to us, and all the poor Jews stuck in La belle France. Because of bastards like you, there's more of them getting out from this country than any other in Europe. They know what's coming, unlike the poor fuckers fifty years ago. That's why we need people like her."

"Yep. She's going to be brilliant." Brigitte Caumartin stepped in. His former Confirmation pupil now relishing her bit of power.

"Colette?" Vidal looked around as he gripped a tombstone loose in the wet earth.

"She's gone. Sorry. Got work to do. Taking over where Bertrand left off."

Jalibert kicked him again.

"What do you mean?" Vidal cried.

"He was one of us. Didn't you know? One of our best. You really should have left him alone."

Vidal gaped.

"His death was nothing to do with me."

"That's what they all still say. Vichy murderers."

"I tried to rescue him from the river. I really did. Colette believe me!" he yelled into the night.

"Well, you didn't try hard enough, Father," Jalibert sneered. "So there we are. And now it's just you and us. L'Armée Contre Juifs – just one – against our twenty-two. How it should be, but one Devil is still one too bloody many in my book."

Vidal took deep breaths, tried to rationalise, to remember Number 26, Rue Salacroux, and the keen, knowledgeable associate with a gift for drawing.

"I don't believe this. *You* helped plan the attack at the Pont de l'Alma. You were there and your papa. We all saw you. For fuck's sake, Marcel Jalibert."

A murmur of disbelief rose up from those behind, but no-one intervened as the leader steadied himself, tilting his head into the sight while Vidal continued.

"So you betrayed him, even your friends here, by giving us information. It was you who drew up the tidal chart amongst other things. Very useful indeed. Even your foreplay to sweeten up old Hermans on the boat. I bet Déchaux paid you well for that. No wonder you let Bertrand Bataille die…"

His syllables were lost among the first hail of bullets that cracked towards the steeple and the smell of carbine hung in the air. But he kept going. "And why didn't Déchaux cotton on after you'd messed up my father's flat? I'll tell you. No-one's ever taken you seriously. You're just a bunch of hot-head wankers."

"The next is for you, *mon curé*," Jalibert laughed, cocking his rifle, taking aim. "Better say your prayers pretty damned quick. What will it be, an Acte de Contrition? An Acte d'Offrande? What do you think is best, Brigitte?"

But the former supermarket cashier had gone, and the rest were following, their flames diminished to little more than sparks beyond the ranks of graves. Their fifth columnist was on his own

"Come back!" Jalibert yelled after them. "What you playing at? We've not finished." He looked at Vidal then at his deserters. Panic flickered behind the mask and for a moment he seemed unsure what to do.

That moment was all she needed.

With the strength of a woman reborn, Colette wrenched his rifle from his grasp and threw it for Vidal.

"Poor Bertrand. You just used him for your own ends, like you'd have used me. Except that I've not been unemployed, without hope of ever finding work. You're no better than this man you were going to kill, but you think by taking the moral high ground you can destroy people's lives."

Jalibert tried to move, then stopped when Vidal approached with the rifle cocked.

"Your dear precious son even bugged your flat." Jalibert taunted, and Colette's umbrella fell to the ground, her thoughts spinning guilt and betrayal into a grotesque aftermath. "He had all the time in the world with you conveniently out of the way, working. And blow me, was he keen." Another sick laugh infected the silence. "He thought more of us than you. Didn't you realise that?" Jalibert grunted before Vidal tore the mask from his face and slapped his mouth shut.

He then aimed at Jalibert's foot and fired. Warm blood sprayed his hand as he grabbed Colette and began to run away from the shriek of pain that hung in the night like a dying shofar.

Nor did the dead sleepers of his parish hinder them. Instead they lay in calm disorder, spared the losses and betrayals of future years, content with the seasons and the call of crows. No more nightmares, just the lull of time curled into a void beyond their understanding.

LXV

Saturday October 11th

Six hours later, as dawn was surreptitiously capturing the sky, the Dominican, Francke Victor Duvivier, safely ensconced in the Presbytery of Ste Trinité, prepared himself for the most meaningful moment in his life.

He'd taken down all the black-and-white enlargements of his mother's wounds and set a match to each corner. He then blew the ashes into the air.

Time was of the essence, nevertheless, he himself must be perfect. As perfect as when he'd first entered the world, when his mother had held him and put him to the breast, her hot-red nipple filling his mouth. If he'd been born full of sin, her milk had surely cleansed him.

"Ouch!"

The razor tugged at his chest hair, but he endured it, rubbing in blobs of Nivea cream until the pink flesh glistened. Next, his scrotum. Ripe, but unused since the Bataille tart. Onanism was only for when he felt God was otherwise engaged, and now the sac weighed comfortingly in his hand as the crinkly outcrop of middle-age fell away. Powdered, softly white, like early snow on the Pic de la Verne, he smiled.

He'd known all along what to wear. No need for the habitual black, that was for Hubert, buried in his Brigade des Jeunes uniform. Duvivier folded up his robe that hung like a shadow on the door, and squashed it into the bin for Renate Javel to deal with.

The voluminous nappy created from one of his bed sheets bulked out his hips, but four safety pins at the front held it all securely in place.

Practice makes perfect, right, maman?

Then, with the help of a large cognac, he swallowed his mother's ring, so her gift would always be part of him. Inviolate. He coughed. It had gone down nicely, and even though Doctor Brébisson had once told him that the body excretes immediately after death, it was better than leaving it lying around for the Javels' grasping fingers.

Duvivier grinned at the transformation in the mirror. He was ready, and eagerness bore him out into the cool morning, down the short drive to the kissing gate and into the graveyard, where his father lay cramped ignominiously against the wall.

A magpie worried at the ground nearby, but today it didn't concern him.

What harm can it do me now? Live and let live, I say.

He felt his old self returning. A beatific glow glazed his features, and for the first time since his affliction, his left cheek felt normal to the touch. The dough was working even if it was now limiting his expression to a happy rigor mortis.

Loose grass from Javel's mowing stuck to his bare feet like iron filings to a magnet but again the priest was unconcerned, focussing only on the freshly dug oblong that awaited. At first, the handyman had objected to the extra labour, but for 5,000 new francs had put his old muscle behind the shovel, and now as Duvivier looked into his new home, he noted with pleasure the sharp corners and nicely finished interior.

He looked around checking for the odd itinerant who'd occasionally emerge from the hills hoping for a meal and a wash. Duvivier too, sat on the edge, like a child contemplating the pool. No rosary, no breviary, just his own thoughts conjoining with those of Madeleine Irma Büber, whose beauty was now more real than the soil under his hands.

Come, my son. It is time... It is time... See how she welcomes me... See the light in her eyes...

He lowered himself in and gasped as the floor's dampness met his bones, but not a moment of regret altered his purpose. He lay with room to spare at either end, savouring the new earth, its deep, timeless secrets, and as the sky cleared between the cedar and the yews, casting the baby pale and without blemish, he drifted towards his last and sweetest Communion...

DOXOLOGY

Robert Vidal checked his watch. 7.09 hrs. Not ideal, in fact there was far too much daylight, but the overnight train from Metz had stopped outside Mâcon for the line to be cleared of an asphalt spillage. Colette had slept through it all, fused against his body, her funeral wig tilting on his shoulder whenever nightmares had stirred her. But during two separate visits by the Gendarmes, she'd revived and acted her part well enough for them to leave, even apologise for the inconvenience.

Now, they walked step-in-step, not hand-in-hand as he hoped, towards the hills above Cavalaire. Her face set hard, older somehow in the southern light. She'd persuaded him to leave Jalibert's cumbersome rifle behind, but she was ready to kill, he knew.

His face, too, was fixed, numbed more by the loss of his house, his bike and the music so carefully stored in the spare room – all ashes now, dusting the Rue Fosse and neighbouring roofs in a fine impermanence.

The motorbike had blown a hole to the sky oxygenating the early feeble flames to an inferno that had merely mocked the water hoses. They'd both heard it, helpless from their hiding place in the Petits Jardins. He'd wondered about his father. Maybe the fool had gone back to the house, maybe not. He'd probably never know.

Neither spoke as the church of Ste Trinité and its bell tower's grotesque ironwork came into view. Vidal still weighted by his damp clothes forced his tired body forwards to keep pace with the woman alongside who was trying to increase her advantage.

"Come on, Colette. Let me touch you." He tried, but she moved faster, keeping him at an even greater arm's length.

The road was deserted. Too early for the *chasseurs* still sleeping off the wild boar blood that had reddened their gums and pinked their teeth the night before. But by noon, the covered trucks would again be crawling the trails of Les Pradels, ex-army green against green, and soon the killing rifle shots would sing out above the church bells.

"I'll try here," she said, reaching the Presbytery, as he shed his jacket and hooked it over his shoulder with one finger. "I bet the cowardly bastard's come home."

The Huntress stood on tiptoe by the window – her well-turned legs bearing dark diagonals under each calf muscle, blue heels still swollen. Yet she was all he had – this woman with no hair, no eyelashes, dressed in black for her son who'd given Moussac his passport to Eternity. Yet he would try to love her again, because otherwise there was no-one. Not even God. And he knew that given time, he would.

She reached the front door and pushed it open on to a thick white carpet. No alarm. No lock. Something was up.

"Colette, come back," he said, fear already sharpening his tongue. He gripped her shoulders to stop her going any further. "Let me go first." But she pushed him away and he watched, helpless as she went in.

Emptiness, emptiness. All is emptiness...

"Look, I'll find Duvivier for you. You go and wait outside, please." But she ignored him, looking from left to right then up the drift of stairs. Her business now. The one thing the Provençal had got right.

"Please!"

She turned too late, and suddenly her mouth fell open in a silent scream.

Three figures stood behind him, booted feet apart. Motionless silhouettes save for three balaclava'd pairs of eyes. Liquid hate distilled, pure and terrible. The one who held him like a goat, also held a knife. Its bright curved blade settled against his throat.

"At least Dominique Mathieu has done the decent thing, unlike his father," the butcher said. Colette gasped in horror. "So you're the last, Robert Vidal. Such a pity you gave too much of your *yeitzer hara* to Satan, like all the others. Michel Plagnol, who'd suffocated his old grandmother, made a good meal for the Cressy's dogs after he'd been most helpful. Éric Cacheux, whose own brave mother had even named him after one of us, strung him up. Francke Duvivier, Philippe Toussirot, Georges Déchaux... all the mad bitches of Libourne, save the switchboard operator who won't last long even under police guard."

"Mademoiselle Zeresche?"

A nod. "Not her real name of course. Like all cowards."

The priest searched her face, but she gave him nothing.

"Mercifully, Zyklon B still has its uses... Oh I forgot. We have our friend Yves Jalibert with us, too; you'll be pleased to hear, but he won't be saying much from now on."

Vidal made no attempt to move. They frisked him for the Browning before the knife point pierced beneath his jaw and warm blood trickled down his neck.

"And still the Milk-White Hind suckles too many fools like you who cling to her teats. You'd think after harbouring murderers who'd slipped through the Nüremberg net, she would now desist. But Satan is insatiable. He prefers white meat however it is prepared. And now he can have all of you. Mens et Corpus. Just like your idol Eichmann. How about that for a feast?"

Robert Vidal's beautiful animal eyes pleaded with her, deep, dark and never more deadly, to no avail. She watched her lover's hands hang limp and brown like old leaves, until suddenly in time to the glide of steel, they splayed and jerked on a final unheard cry.

Colette.

***

In the aftermath, the gloating silence, she swayed for a moment, then steadied herself. "There's something I've got to do," she whispered, "before I forget. I need to take his shadow. Please."

Hesitation.

One of them aimed Vidal's semi-automatic at his shortened silhouette on the ground behind, and when it was done, allowed the man to fall, soulless at her feet.

But because they owed her one, because when Leila Fraenkel had asked, she'd given, the Israelis let her go. So, winged like the swallow, Colette Bataille flew under the cedar, past Duvivier still smiling up at the sky, out into the autumn sunlight.

FINIS

Sparkling Books

Young adult fiction

Cheryl Bentley, *Petronella & The Trogot*

Brian Conaghan, *The Boy Who Made it Rain*

Luke Hollands, *Peregrine Harker and the Black Death*

Vitali Vitaliev, *Granny Yaga*

Crime, mystery and thriller fiction

Nikki Dudley, *Ellipsis*

Sally Spedding, *Cold Remains*

Other fiction

Amanda Sington-Williams, *The Eloquence of Desire*

Non-fiction

Daniele Cuffaro, *American Myths in Post-9/11 Music*

David Kauders, *The Greatest Crash: How contradictory policies are sinking the global economy*

Revivals

Carlo Goldoni, *Il vero amico / The True Friend*

Gustave Le Bon, *Psychology of Crowds*

For full list of titles and more information visit:

www.sparklingbooks.com

Sparkling Books